Cursed By A Fortune

By

George Manville Fenn

Cursed By A Fortune
by George Manville Fenn

ISBN: 978-93-59955-71-1
Published by

DOUBLE 9 BOOKS

2/13-B, Ansari Road
Daryaganj, New Delhi – 110002
info@double9books.com
www.double9books.com
Tel. 011-40042856

ABOUT THE AUTHOR

George Manville Fenn was a very productive author of novels, a writer, an editor, and an educator from England. He was born on January 3, 1831, in Pimlico, London. He mostly learned on his own; he taught himself Italian, French, and German. During the years 1851–1854, he went to Battersea Training College for Teachers and then became the head of a state school in Alford, Lincolnshire. In the early 1850s, Fenn started to write short stories and pieces for newspapers and magazines. The Old Forest Ranger, his first book, came out in 1856. Afterward, he wrote more than 100 books, many of them for teenagers and young adults. He was one of the most famous writers of his time, and his books were well-liked and read by many people. He also worked as a reporter and writer for Fenn. Among the newspapers and magazines, he worked for was The Boy's Own Paper, which he ran from 1866 to 1874. He worked hard to make children's books better and was a strong supporter of education and reading. The Englishman Fenn passed away on August 26, 1909, in Isleworth.

CONTENTS

Chapter One

"Yes, James; this is my last dying speech and confession."

"Oh, papa!" with a burst of sobbing.

"Be quiet, Kitty, and don't make me so miserable. Dying is only going to sleep when a man's tired out, as I am, with the worries of the world, money-making, fighting for one's own, and disappointment. I know as well as old Jermingham that it's pretty nearly all over. I'm sorry to leave you, darling, but I'm worn out, and your dear mother has been waiting for nearly a year."

"Father, dearest father!" and two white arms clung round the neck of the dying man, as their owner sank upon her knees by the bedside.

"I'd stay for your sake, Kitty, but fate says no, and I'm so tired, darling, it will be like going into rest and peace. She always was an angel, Kitty, and she must be now; I feel as if I must see her afterwards. For I don't think I've been such a very bad man, Will."

"The best of fellows, Bob, always," said the stout, florid, country-looking gentleman seated near the great heavily-curtained four-post bed.

"Thanks, James. I don't want to play the Pharisee, but I have tried to be an honest man and a good father."

"Your name stands highest in the city, and your charities—"

"Bother! I made plenty of money by the bank, and I gave some away, and I wish it had done more good. Well, my shares in the bank represent a hundred and fifty thousand; those are Kitty's. There's about ten thousand pounds in India stock and consols."

"Pray, pray don't talk any more, papa, dear."

"Must, Kitty, while I can. That money, Will, is yours for life, and after death it is for that boy of yours, Claud. He doesn't deserve it, but perhaps he'll be a better boy some day. Then there's the lease of this house, my furniture, books, plate, pictures, and money in the private account. You will sell and realise everything; Kitty does not want a great gloomy house in Bedford Square—out of proceeds you will pay the servants' legacies, and the expenses, there will be ample; and the residue is to be given to your wife for her use. That's all. I have made you my sole executor, and I thought it better to send for you to tell you than for you to wait till the will was read. Give me a little of that stuff in some water, Kitty."

His head was tenderly raised, and he drank and sank back with a sigh.

"Thank you, my darling. Now, Will, I might have joined John Garstang with you as executor, but I thought it better to give you full control, you being a quiet country squire, leading your simple, honest, gentleman-farmer's life, while he is a keen speculative man."

James Wilton, the banker's brother, uttered something like a sigh, muttered a few words about trying to do his duty, and listened, as the dying man went on—

"I should not have felt satisfied. You two might have disagreed over some marriage business, for there is no other that you will have to control. And I said to myself that Will would not try to play the wicked uncle over my babe. So you are sole executor, with very little to do, for I have provided for everything, I think. Her money stays in the old bank I helped to build up, and the dividends will make her a handsome income. What you have to see to is that she is not snapped up by some plausible scoundrel for the sake of her money. When she does marry—"

"Oh, papa, dear, don't, don't! You are breaking my heart. I shall never marry," sobbed the girl, as she laid her sweet young face by the thin, withered countenance on the pillow.

"Yes, you will, my pet. I wish it, when the right man comes, who loves you for yourself. Girls like you are too scarce to be wasted. But your uncle will watch over you, and see to that. You hear, Will?"

"Yes, I will do my duty by her."

"I believe you."

"But, papa dear, don't talk more. The doctor said you must be kept so quiet."

"I must wind up my affairs, my darling, and think of your future. I've had quite enough of the men hanging about after the rich banker's daughter. When my will is proved, the drones and wasps will come swarming round you for the money. There is no one at all, yet, is there?" he said, with a searching look.

"Oh, no, papa, I never even thought of such a thing."

"I know it, my darling. I've always been your sweetheart, and we've lived for one another, and I'm loth to leave you, dear."

"Oh, father, dearest father, don't talk of leaving me," she sobbed.

He smiled sadly, and his feeble hand played with her curls.

"God disposes, my own," he said. "But there, I must talk while I can. Now, listen. These are nearly my last words, Will."

His brother started and bent forward to hear his half-whispered words, and he wiped the dew from his sun-browned forehead, and shivered a little, for the chilly near approach of death troubled the hale, hearty-looking man, and gave a troubled look to his florid face.

"When all is over, Will, as soon as you can, take her down to Northwood, and be a father to her. Her aunt always loved her, and she'll be happy there. Shake hands upon it, Will."

The thin, white, trembling hand was placed in the fat, heavy palm extended, and rested there for some minutes before Robert Wilton spoke again.

"Everything is set down clearly, Will. The money invested in the bank is hers—one hundred and fifty thousand pounds, strictly tied up. I have seen to that. There, you will do your duty by her, and see that all goes well."

"Yes."

"I am satisfied, brother; I exact no oaths. Kate, my child, your uncle will take my place. I leave you in his hands." Then in a low voice, heard only by her who clung to him, weeping silently, he whispered softly, "And in Thine, O God."

The next morning the blinds were all down in front of Number 204, Bedford Square, which looked at its gloomiest in the wet fog, with the withered leaves falling fast from the great plane trees; and the iron shutters were half drawn up at the bank in Lothbury, for the old leather-covered chair in the director's rom was vacant, waiting for a new occupant—the chairman of the Great British and Bengalie Joint Stock Bank was dead.

"As good and true a man as ever breathed," said the head clerk, shaking his grey head; "and we've all lost a friend. I wonder who will marry Miss Kate!"

Chapter Two

"Morning, Doctor. Hardly expected to find you at home. Thought you'd be on your rounds."

The speaker was mounted on a rather restive cob, which he now checked by the gate of the pretty cottage in one of the Northwood lanes; and as he spoke he sprang down and placed his rein through the ring on the post close by the brass plate which bore the words—"Pierce Leigh, M.D., Surgeon, etc.," but he did not look at the ring, for his eyes gave a furtive glance at the windows from one to the other quickly.

He was not a groom, for his horse-shoe pin was set with diamonds, and a large bunch of golden charms hung at his watch chain, but his coat, hat, drab breeches, and leggings were of the most horsey cut, and on a near approach anyone might have expected to smell stables. As it was, the odour he exhaled was Jockey Club, emanating from a white pocket handkerchief dotted with foxes' heads, hunting crops and horns, and saturated with scent.

"My rounds are not very regular, Mr Wilton," said the gentleman addressed, and he looked keenly at the commonplace speaker, whose ears stood out widely from his closely-cropped hair. "You people are dreadfully healthy down here," and he held open the garden gate and drew himself up, a fairly handsome, dark, keen-eyed, gentlemanly-looking man of thirty, slightly pale as if from study, but looking wiry and strong as an athlete. "You wished to see me?"

"Yes. Bit off my corn. Headache, black spots before my eyes, and that sort of thing. Thought I'd consult the Vet."

"Will you step in?"

"Eh? Yes. Thankye."

The Doctor led the way into his flower-decked half-study, half-consulting room, where several other little adornments suggested the near presence of a woman; and the would-be patient coughed unnecessarily, and kept on tapping his leg with the hunting crop he carried, as he followed, and the door was closed, and a chair was placed for him.

"Eh? Chair? Thanks," said the visitor, taking it by the back, swinging it round, and throwing one leg across as if it were a saddle, crossing his arms and resting his chin there—the while he stared rather enviously at the man before him. "Not much the matter, and you mustn't make me so that I can't get on. Got a chap staying with me, and we're going after the pheasants. I say, let me send you a brace."

"You are very good," said the Doctor, smiling rather contemptuously, "but as I understand it they are not yet shot?"

"Eh? Oh, no; but no fear of that. I can lick our keeper; pretty sure with a gun. Want to see my tongue and feel my pulse?"

"Well, no," said the Doctor, with a slight shrug of his shoulders. "I can pretty well tell."

"How?"

"By your looks."

"Eh? Don't look bad, do I?"

"Rather."

"Something nasty coming on?" said the young man nervously.

"Yes; bad bilious attack, if you are not careful. You have been drinking too much beer and smoking too many strong cigars."

"Not a bad guess," said the young man with a grin. "Last boxes are enough to take the top of your head off. Try one."

"Thank you," was the reply, and a black-looking cigar was taken from the proffered case.

"Mind, I've told you they are roofers."

"I can smoke a strong cigar," said the Doctor, quietly.

"You can? Well, I can't. Now then, mix up something; I want to be off."

"There is no need to give you any medicine. Leave off beer and tobacco for a few days, and you will be all right."

"But aren't you going to give me any physic?"

"Not a drop."

"Glad of it. But I say, the yokels down here won't care for it if you don't give them something."

"I have found out that already. There, sir, I have given you the best advice I can."

"Thankye. When am I to come again?"

"Not until you are really ill. Not then," said the Doctor, smiling slightly as he rose, "for I suppose I should be sent for to you."

"That's all then?"

"Yes, that is all."

"Well, send in your bill to the guv'nor," said the young man, renewing his grin; "he pays all mine. Nice morning, ain't it, for December? Soon have Christmas."

"Yes, we shall soon have Christmas now," said the Doctor, backing his visitor toward the door.

"But looks more like October, don't it?"

"Yes, much more like October."

"Steady, Beauty! Ah, quiet, will you!" cried the young man, as he mounted the restive cob. "She's a bit fresh. Wants some of the dance taken out of her. Morning.—Sour beggar, no wonder he don't get on," muttered the patient. "Take that and that. Coming those games when I'm mounting! How do you like that? Wanted to have me off."

There was a fresh application of the spurs, brutally given, and after plunging heavily the little mare tore off as hard as she could go, while the Doctor watched till his patient turned a corner, and then resumed his walk up and down the garden—a walk interrupted by the visit.

"Insolent puppy!" he muttered, frowning. "A miserable excuse."

"Pierce, dear, where are you?" cried a pleasant voice, and a piquant little figure appeared at the door. "Oh, there you are. Shall I want a hat? Oh, no, it's quite mild." The owner of the voice hurried out like a beam of sunshine on the dull grey morning, and taking the Doctor's arm tried to keep step with him, after glancing up in his stern face, her own looking merry and arch with its dimples.

"What is it, Jenny?" he said.

"What is it, sir? Why, I want fresh air as well as you; but don't stride along like that. How can I keep step? You have such long legs."

"That's better," he said, trying to accommodate himself to the little body at his side.

"Rather. So you have had a patient," she said.

"Yes, I've had a patient, Sis," he replied, looking down at her; and a faint colour dawned in her creamy cheeks.

"And you always grumbling, sir! There, I do believe that is the beginning of a change. Who was the patient?"

The Doctor's hand twitched, and he frowned, but he said, calmly enough, "That young cub from the Manor."

"Mr Claud Wilton?" said the girl innocently; "Oh, I am glad. Beginning with the rich people at the Manor. Now everyone will come."

"No, my dear; everyone will not come, and the sooner we pack up and go back to town the better."

"What, sell the practice?"

"Sell the practice," he cried contemptuously. "Sell the furniture, Sis. One man—fool, I mean—was enough to be swindled over this affair. Practice! The miserable scoundrel! Much good may the money he defrauded me of do him. No, but we shall have to go."

"Don't, Pierce," said the girl, looking up at him wistfully.

"Why?" he said angrily.

"Because it did do me good being down here, and I like the place so much."

"Any place would be better than that miserable hole at Westminster, where you were getting paler every day, but I ought to have been more businesslike. It has not done you good though; and if you like the place the more reason why we should go," he cried angrily.

"Oh, Pierce, dear, what a bear you are this morning. Do be patient, and I know the patients will come."

"Bah! Not a soul called upon us since we've been here, except the tradespeople, so that they might get our custom."

"But we've only been here six months, dear."

"It will be the same when we've been here six years, and I'm wasting time. I shall get away as soon as I can. Start the New Year afresh in town."

"Pierce, oh don't walk so fast. How can I keep up with you?"

"I beg your pardon."

"That's better. But, Pierce, dear," she said, with an arch look; "don't talk like that. You wouldn't have the heart to go."

"Indeed! But I will."

"I know better, dear."

"What do you mean?"

"You couldn't go away now. Oh, Pierce, dear, she is sweet! I could love her so. There is something so beautiful and pathetic in her face as she sits there in church. Many a time I've felt the tears come into my eyes, and as if I could go across the little aisle and kiss her and call her sister."

He turned round sharply and caught her by the arm, his eyes flashing with indignation.

"Jenny," he cried, "are you mad?"

"No, only in pain," she said, with her lip quivering. "You hurt me. You are so strong."

"I—I did not mean it," he said, releasing her.

"But you hurt me still, dear, to see you like this. Oh, Pierce, darling," she whispered, as she clung to his arm and nestled to him; "don't try and hide it from me. A woman always knows. I saw it from the first when she came down, and we first noticed her, and she came to church looking like some dear, suffering saint. My heart went out to her at once, and the more so that I saw the effect it had on you. Pierce, dear, you do love me?"

"You know," he said hoarsely.

"Then be open with me. What could be better?"

He was silent for a few moments, and then he answered the pretty, wistful eyes, gazing so inquiringly in his.

"Yes," he said. "I will be open with you, Sis, for you mean well; but you speak like the pretty child you have always been to me. Has it ever crossed your mind that I have never spoken to this lady, and that she is a rich heiress, and that I am a poor doctor who is making a failure of his life?"

"What!" cried the girl proudly. "Why, if she were a princess she would not be too grand for my brave noble brother."

"Hah!" he cried, with a scornful laugh; "your brave noble brother! Well, go on and still think so of me, little one. It's very pleasant, and does not hurt anyone. I hope I'm too sensible to be spoiled by my little flatterer. Only keep your love for me yet awhile," he said meaningly. "Let's leave love out of the question till we can pay our way and have something to spare, instead of having no income at all but what comes from consols."

"But Pierce—"

"That will do. You're a dear little goose. We must want the Queen's Crown from the Tower because it's pretty."

"Now you're talking nonsense, Pierce," she said, firmly, and she held his arm tightly between her little hands. "You can't deny it, sir. You fell in love with her from the first."

"Jenny, my child," he said quietly. "I promised our father I would be an honorable man and a gentleman."

"And so you would have been, without promising."

"I hope so. Then now listen to me; never speak to me in this way again."

"I will," she cried flushing. "Answer me this; would it be acting like an honorable man to let that sweet angel of a girl marry Claud Wilton?"

"What!" he cried, starting, and gazing at his sister intently. "Her own cousin? Absurd."

"I've heard that it is to be so."

"Nonsense!"

"People say so, and where there's smoke there's fire. Cousins marry, and I don't believe they'll let a fortune like that go out of the family."

"They're rich enough to laugh at it."

"They're not rich; they're poor, for the Squire's in difficulties."

"Petty village tattle. Rubbish, girl. Once more, no more of this. You're wrong, my dear. You mean well, but there's an ugly saying about good intentions which I will not repeat. Now listen to me. The coming down to Northwood has been a grave mistake, and when people blunder the sooner they get back to the right path the better. I have made up my mind to go back to London, and your words this morning have hastened it on. The sooner we are off the better."

"No, Pierce," said the girl firmly. "Not to make you unhappy. You shall not take a step that you will repent to the last day of your life, dear. We must stay."

"We must go. I have nothing to stay for here. Neither have you," he added, meaningly.

"Pierce!" she cried, flushing.

"Beg pardon, sir; Mr Leigh, sir."

They had been too much intent upon their conversation to notice the approach of a dog-cart, or that the groom who drove it had pulled up on seeing them, and was now talking to them over the hedge.

"Yes, what is it?" said Leigh, sharply.

"Will you come over to the Manor directly, sir? Master's out, and Missus is in a trubble way. Our young lady, sir, Miss Wilton, took bad—fainting and nervous. You're to come at once."

Jenny uttered a soft, low, long-drawn "Oh!" and, forgetful of everything he had said, Pierce Leigh rushed into the house, caught up his hat, and hurried out again, to mount into the dog-cart beside the driver.

"Poor, dear old brother!" said Jenny, softly, as with her eyes half-blinded by the tears which rose, she watched the dog-cart driven away. "I don't believe he will go to town. Oh, how strangely things do come about. I wish I could have gone too."

Chapter Three

John Garstang stood with his back to the fire in his well furnished office in Bedford Row, tall, upright as a Life Guardsman, but slightly more prominent about what the fashionable tailor called his client's chest. He was fifty, but looked by artificial aid, forty. Scrupulously well-dressed, good-looking, and with a smile which won the confidence of clients, though his regular white teeth were false, and the high foreheaded look which some people would have called baldness was so beautifully ivory white and shiny that it helped to make him look what he was—a carefully polished man of the world.

The clean japanned boxes about the room, all bearing clients' names, the many papers on the table, the waste-paper basket on the rich Turkey carpet, chock full of white fresh letters and envelopes, all told of business; and the handsome morocco-covered easy chairs suggested occupancy by moneyed clients who came there for long consultations, such as would tell up in a bill.

John Garstang was a family solicitor, and he looked it; but he would have made a large fortune as a physician, for his presence and urbane manner would have done anyone good.

The morning papers had been glanced at and tossed aside, and the gentleman in question, while bathing himself in the warm glow of the fire, was carefully scraping and polishing his well-kept nails, pausing from time to time to blow off tiny scraps of dust; and at last he took two steps sideways noiselessly and touched the stud of an electric bell.

A spare-looking, highly respectable man answered the summons and stood waiting till his principal spoke, which was not until the right hand little finger nail, which was rather awkward to get at, had been polished, when without raising his eyes, John Garstang spoke.

"Mr Harry arrived?"

"No, sir."

"What time did he leave yesterday?"

"Not here yesterday, sir."

"The day before?"

"Not here the day before yesterday, sir."

"What time did he leave on Monday?"

"About five minutes after you left for Brighton, sir."

"Thank you, Barlow; that will do. By the way—"

The clerk who had nearly reached the door, turned, and there was again silence, while a few specks were blown from where they had fallen inside one of the spotless cuffs.

"Send Mr Harry to me as soon as he arrives."

"Yes, sir," and the man left the room; while after standing for a few moments thinking, John Garstang walked to one of the tin boxes in the rack and drew down a lid marked, "Wilton, Number 1."

Taking from this a packet of papers carefully folded and tied up with green silk, he seated himself at his massive knee-hole table, and was in the act of untying the ribbon, when the door opened and a short, thick-set young man of five-and-twenty, with a good deal of French waiter in his aspect, saving his clothes, entered, passing one hand quickly over his closely-shaven face, and then taking the other to help to square the great, dark, purple-fringed, square, Joinville tie, fashionable in the early fifties.

"Want to see me, father?"

"Yes. Shut the baize door."

"Oh, you needn't be so particular. It won't be the first time Barlow has heard you bully me."

"Shut the baize door, if you please, sir," said Garstang, blandly.

"Oh, very well!" cried the young man, and he unhooked and set free a crimson baize door whose spring sent it to with a thud and a snap.

Then John Garstang's manner changed. An angry frown gathered on his forehead, and he placed his elbows on the table, joined the tips of his fingers to form an archway, and looked beneath it at the young man who had entered.

"You are two hours late this morning."

"Yes, father."

"You did not come here at all yesterday."

"No, father."

"Nor the day before."

"No, father."

"Then will you have the goodness to tell me, sir, how long you expect this sort of thing to go on? You are not of the slightest use to me in my professional business."

"No, and never shall be," said the young man coolly.

"That's frank. Then will you tell me why I should keep and supply with money such a useless drone?"

"Because you have plenty, and a lot of it ought to be mine by right."

"Why so, sir? You are not my son."

"No, but I'm my mother's."

"Naturally," said Garstang, with a supercilious smile.

"You need not sneer, sir. If you hadnt deluded my poor mother into marrying you I should have been well off."

"Your mother had a right to do as she pleased, sir. Where have you been?"

"Away from the office."

"I know that. Where to?"

"Where I liked," said the young man sulkily, "I'm not a child."

"No, and this conduct has become unbearable. It is time you went away for good. What do you say to going to Australia with your passage paid and a hundred pounds to start you?"

"'Tisn't good enough."

"Then you had better execute your old threat and enlist in a cavalry regiment. I promise you that I will not buy you out."

"Thank you, but it isn't good enough."

"What are you going to do then?"

"Never mind."

Garstang looked up at him sharply, this time from outside the finger arch.

"Don't provoke me, Harry Dasent, for your own sake. What are you going to do?"

"Get married."

"Indeed? Well, that's sensible. But are there not enough pauper children for the parish to keep?"

"Yes, but I am not going to marry a pauper. You have my money and will not disgorge it, so I must have somebody's else."

"Indeed! Then you are going to look out for a lady with money?"

"No. I have already found one."

"Anyone I know?"

"Oh, yes."

"Who is it, pray?"

"Katherine Wilton."

Garstang's eyes contracted, and he gazed at his stepson for some moments in silence. Then a contemptuous smile dawned upon his lip.

"I was not aware that you were so ambitious, Harry. But the lady?"

"Oh, that will be all right."

"Indeed! May I ask when you saw her last?"

"Yesterday evening at dinner."

"You have been down to Northwood?"

"Yes; I was there two days."

"Did your Uncle Wilton invite you down?"

"No, but Claud did, for a bit of shooting."

"Humph!" ejaculated Garstang thoughtfully, and the young man stood gazing at him intently. Then his manner changed, and he took one of the easy chairs, drew it forward, and seated himself, to sit leaning forward, and began speaking confidentially.

"Look here, step-father," he half-whispered, "I've been down there twice. I suspected it the first time; yesterday I was certain. They're playing a deep game there."

"Indeed?"

"Yes. I saw through it at once. They're running Claud for the stakes."

"Please explain yourself, my good fellow; I do not understand racing slang."

"Well, then, they mean Claud to marry Kate, and I'm not going to stand by and see that done."

"By the way, I thought Claud was your confidential friend."

"So he is, up to a point; but it's every man for himself in a case like this. I'm in the race myself, and I mean to marry Kate Wilton myself. It's too good a prize to let slip."

"And does the lady incline to my stepson's addresses?"

"Well, hardly. I've had no chance. They watched me like cats do mice, and she has been so sickly that it would be nonsense to try and talk to her."

"Then your prospects are very mild indeed."

"Oh, no, they're not. This is a case where a man must play trumps, high and at once. I may as well speak out, and you'll help me. There's no time shilly-shallying. If I hesitate my chance would be gone. I shall make my plans, and take her away."

"With her consent, of course."

"With or without," said the young man, coolly.

"How?"

"Oh, I'll find a means. Girls are only girls, and they'll give way to a stronger will. Once I get hold of her she'll obey me, and a marriage can soon be got through."

"But suppose she refuses?"

"She'll be made," said the young man, sharply. "The stakes are worth some risk."

"But are you aware that the law would call this abduction?"

"I don't care what the law calls it if I get the girl."

"And it would mean possibly penal servitude."

"Well, I'm suffering that now, situated as I am. There, father, never mind the law. Don't be squeamish; a great fortune is at stake, and it must come into our family, not into theirs."

"You think they are trying that?"

"Think? I'm sure. Claud owned to as much, but he's rather on somewhere else. Come, you'll help me? It would be a grand coup."

"Help you? Bah! you foolish young ass! It is impossible. It is madness. You don't know what you are talking about. The girl could appeal to the first policeman, and you would be taken into custody. You and Claud Wilton must have been having a drinking bout, and the liquor is still in your head. There, go to your own room, and when you can talk sensibly come back to me."

"I can talk sensibly now. Will you help me with a couple of hundred pounds to carry this through? I should want to take her for a couple of months on the Continent, and bring her back my wife."

"Two hundred pounds to get you clapped in a cell at Bow Street."

"No; to marry a hundred and fifty thousand pounds."

"No, no, no. You are a fool, a visionary, a madman. It is impossible, and I shall feel it my duty to write to James Wilton to forbid, you the house."

"Once more; will you help me?"

"Once more, no. Now go, and let me get on with my affairs. Someone must work."

"Then you will not?"

"No."

"Then listen to me: I've made up my mind to it, and do it. I will, at any cost, at any risk. She shan't marry Claud Wilton, and she shall marry me. Yes, you may smile, but if I die for it I'll have that girl and her money."

"But it would cost two hundred pounds to make the venture, sir. Perhaps you had better get that first. Now please go."

The young man rose and looked at him fiercely for a few minutes, and Garstang met his eyes firmly.

"No," he said, "that would not do, Harry. The law fences us round against robbery and murder, just as it does women against abduction. You are not in your senses. You were drinking last night. Go back home and have a long sleep. You'll be better then."

The young man glanced at him sharply and left the room.

Ten minutes spent in deep thought were passed by Garstang, who then rose, replaced the papers in the tin case, and crossed and rang the bell.

"Send Mr Harry here."

"He went out as soon as he left your room, sir."

"Thank you; that will do." Then, as the door closed upon the clerk, Garstang said softly:

"So that's it; then it is quite time to act."

Chapter Four

"Will that Doctor never come!" muttered plump Mrs Wilton, who had been for the past ten minutes running from her niece's bedside to one of the front casement windows of the fine old Kentish Manor House, to watch the road through the park. "He might have come from London by this time. There, it's of no use; it's fate, and fate means disappointment. She'll die; I'm sure she'll die, and all that money will go to those wretched Morrisons. Why did he go out to the farms this morning? Any other morning would have done; and Claud away, too. Was ever woman so plagued?—Yes, what is it? Oh, it's you, Eliza. How is she?"

"Quite insensible, ma'am. Is the Doctor never coming?"

"Don't ask me, Eliza. I sent the man over in the dog-cart, with instructions to bring him back."

"Then pray, pray come and stay with me in the bedroom, ma'am."

"But I can't do anything, Eliza, and it isn't as if she were my own child. I couldn't bear to see her die."

"Mrs Wilton!" cried the woman, wildly. "Oh, my poor darling young mistress, whom I nursed from a babe—die!"

"Here's master—here's Mr Wilton," cried the rosy-faced lady from the window, and making a dash at a glass to see that her cap was right, she hurried out of the room and down the broad oaken stairs to meet her lord at the door.

"Hallo, Maria, what's the matter?" he cried, meeting her in the hall, his high boots splashed with mud, and a hunting whip in his hand.

"Oh, my dear, I'm so glad you've come! Kate—fainting fits—one after the other—dying."

"The devil! What have you done?"

"Cold water—vinegar—burnt—"

"No, no. Haven't you sent for the Doctor?"

"Yes, I sent Henry with the dog-cart to fetch Mr Leigh."

"Mr Leigh! Were you mad? What do you know about Mr Leigh? Bah, you always were a fool!"

"Yes, my dear, but what was I to do? It would have taken three hours to get—Oh, here he is."

For there was the grating of carriage wheels on the drive, the dog-cart drew up, and Pierce Leigh sprang down and entered the hall.

Mrs Wilton glanced timidly at her husband, who gave her a sulky nod, and then turned to the young Doctor.

"My young niece—taken bad," he said, gruffly, "You'd better go up and see her. Here, Maria, take him up."

Unceremonious; but businesslike, and Leigh showed no sign of resentment, but with a peculiar novel fluttering about the region of the heart he followed the lady, who, panting the while, led the way upstairs, and breathlessly tried to explain how delicate her niece was, and how after many days of utter despondency, she had suddenly been seized with an attack of hysteria, which had been succeeded by fit after fit.

The next minute they were in the handsome bedroom at the end of a long, low corridor, where, pale as death, and with her maid—erst nurse—kneeling by her and fanning her, Kate Wilton, in her simple black, lay upon a couch, looking as if the Doctor's coming were too late.

He drew a deep breath, and set his teeth as he sank on one knee by the insensible figure, which he longed with an intense longing to clasp to his breast. Then his nerves were strung once more, and he was the calm, professional man giving his orders, as he made his examination and inspired aunt and nurse with confidence, the latter uttering a sigh of relief as she opened the window, and obeyed sundry other orders, the result being that at the end of half an hour the sufferer, who twice over unclosed her eyes, and responded to her aunt's questions with a faint smile, had sunk into the heavy sleep of exhaustion.

"Better leave her now, madam," said Leigh, softly. "Sleep is the great thing for her." Then, turning to the maid—"You had better stay and watch by her, though she will not wake for hours."

"God bless you, sir," she whispered, with a look full of gratitude which made Leigh give her an encouraging smile, and he then followed Mrs Wilton downstairs.

"Really, it's wonderful," she said. "Thank you so much, Doctor. I'm sure you couldn't have been nicer if you'd been quite an old man, and I really think that next time I'm ill I shall—Oh, my dear, she's ever so much better now."

"Humph!" ejaculated Wilton; and then he gave his wife an angry look, as she pushed him in the chest.

"Come in here and sit down, Mr Leigh. I want you to tell us all you think."

The Doctor followed into the library, whose walls were covered with books that were never used, while, making an effort to be civil, their owner pointed to a chair and took one himself, Leigh waiting till his plump, amiable-looking hostess had subsided, and well-filled that nearest the fire.

"Found her better then?" said Wilton.

"No, sir," said Leigh, smiling, "but she is certainly better now."

"That's what I meant. Nothing the matter, then. Vapours, whims, young girls' hysterics, and that sort of thing? What did she have for breakfast, Maria?"

"Nothing at all, dear. I can't get her to eat."

"Humph! Why don't you make her? Can't stand our miserable cookery, I suppose. Well, Doctor, then, it's a false alarm?"

"No, sir; a very serious warning."

"Eh? You don't think there's danger? Here, we'd better send for some big man from town."

"That is hardly necessary, sir, though I should be happy to meet a man of experience in consultation."

"My word! What airs!" said Wilton, to himself.

"As far as I could I have pretty well diagnosed the case, and it is very simple. Your niece has evidently suffered deeply."

"Terribly, Doctor; she has been heart-broken."

"Now, my dear Maria, do pray keep your mouth shut, and let Mr Leigh talk. He doesn't want you to teach him his business."

"But James, dear, I only just—"

"Yes, you always will only just! Go on, please, Doctor, and you'll send her some medicine?"

"It is hardly a case for medicine, sir. Your niece's trouble is almost entirely mental. Given rest and happy surroundings, cheerful female society of her own age, fresh air, moderate exercise, and the calmness and peace of a home like this, I have no doubt that her nerves will soon recover their tone."

"Then they had better do it," said Wilton, gruffly. "She has everything a girl can wish for. My son and I have done all we can to amuse her."

"And I'm sure I have been as loving as a mother to her," said Mrs Wilton.

"Yes, but you are mistaken, sir. There must be something more. I'd better take her up to town for advice."

"By all means, sir," said Leigh, coldly. "It might be wise, but I should say that she would be better here, with time to work its own cure."

"Of course, I mean no disrespect to you, Mr Leigh, but you are a young man, and naturally inexperienced."

"Now I don't want to hurt your feelings, James," broke in Mrs Wilton, "but it is you who are inexperienced in what young girls are. Mr Leigh has spoken very nicely, and quite understands poor Kate's case. If you had only seen the way in which he brought her round!"

"I really do wish, Maria, that you would not interfere in what you don't understand," cried Wilton, irascibly.

"But I'm obliged to when I find you going wrong. It's just what I've said to you over and over again. You men are so hard and unfeeling, and don't believe there are such things as nerves. Now, I'm quite sure that Mr Leigh could do her a great deal of good, if you'd only attend to your out-door affairs and leave her to me — You grasped it all at once, Mr Leigh. Poor child, she has done nothing but fret ever since she has been here, and no wonder. Within a year she has lost both father and mother."

"Now, Maria, Mr Leigh does not want to hear all our family history."

"And I'm not going to tell it to him, my dear; but it's just as I felt. It was only last night, when she had that fit of hysterical sobbing, I said to myself, Now if I had a dozen girls — as I should have liked to, instead of a boy, who is really a terrible trial to one, Mr Leigh — I should —"

"Maria!"

"Yes, my dear; but you should let me finish. If poor dear Kate had come here and found a lot of girls she would have been as happy as the day is long. — And you don't think she wants physic, Mr Leigh? No, no, don't hurry away."

"I have given you my opinion, madam," said Leigh, who had risen.

"Yes, and I'm sure it is right. I did give her some fluid magnesia yesterday, the same as I take for my acidity—"

"Woman, will you hold your tongue!" cried Wilton.

"No, James, certainly not. It is my duty, as poor Kate's aunt, to do what is best for her; and you should not speak to me like that before a stranger. I don't know what he will think. The fluid magnesia would not do her any harm, would it, Mr Leigh?"

"Not the slightest, madam; and I feel sure that with a little motherly attention and such a course of change as I prescribed, Miss Wilton will soon be well."

"There, James, we must have the Morrison girls to stay here with her. They are musical and—"

"We shall have nothing of the kind, Maria," said her husband, with asperity.

"Well, I know you don't like them, my dear, but in a case of urgency— by the way, Mr Leigh, someone told me your sister played exquisitely on the organ last Sunday because the organist was ill."

"My sister does play," said Leigh, coldly.

"I wish I had been at church to hear her, but my poor Claud had such a bad bilious headache I was nearly sending for you, and I had to stay at home and nurse him. I'm sure the cooking must be very bad at those cricket match dinners."

"Now, my dear Maria, you are keeping Mr Leigh."

"Oh, no, my dear, he was sent for to give us his advice, and I'm sure it is very valuable. By the way, Mr Leigh, why has not your sister called here?"

"I—er—really—my professional duties have left me little time for etiquette, madam, but I was under the impression that the first call should be to the new-comer."

"Why, of course. Do sit down, James. You are only kicking the dust out of this horrid thick Turkey carpet—they are such a job to move and get beaten, Mr Leigh. Do sit down, dear; you know how it fidgets me when you will jump up and down like a wild beast in a cage."

"Waffle!" said Mr Wilton aside.

"You are quite right, Mr Leigh; I ought to have called, but Claud does take up so much of my time. But I will call to-morrow, and then you two come up here the next day and dine with us, and I feel sure that our poor dear Kate will be quite pleased to know your sister. Tell her—no; I'll ask her to bring some music. She seems very nice, and young girls do always get on so well together. I know she'll do my niece a deal of good. But, of course, you will come again to-day, and keep on seeing her as much as you think necessary."

"Really I—" said Leigh, hesitating, and glancing resentfully at the master of the house.

"Oh, yes, come on, Mr Leigh, and put my niece right as soon as you can," he said.

"But your regular medical attendant—Mr Rainsford, I believe?"

"You may believe he's a pig-headed, obstinate old fool," growled Wilton. "Wanted to take off my leg when I had a fall at a hedge, and the horse rolled over it. Simple fracture, sir; and swore it would mortify. I mortified him."

"Yes, Mr Leigh, and the leg's stronger now than the other," interposed Mrs Wilton.

"How do you know, Maria?" said her husband gruffly.

"Well, my dear, you've often said so."

"Humph! Come in again and see Miss Wilton, Doctor, and I shall feel obliged," said the uncle. "Good morning. The dog-cart is waiting to drive you back. I'll send and have you fetched about—er—four?"

"It would be better if it were left till seven or eight, unless, of course, there is need."

"Eight o'clock, then," said Wilton; and Pierce Leigh bowed and left the room, with the peculiar sensation growing once more in his breast, and lasting till he reached home, thinking of how long it would be before eight o'clock arrived.

Chapter Five

"I should very much like to know what particular sin I have committed that I should have been plagued all my life with a stupid, garrulous old woman for a wife, who cannot be left an hour without putting her foot in it some way or another."

"Ah, you did not say so to me once, James," sighed Mrs Wilton.

"No, a good many hundred times. It's really horrible."

"But James—"

"There, do hold your tongue—if you can, woman. First you get inviting that young ruffian of John Garstang's to stay when he comes down."

"But, my dear, it was Claud. You know how friendly those two always have been."

"Yes, to my sorrow; but you coaxed him to stay."

"Really, my dear, I could not help it without being rude."

"Then why weren't you rude? Do you want him here, fooling about that girl till she thinks he loves her and marries him?"

"Oh, no, dear, it would be horrid. But you don't think—"

"Yes, I do, fortunately," snapped Wilton. "Why don't you think?"

"I do try to, my dear."

"Bah! Try! Then you want to bring in those locusts of Morrisons. It's bad enough to know that the money goes there if Kate dies, without having them hanging about and wanting her to go."

"I'm very, very sorry, James. I wish I was as clever as you."

"So do I. Then, as soon as you are checked in that, you dodge round and invite that Doctor, who's a deuced sight too good-looking, to come again, and ask him to bring his sister."

"But, my dear, it will do Kate so much good, and she really seems very nice."

"Nice, indeed! I wish you were. I believe you are half mad."

"Really, James, you are too bad, but I won't resent it, for I want to go up to Kate; but if someone here is mad, it is not I."

"Yes, it is. Like a weak fool I spoke plainly to you about my plans."

"If you had always done so we should have been better off and not had to worry about getting John Garstang's advice, with his advances and interests, and mortgages and foreclosures."

"You talk about what you don't understand, woman," said Wilton, sharply. "Can't you see that it is to our interest to keep the poor girl here? Do you want to toss her amongst a flock of vulture-like relatives, who will devour her?"

"Why, of course not, dear."

"But you tried to."

"I'm sure I didn't. You said she was so ill you were afraid she'd die and slip through our fingers."

"Yes, and all her money go to the Morrisons."

"Oh, yes, I forgot that. But I gave in directly about not having them here; and what harm could it do if Miss Leigh came? I'm sure it would do poor Kate a lot of good."

"And Claud, too, I suppose."

"Claud?"

"Ugh! You stupid old woman! Isn't she young and pretty? And artful, too, I'll be bound; poor Doctor's young sisters always are."

"Are they, dear?"

"Of course they are; and before she'd been here five minutes she'd be making eyes at that boy, and you know he's just like gunpowder."

"James, dear, you shouldn't."

"I was just as bad at his age—worse perhaps;" and Mr James Wilton, the stern, sage Squire of Northwood Manor, J.P., chairman of the Quarter Sessions, and several local institutions connected with the morals of the poor, chuckled softly, and very nearly laughed.

"James, dear, I'm surprised at you."

"Humph! Well, boys will be boys. You know what he is."

"But do you really think—"

"Yes, I do really think, and I wish you would too. Kate does not take to our boy half so well as I should like to see, and nothing must occur to set her against him. It would be madness."

"Well, it would be very disappointing if she married anyone else."

"Disappointing? It would be ruin. So be careful."

"Oh, yes, dear, I will indeed. I have tried to talk to her a little about what a dear good boy Claud is, and—why, Claud, dear, how long have you been standing there?"

"Just come. Time to hear you say what a dear good boy I am. Won't father believe it?"

Chapter Six

Claud Wilton, aged twenty, with his thin pimply face, long narrow jaw, and closely-cropped hair, which was very suggestive of brain fever or imprisonment, stood leering at his father, his appearance in no wise supporting his mother's high encomiums as he indulged in a feeble smile, one which he smoothed off directly with his thin right hand, which lingered about his lips to pat tenderly the remains of certain decapitated pimples which redly resented the passage over them that morning of an unnecessary razor, which laid no stubble low.

The Vicar of the Parish had said one word to his lady re Claud Wilton—a very short but highly expressive word that he had learned at college. It was "cad,"—and anyone who had heard it repeated would not have ventured to protest against its suitability, for his face alone suggested it, though he did all he could to emphasise the idea by adopting a horsey, collary, cuffy style of dress, every article of which was unsuited to his physique.

"Has Henry Dasent gone?"

"Yes, guvnor, and precious glad to go. You were awfully cool to him, I must say. He said if it wasn't for his aunt he'd never darken the doors again."

"And I hope he will not, sir. He is no credit to your mother."

"But I think he means well, my dear," said Mrs Wilton, plaintively. "It is not his fault. My poor dear sister did spoil him so."

"Humph! And she was not alone. Look here, Claud, I will not have him here. I have reasons for it, and he, with his gambling and racing propensities, is no proper companion for you."

"P'raps old Garstang says the same about me," said the young man, sulkily.

"Claud, my dear, for shame," said Mrs Wilton. "You should not say such things."

"I don't care what John Garstang says; I will not have his boy here. Insolent, priggish, wanting in respect to me, and—and—he was a deal too attentive to Kate."

"Oh, my dear, did you think so?" cried Mrs Wilton.

"Yes, madam, I did think so," said her husband with asperity, "and, what was ten times worse, you were always leaving them together in your blundering way."

"Don't say such things to me, dear, before Claud."

"Then don't spend your time making mistakes. Just come, have you, sir?"

"Oh, yes, father, just come," said the young man, with an offensive grin.

"You heard more than you said, sir," said the Squire, "so we may as well have a few words at once."

"No, no, no, my dear; pray, pray don't quarrel with Claud now; I'm sure he wants to do everything that is right."

"Be quiet, Maria," cried the Squire, angrily.

"All right, mother; I'm not going to quarrel," said the son.

"Of course not I only want Claud to understand his position. Look here, sir, you are at an age when a bo—, when a man doesn't understand the value of money."

"Oh, I say, guv'nor! Come, I like that."

"It's quite true, sir. You boys only look upon money as something to spend."

"Right you are, this time."

"But it means more, sir—power, position, the respect of your fellows—everything."

"Needn't tell me, guv'nor; I think I know a thing or two about tin."

"Now, suppose we leave slang out of the matter and talk sensibly, sir, about a very important matter."

"Go on ahead then, dad; I'm listening."

"Sit down then, Claud."

"Rather stand, guv'nor; stand and grow good, ma."

"Yes, my dear, do then," said Mrs Wilton, smiling at her son fondly. "But listen now to what papa says; it really is very important."

"All right, mother; but cut it short, father, my horse is waiting and I don't want him to take cold."

"Of course not, my boy; always take care of your horse. I will be very brief and to the point, then. Look here, Claud, your cousin, Katherine—"

"Oh! Ah, yes; I heard she was ill. What does the Doctor say?"

"Never mind what the Doctor says. It is merely a fit of depression and low spirits. Now this is a serious matter. I did drop hints to you before. I must be plain now about my ideas respecting your future. You understand?"

"Quite fly, dad. You want me to marry her."

"Exactly. Of course in good time."

"But ain't I 'owre young to marry yet,' as the song says?"

"Years do not count, my boy," said his father, majestically. "If you were ten years older and a weak, foolish fellow, it would be bad; but when it is a case of a young man who is bright, clever, and who has had some experience of the world, it is different."

Mrs Wilton, who was listening intently to her husband's words, bowed her head, smiled approval, and looked with the pride of a mother at her unlicked cub.

But Claud's face wrinkled up, and he looked inquiringly at his elder.

"I say, guv'nor," he said, "does this mean chaff?"

"Chaff? Certainly not, sir," said the father sternly. "Do I look like a man who would descend to—to—to chaff, as you slangly term it, my own son?"

"Not a bit of it, dad; but last week you told me I was the somethingest idiot you ever set eyes on."

"Claud!"

"Well, he did, mother, and he used that favourite word of his before it. You know," said the youth, with a grin.

"Claud, my dear, you shouldn't."

"I didn't, mother; it was the dad. I never do use it except in the stables or to the dogs."

"Claud, my boy, be serious. Yes, I did say so, but you had made me very angry, and—er—I spoke for your good."

"Yes, I'm sure he did, my dear," said Mrs Wilton.

"Oh, all right, then, so long as he didn't mean it. Well, then, to cut it short, you both want me to marry Kate?"

"Exactly."

"Not much of a catch. Talk about a man's wife being a clinging vine; she'll be a regular weeping willow."

"Ha! ha! very good, my boy," said Wilton, senior; "but no fear of that. Poor girl, look at her losses."

"But she keeps going on getting into deeper misery. Look at her."

"It only shows the sweet tenderness of her disposition, Claud, my dear," said his mother.

"Yes, of course," said his father, "but you'll soon make her dry her eyes."

"And she really is a very sweet, lovable, and beautiful girl, my dear," said Mrs Wilton.

"Tidy, mother; only her eyes always look as red as a ferret's."

"Claud, my dear, you shouldn't—such comparisons are shocking."

"Oh, all right, mother. Very well; as I am such a clever, man-of-the-world sort of a chap, I'll sacrifice myself for the family good. But I say, dad, she really has that hundred and fifty thou—?"

"Every shilling of it, my boy, and—er—really that must not go out of the family."

"Well, it would be a pity. Only you will have enough to leave me to keep up the old place."

"Well—er—I—that is—I have been obliged to mortgage pretty heavily."

"I say, guv'nor," cried the young man, looking aghast; "you don't mean to say you've been hit?"

"Hit? No, my dear, certainly not," cried Mrs Wilton.

"Oh, do be quiet, ma. Father knows what I mean."

"Well, er—yes, my boy, to be perfectly frank, I have during the past few years made a—er—two or three rather unfortunate speculations, but, as John Garstang says—"

"Oh, hang old Garstang! This is horrible, father; just now, too, when I wanted to bleed you rather heavily."

"Claud, my darling, don't, pray don't use such dreadful language."

"Will you be quiet, ma! It's enough to make a fellow swear. Are you quite up a tree, guv'nor?"

"Oh, no, no, my boy, not so bad as that. Things can go oh for years just as before, and, er—in reason, you know—you can have what money you require; but I want you to understand that you must not look forward to having this place, and er—to see the necessity for thinking seriously about a wealthy marriage. You grasp the position now?"

"Dad, it was a regular smeller, and you nearly knocked me out of time. I saw stars for the moment."

"My dearest boy, what are you talking about?" asked Mrs Wilton, appealingly.

"Oh, bother! But, I say, guv'nor, I'm glad you spoke out to me—like a man."

"To a man, my boy," said the father, holding out his hand, which the son eagerly grasped. "Then now we understand each other?"

"And no mistake, guv'nor."

"You mustn't let her slip through your fingers, my boy."

"Likely, dad!"

"You must be careful; no more scandals—no more escapades—no follies of any kind."

"I'll be a regular saint, dad. I say, think I ought to read for the church?"

"Good gracious me, Claud, my dear, what do you mean?"

"White choker, flopping felt, five o'clock tea, and tennis, mother. Kate would like that sort of thing."

Wilton, senior, smiled grimly.

"No, no, my boy, be the quiet English gentleman, and let her see that you really care for her and want to make her happy. Poor girl, she wants love and sympathy."

"And she shall have 'em, dad, hot and strong. A hundred and fifty thou—!"

"Would clear off every lien on the property, my boy, and it would be a grand thing for my poor deceased brother's child."

"You do think so, don't, you, my dear?" said Mrs Wilton, mentally extending a tendril, to cling to her husband, "because I—"

"Decidedly, decidedly, my dear," said the Squire, quickly. "Thank you, Claud, my boy," he continued. "I shall rely upon your strong common sense and judgment."

"All right, guv'nor. You give me my head. I'll make it all right. I'll win the stakes with hands down."

"I do trust you, my boy; but you must be gentle, and not too hasty."

"I know," said the young man with a cunning look. "You leave me alone."

"Hah! That's right, then," said the Squire, drawing a deep breath as he smiled at his son; but all the same his eyes did not look the confidence expressed by his words.

Chapter Seven

"Why, there then, my precious, you are ever so much better. You look quite bright this morning."

"Do I, 'Liza?" said Kate sadly, as she walked to her bedroom window and stood gazing out at the sodden park and dripping trees.

"Ever so much, my dear. Mr Leigh has done you a deal of good. I do wonder at finding such a clever gentlemanly Doctor down in an out-of-the-way place like this. You like him, don't you?"

The girl turned slowly and gazed at the speaker, her brow contracting a little at the inner corners of her straight eyebrows, which were drawn up, giving her face a troubled expression.

"I hardly thing I do, nurse, dear; he is so stern and firm with me. He seems to talk to me as if it were all my fault that I have been so weak and ill; and he does not know—he does not know."

The tears rose to her eyes, ready to brim over as she spoke.

"Ah! naughty little girl!" cried the woman, with mock anger; "crying again! I will not have it. Oh! my own pet," she continued, changing her manner, as she passed her arm lovingly about the light waist and tenderly kissed her charge. "Please, please try. You are so much better. You must hold up."

"Yes, yes, nurse, I will," cried the girl, making an effort, and kissing the homely face lovingly.

"And what did I tell you? I'm always spoken of as your maid now—lady's maid. It must not be nurse any longer."

"Ah!" said Kate, with the wistful look coming in her eyes again; "it seems as if all the happy old things are to be no more."

"No, no, my dear; you must not talk so. You not twenty, and giving up so to sadness! You must try and forget."

"Forget!" cried the girl, reproachfully.

"No, no, not quite forget, dear; but try and bear your troubles like a woman now. Who could forget dear old master, and your poor dear mother?

But would they like you to fret yourself into the grave with sorrow? Would they not say if they could come to you some night, 'Never forget us, darling; but try and bear this grief as a true woman should'?"

"Yes," said the girl, thoughtfully, "and I will. But I don't feel as if I could be happy here."

The maid sighed.

"Uncle is very kind, and my aunt is very loving in her way, but I feel as if I want to be alone somewhere—of course with you. I have lain awake at night, longing to be back home."

"But that is impossible now, darling. Cook wrote to me the other day, and she told me that the house and furniture had been sold, and that the workmen were in, and—oh, what a stupid woman I am. Pretty way to try and comfort you!"

"It's nothing, 'Liza. It's all gone now," said the girl, smiling piteously.

"That's nice and brave of you; but I am very stupid, my dear. There, there, you will try and be more hopeful, and to think of the future?"

"Yes, I will; but I'm sure I should be better and happier if I went away from here. Couldn't we have a cottage somewhere—at the seaside, perhaps, and live together?"

"Well, yes, you could, my dear; but it wouldn't be nice for you, nor yet proper treatment to your uncle and aunt. Come, try and get quite well. So you don't like Doctor Leigh?"

"No, I think not."

"Nor yet Miss Jenny?"

"Oh, yes, I like her," said Kate, with animation. "She is very sweet and girlish. Oh, nurse, dear, I wish I could be as happy, and light-hearted as she is!"

"So you will be soon, my darling. I don't want to see you quite like her. You are so different; but she is a very nice girl, and by-and-by perhaps you'll see more of her. You do want more of a companion of your own age. There goes the breakfast bell! What a wet, soaking morning; but it isn't foggy down here like it used to be in the Square, and the sun shines more; and Miss Kate—"

"Oh, don't speak like that, nurse!"

"But I must, my dear. I have to keep my place down here."

"Well, when we are alone then. What were you going to say?"

"I want you to try and make me happy down here."

"I? How can I?"

"By letting the sunshine come back into your face. You've nearly broken my heart lately, what with seeing you crying and being so ill."

"I'm going to try, nurse."

"That's right. What's that? Hail?"

At that moment there was a tap at the door.

"Nearly ready to go down, my darling?"

The door opened, and Mrs Wilton appeared.

"May I come in? Ah, quite ready. Come, that's better, my pretty pet. Why, you look lovely and quite a colour coming into your face. Now, don't she look nice this morning?"

"Yes, ma'am; I've been telling her so."

"I thought we should bring her round. I am pleased, and you're a very good girl. Your uncle will be delighted; but come along down, and let's make the tea, or he'll be going about like a roaring lion for his food. Oh! bless me, what's that?"

"That" was a sharp rattling, for the second time, on the window-pane.

"Not hail, surely. Oh, you naughty boy," she continued, throwing open the casement window. "Claud, my dear, you shouldn't throw stones at the bedroom windows."

"Only small shot. Morning. How's Kate? Tell her the breakfast's waiting."

"We're coming, my dear, and your cousin's ever so much better. Come here, my dear."

Kate coloured slightly, as she went to the open window, and Claud stood looking up, grinning.

"How are you? Didn't you hear the shot I pitched up before?"

"Yes, I thought it was hail," said Kate, coldly.

"Only number six. But come on down; the guv'nor's been out these two hours, and gone to change his wet boots."

"We're coming, my dear," cried Mrs Wilton; "and Claud, my dear, I'm sure your feet must be wet. Go in and change your boots at once."

"Bother. They're all right."

"Now don't be obstinate, my dear; you know how delicate your throat is, and—There, he's gone. You'll have to help me to make him more obedient, Kate, my dear. I've noticed already how much more attention he pays to what you say. But there, come along."

James Wilton was already in the breakfast-room, looking at his letters, and scowling over them like the proverbial bear with the sore head.

"Come, Maria," he growled, "are we never to have any—Ah, my dear, you down to breakfast! This makes up for a wet morning," and he met and kissed his niece, drew her hand under his arm, and led her to a chair on the side of the table nearest the fire. "That's your place, my dear, and it has looked very blank for the past fortnight. Very, very glad to see you fill it again. I say," he continued, chuckling and rubbing his hands, "you're quite looking yourself again."

"Yes," said Mrs Wilton, "but you needn't keep all the good mornings and kisses for Kitty. Ah, it's very nice to be young and pretty, but if Uncle's going to pet you like this I shall grow quite jealous." This with a good many meaning nods and smiles at her niece, as she took her place at the table behind the hissing urn.

"You've been too much petted, Maria. It makes you grow too plump and rosy."

"James, my dear, you shouldn't."

"Oh, yes, I should," said her husband, chuckling. "I know Kitty has noticed it. But is that boy coming in to breakfast?"

"Yes, yes, yes, my dear; but don't shout so. You quite startle dear Kitty. Recollect, please, that she is an invalid."

"Bah! Not she. Going to be quite well again directly, and come for rides and drives with me to the farms. Aren't you, my dear?"

"I shall be very pleased to, Uncle—soon."

"That's right. We'll soon have some roses among the lilies. Ha! ha! You must steal some of your aunt's. Got too many in her cheeks, hasn't she, my dear—Damask, but we want maiden blush, eh?"

"Do be quiet, James. You really shouldn't."

"Where is Claud? He must have heard the bell."

"Oh, yes, and he, came and called Kitty. He has only gone to change his wet boots."

"Wet boots! Why, he wasn't down till nine. Oh, here you are, sir. Come along."

"Did you change your boots, Claud?"

"No, mother," said that gentleman, seating himself opposite Kate.

"But you should, my dear."

Wilton gave his niece a merry look and a nod, which was intended to mean, "You attend to me."

"Yes, you should, my dear," he went on, imitating his wife's manner; "and why don't you put on goloshes when you go out?"

Claud stared at his father, and looked as if he thought he was a little touched mentally.

"Isn't it disgusting, Kitty, my dear?" said Wilton. "She'd wrap him up in a flannel and feed him with a spoon if she had her way with the great strong hulking fellow."

"Don't you take any notice of your uncle's nonsense, my dear. Claud, my love, will you take Kitty's cup to her?"

"She'd make a regular molly-coddle of him. And we don't want doctoring here. Had enough of that the past fortnight. I say, you're going to throw Leigh overboard this morning. Don't want him any more, do you?"

"Oh, no, I shall be quite well now."

"Yes," said her uncle, with a knowing look. "Don't you have any more of it. And I say, you'll have to pay his long bill for jalap and pilly coshy. That is if you can afford it."

"I do wish, my dear, you'd let the dear child have her breakfast in peace; and do sit down and let your cousin be, Claud, dear; I'm sure she will not eat bacon. It's so fidgeting to have things forced upon you."

"You eat your egg, ma! Kitty and I understand each ether. She wants feeding up, and I'm going to be the feeder."

"That's right, boy; she wants stamina."

"But she can't eat everything on the table, James."

"Who said she could? She isn't a stout elderly lady."

The head of the family looked at his niece with a broad smile, as if in search of a laugh for his jest, but the smile that greeted him was very wan and wintry.

"Any letters, my dear?" said Mrs Wilton, as the breakfast went on, with Kate growing weary of her cousin's attentions, all of which took the form of a hurried movement to her side of the table, and pressure brought to bear over the breakfast delicacies.

The wintry look appeared to be transferred from Kate's to her uncle's face, but it was not wan; on the contrary, it was decidedly stormy.

"Yes," he said, with a grunt.

"Anything particular?"

"Yes, very."

"What is it, my dear?"

"Don't both—er—letter from John Garstang."

"Oh, dear me!" said Mrs Wilton, looking aghast; and her husband kicked out one foot for her special benefit, but as his leg was not eight feet long the shot was a miss.

"Says he'll run down for a few days to settle that little estate business; and that it will give him an opportunity to have a few chats with Kate here. You say you like Mr Garstang, my dear?"

"Oh, yes," said Kate, quietly; "he was always very nice and kind to me."

"Of course, my darling; who would not be?" said Mrs Wilton.

"Claud, boy, I suppose the pheasants are getting scarce."

"Oh, there are a few left yet," said the young man.

"You must get up a beat and try and find a few hares, too. Uncle Garstang likes a bit of shooting. Used to see much of John Garstang, my dear, when you were at home?"

"No, uncle, not much. He used to come and dine with us sometimes, and he was always very kind to me from the time I was quite a little girl, but my father and he were never very intimate."

"A very fine-looking man, my dear, and so handsome," said Mrs Wilton.

"Yes, very," said her husband, dryly; "and handsome is as handsome does."

"Yes, my dear, of course," said Mrs Wilton; and very little more was said till the end of the breakfast, when the lady of the house asked what time the guest would be down.

"Asks me to send the dog-cart to meet the mid-day train. Humph! rain's over and sun coming out. Here, Claud, take your cousin round the greenhouse and the conservatory. She hasn't seen the plants."

"All right, father. Don't mind me smoking, do you, Kitty?"

"Of course she'll say no," said Wilton testily; "but you can surely do without your pipe for an hour or two."

"Oh, very well," said Claud, ungraciously; and he offered his cousin his arm.

She looked surprised at the unnecessary attention, but took it; and they went out through the French window into the broad verandah, the glass door swinging to after them.

"What a sweet pair they'll make, James, dear," said Mrs Wilton, smiling fondly after her son. "How nicely she takes to our dear boy!"

"Yes, like the rest of the idiots. Girl always says snap to the first coat and trousers that come near her."

"Oh, James, dear! you shouldn't say that I'm sure I didn't!"

"You! Well, upon my soul! How you can stand there and utter such a fib! But never mind; it's going to be easy enough, and we'll get it over as soon as we decently can, if you don't make some stupid blunder and spoil it."

"James, dear!"

"Be just like you. But a nice letter I've had from John Garstang about that mortgage. Never mind, though; once this is over I can snap my fingers at him. So be as civil as you can; and I suppose we must give him some of the best wine."

"Yes, dear, and have out the china dinner service."

"Of course. But I wish you'd put him into a damp bed."

"Oh, James, dear! I couldn't do that."

"Yes, you could; give him rheumatic fever and kill him. But I suppose you won't."

"Indeed I will not, dear. There are many wicked things that I feel I could do, but put a Christian man into a damp bed—no!"

"Humph! Well, then, don't; but I hope that boy will be careful and not scare Kitty."

"What, Claud? Oh, no, my dear, don't be afraid of that. My boy is too clever; and, besides, he's beginning to love the very ground she walks on. Really, it seems to me quite a Heaven-made matter."

"Always is, my dear, when the lady has over a hundred thousand pounds," said Wilton, with a grim smile; "but we shall see."

Chapter Eight

"I say, don't be in such a jolly hurry. You're all right here, you know. I want to talk to you."

"You really must excuse me now, Claud; I have not been well, and I'm going back to my room."

"Of course you haven't been well, Kitty—I say, I shall call you Kitty, you know—you can't expect to be well moping upstairs in your room. I'll soon put you right, better than that solemn-looking Doctor. You want to be out in the woods and fields. I know the country about here splendidly. I say, you ride, don't you?"

"I? No."

"Then I'll teach you. Get your old maid to make you a good long skirt— that will do for a riding-habit at first—I'll clap the side-saddle on my cob, and soon show you how to ride like a plucky girl should. I say, Kitty, I'll hold you on at first—tight."

The speaker smiled at her, and the girl shrank from him, but he did not see it.

"You'll soon ride, and then you and I will have the jolliest of times together. I'll make you ride so that by this time next year you'll follow the hounds, and top a hedge with the best of them."

"Oh, no, I have no wish to ride, Claud."

"Yes, you have. You think so now, because you're a bit down; but you wait till you're on the cob, and then you'll never want to come off. I don't. I say, you haven't seen me ride."

"No, Claud; but I must go now."

"You mustn't, coz. I'm going to rouse you up. I say, though, I don't want to brag, but I can ride—anything. I always get along with the first flight, and a little thing like you after I've been out with you a bit will astonish some of them. I shall keep my eye open, and the first pretty little tit I see that I think will suit you, I shall make the guv'nor buy."

"I beg that you will not, Claud."

"That's right, do. Go down on your poor little knees and beg, and I'll get the mount for you all the same. I know what will do you good and bring the blood into your pretty cheeks. No, no, don't be in such a hurry. I won't let you go upstairs and mope like a bird with the pip. You never handled a gun, I suppose?"

"No, never," said Kate, half angrily now; "of course not."

"Then you shall. You can have my double-barrel that father bought for me when I was a boy. It's light as a feather, comes up to the shoulder splendidly, and has no more kick in it than a mouse. I tell you what, if it's fine this afternoon you shall put on thick boots and a hat, and we'll walk along by the fir plantations, and you shall have your first pop at a pheasant."

"I shoot at a pheasant!" cried Kate in horror.

"Shoo!" exclaimed Claud playfully. "Yes, you have your first shot at a pheasant. Shuddering? That's just like a London girl. How horrid, isn't it?"

"Yes, horrible for a woman."

"Not a bit of it. You'll like it after the first shot. You'll be ready enough to shove in the cartridges with those little hands, and bring the birds down. I say, I'll teach you to fish, too, and throw a fly. You'll like it, and soon forget all the mopes. You've been spoiled; but after a month or two here you won't know yourself. Don't be in such a hurry, Kitty."

"Don't hold my hand like that, Claud; I must really go now," said Kate, whose troubled face was clouded with wonder, vexation, and something approaching fear. "I really wish to go into the house."

"No, you don't; you want to stop with me. I shan't have a chance to talk to you again, with old Garstang here. I say, I saw you come out to have this little walk up and down here. I was watching and came after you to show you the way about the grounds."

"It was very kind of you, Claud. Thank you; but let me go in now."

"Shan't I don't get a chance to have a walk with such a girl as you every day. I am glad you've come. It makes our house seem quite different."

"Thank you for saying so—but I feel quite faint now."

"More need for you to stop in the fresh air. You faint, and I'll bring you to again with a kiss. That's the sort of thing to cure a girl who faints."

She looked at him in horror and disgust, as he burst into a boisterous laugh.

"I suppose old Garstang isn't a bad sort but we don't much like him here. I say, what do you think of Harry Dasent?"

"I—I hardly know," said Kate, who was trying her best to get back along the path by some laurels to where the conservatory door by the drawing-room stood open. "I have seen so little of him."

"So much the better for you. He's not a bad sort of a fellow for men to know, but he's an awful cad with girls. Not a bit of a gentleman. You won't see much more of him, though, for the guv'nor says he won't have him here. I say, a month ago it would have made me set up on bristles, because I want him for a mate, but I don't mind now you've come. We'll be regular pals, and go out together everywhere. I'll soon show you what country life is. Oh, well, if you will go in now I won't stop you. I'll go and have the little gun cleaned up, and—I say, come round the other way; I haven't shown you the dogs."

"No, no—not now, please, Claud. I really am tired out and faint."

He still kept her hand tightly under his arm, in spite of her effort to withdraw it, and followed her into the conservatory, which was large and well-filled with ornamental shrubs and palms.

"Well, you do look a bit tired, dear, but it becomes you. I say, I am so glad you've come. What a pretty little hand this is. You'll give me a kiss before you go?"

She started from him in horror.

"Nobody can't see here. Just one," he whispered, as he passed his arm round her waist; and before she could struggle free he had roughly kissed her twice.

"Um-m-m," exclaimed Mrs Wilton, in a soft simmering way. "Claud, Claud, my dear, shocking, shocking! Oh, fie, fie, fie! You shouldn't, you know. Anyone would think you were an engaged couple."

"Aunt, dear!" cried Kate, in an agitated voice, as she clung to that lady, but no further words would come.

"Oh, there, there, my dear, don't look like that," cried Mrs Wilton. "I'm not a bit cross. Why, you're all of a flutter. I wasn't blaming you, my dear, only that naughty Claud. It was very rude of him, indeed. Really, Claud, my dear, it is not gentlemanly of you. Poor Kate is quite alarmed."

"Then you shouldn't have come peeping," cried the oaf, with a boisterous laugh.

"Claud! for shame! I will not allow it. It is not respectful to your mamma. Now, come in, both of you. Mr Garstang is here—with your father, Claud, my love; and I wish you to be very nice and respectful to him, for who knows what may happen? Kate, my dear, I never think anything of money, but when one has rich relatives who have no children of their own, I always say that we oughtn't to go out of our way to annoy them. Henry Dasent certainly is my sister's child, but one can't help thinking more of one's own son; and as Harry is nothing to Mr Garstang, I can't see how he can help remembering Claud very strongly in his will."

"Doesn't Claud wish he may get it!" cried that youth, with a grin. "I'm not going to toady old Garstang for the sake of his coin."

"Nobody wishes you to, my dear; but come in; they must be done with their business by now. Come, my darling. Why, there's a pretty bloom on your cheeks already. I felt that a little fresh air would do you good. They're in the library; come along. We can go in through the verandah. Don't whistle, Claud, dear; it's so boyish."

They passed together out of the farther door of the conservatory into the verandah, and as they approached an open window, a smooth bland voice said:

"I'll do the best I can, Mr Wilton; but I am only the agent. If I stave it off, though, it can only be for a short time, and then—Ah, my dear child!"

John Garstang, calm, smooth, well-dressed and handsome, rose from one of the library chairs as Kate entered with her aunt, and held out both his hands: "I am very glad to see you again—very, very sorry to hear that you have been so ill. Hah!" he continued, as he scrutinised the agitated face before him in a tender fatherly way, "not quite right yet, though," and he led her to a chair near the fire. "That rosy tinge is a trifle too hectic, and the face too transparently white. You must take care of her, Maria Wilton, and see that she has plenty of this beautiful fresh air. I hope she is a good obedient patient."

"Ve-ry, ve-ry, good indeed, John Garstang, only a little too much disposed to keep to her room."

"Oh, well, quite natural, too," said Garstang, smiling. "What we all do when we are ailing. But there, we must not begin a discussion about ailments. I'm very glad to see you again, though, Kate, and congratulate you upon being here."

"Thank you, Mr Garstang," she replied, giving him a wistful look, as a feeling of loneliness amongst these people made her heart seem to contract.

"Well, Wilton, I don't think we need talk any more about business?"

"Oh, we're not going to stay," cried Mrs Wilton. "Come, Kate, my child, and let these dreadful men talk."

"By no means," said Garstang; "sit still, pray. We shall have plenty of time for anything more we have to say over a cigar to-night, for I've come down to throw myself upon your hospitality for a day or two."

"Of course, of course," said Wilton, quickly; "Maria has a room ready for you."

"Yes, your old room, John Garstang; and it's beautifully aired, and just as you like it."

"Thank you, Maria. You aunt always spoils me, Kate, when I come down here. I look upon the place as quite an oasis in the desert of drudgery and business; and at last I have to drag myself away, or I should become a confirmed sybarite."

"Well, why don't you?" said Claud. "Only wish I had your chance."

"My dear Claud, you speak with the voice of one-and-twenty. When you are double your age you will find, as I do, that money and position and life's pleasures soon pall, and that the real enjoyment of existence is really in work."

"Walker!" said Claud, contemptuously.

Garstang laughed merrily, and while Wilton and his wife frowned and shook their heads at their son, he turned to Kate.

"It is of no use to preach to young people," he said, "but what I say is the truth. Not that I object to a bit of pleasure, Claud, boy. I'm looking forward to a few hours with you, my lad—jolly ones, as you call them, and as I used. How about the pheasants?"

"More than you'll shoot."

"Sure to be. My eye is not so true as it was, Maria."

"Stuff! You look quite a young man still."

"Well, I feel so sometimes. What about the pike in the lake, Claud? Can we troll a bit?"

"It's chock full of them. The weeds are rotten and the pike want thinning down. Will you come?"

"Will I come! Indeed I will; and I'd ask your cousin to come on the lake with us to see our sport, but it would not be wise. How is the bay?"

"Fit as a fiddle. Say the word and I'll have him round if you're for a ride."

"After lunch, my dear, after lunch," said Mrs Wilton.

"Yes, after lunch I should enjoy it," said Garstang.

"Two, sharp, then," said Claud.

"Yes, two, sharp," replied Garstang, consulting his watch. "Quarter to one now."

"Yes, and lunch at one."

"By the way," said Garstang, "Harry said he had been down here, and you gave him some good sport. I'm afraid I have made a mistake in tying him down to the law."

Wilton moved uneasily in his chair and darted an angry look at his wife, who began to fidget, and looked at Kate and then at her son.

Garstang did not seem to notice anything, but smiled blandly, as he leaned back in his chair.

"Oh, yes, he blazed away at the pheasants," said Claud, sneeringly; "but he only wounded one, and it got away."

"That's bad," said Garstang. "But then he has not had your experience, Master Claud. It's very good of you, though, James, to have him down, and of you, Maria, to make the boy so welcome. He speaks very gratefully about you."

"Oh, it isn't my doing, John Garstang," said the lady, hurriedly; "but of course I am bound to make him welcome when he comes;" and she uttered a little sigh as she glanced at her lord again, as if feeling satisfied that she had exonerated herself from a serious charge.

"Ah, well, we'll thank the lord of the manor, then," said Garstang, smiling at Kate.

"Needn't thank me," said Wilton, gruffly. "I don't interfere with Claud's choice of companions. If you mean that I encourage him to come and neglect his work you are quite out. You must talk to Claud."

"I don't want him," cried that gentleman.

"But I think I understood him to say that you had asked him down again."

"Not I," cried Claud. "He'd say anything."

"Indeed! I'm sorry to hear this. In fact, I half expected to find him down here, and if I had I was going to ask you, James, if you thought it would be possible for you to take him as—as—well, what shall I say?—a sort of farm pupil."

"I?" cried Wilton, in dismay. "What! Keep him here?"

"Well—er—yes. He has such a penchant for country life, and I thought he would be extremely useful as a sort of overlooker, or bailiff, while learning to be a gentleman-farmer."

"You keep him at his desk, and make a lawyer of him," said Wilton sourly. "He'll be able to get a living then, and not have to be always borrowing to make both ends meet. There's nothing to be made out of farming."

"Do you hear this, Kate, my dear?" said Garstang, with a meaning smile. "It is quite proverbial how the British farmer complains."

"You try farming then, and you'll see."

"Why not?" said Garstang, laughingly, while his host writhed in his seat. "It always seems to me to be a delightful life in the country, with horses to ride, and hunting, shooting and fishing."

"Oh, yes," growled Wilton, "and crops failing, and markets falling, and swine fever, and flukes in your sheep, and rinderpest in your cattle, and the bank refusing your checks."

"Oh, come, come, not so bad as that! You have fine weather as well as foul," said Garstang, merrily. "Then Harry has not been down again, Claud?"

"No, I haven't seen him since he went back the other day," said Claud, and added to himself, "and don't want to."

"That's strange," said Garstang, thoughtfully. "I wonder where he has gone. I daresay he will be back at the office, though, by now. I don't like for both of us to be away together. When the cat's away the mice will play, Kate, as the old proverb says."

"Then why don't you stop at the office, you jolly old sleek black tom, and not come purring down here?" said Claud to himself. "Bound to say you can spit and swear and scratch if you like."

There was a dead silence just then, which affected Mrs Wilton so that she felt bound to say something, and she turned to the visitor.

"Of course, John Garstang, we don't want to encourage Harry Dasent here, but if—"

"Ah, here's lunch ready at last," cried Wilton, so sharply that his wife jumped and shrank from his angry glare, while the bell in the little wooden turret went on clanging away.

"Oh, yes, lunch," she said hastily. "Claud, my dear, will you take your cousin in?"

But Garstang had already arisen, with bland, pleasant smile, and advanced to Kate.

"May I?" he said, as if unconscious of his sister-in-law's words; and at that moment a servant opened the library door as if to announce the lunch, but said instead:

"Mr Harry Dasent, sir!"

That gentleman entered the room.

Chapter Nine

"Hello, Harry!" said Claud, breaking up what is generally known as an awkward pause, for the fresh arrival had been received in frigid silence.

"Ah, Harry, my boy," said Garstang, with a pleasant smile, "I half expected to find you here."

"Did you?" said the young man, making an effort to be at his ease. "Rather a rough morning for a walk—roads so bad. I've run down for a few hours to see how Kate Wilton was. Thought you'd give me a bit of lunch."

"Of course, my dear," said Mrs Wilton, stiffly, and glancing at her husband afterwards as if to say, "Wasn't that right?"

"One knife and fork more or less doesn't make much difference at my table," said Wilton, sourly.

"And he does look pretty hungry," said Claud with a grin.

"Glad to see you looking better, Kate," continued the young man, holding out his hand to take that which was released from his step-father's for the moment.

"Thank you, yes," said Kate, quietly; "I am better."

"Well, we must not keep the lunch waiting," said Garstang. "Won't you take in your aunt, Harry? And, by the way, I must ask you to get back to-night so as to be at the office in good time in the morning, for I'm afraid my business will keep me here for some days."

"Oh, yes, I'll be there," replied the young man, with a meaning look at Garstang; and then offering his arm to Mrs Wilton, they filed off into the dining-room, to partake of a luncheon which would have been eaten almost in silence but for Garstang. He cleverly kept the ball rolling with his easy, fluent conversation, seeming as he did to be a master of the art of drawing everyone out in turn on his or her particular subject, and as if entirely for the benefit of the convalescent, to whom he made constant appeals for her judgment.

The result was that to her own surprise the girl grew more animated, and more than once found herself looking gratefully in the eyes of the courtly man of the world, who spoke as if quite at home on every topic he started, whether it was in a discussion with the hostess on cookery and preserves, with Wilton on farming and the treatment of cattle, or with the young men on hunting, shooting, fishing and the drama.

And it was all so pleasantly done that a load seemed to be lifted from the sufferer's breast, and she found herself contrasting what her life was with what it might have been had Garstang been left her guardian, and half wondered why her father, who had been one of the most refined and scrupulous of men, should have chosen her Uncle James instead of the polished courtly relative who set her so completely at her ease and listened with such paternal deference to her words.

"Wish I could draw her out like he does," thought Claud.—"These old fogies! they always seem to know what to say to make a wench grin."

"He'll watch me like a cat does a mouse," said Harry to himself, "but I'll have a turn at her somehow."

James Wilton said little, and looked glum, principally from the pressure of money on the brain; but Mrs Wilton said a great deal, much more than she should have said, some of her speeches being particularly unfortunate, and those which followed only making matters worse. But Garstang always came to her help when Wilton's brow was clouding over; and the lady sighed to herself when the meal was at an end.

"If Harry don't come with us I shall stop in," said Claud to himself; and then aloud, "Close upon two. You'd like a turn with us, Harry, fishing or shooting?"

"I? No. I'm tired with my walk, and I've got to do it again this evening."

"No, you haven't," said Claud, sulkily; "you know you'll be driven back."

"Oh, yes," said Garstang; "your uncle will not let you walk. Better come, Harry."

"Thanks, no, sir; I'll stop and talk to Aunt and Kate, here."

"No, my dear; we must not tire Kate out, she'll have to go and lie down this afternoon."

"Oh, very well then, Aunt; I'll stop and talk to you and Uncle."

"Then you'll have to come round the farms with me if you do," growled Wilton.

"Thanks, no; I've walked enough through the mud for one day."

"Let him have his own way, Claud, my lad," cried Garstang. "We must be off. See you down to dinner, I hope, Kate, my child?"

She smiled at him.

"Yes, I hope to be well enough to come down," she replied.

"That's right; and we'll see what we can get to boast about when we come back. Come along, boy."

Claud was ready to hesitate, but he could not back out, and he followed Garstang, the young men's eyes meeting in a defiant gaze.

But he turned as he reached the door.

"Didn't say good-bye to you, Mamma. All right," he cried, kissing her boisterously. "I won't let them shoot me, and I'll mind and not tumble out of the boat. I say," he whispered, "don't let him get Kate alone."

"Oh, that's your game, is it?" said Harry to himself; "treats it with contempt. All right, proud step-father; you haven't all the brains in the world."

He followed the gentlemen into the hall, and then stood at the door to see them off, hearing Garstang say familiarly: "Let's show them what we can do, Harry, my lad. It's just the day for the pike. Here, try one of these; they tell me they are rather choice."

"Oh, I shall light my pipe," said the young man sulkily.

"Wise man, as a rule; but try one of these first, and if you don't like it you can throw it away."

Claud lit the proffered cigar rather sulkily, and they went off; while Harry, after seeing Wilton go round to the stables, went back into the hall, and was about to enter the drawing-room, but a glance down at his muddy boots made him hesitate.

He could hear the voice of Mrs Wilton as she talked loudly to her niece, and twice over he raised his hand to the door knob, but each time lowered it; and going back into the dining-room, he rang the bell.

"Can I have my boots brushed?" he said to the footman.

"Yes, sir, I'll bring you a pair of slippers."

"Oh, no, I'll come to the pantry and put my feet up on a chair."

The man did not look pleased at this, but he led the way to his place, fetched the blacking and brushes, and as he manipulated them he underwent a kind of cross-examination about the household affairs, answering the first question rather shortly, the rest with a fair amount of eagerness. For the visitor's hand had stolen into his pocket and come out again with half-a-crown, which he used to rasp the back of the old Windsor chair on which he rested his foot, and then, balancing it on one finger, he tapped it softly, making it give forth a pleasant jingling sound that was very grateful to the man's ear, for he brushed away most diligently, blacked, polished, breathed on the leather, and brushed again.

"Keep as good hours as ever?" said Dasent, after several questions had been put.

"Oh, yes, sir. Prayers at ha'-past nine, and if there's a light going anywhere with us after ten the governor's sure to see it and make a row. He's dreadful early, night and morning, too."

"Yes, he is very early of a morning, I noticed. Well, it makes the days longer."

"Well, sir, it do; but one has to be up pretty sharp to get his boots done and his hot water into his room by seven, for if it's five minutes past he's there before you, waiting, and looking as black as thunder. My predecessor got the sack, they say, for being quarter of an hour late two or three times, and it isn't easy to be ready in weather like this."

"What, dark in the mornings?"

"Oh, no, sir, I don't mean that. It's his boots. He gets them that clogged and soaked that I have to wash 'em overnight and put 'em to the kitchen fire, and if that goes out too soon it's an awful job to get 'em to shine. They don't have a hot pair of feet in 'em like these, sir. Your portmanteau coming on by the carrier?"

"Oh, no, I go back to-night. And that reminds me—have they got a good dog-cart in the village?"

"Dog-cart, sir?" said the man, with a laugh; "not here. The baker's got a donkey-cart, and there's plenty of farmers' carts. That's all there is near."

"I thought so, but I've been here so little lately."

"But you needn't mind about that, sir. Master's sure to order our trap to be round to take you to the station, and Tom Johnson'll be glad enough to drive you."

"Oh, yes; of course; but I like to be independent. I daresay I shall walk back."

"I wouldn't, sir, begging your pardon, for it's an awkward road in the dark. Tell you what, though, sir, if you did, there's the man at Barber's Corner, at the little pub, two miles on the road. He has a very good pony and trap. He does a bit of chicken higgling round the country. You mention my name, sir, and he'd be glad enough to drive you for a florin or half-a-crown."

"Ah, well, we shall see," said Dasent, putting down his second leg. "Look a deal better for the touch-up. Get yourself a glass."

"Thankye, sir. Much obliged, sir. But beg your pardon, sir, I'll just give Tom Johnson a 'int and he'll have the horse ready in the dog-cart time enough for you. He'll suppose it'll be wanted. It'll be all right, sir. I wouldn't go tramping it on a dark night, sir, and it's only doing the horse good. They pretty well eat their heads off here sometimes."

"No, no, certainly not," said Dasent. "Thank you, though, er—Samuel, all the same."

"Thank you, sir," said the man, and the donor of half-a-crown went back through the swing baize-covered door, and crossed the hall.

"Needn't ha' been so proud; but p'raps he ain't got another half-crown. Lor', what a gent will do sooner than be under an obligation!"

Even that half-crown seemed to have been thrown away, for upon the giver entering the drawing-room it was to find it empty, and after a little hesitation he returned to the hall, where he was just in time to encounter the footman with a wooden tray, on his way to clear away the lunch things.

"Is your mistress going out?" he said. "There is no one in the drawing-room."

"Gone upstairs to have her afternoon nap, sir," said the man, in a low tone. "I suppose Miss Wilton's gone up to her room, too?"

Dasent nodded, took his hat, and went out, lit a cigar, and began walking up and down, apparently admiring the front of the old, long, low, red-brick house, with its many windows and two wings covered with wistaria and roses. One window—that at the end of the west wing—took his attention greatly, and he looked up at it a good deal before slowly making his way round to the garden, where he displayed a great deal of interest in the vineries and the walls, where a couple of men were busy with their ladders, nailing.

Here he stood watching them for some minutes—the deft way in which they used shreds and nails to rearrange the thin bearing shoots of peach and plum.

After this he passed through an arched doorway in the wall, and smoked in front of the trained pear-trees, before going on to the yard where the tool shed stood, and the ladders used for gathering the apples in the orchard hung beneath the eaves of the long, low mushroom house.

Twice over he went back to the hall, but the drawing-room stood open, and the place was wonderfully quiet and still.

"Anyone would think he was master here," said one of the men, as he saw Dasent pass by the third time. "Won't be much he don't know about the place when he's done."

"Shouldn't wonder if he is," said the other. "Him and his father's lawyers, and the guv'nor don't seem none too chirpy just now. They say he is in Queer Street."

"Who's they?" said his companion, speaking indistinctly, consequent upon having two nails and a shred between his lips.

"Why, they. I dunno, but it's about that they've been a bit awkward with the guv'nor at Bramwich Bank."

"That's nothing. Life's all ups and downs. It won't hurt us. We shall get our wages, I dessay. They're always paid."

The afternoon wore on and at dusk Garstang and Claud made their appearance, followed by a labourer carrying a basket, which was too short to hold the head and tail of a twelve-pound pike, which lay on the top of half-a-dozen more.

"Better have come with us, Harry," said Claud. "Had some pretty good sport. Found it dull?"

"I? No," was the reply. "I say, what time do you dine to-night?"

"Old hour—six."

"Going to stay dinner, Harry?" said Garstang.

"Oh, yes; I'm going to stay dinner," said the young man, giving him a defiant look.

"Well, it will be pleasanter, but it is a very dark ride."

"Yes, but I'm going to walk."

"No, you aren't," said Claud, in a sulky tone of voice; "we're going to have you driven over."

"There is no need."

"Oh, yes, there is. I want a ride to have a cigar after dinner, and I shall come and see you off. We don't do things like that, even if we haven't asked anyone to come."

Kate made her appearance again at dinner, and once more Garstang was the life and soul of the party, which would otherwise have been full of constraint. But it was not done in a boisterous, ostentatious way. Everything was in good taste, and Kate more than once grew quite animated, till she saw that both the young men were eagerly listening to her, when she withdrew into herself.

Mrs Wilton got through the dinner without once making her lord frown, and she was congratulating herself upon her success, as she rose, after making a sign, when her final words evolved a tempestuous flash of his eyes.

"Don't you think you had better stop till the morning, Harry Dasent?" she said.

But his quick reply allayed the storm at once.

"Oh, no, thank you, Aunt," he said, with a side glance at Garstang. "I must be back to look after business in the morning."

"But it's so dark, my dear."

"Bah! the dark won't hurt him, Maria, and I've told them to bring the dog-cart round at eight."

"Oh, that's very good of you, sir," said the young man; "but I had made up my mind to walk."

"I told you I should ride over with you, didn't I?" growled Claud.

"Yes, but—"

"I know. There, hold your row. We needn't start till half-past eight, so there'll be plenty of time for coffee and a cigar."

"Then I had better say good-night to you now, Mr Dasent," said Kate, quietly, holding out her hand.

"Oh, I shall see you again," he cried.

"No; I am about to ask Aunt to let me go up to my room now; it has been a tiring day."

"Then good-night," he said impressively, and he took and pressed her hand in a way which made her colour slightly, and Claud twitch one arm and double his list under the table.

"Good-night. Good-night, Claud." She shook hands; then crossed to her uncle.

"Good-night, my dear," he said, drawing her down to kiss her cheek. "Glad you are so much better."

"Thank you, Uncle.—Good-night, Mr Garstang." Her lip was quivering a little, but she smiled at him gratefully as he rose and spoke in a low affectionate way.

"Good-night, my dear child," he said. "Let me play doctor with a bit of good advice. Make up your mind for a long night's rest, and ask your uncle and aunt to excuse you at breakfast in the morning. You must hasten slowly to get back your strength. Good-night."

"You'll have to take great care of her, James," he continued, as he returned to his seat. "Umph! Yes, I mean to," said the host. "A very, very sweet girt," said Garstang thoughtfully, and his face was perfectly calm as he met his stepson's shifty glance.

Then coffee was brought in; Claud, at a hint from his lather, fetched a cigar box, and was drawn out by Garstang during the smoking to give a lull account of their sport that afternoon with the pike.

"Quite bent the gaff hook," he was saying later on, when the grating of wheels was heard; and soon after the young men started, Mrs Wilton coming into the hall to see them off and advise them both to wrap up well about their chests.

That night John Garstang broke his host's rules by keeping his candle burning late, while he sat thinking deeply by the bedroom fire; for he had a good deal upon his brain just then. "No," he said at last, as he rose to wind up his watch; "she would not dare. But fore-warned is fore-armed, my man. You were never meant for a diplomat. Bah! Nor for anything else."

But it was a long time that night before John Garstang slept.

Chapter Ten

"I say, guv'nor, when's old Garstang going?"

"Oh, very soon, now, boy," said James Wilton testily.

"But you said that a week ago, and he seems to be settling down as if the place belonged to him."

The father uttered a deep, long-drawn sigh.

"It's no use for you to snort, dad; that doesn't do any good. Why don't you tell him to be off?"

"No, no; impossible; and mind what you are about; be civil to him."

"Well, I am. Can't help it; he's so jolly smooth with a fellow, and has such good cigars—I say, guv'nor, rather different to your seventeen-and-six-penny boxes of weeds. I wouldn't mind, only he's in the way so. Puts a stop to, you know what. I never get a chance with her alone; here are you two shut up all the morning over the parchments, and she don't come down; and when she does he carries me off with him. Then at night you're all there."

"Never mind! he will soon go now; we have nearly done."

"I'm jolly glad of it. I've been thinking that if it's going on much longer I'd better do without the four greys."

"Eh?"

"Oh, you know, guv'nor; toddle off to Gretna Green, or wherever they do the business, and get it over."

"No, no, no, no. There must be no nonsense, my boy," said Wilton, uneasily. "Don't do anything rash."

"Oh, no, I won't do anything rash," said Claud, with an unpleasant grin; "only one must make one's hay when the sun shines, guv'nor."

"There's one thing about his visit," said Wilton hurriedly; "it has done her a great deal of good; she isn't like the same girl."

"No; she has come out jolly. Makes it a little more bearable."

"Eh, what, sir?—bearable?"

"Yes. Fellow wants the prospect of some sugar or jam afterwards, to take such a sickly dose as she promised to be."

"Oh, nonsense, nonsense. But—er—mind what you're about; nothing rash."

"I've got my head screwed on right, guv'nor. I can manage a girl. I say, though, she has quite taken to old Garstang; he has got such a way with him. He can be wonderfully jolly when he likes."

"Yes, wonderfully," said Wilton, with a groan.

"You've no idea how he can go when we're out. He's full of capital stories, and as larky when we're fishing or shooting as if he were only as old as I am. Ever seen him jump?"

"What, run and jump?"

"Yah! When he is mounted. He rides splendidly. Took Brown Charley over hedge after hedge yesterday like a bird. Understands a horse as well as I do. I like him, and we get on swimming together; but we don't want him here now."

"Well, well, it won't be long before he has gone," said Wilton, hurrying some papers away over which he and Garstang had been busy all the morning. "Where are you going this afternoon?"

"Ride. He wants to see the Cross Green farm."

"Eh?" said Wilton, looking up sharply, and with an anxious gleam in his eyes. "Did he say that?"

"Yes; and we're off directly after lunch. I say, though, what was that letter about?"

"What letter?" said Wilton, starting nervously.

"Oh, I say; don't jump as if you thought the bailiffs were coming in. I meant the one brought over from the station half-an-hour ago."

"I had no letter."

"Sam said one came. It must have been for old Garstang then."

"Am I intruding? Business?" said Garstang, suddenly appearing at the door.

"Eh? No; come in. We were only talking about ordinary things. Sit down. Lunch must be nearly due. Want to speak to me?"

All this in a nervous, hurried way.

"Never mind lunch," said Garstang quietly; "I want you to oblige me, my dear James, by ordering that brown horse round."

Wilton uttered a sigh of relief, and his face, which had been turning ghastly, slowly resumed its natural tint.

"But I understood from Claud here that you were both going out after lunch."

"I've had a particular letter sent down in a packet, and I must ride over and telegraph back at some length."

"We'll send Tom over for you," said Claud; and then he felt as if he would have given anything to withdraw the words.

"It's very good of you," said Garstang, smiling pleasantly, "but the business is important. Oblige me by ordering the horse at once."

"Oh, I'll run round. Have Brown Charley here in five minutes."

"Thank you, Claud; and perhaps you'll give me a glass of sherry and a biscuit, James?"

"Yes, yes, of course; but you'll be back to dinner?"

"Of course. We must finish what we are about."

"Yes, we must finish what we are about," said Wilton, with a dismal look; and he rang the bell, just as Claud passed the window on the way to the stables.

A quarter of an hour later Garstang was cantering down the avenue, just as the lunch-bell was ringing; and Claud winked at his father as they crossed to the drawing-room, where his mother and Kate were seated, and chuckled to himself as he thought of the long afternoon he meant to have.

"Oh, I say, guv'nor, it's my turn now," he cried, as Wilton crossed smiling to his niece, and offered her his arm.

"All in good time, my boy; all in good time. You bring in your mother. I don't see why I'm always to be left in the background. Come along, Kate, my dear; you must have me to-day."

"Why, where is John Garstang?" cried Mrs Wilton.

"Off on the horse, mother," said Claud, with a grin. "Gone over to the station to wire."

"Gone without saying good-bye?"

"Oh, he's coming back again, mother; but we can do without him for once in the way. I say, Kate, I want you to give me this afternoon for that lesson in riding."

"Riding, my dear?"

"Yes, mother, riding. I'm going to give Kitty some lessons on the little mare."

"No, no; not this afternoon," said the girl nervously, as they entered the dining-room.

"Yes, this afternoon. You've got to make the plunge, and the sooner you do it the better."

"Thank you; you're very good, but I was going to read to aunt."

"Oh, never mind me, my dear; you go with Claud. It's going to be a lovely afternoon."

"I should prefer not to begin yet," said Kate, decisively.

"Get out," cried Claud. "What a girl you are. You'll come."

"I'm sure Claud will take the greatest care of you, my darling."

"Yes, aunt, I am sure he would; but the lessons must wait for a while."

"All right, Kitty. Come for a drive, then. I'll take you a good round."

"I should prefer to stay at home this afternoon, Claud."

"Very well, then, we'll go on the big pond, and I'll teach you how to troll."

She turned to speak to her uncle, to conceal her annoyance, but Claud persevered.

"You will come, won't you?" he said.

"Don't worry your cousin, Claud, my dear, if she would rather not," said Mrs Wilton.

"Who's worrying her?" said Claud, testily. "I say, Kate, say you'll come."

"I would rather not to-day," she said, quietly.

"There now, you're beginning to mope again, and I mean to stop it. I tell you what; we'll have out the guns, and I'll take you along by the fir plantation."

"No, no, my boy," said Wilton, interposing. "Kate isn't a boy."

"Who said she was?" said the young man, gruffly. "Can't a woman pull a trigger if she likes?"

"I daresay she could, my dear," said Mrs Wilton; "but I'm sure I shouldn't like to. I've often heard your papa say how badly guns kicked."

"So do donkeys, mother," said Claud, sulkily; "but I shouldn't put her on one that did. You'll come, won't you, dear?"

"No, Claud," said Kate, very quietly and firmly. "I could not find any pleasure in trying to destroy the life of a beautiful bird."

"Ha, ha! I say, we are nice. Don't you eat any pheasant at dinner, then. There's a brace for to-night. Old Garstang shot 'em—a cruel wretch."

Kate looked at him indignantly, and then began conversing with her uncle, while her cousin relapsed into sulky silence, and began to eat as if he were preparing for a famine to come, his mother shaking her head at him reproachfully every time she caught his eye.

The lunch at an end, Kate took her uncle's arm and went out into the veranda with him for a few minutes as the sun was shining, and as soon as they were out of hearing Claud turned fiercely upon his mother.

"What were you shaking your head at me like that for?" he cried. "You looked like some jolly old Chinese figure."

"For shame, my dear. Don't talk to me like that, or I shall be very, very cross with you. And look here, Claud, you mustn't be rough with your cousin. Girls don't like it."

"Oh, don't they? Deal you know about it."

"And there's another thing I want to say to you. If you want to win her you must not be so attentive to that Miss Leigh."

"Who's attentive to Miss Leigh?" said the young man, savagely.

"You are, my dear; you quite flirted with her when she was here with her brother last night, and I heard from one of the servants that you were seen talking to her in Lower Lane on Monday."

"Then it was a lie," he cried, sharply. "Tell 'em to mind their own business. Now, look here, mother, you want me to marry Katey, don't you?"

"Of course, my dear."

"Then you keep your tongue still and your eyes shut. The guv'nor 'll be off directly, and you'll be taking her into the drawing-room."

"Yes, my dear."

"Well, I'm not going out; I'm going to have it over with her this afternoon, so you slip off and leave me to my chance while there is one. I'm tired of waiting for old Garstang to be out of the way."

"But I don't think I ought to, my dear."

"Then I do. Look here, she knows what's coming, and that's why she wouldn't come out with me, you know. It's all gammon, to lead me on. She means it. You know what girls are. I mean to strike while the iron's hot."

"But suppose—"

"I shan't suppose anything of the kind. She only pretends. We understand one another with our eyes. I know what girls are; and you give me my chance this afternoon, and she's mine. She's only holding off a bit, I tell you."

"Perhaps you are right, my dear; but don't hurt her feelings by being too premature."

"Too gammon! You do what I say, and soon. I don't want old Garstang back before we've got it all over. Keep dark; here they come."

Kate entered with her uncle as soon as he had spoken, and Claud attacked her directly.

"Altered your mind?" he said.

"No, Claud; you must excuse me, please," was the reply.

"All right. Off, father?"

"Yes, my boy. In about half an hour or so; I have two or three letters to write."

"Two or three letters to write!" muttered the young man, as he went out into the veranda, to light his pipe, and keep on the watch for the coveted opportunity; "haven't you any brains in your head?"

But James Wilton's half-hour proved to be an hour, and when, after seeing him off, the son returned to the hall, he heard voices in the drawing-room, and gave a vicious snarl.

"Why the devil don't she go?" he muttered.

There were steps the next moment, and he drew back into the dining-room to listen, the conversation telling him that his mother and cousin were going into the library to get some particular book.

There, to the young man's great disgust, they stayed, and he waited for quite half an hour trying to control his temper, and devise some plan for trying to get his mother away.

At last she appeared, saying loudly as she looked back, "I shall be back directly, my dear," and closed the door.

Claud appeared at once, and with a meaning smile at his mother, she crossed to the stairs, while as she ascended to her room the son went straight to the library and entered.

As he threw open the door he found himself face to face with his cousin, who, book in hand, was coming out of the room.

"Hallo!" he cried, with a peculiar laugh; "Where's the old lady?"

"She has just gone to her room, Claud," said Kate, quietly.

"Here, don't be in such a hurry, little one," he cried, pushing to the door. "What's the matter?"

"Nothing," she said, quietly, though her heart was throbbing heavily; "I was going to take my book into the drawing-room."

"Oh, bother the old books!" he cried, snatching hers away, and catching her by the wrist; "come and sit down; I want to talk to you."

"You can talk to me in the drawing-room," she said, trying hard to be firm.

"No, I can't; it's better here. I say, Kitty, when shall it be?"

"When shall what be?"

"Our wedding. You know."

"Never," she said, gravely, fixing her eyes upon his.

"What?" he cried. "What nonsense! You know how I love you. I do, 'pon my soul. I never saw anyone who took my fancy so before."

"Do your mother and father know that you are talking to me in this mad way?—you, my own cousin?" she said, firmly.

"What do I care whether they do or no?" he said, with a laugh; "I've been weaned for a long time. I say, don't hold me off; don't play with a fellow like silly girls do. I love you ever so, and I'm always thinking about your beautiful eyes till I can't sleep of a night. It's quite right for you to hold me off for a bit, but there's been enough of it, and I know you like me."

"I have tried to like you as my cousin," she said, gravely.

"That'll do for a beginning," he replied, laughingly; "but let's get a little farther on now, I say. Kitty, you are beautiful, you know, and whenever I see you my heart goes pumping away tremendously. I can't talk like some fellows do, but I can love a girl with the best of them, and I want you to pitch over all shilly-shally nonsense, and let's go on now like engaged people."

"You are talking at random and of what is unnatural and impossible. Please never to speak to me again like this, Claud; and now loose my wrist, and let me go."

"Likely, when I've got you alone at last I say, don't hold me off like this; it's so silly."

She made a brave effort to hide the alarm she felt; and with a sudden snatch she freed her wrist and darted across the room.

The flight of the hunted always gives courage to the hunter, and in this case he sprang after her, and the next minute had clasped her round the waist.

"Got you!" he said, laughingly; "no use to struggle; I'm twice as strong as you."

"Claud! How dare you?" she cried, with her eyes flashing.

"'Cause I love you, darling."

"Let go. It is an insult. It is a shame to me. Do you know what you are doing?"

"Yes; getting tighter hold of you, so as to kiss those pretty lips and cheeks and eyes—There, and there, and there!"

"If my uncle knew that you insulted me like this—"

"Call him; he isn't above two miles off."

"Aunt—aunt!" cried the girl, excitedly, and with the hot, indignant tears rising to her eyes.

"Gone to lie down, while I have a good long loving talk with you, darling. Ah, it's of no use to struggle. Don't be so foolish. There, you've fought long enough. All girls do the same, because it is their nature to fool it. There! now I'm master; give me a nice, pretty, long kiss, little wifie-to-be. I say, Kitty, you are a beauty. Let's be married soon. You don't know how happy I shall make you."

Half mad now with indignation and fear, she wrested herself once more free, and, scorning to call for help, she ran toward the fire place. But before she could reach the bell he struck her hand on one side, caught her closely now in his arms, and covered her face once more with kisses.

This time a loud cry escaped her as she struggled hard, to be conscious the next moment of some one rushing into the room, feeling herself dragged away, and as the word "Hound!" fell fiercely upon her ear there was the sound of a heavy blow, a scuffling noise, and a loud crash of breaking wood and glass.

Chapter Eleven

"My poor darling child!—Lie still, you miserable hound, or I'll half strangle you."

The words—tender and gentle as if it were a woman's voice, fierce and loud as from an enraged man—seemed to come out of a thick mist in which Kate felt as if she were sick unto death. Then by degrees she grew conscious that she was being held tightly to the breast of of some one who was breathing hard from exertion, and tenderly stroking and smoothing her dishevelled hair.

The next moment there was a wild cry, and she recognised her aunt's voice, as, giddy and exhausted, she clung to him who held her.

"What is it? What is it? Oh, Claud, my darling! Help, help, help! He's killed him—killed."

"Here, what's the matter? Who called?" came from a little distance. Then from close at hand Kate heard her uncle's voice through the mist. "What's all this, Maria—John Garstang—Claud? Damn it all, can no one speak?—Kate, what is it?"

"This," cried Garstang, sternly. "I came back just now, and hearing shrieks rushed in here, just in time to save this poor, weak, suffering child from the brutal insulting attack of that young ruffian."

"He has killed him. James—he has killed him," shrieked Mrs Wilton. "On, my poor dear darling boy!"

"Back, all of you. Be off," roared Wilton, as half a dozen servants came crowding to the door, which he slammed in their faces, and turned the key. "Now, please let's have the truth," he cried, hotly. "Here, Kate, my dear; come to me."

She made no reply, but Garstang felt her cling more closely to him.

"Will some one speak?" cried Wilton, again.

"The Doctor—send for the Doctor; he's dead, he's dead," wailed Mrs Wilton, who was down upon her knees now, holding her son's head in her lap; while save for a slight quiver of the muscles, indicative of an effort to keep his eyes closed, Claud made no sign.

"He is not dead," said Garstang, coldly; "a knockdown blow would not kill a ruffian of his calibre."

"Oh," exclaimed Mrs Wilton, turning upon him now in her maternal fury; "he owns to it, he struck him down—my poor, poor boy. James, why don't you send for the police at once? The cruelty—the horror of it! Kate, Kate, my dear, come away from the wretch at once."

"Then you own that you struck him down?" cried Wilton, whose face was now black with a passion which made him send prudence to the winds, as he rose in revolt against one who had long been his master.

"Yes," said Garstang, quietly, and without a trace of anger, though his tone was full of contempt; "I told you why."

"Yes, and by what right did you interfere? Some foolish romping connected with a boy and girl love, I suppose. How dared you interfere?"

"Boy and girl love!" cried Garstang, scornfully, as he laid one hand upon Kate's head and pressed it to his shoulder, where she nestled and hid her face. "Shame upon you both; it was scandalous!"

"Shame upon us? What do you mean, sir? What do you mean?—Will you come away from him, Kate?"

"I mean this," said Garstang, with his arm firmly round the poor girl's waist, "that you and your wife have failed utterly in your duties towards this poor suffering child."

"It isn't true," cried Mrs Wilton. "We've treated her as if she were our own daughter; and my poor boy told me how he loved her, and he had only just come to talk to her for a bit. Oh, Claud, my darling! my precious boy!"

"Did I not tell you that your darling—your precious boy—was insulting her grievously? Shame upon you, woman," cried Garstang. "It needed no words of mine to explain what had taken place. Your own woman's nature ought to have revolted against such an outrage to the weak invalid placed by her poor father's will in your care."

"Don't you speak to my wife like that!" cried Wilton, angrily.

"I will speak to your wife like that, and to you as well. I forbore to speak before: I had no right; but do you think I have been blind to the scandal going on here? The will gives you full charge of the poor child and her fortune, and what do I find when I come down? A dastardly cruel plot to ensnare her—to force on a union with an unmannerly, brutally coarse young ruffian, that he may—that you may, for your own needs and ends, lawfully gain possession of the fortune, to scatter to the winds."

"It's a lie—it's a lie!" roared Wilton.

"It is the truth, sir. Your wife's words just now confirmed what I had noted over and over again, till my very gorge rose at being compelled to accept the hospitality of such people, while I writhed at my own impotence, my helplessness when I wished to interfere. You know—she knows—how I have kept silence. Not one word of warning have I uttered to her. She must have seen and felt what was being hatched, but neither she nor I could have realised that the cowardly young ruffian lying there would have dared to insult a weak gentle girl whose very aspect claimed a man's respect and protection. A lie? It is the truth, James Wilton."

"Oh, my poor, poor boy!" wailed Mrs Wilton; "and I did beg and pray of you not to be too rash."

"Will you hold your tongue, woman?" roared Wilton.

"Yes, for heaven's sake be silent, madam," cried Garstang; "there was no need for you to indorse my words, and lower yourself more in your poor niece's eyes."

"Look here," cried Wilton, who was going to and fro beyond the library table, writhing under the lash of his solicitor's tongue; "it's all a bit of nonsense; the foolish fellow snatched a kiss, I suppose."

"Snatched a kiss!" cried Garstang, scornfully. "Look at her: quivering with horror and indignation."

"I won't look at her. I won't be talked to like this in my own house."

"Your own house!" said Garstang, contemptuously.

"Yes, sir; mine till the law forces me to give it up. I won't have it. It's my house, and I won't stand here and be bullied by any man."

"Oh, don't, don't, don't make things worse, James," wailed Mrs Wilton. "Send for the Doctor; his heart is beating still."

"You hold your tongue, and don't you make things worse," roared her husband. "As for him—curse him!—it's all his doing."

"But he's lying here insensible, and you won't send for help."

"No, I won't. Do you think I want Leigh and his sister, and then the whole parish, to know what has been going on? The servants will talk enough."

"But he's dying, James."

"You said he was dead just now. Chuck some cold water over the idiot, and bring him to. Damn him! I should like to horsewhip him!"

"You should have done it often, years ago," said Garstang, bitterly. "It is too late now."

"You mind your own business," shouted Wilton, turning upon him; "I can't talk like you do, but I can say what I mean, and it's this: I'm master here yet, and I'll stand no more of it. I don't care for your deeds and documents. I won't have you here to insult me and my wife, and what's more, if you've done that boy a mischief we'll see what the law can do. You shall suffer as well as I. Now then: off with you; pack and go, and I'll show you that the law protects me as well as you. Kate, my girl, you've nothing to be frightened about. Come to me here."

She clung the more tightly to her protector.

"Then come to your aunt," said Wilton, fiercely. "Get up, Maria," he shouted. "Can't you see I want you here?"

"Get up? Oh, James, James, I can't leave my boy."

"Get up, before you put me in a rage," he yelled. "Now, then, Kate, come here; and I tell you this, John Garstang. I give you a quarter of an hour, and if you're not gone then, the men shall throw you out."

"What!" cried Garstang, sternly, as he drew himself up. "Go and leave this poor girl here to your tender mercies?"

"Yes, sir; go and leave 'this poor girl,' as you call her, to my tender mercies."

"I can not; I will not," said Garstang, firmly.

"But I say you shall, Mr Lawyer. You know enough of such things to feel that you must. Curse you and your interference. Kate, my dear, I am your poor dead father's executor, and your guardian."

"Yes, it is true," said Garstang, bitterly. "Poor fellow, it was the one mistake of a good, true life. He had faith in his brother."

"More than he had in you," cried Wilton. "Do you hear what I say, Kate? Don't visit upon your aunt and me the stupid folly of that boy, whose sin is that he is very fond of you, and frightened you by a bit of loving play."

"Loving play!" cried Garstang, scornfully.

"Yes, my dear, loving play. I vouch for it, and so will his mother."

"Yes, yes, yes, Kate, dear. He does love you. He told me so, and if he did wrong, poor, poor boy, see how he has been punished."

"There, my dear, you hear," cried Wilton, trying hard to speak gently and winningly to her, but failing dismally. "Come to your aunt now."

"Yes, Kate, darling, do, do please, and help me to try and bring him round. You don't want to see him lie a corpse at his sorrowing mother's feet?"

"Come here, Kate," cried Wilton, fiercely now. "Don't you make me angry. I am your guardian, and you must obey me. Come away from that man."

She shuddered, and began to sob now violently.

"Ah, that's better. You're coming to your senses now, and seeing things in their proper light. Now, John Garstang, you heard what I said—go."

"Yes, my child," said Garstang, taking one of Kate's hands, and raising it tenderly to his lips, "your uncle is right. I have no place here, no right to protect you, and I must go, trusting that good may come out of evil, and that what has passed, besides opening your eyes to what is a thorough conspiracy, will give you firmness to protect yourself, and teach them that such a project as theirs is an infamy."

"Don't stand preaching there, man. Your time's nearly up. Go, before you are made. Come here to your aunt, Kate."

"No, my dear, do nothing of the sort," said Garstang, gently, as she slowly raised her head and gazed imploringly in his face. "You are but a girl, but you must play the woman now—the firm, strong woman who has to protect herself. Go up to your room and insist upon staying there until you have a guarantee that this insolent cub, who is lying here pretending to be insensible, shall cease his pretensions or be sent away. There, go, and heaven protect you; I can do no more."

Kate drew herself up erect and gazed at him mournfully for a few moments, and then said firmly:

"Yes, Mr Garstang, I will do as you say. Good-bye."

"Good-bye," he said, as he bent down and softly kissed her forehead. Then she walked firmly from the room.

"Brave girl!" said Garstang; "she will be a match for you and your plans now, James Wilton."

"Will you go, sir?" roared the other.

"Yes, I will go. Then it is to be war between us, is it?"

"What you like; I'm reckless now; but you can't interfere with me there."

"No, and I will not trample upon a worm when it is down. I shall take no petty revenge, and you dare not persecute that poor girl. Good-bye to you both, and may this be a lesson to you and your foolish wife. As for you,

you cur, if I hear that you have insulted your cousin again—a girl that any one with the slightest pretension to being a man would have looked upon as a sister—law or no law, I'll come down and thrash you within an inch of your life. I'm a strong man yet, as you know."

He turned and walked proudly out of the room; and as soon as his step had ceased to ring on the oaken floor of the hall Wilton turned savagely upon his son, where he lay upon the thick Turkey carpet, and roared:

"Get up!"

Mrs Wilton shrieked and caught at her husband's leg, but in vain, for he delivered a tremendous kick at the prostrate youth, which brought him to his senses with a yell.

"What are you doing?" he roared.

"A hundred and fifty thousand pounds!" cried Wilton. "Curse you, I should like to give you a hundred and fifty thousand of those."

Within half an hour the dog-cart bearing John Garstang and his portmanteau was grating over the gravel of the drive, and as he passed the further wing he looked up at an open window where Kate was standing pale and still.

He raised his hat to her as he passed, but she did not stir, only said farewell to him with her eyes.

But as the vehicle disappeared among the trees of the avenue she shrank away, to stand thinking of her position, of Garstang's words, and how it seemed now that her girlish life had come to an end that day. For she felt that she was alone, and that henceforth she must knit herself together to fight the battle of her life, strong in her womanly defence, for her future depended entirely upon herself.

And through the rest of that unhappy afternoon and evening, as she sat there, resisting all requests to come down, and taking nothing but some slight refreshment brought up by her maid, she was trying to solve the problem constantly before her:

What should she do now?

Chapter Twelve

Kate was not the only one at the Manor House who declined to come down to dinner.

The bell had rung, and after Mrs Wilton had been up twice to her niece's room, and reported the ill success of her visits to her lord, Wilton growled out:

"Well, I want my dinner. Let her stay and starve herself into her senses. But here," he cried, with a fresh burst of temper, "why the devil isn't that boy here? I'm not going to be kept waiting for him. Do you hear? Where is he?"

"He was so ill, dear, he said he was obliged to go upstairs and lie down."

"Bah! Rubbish! He wasn't hurt."

"Oh, my dear, you don't know," sobbed Mrs Wilton.

"Yah! You cry if you dare. Wipe your eyes. Think I haven't had worry enough to-day without you trying to lay the dust? Ring and tell Samuel to fetch him down."

"Oh, pray don't do that, dear; the servants will talk enough as it is."

"They'd better. I'll discharge the lot. I've been too easy with everybody up to now, and I'll begin to turn over a new leaf. Stand aside, woman, and let me get to that bell."

"No, no, don't, pray don't ring. Let me go up and beg of him to come down."

"What! Beg? Go up and tell him that if he don't come down to dinner in a brace of shakes I'll come and fetch him with a horsewhip."

"James, my dear, pray, pray don't be so violent."

"But I will be violent. I am in no humour to be dictated to now. I'll let some of you see that I'm master."

"But poor dear Claud is so big now."

"I don't care how big he is—a great stupid oaf! Go and tell him what I say. And look here, woman."

"Yes, dear," said Mrs Wilton, plaintively.

"I mean it. If he don't come at once, big as he is, I'll take up the horsewhip."

Mrs Wilton stifled a sob, and went up to her son's room and entered, to find him lying on his bed with his boots resting on the bottom rail, a strong odour of tobacco pervading the room, and a patch or two of cigar ashes soiling the counterpane.

"Claud, my dearest, you shouldn't smoke up here," she said, tenderly, as she laid her hand upon her son's forehead. "How are you now, darling?"

"Damned bad."

"Oh, not quite so bad as that, dearest. Dinner is quite ready."

"—The dinner!"

"Claud, darling, don't use such dreadful language. But please get up now, and let me brush your hair. Your father is so angry and violent because you are keeping him waiting. Pray come down at once."

"Shan't!"

"Claud, dearest, you shouldn't say that. Please come down."

"Shan't, I tell you. Be off, and don't bother me."

"I am so sorry, my dear, but I must. He sent me up, dear."

"I—shan't—come—down. There!"

"But Claud, my dear, he is so angry. I dare not go without you. What am I to say?"

"Tell him I say he's an old beast."

"Oh, Claud, I can't go and tell him that. You shouldn't—you shouldn't, indeed."

"I'm too bad to eat."

"Yes—yes; I know, darling, but do—do try and come down and have a glass of wine. It will do you good, and keep poor papa from being so violent."

"I don't want any wine. And I shan't come. There!"

"Oh, dear me! Oh, dear me!" sighed Mrs Wilton; "what am I to do?"

"Go and tell him I won't come. Bad enough to be hit by that beastly old prize fighter, without him kicking me as he did. I'm not a door mat."

"No, no, my dear; of course not."

"An old brute! I believe he has injured my liver."

"Claud, my darling, don't, pray don't say that."

"Why not? The doctor ought to be fetched; I'm in horrid pain."

"Yes, yes, my dear; and it did seem very hard."

"Hard? I should think it was. I'm sure there's a rib broken, if not two."

"Oh, my own darling boy!" cried Mrs Wilton, embracing him.

"Don't, mother; you hurt. Be off, and leave me alone. Tell him I shan't come."

"No, no, my dear; pray make an effort and come down."

"Shan't, I tell you. Now go!"

"But—but—Claud, dear, he threatened to come up with a horse whip and fetch you."

"What!" cried Claud, springing up on the bed without wincing, and staring at his mother; "did he say that?"

"Yes, my love," faltered the mother.

"Then you go down and tell him to come, and I'll knock his old head off."

"Oh, Claud, my dear boy, you shouldn't. I can not sit here and listen to such parricidical talk."

"Stand up then, and now be off."

"But, my darling, you will come?"

"No, I won't."

"For my sake?"

"I won't, for my own. I'm not going to stand it. He shan't bully and knock me about I'm not a boy now. I'll show him."

"But, Claud, darling, for the sake of peace and quietness; I don't want the servants to know."

But dear Claud—his mother's own darling—was as obstinate now as his father, whom he condemned loudly, then condemned peace and quietness, then the servants, and swore that he would serve Kate out for causing the trouble.

"I'll bring her down on her knees—I'll tame her, and make her beg for a kiss next time."

"Yes, yes, my dear, you shall, but not now. You must be humble and patient."

"Are you coming down, Maria?" ascended in a savage roar.

"Yes, yes, my dear, directly," cried the trembling woman. "There, you hear, darling. He is in a terrible fury. Come down with me."

"I won't, I tell you," cried the young man, making a snatch at the pillow, to raise it threateningly in his hands; "go, and tell him what I said."

"Maria! Am I to come up?" ascended in a roar.

"Yes—no—no, my dear," cried Mrs Wilton. "I'm—I'm coming down."

She hurried out of the room, dabbed her eyes hastily, and descended to where the Squire was tramping up and down the hall, with Samuel, the cook, housemaid, and kitchen maid in a knot behind the swing baize door, which cut off the servants' offices, listening to every word of the social comedy.

"Well," roared Wilton, "is he coming?"

"N-n-not just now, my d-dear. He feels so ill and shaken that he begs you will excuse him."

"Humbug, woman! My boy couldn't have made up such a message. He said he wouldn't, eh? Now then; no prevarication. That's what he said."

"Y-yes, my dear," faltered the mother. "Oh, James dearest, pray—pray don't."

She clung to him, but he shook her off, strode to the umbrella stand, and snatched a hunting whip from where it hung with twisted thong, and stamped up the stairs, with his trembling wife following, sobbing and imploring him not to be so violent; but all in vain, for he turned off at the top of the old oaken staircase and stamped away to the door of his son's bedroom—that at the end of the wing which matched to Kate's.

Here Mrs Wilton made a last appeal in a hurried whisper.

"He is so bad—says his ribs are broken from the kick."

"Bah!" roared the Squire; "he has no ribs in his hind legs—Here, you, Claud; come down to dinner directly or—Here, unlock this door."

He rattled the handle, and then thumped and banged in vain, while Mrs Wilton, who had been ready to shriek with horror, began to breathe more freely.

"I thought you said he was lying down, too bad to get up?"

"Yes, yes, dear, he is," faltered the poor woman.

"Seems like it. Able to lock himself in. Here, you sir; come down."

But there was no reply; not a sound in answer to his rattling and banging; and at last, in the culmination of his rage, the Squire drew back to the opposite wall to gain force so as to dash his foot through the panel if he could, but just then Eliza opened Kate's door at the far end of the long corridor, and peered out.

That ended the disturbance.

"Come on down to dinner, Maria," said the Squire.

"Yes, my dear," she faltered, and they descended to dine alone, Mrs Wilton on water, her husband principally on wine, and hardly a word was spoken, the head of the house being very quiet and thoughtful in the calm which followed the storm.

Just as the untasted pheasants were being taken away, after the second course, Wilton suddenly said to the footman:

"Tell Miss Kate's maid to come here."

Mrs Wilton looked at her husband wonderingly, but he sat crumbling his bread and sipping his claret till the quiet, grave, elderly servant appeared.

"How is your mistress?" he said.

"Very unwell, sir."

"Think the doctor need be sent for?"

"Well, no, sir, I hardly think that. She has been very much agitated."

"Yes, of course; poor girl," said Wilton, quietly.

"But I think she will be better after a good night's rest, sir."

"So do I, Eliza. You will see, of course, that she has everything she wants."

"Oh, yes, sir. I did take her up some dinner, but I could not prevail upon her to touch it."

"Humph! I suppose not. That will do, thank you.—No, no, Maria, there is no occasion to say any more."

Mrs Wilton's mouth was open to speak, but she shut it again quickly, fearing to raise another storm, and the maid left the room. But the mother would speak out as soon as they were alone.

"I should like to order a tray with one of the pheasants to be sent up to Claud, dear."

"I daresay you would," he replied. "Well, I shouldn't."

"May I send for Doctor Leigh?"

"What for? You heard what the woman said?"

"I meant for Claud, dear."

"Oh, I'll see to him in the morning. I shall have a pill ready for him when I'm cooled down. It won't be so strong then."

"But, James, dear—"

"All right, old lady, I'm getting calm now; but listen to me. I mean this: you are not to go to his room to-night."

"James!"

"Nor yet to Kate's, till I go with you."

"My dear James!"

"That's me," he said, with a faint smile, "and you're a very good, affectionate, well meaning old woman; but if ever there was one who was always getting her husband into scrapes, it is you."

"Really, dear!" she cried, appealingly.

"Yes, and truly. There, that will do. Done dinner?"

"Yes, dear."

"Don't you want any cheese or dessert?"

"No, dear."

"Then let's go. You'll come and sit with me in the library to-night and have your cup of tea there."

"Yes, dear, but mayn't I go and just see poor Kate?"

"No."

The word was said quietly, but with sufficient emphasis to silence the weak woman, who sat gazing appealingly at her husband, whom she followed meekly enough to the library, where she sat working, and later on sipped her tea, while he was smoking and gazing thoughtfully at the fire, reviewing the events of the day, and, to do him justice, repenting bitterly a great deal that he had said. But as the time went on, feeling as he did the urgency of his position and the need to be able to meet the demands which would be made upon him before long, he grew minute by minute more stubbornly determined to carry out his plans with respect to his ward.

"He's only a boy yet," he said to himself, "and he's good at heart. I don't suppose I was much better when I was his age, and excepting that I'm a bit arbitrary I'm not such a bad husband after all."

At that moment he looked up at his wife, just in time to see her bow gently towards him. But knowing from old experience that it was not in acquiescence, he glanced at his watch and waited a few minutes, during which time Mrs Wilton nodded several times and finally dropped her work into her lap.

This woke her up, and she sat up, looking very stern, and as if going to sleep with so much trouble on the way was the last thing possible. But nature was very strong, and the desire for sleep more powerful than the sorrow from which she suffered; and she was dozing off again when her husband rose suddenly to ring the bell, the servants came in, prayers were read, and at a few minutes after ten Wilton took a chamber candlestick and led the way to bed.

He turned off, though, signing to Mrs Wilton to follow him, and on reaching his niece's room, tapped at the door gently.

"Kate—Kate, my dear," he said, and Mrs Wilton looked at him wonderingly.

"Yes, uncle."

"How are you now, my child?"

"Not very well, uncle."

"Very sorry, my dear. Can your aunt get you anything?"

"No; I thank you."

"Wish you a good night, then. I am very sorry about that upset this afternoon.—Come, my dear."

"Good-night, Kate, my love," said Mrs Wilton, with her ear against the panel; "I do hope you will be able to sleep."

"Good-night, aunt," said the girl quietly; and they went back to their own door.

"Won't you come and say 'good-night' to poor Claud, dear?" whispered Mrs Wilton.

"No, 'poor Claud' has to come to me first.—Go in."

He held open the door for his wife to enter, and then followed and locked it, and for some hours the Manor House was very still.

The next morning James Wilton was out a couple of hours before breakfast, busying himself around his home farm as if nothing whatever had happened and there was no fear of a foreclosure, consequent upon any action by John Garstang. He was back ready for breakfast rather later than his usual time, just as Mrs Wilton came bustling in to unlock the tea-caddy, and he nodded, and spoke rather gruffly:

"Claud not down?" he said.

"No, my dear; I saw you coming across the garden just as I was going to his room to see how he was."

"Oh, Samuel,"—to the man, who entered with a dish and hot plates,—"go and tell Mr Claud that we're waiting breakfast."

The man went.

"Let me go up, my dear. Poor boy! he must feel a bit reluctant to come down and meet you this morning."

"Poor fellow! he always was afflicted with that kind of timid shrinking," said Wilton, ironically. "No, stop. How is Kate?"

"I don't know, my dear; Eliza said that she had been twice to her room, but she was evidently fast asleep, and she would not disturb her."

"Humph! I shall be glad when she can come regularly to her meals."

"What shall you say to her this morning?"

"Wait and see—Well, is he coming down?"

"Beg pardon, sir," said the footman. "I've been knocking ever so long at Mr Claud's door, and I can't get any answer."

Mrs Wilton's hand dropped from the tap of the tea urn, and the boiling water began to flow over the top of the pot.

"Humph! Sulky," muttered Wilton—"Eh? What are you staring at?"

"Beg pardon, sir, but he didn't put his boots outside last night, and he never took his hot water in."

"Oh, James, James!" cried Mrs Wilton, wildly, "I knew it, I knew it. I dreamed about the black cow all last night, and there's something wrong."

"Stop a minute: I'll come," said Wilton, quickly, and a startled look came into his face.

"Take me—take me, too," sobbed his wife. "Oh, my poor boy! If anything has happened to him in the night. I shall never forgive myself. Samuel—Samuel!"

"Yes, ma'am."

"Run round to the stables and send one of the men over for Doctor Leigh at once."

Wilton felt too much startled to counter-order this, but before the man had gone a dozen steps he shouted to him.

"Tell the gardener to bring a mallet and cold chisel from the tool shed."

"Yes, sir," and full of excitement the man ran off, while his master and mistress hurried upstairs to their son's door. But before they reached it Wilton had recovered his calmness.

"What nonsense," he muttered. Then softly: "Here, you speak to him. Gently. Only overslept himself."

He tapped, and signed to his wife.

But her voice sounded full of agitation, as she said:

"Claud, dear; it's getting very late." Then louder: "Claud! Claud, my dear, are you unwell?" Then with aery of agony, "Claud! Claud, my darling! Oh, pray, pray speak to me, or you'll break my poor heart!"

"Here, stand aside," cried Wilton, who was thoroughly startled now. He seized the handle of the door, turned it, and tried to force it open, but in vain. The next moment he was about to lay his shoulder close down to the keyhole, when Kate's maid came running up to them.

"Mrs Wilton! Mrs Wilton!" she cried; "pray, pray come! My dear young lady! Oh, help, help! I ought to have spoken sooner. What shall I do?"

Chapter Thirteen

Wilton pere and mere had not been gone five minutes when there was a gentle tap at Kate's door, and she started and turned her fearful face in that direction, but made no reply. The tap was repeated,

"Miss Kate," came in a sharp whisper; "it is only me, my dear."

"Ah," sighed the girl, as if in relief; and she nearly ran to the door, turned the key, and admitted the old servant, locked the door again, and flung her arms about the woman's neck, to bury her face in her breast, and sob as if her heart would break.

"There, there, there," cooed the woman, as if to the little child she had nursed long years before; and she led her gently to a couch, and drew the weeping girt down half reclining upon her breast. "Cry then, my precious; it will do you good; and then you must tell Liza all about it—what has been the matter, dear?"

"Matter!" cried Kate, starting up, and gazing angrily in the woman's face. "Liza, it's horrible. Why did I ever come to this dreadful house?"

"Hush, hush, my own; you will make yourself had again. We must not have you ill."

"Bad—ill?" cried Kate. "Better dead and at rest. Oh, I hate him! I hate him! How dare he touch me like that! It was horrible—an outrage!"

The woman's face flushed, and her eyes sparkled angrily, then her lips moved as if to question, but she closed them tightly into a thin line and waited, knowing from old experience that it would not be long before her young mistress' grief and trouble would be poured into er ear.

She was quiet, and clasping the agitated girl once lore in her arms, she began to rock herself slowly to and fro.

"No, no! don't," cried Kate, peevishly, and she raised her head once more, looking handsomer than ever in her anger and indignation. "I am no longer a child. Aunt and uncle have encouraged it. This hateful money is at the bottom of it all. They wish me to marry him. Pah! he makes me shudder with disgust. And how could I even think of such a horror with all this terrible trouble so new."

Eliza half closed her eyes and nodded her head, while her mouth seemed almost to disappear.

"It is cruel—it is horrible," Kate continued. "They have encouraged it all through. Even aunt, with her sickly worship of her wretched spoiled boy. Oh, what a poor, pitiful, weak creature she must have thought me. No one seemed to understand me but Mr Garstang."

Eliza knit her brows a little at his name, but she remained silent, and by slow degrees she was put in possession of all that had taken place; and then, faint and weary, Kate let her head sink down till her forehead rested once more upon the breast where she had so often sunk to rest.

"Oh, the hateful money!" she sighed, as the tears came at last. "Let him have it. What is it to me? But I cannot stop here, nurse; it is impossible. We must go at once. Uncle is my guardian, but surely he cannot force me to stay against my inclination. If I remained here it would kill me. Nurse," she cried, with a display of determination that the woman had never seen in her before, "you must pack up what is necessary, and to-morrow we will go. It would be easy to stay at some hotel till we found a place—a furnished cottage just big enough for us two; anywhere so that we could be at peace. We could be happier then—Why don't you speak to me when I want comfort in my trouble?"

"Because no words of mine could give you the comfort you need, my dear. Don't you know that my heart bleeds for you, and that always when my poor darling child has suffered I have suffered, too?"

"Yes, yes, dear; I know," said Kate, raising her face to kiss the woman passionately. "I do know. Don't take any notice of what I said. All this has made me feel so wickedly angry, and as if I hated the whole world."

"Don't I know my darling too well to mind a few hasty words?" said the woman, softly. "Say what you please. If it is angry I know it only comes from the lips, and there is something for me always in my darling's heart."

"That does me good, nurse," said the girl, clinging to her affectionately for a few moments, and then once more sitting up, to speak firmly. "It makes me feel after all that I am not alone, and that my dear, dead mother was right when she said, 'Never part from Eliza. She is not our servant; she has always been our faithful, humble, trusty friend.'"

The woman's face softened now, and a couple of tears stole down her cheeks.

"Now, nurse, we must talk and make our plans. I wish I could see Mr Garstang, and ask his advice."

"Do you like Mr Garstang, my dear?" said the woman, gently.

"Yes; he is a gentleman. He seems to me the only one who can talk to me as what I am, and without thinking I am what they call me—an heiress."

"But poor dear master never trusted Mr Garstang."

"Perhaps he had no need to. He always treated him as a friend, and he has proved himself one to-day by the brave way in which he defended me, and spoke out to open my eyes to all this iniquity."

"But dear master did not make him his executor."

"How could he when he had his brother to think of? How could my dear father suspect that Uncle James would prove so base? It was a mistake. You ought to have heard Mr Garstang speak to-day."

Eliza sighed.

"I don't think I should put all my trust in Mr Garstang, my dear," she said.

"Is not that prejudice, nurse?"

"I hope not my dear; but my heart never warmed to Mr Garstang, and it has always felt very cold toward that young man, his stepson."

"Harry Dasent? Well," said Kate, with a faint smile, "perhaps mine has been as cold. But why should we trouble about this? It would be no harm if I asked Mr Garstang's advice; but if we do not like it, nurse, we can take our own. One thing we decide upon at once: we will leave here."

"Can we, my dear? You have money, but—"

"Oh, don't talk about the hateful thing," cried the girl, passionately.

"I must, my dear. We cannot take even a cottage without. This money is in your uncle's charge; you, as a girl under age, can not touch a penny without your Uncle James' consent."

"But surely he can not keep me here against my will—a prisoner?"

"I don't know, my dear," said the woman, with a sigh.

"Then that is where we want help and advice—that is where Mr Garstang could assist me and tell me what to do."

Eliza sighed.

"Well, if the worst comes to the worst, I can take a humble place where you can keep house and do needlework to help, while I go out as daily governess."

"You! A daily governess?"

"Well," said the girl, proudly, "I can play—brilliantly, they say—I know three languages, and—"

"You have a hundred and fifty thousand pounds in your own right."

"What are a hundred and fifty thousand pounds to a miserable prisoner who is being persecuted? Liberty is worth millions, and come what may, I will be free."

"Yes, you shall be free, darling; but you must do nothing rash. To-day has taught me that my dear girl is a woman of firmness and spirit; and, please God, all will come right in the end. There, this is enough. You are fluttered and feverish now, and delicate as you are, you require rest. It is getting late. Let me help you to undress for a good long night's rest. Sleep on it all, my child; out of the evil good will come, and you have shown them that they have not a baby to deal with, but a true woman, so matters are not so bad as they seem. Come, my little one."

"I must and will leave here, nurse," said Kate, firmly.

"Sleep on it, my child, and remember that after all you have won the day. Come, let me help you."

"No, Liza, go now. I must sit for a while and think."

"Better sleep, and think after a long rest."

"No, dear; I wish to sit here in the quiet and silence first. Look, the moon is rising over the trees, and it seems to bring light into my weary brain. I'll go to bed soon. Please do as I wish, and leave me now—Nurse, dear, do you think those who have gone from us ever come back in spirit to help us when we are in need?"

"Heaven only knows, my darling," said the woman, looking startled. "But please don't talk like this—You really wish me to go?"

"Yes, leave me now. I am going to make my plans for to-morrow."

"To-morrow."

"No, before I lie down to rest. Good-night."

"You are mistress, and I am servant, my child. Good-night, then—good-night."

"Good-night," said Kate, and a minute later she had closed and re-locked the door, to turn and stand gazing at the window, whose blind was suffused with the soft silvery light of the slowly rising moon.

Chapter Fourteen

"Who's the letter from, Pierce?"

"One of the medical brokers, as they call themselves—the man I wrote to;" and the young doctor tossed the missive contemptuously across the breakfast table to his sister, who caught it up eagerly and read it through.

"Of course," she cried, with her downy little rounded cheeks flushing, and a bright mocking look in her eyes; "and I quite agree with him. He says you are too modest and diffident about your practice; that the very fact of its being established so many years makes it of value; that no one would take it on the terms you propose, and that you must ask at least five hundred pounds, which would be its value plus a valuation of the furniture. How much did you ask?"

"Nothing at all."

"What!" cried Jenny, dropping her bread and butter.

"I said I was willing to transfer the place to any enterprising young practitioner who would take the house off my hands, and the furniture."

"Oh, you goose—I mean gander!"

"Thank you, Sissy."

"Well, so you are—a dear, darling, stupid old brother," cried the girl, leaping up to go behind the young doctors chair, covered his eyes with her hands, and place her little soft white double chin on the top of his head. "There you are! Blind as a bat! Five hundred pounds! Pooh! Rubbish! Stuff! Why, it's worth thousands and thousands, and, what is more, happiness to my own old Pierce."

"I thought that subject was tabooed, Sissy."

"I don't care; I have broken the taboo. I have risen in rebellion, and I'll fight till I die for my principles."

"Brave little baby," he said mockingly, as he took the little hands from his eyes and prisoned them.

"Yes," she said, meaningly, "braver than you know."

"Jenny! You have not dared to speak about such a thing?" he cried, turning upon her angrily.

"Not such a little silly," she replied. "What! make her draw in her horns and retire into her shell, and begin thinking my own dear boy is a miserable money-hunter? Not I, indeed. For shame, sir, to think such a thing of me! I never even told her what a dear good fellow you are, worrying yourself to death to keep me, and bringing me to live in the country, because you thought I was pining and growing pale in nasty old Westminster and its slums."

"That's right," said Pierce, with a faint sigh.

"Let her find out naturally what you are; and she is finding it out, for don't you make any mistake about it, Miss Katherine Wilton is young, but she has plenty of shrewd common sense, as I soon found out, and little as I have seen of her I soon saw that she was quite awake to her position. Girls of sense who have fortunes soon smell out people's motives; and if they think they are going to marry her right off to that out-door sport, Claud, they have made a grand mistake."

"But you have not dared to talk about your foolish ideas to her, Jenny?"

"Not a word. Oh, timid, modest frere! I put on my best frock and my best manners when we went there to dinner, and I was as nice and ladylike as a girl could be. Reward:—Kate took to me at once, and we became friends."

Leigh uttered a sigh of relief.

"But if I had dared I could have told her what a coward you are, and how ashamed I am of you."

"For not playing the part of a contemptible schemer, Sis?"

"Who wants you to, sir? Why, money has nothing to do with it. Now, answer me this, Pierce. If she were only Miss Wilton without a penny, wouldn't you propose for her at once?"

"No, Sis; I would not."

"You wouldn't?"

"No, I wouldn't be so contemptible as to take such a step when I am little better than a pauper."

"Boo! What nonsense. You a pauper! An educated gentleman, acknowledged to be talented in his profession. But I know you'd marry her to-morrow and turn your poor little sister out of doors if you had an income. Bother incomes and money! It's all horrid, and causes all the misery there is in the world. Pierce, you shan't run away from here and leave the poor girl to be married to that wretched boy."

"Jenny, dear, be serious. I really must get away from here as soon as I can."

"Oh, Pierce! Don't talk about it, dear. It is only to make yourself miserable through these silly ideas of honour; and it is to make me wretched, too, just when I am so well and so happy, and all that nasty London cough gone. I declare if you take me away I'll pine away and die."

"No, you shan't, Sissy. You can't, with your own clever special physician at your side," he said merrily.

"Not if you could help it, I know. But Pierce, darling, don't be such a coward. It's cruel to her to run away, and leave her unprotected."

"Hold your tongue!" said Leigh peremptorily. "I tell you that is all imagination on your part."

"And I tell you it is a fact I've seen and heard quite enough. Old Wilton is very poor, and he wants to get the money safe in his family. Mrs Wilton is only the old puss whose paws he is using for tongs. As for Claud—Ugh! I could really enjoy existence if I might box his big ears. Now look here, big boy," cried Jenny, impulsively snatching up the agent's letter: "I am going to burn this, for you shan't go away and make a medical martyr of yourself, just because the dearest girl in the world—who likes you already for your straightforward manly conduct towards her—happens to have a fortune, and your practice beginning to improve, too."

"My practice beginning to improve!" he cried, contemptuously.

"Yes, sir, improve; didn't you have a broken boy to mend yesterday? and haven't you a chance of the parish practice, which is twenty pounds a year? and oh, hooray, hooray! I am so glad, there's somebody ill at the Manor again. I hope it's Clodpole Claud this time," and she wildly waltzed round the room, waving the letter over her head, before stopping by the fire, throwing the paper in, and plumping down in a chair, looking demure and solemn as a nun.

For Tom Jonson, the groom from the Manor, had driven over in the dog-cart, pulled up short, and now rang sharply at the bell.

Leigh turned pale, for the man's manner betokened emergency, and he could only associate this with the patient to whom he had been called before.

"Will you come over at once, sir, please?"

"Miss Wilton worse?"

"Oh, no, sir. Something wrong with young Master." Leigh uttered a sigh of relief, and stepped back for his hat.

"Mr Wilton, junior, taken ill, dear," he said. "I heard, Pierce. Do kill him, or send him into a consumption."

Chapter Fifteen

Leigh hardly heard his sister's words, for he hurried out and sprang into the dog-cart, where the groom was full of the past day's trouble, and ready to pour into unwilling ears what he had heard from Samuel, who knew that Mr Garstang, the solicitor from London, knocked down young Master about money, he thought, and that he had heard Mr Claud say something about his father kicking him.

"Missus wanted to send for you last night, sir, but Master wouldn't have it, and this morning they couldn't make him hear in his room. Poor chap, I expect he's very bad."

The man would have gone on talking, but finding his companion silent and thoughtful, he relapsed into a one-sided conversation with the horse he drove, bidding him "come on," and "look alive," and "be steady," till he turned in at the avenue and cantered up to the hall door.

Mrs Wilton was there, tearful and trembling.

"Oh, do make haste, Mr Leigh," she cried. "How long you have been!"

"I came at once, madam; is your son in his room?"

"Yes, yes—dead by this time. Pray, come up."

He sprang up the stairs in a very unprofessional way, forgetting the necessity for a medical man being perfectly calm and cool, and Wilton met him on the landing.

"Oh, here you are. Haven't got the door open yet. Curse the old wood! It's like iron. Maria, go and get all the keys you can find."

"Yes, dear, but while the men are doing that hadn't we better try and get poor Claud's door open?"

"No, hers first," cried Wilton, and Leigh started.

"I understood that it was your son who needed help," he said.

"Never mind him for a bit. You must see to my niece first;" and in a few seconds Leigh was in possession of the fact that the maid had been unable to make her mistress hear; that since then they could get no response to constant calling and knocking, and the door had resisted all their efforts to get it open.

On reaching the end of the corridor Leigh found the maid, white and trembling, holding her apron pressed hard to her lips, while the footman and two gardeners, after littering the floor with unnecessary tools, were now trying to make a hole with a chisel large enough to admit the point of a saw, so as to cut round the lock.

"Wood's like iron, sir," said the gardener, who was operating.

"But would it not be easier to put a ladder to the window, and break a pane of glass?" said Leigh, impatiently.

"Oh, Lord!" cried Wilton, "who would be surrounded with such a set of fools! Come along. Of course. Here, one of you, go and fetch a ladder."

The second gardener hurried off down the back stairs, while his master led the way to the front, leaving Mrs Wilton and the maid tapping at the bedroom door.

"Oh, do, do speak, my darling," sobbed Mrs Wilton. "If it's only one word, to let us know you are alive."

"Oh, don't, don't pray say that ma'am," sobbed the maid. "My poor dear young mistress! What shall I do—what shall I do?"

Mrs Wilton made no reply, but, free from her husband's coercion now, she hurried along the corridor to the other wing, to begin knocking at her son's door, and then went down upon her knees, with her lips to the keyhole, begging him within to speak.

"Such a set of blockheads," growled Wilton; "and I was just as bad, Doctor. In the hurry and excitement that never occurred to me. You see you've come in cool, and ready to grasp everything. Poor girl, she was a bit upset yesterday, and I suppose it was too much for her. Boys will be boys, and I had a quarrel with my son."

This in a confidential whisper, as they crossed the hall, but Leigh hardly heard him in his anxiety, and as they passed out and along the front of the house he said, hurriedly:

"I'll go on, sir. I see they have the ladder there."

"What!" cried Wilton, excitedly, "they can't have got it yet, and—God bless me! what does this mean?"

He broke into a run, for there, in full view now, at the end of the house, with its broad foot in a flower-bed, was one of the fruit-gathering ladders, just long enough to reach the upper windows, and resting against the sill beneath that of Kate's room.

He reached the place first, clapped his hands upon the sides, and ascended a couple of rounds, but stepped back directly, with his florid face mottled with white, and his lips quivering with excitement as he spoke.

"Here, you're a lighter man than I, Doctor; go up. The window's open, too."

Leigh sprang up, mad now with anxiety and a horrible dread; but as he reached the window he paused and hesitated, for more than one reason, the principal being a fear of finding that which he suspected true.

"In with you, man—in with you," cried Wilton; "it is no time for false delicacy now;" and as he spoke he began to ascend in turn.

Leigh sprang in, and at a glance saw that the bed had not been pressed, and that there was no sign of struggle and disturbance in the daintily furnished room. No chair overset, no candlestick upon the floor, but all looking as if ready for its occupant, save that an extinguisher was upon one of the candles beside the dressing-table glass.

"Gone!" cried a hoarse voice behind him, as he stood there, shrinking in the midst of the agony he felt, for it seemed to him like a sacrilege to be present.

Leigh started round, to find Wilton's head at the open casement, and directly after the heavy man stepped in.

"No, no," he shouted back, as the ladder began to bend again. "Not you. Stop below. No; take this ladder to the hall door, and wait."

He banged to, and fastened the casement, after seizing the top of the ladder, and giving it a thrust which sent it over with a crash on to the gravel.

"Don't seem like a doctor's business, sir," continued Wilton, gravely; "but you medical men have to be confidential, so keep your tongue quiet about what you have seen."

Leigh bowed his head, for he could not speak. A horrible sensation, as if he were about to be attacked by a fit, assailed him, and he had to battle with it to think and try to grasp what this meant. One moment there was the fear that violence had been used; the next that it meant a willing flight; and he was fiercely struggling with the bitter thoughts which came, suggesting that his love for this delicate, gentle girl was a mockery, for she was either weak, or had long enough before bound herself to another, when he was brought back to the present by the action of the Squire, who, after a sharp glance round, stooped to pick up the door-key from where it lay on the carpet after being turned and pushed out by means of a piece of wire, in the hope, as suggested by Samuel, that it could be picked out afterwards at the bottom of the door, a plan which had completely failed.

Wilton thrust in the key, turned it, and opened the door, to admit his wife and the maid.

"Miss Kate, Miss Kate," cried the latter.

"Call louder," said Wilton, mockingly. "There's no one here."

"James, James, my dear, what does this mean?" cried Mrs Wilton excitedly.

"Bed not been slept in; window open—ladder outside—can't you see?"

Eliza looked at him wildly, as if she could not grasp his words; then with a cry she rushed to a wardrobe, dragged it open, and examined the hooks and pegs.

"Hat—waterproof!" she cried; and then with a faint shriek—"Gone?"

"Yes, gone," said Wilton brutally. "Here, Maria; this way."

"Yes, yes; Claud's room. Come quickly, Doctor, pray."

Pierce Leigh followed the Wiltons along the corridor, hardly knowing where he was going, in the wild turmoil which raged, in his brain. There were moments when he felt as if he were going mad; others when he was ready to think that he was suffering from some strange aberration which distorted everything he saw and heard, till he was brought back to himself by the Squire's voice which begat an intense desire to know the worst.

"Here, Claud," he shouted, after thumping hard at his son's bedroom door without result. "Claud! No nonsense, sir; I want you. Something serious has happened. Answer at once if you are here."

There was not a sound to be heard, and Mrs Wilton sobbed aloud.

"Oh, my boy, my boy! I'm sure he is dead."

"Bah!" cried Wilton, angrily. "Here, who has been trying to get in this room?"

No one answered, and Wilton bent down and looked through the keyhole.

"Has anyone pushed the key out to make it fall inside?"

A low murmur of inquiry followed the question, but there was no reply.

"Come round to the front, Doctor," said Wilton then, and Leigh followed him in silence downstairs and out to where the men were waiting with the ladder. This was placed up against the window which matched with Kate's at the other end of the house, and at a sign from Wilton, Leigh once more mounted, acting in a mechanical way, as if he were no longer master of his own acts, but completely influenced by his companion.

"Window fastened?" cried Wilton.

"Yes."

"Break it. Mind; don't cut your hand."

But as Wilton spoke there was the crash of glass, Leigh thrust in his hand, and unfastened the casement, which he flung open and stepped in, the Squire following.

In this case the bed was tumbled from Claud having been lying down outside, but it was evident to his father that he had descended in the ordinary way, after locking his room and placing the key in his pocket, so as to make it seem that he was still in the room.

"That will do," said Wilton, gruffly. "We can go down, and it must be by the way we came."

He looked at the young doctor as if expecting him to ask some questions, but Leigh did not speak a word, merely drawing back for his companion to descend.

"You'll hold your tongue about all this, Mr Leigh?" he said.

"Of course, sir," said the young man coldly. "It is no affair of mine."

"No, nor anybody else's but mine," cried Wilton, fiercely. Then as soon as he reached the foot of the ladder he gazed fiercely at his two men.

"Take that ladder back," he said; "and mind this: if I find that any man I employ has been chattering about this business, I discharge him on the instant.—Thank you, Doctor, for coming. Of course, you will make a charge. The young lady seems to prefer fresh air."

Leigh looked at him wildly, and strode rapidly away.

"Disappointed at losing his patient," muttered Wilton, as he went in, to find his wife waiting for him with both her trembling hands extended.

"Quick!" she cried; "tell me the worst," as she caught his arm.

He passed his arm about her waist, and seemed to sweep her into the library, where he closed the door, and pushed her down into an easy chair.

"There is no worst," he said, in a low voice. "Now, look here; you must keep your mouth shut, and be as surprised as I am. It's all right. She was only a bit scared yesterday. The boy knew what he was about. The cunning jade has bolted with him."

"Gone—Kate?" cried Mrs Wilton.

"Yes; Claud was throwing dust in our stupid old eyes. The money won't go out of the family, old girl. They're on the way to be married now, and as for John Garstang—let him do his worst."

"Pierce, darling, what has happened?" cried Jenny, as her brother entered the room and sank into a chair. "Oh," she cried wildly, as she flew to him to throw her arms about his neck and gazed in his ghastly face, "it was for Kate. Oh, Pierce, don't say she's dead!"

"Yes," he said, in a voice full of agony; "dead to me."

Chapter Sixteen

"Dead? Dead to you? Pierce, speak to me," cried Jenny. "What do you mean?"

"What I say. They are a curious mixture of weakness and duplicity."

"Who are, dear?" said Jenny, with a warm colour taking the place of the pallor which her brother's words had produced. "Why will you go on talking in riddles?"

"Women. Their soft, quiet ways force you to believe in them, and then comes some sudden enlightening to prove what I say."

Jenny caught him by the shoulder as he sat in his chair, looking ghastly.

"Tell me what you mean," she cried excitedly.

"Only the falling to pieces of your castle in the air," he said, with a mocking laugh. "The marriage you arranged between the pauper physician and the rich heiress. I can easily be strictly honorable now."

"Will you tell me what you mean, Pierce?" cried the girl, angrily. "What has happened? Is someone ill at the Manor House?"

"No," he said, bitterly.

"Then why were you sent for?"

"To see an imaginary patient."

"Pierce, if you do not wish me to go into a fit of hysterical passion," cried the girl, "tell me what you mean. Why—were—you—sent—for?"

"Because," replied Leigh, imitating his sister's manner of speaking, "Mise—Katherine—Wilton—and—Mr   Claud—were—supposed—to—be—lying—speechless in their rooms, and—ha-ha-ha! their doors could not be forced."

"Pierce, what is the matter with you?" cried Jenny, excitedly; "do you know what you are saying?"

"Perfectly," he cried, his manner changing from its mocking tone to one of fierce passion. "When I reached the place, a way was found in, and the birds were flown."

"Birds—flown," cried Jenny, looking more and more as if she doubted her brother's sanity; "what birds?"

"The fair Katherine, and that admirable Crichton, Claud."

"Flown?" stammered Jenny, who looked now half stunned.

"Well, eloped," he cried, savagely, "to Gretna Green, or a registry office. Who says that Northwood is a dull place, without events?"

"Kate Wilton eloped with her cousin Claud!"

"Yes, my dear," said Pierce, striving hard to speak in a careless, indifferent tone, but failing dismally, for every word sounded as if torn from his breast, his quivering lips bespeaking the agony he felt.

There was silence for a few moments, and then Jenny exclaimed:

"Pierce, is this some cruel jest?"

"Do I look as if I were jesting?" he cried wildly, and springing up he cast aside the mask beneath which he had striven to hide the agony which racked him. "Jesting! when I am half mad with myself for my folly. Driveling pitiful idiot that I was, ready to believe in the first pretty face I see, and then, as I have said, I find how full of duplicity and folly a woman is."

"Mind what you are saying, Pierce," cried his sister, who seemed to be strangely moved; "don't say words which will make you bitterly repent. Tell me again; I feel giddy and sick. I must be going to be taken ill, for I can't have heard you aright, or there must be some mistake."

"Mistake!" he cried, with a savage laugh. "Don't I tell you—I have just come from there? Has not old Wilton hid me keep silence? And I came babbling it all to you."

"Stop!" said Jenny thoughtfully; "Kate could not do such a thing. When was it?"

"Who can tell?—late last night—early this morning. What does it matter?"

"It is not true," cried Jenny, with her eyes flashing. "How dare you, who were ready to go down on your knees and worship her, utter such a cruel calumny."

"Very well," he cried bitterly; "then it is not true; I have not been there this morning, and have not looked in their empty rooms. Tell me I am a fool and a madman, and you will be very near the truth."

"I don't care," cried Jenny angrily; "and it's cruel—almost blasphemous of you to say such a thing about that poor sweet girl whom I had already grown to love. She elope with her cousin—run away like a silly girl in a romance! It is impossible."

"Yes, impassible," he said mockingly, as he writhed in his despair and agony.

"Pierce, you ought to be ashamed of yourself. There! I can only talk to you in a commonplace way, though all the time I am longing for words full of scorn and contempt with which to crush you. No, I'm not, my poor boy, because I can see how *you* are suffering. Oh, Pierce! Pierce!" she continued, sobbing as she threw her arms about his neck; "how can you torture yourself so by thinking such a thing of her?"

"Good little girl," he said tenderly, moved as he was by her display of affection. "I shall begin to respect myself again now I find that my bright, clever little sister could be as much deceived as I."

"I have not been deceived in her. She is all that is beautiful, and good, and true. Of course, I believe in her, and so do you at heart, only you are half mad now, and deceived."

"Yes, half mad, and deceived!"

"Yes. There is something behind all this—I know," cried Jenny, wildly. "They have persecuted her so, and encouraged that wretched boy to pay her attentions, till in despair she has run away to take refuge with some other friends."

"With Claud Wilton!" said Pierce, bitterly.

"Silence, sir! No. Women are not such weak double-faced creatures as you think. No, it is as I say; and oh! Pierce, dear, he was out late last night, and when he got back found her going away and followed her."

"Fiction—imagination," he said bitterly. "You are inventing all this to try and comfort me, little woman, but your woven basket will not hold water. It leaks at the very beginning. How could you know that he was out late last night?"

Jenny's cheeks were scarlet, and she turned away her face.

"There, you see, you are beaten at once, Jenny, and that I have some reason for what I have said about women; but there are exceptions to every rule, and my little sister is one of them. I did not include her among the weak ones."

To his astonishment she burst into a passionate storm of sobs and tears, and in words confused and only half audible, she accused herself of being as weak and foolish as the rest, and, as he made out, quite unworthy of his trust.

"Oh! Pierce, darling," she cried wildly, as she sank upon her knees in front of his chair; "I'm a wicked, wicked girl, and not deserving of all you think about me. Believe in poor Kate, and not in me, for indeed, indeed, she is all that is good and true."

"A man cannot govern his feelings, Sissy," he said, half alarmed now at the violence of her grief. "I must believe in you always, as my own little girl. How could I do otherwise, when you have been everything to me for so long, ever since you were quite a little girl and I told you not to cry for I would be father and mother to you, both."

"And so you have been, Pierce, dear," she sobbed, "but I don't deserve it—I don't deserve it."

"I don't deserve to have such a loving little companion," he said, kissing her tenderly. "Haven't I let my fancy stray from you, and am I not being sharply punished for my weal mess?"

She suddenly hung back from him and pressed her hair from her temples, as he held her by the waist.

"Pierce!" she said sharply, and there was a look of anger in her eyes, "he is a horrid wretch."

"People do not give him much of a character," said Leigh bitterly, "but that would be no excuse for my following him to wring his neck."

"I believe he would be guilty of any wickedness. Tell me, dear; do you think it possible—such things have been done?"

"What things?" he said, wondering at her excited manner.

"It is to get her money, of course; for it would be his then. Do you think he has taken her away by force?"

Leigh started violently now in turn, and a light seemed to flash into his understanding, but it died out directly, and he said half pityingly, as he drew her to him once again:

"Poor little inventor of fiction," he said, with a harsh laugh. "But let it rest, Sissy; it will not do. These things only occur in a romance. No, I do not think anything of the kind; and what do you say to London now?"

Chapter Seventeen

"What are you going to do, James, dear?" said Mrs Wilton.

"Eh?"

"What are you going to do, dear? Oh, you don't know what a relief it is to me. I was going to beg you to have the pike pond dragged."

James Wilton's strong desire was to do nothing, and give his son plenty of time; but there was a Mrs Grundy even at Northwood, and she had to be studied.

"Do? Errum!" He cleared his throat with a long imposing, rolling sound. "Well, search must be made for them directly, and they must be brought back. It is disgraceful I did mean to sit down and do nothing, but it will not do. I am very angry and indignant with them both, for Kate is as bad as Claud. It must not be said that we connived at the—the—the—what's the word?—escapade."

"Of course not, my dear; and it is such a pity. Such a nice wedding as she might have had, and made it a regular 'at home,' to pay off all the people round I'd quite made up my mind about my dress."

"Oh, I'm glad of that," said Wilton, with a grim smile. "Nothing like being well prepared for the future. Have you quite made up your mind about your dress when I pop off? Crape, of course?"

"James, my darling, you shouldn't. How can you say such dreadful things?"

"You make me—being such a fool."

"James!"

"Hold your tongue, do. Yes, I must have inquiries made."

"But do you feel quite sure that they have eloped like that?"

"Oh, yes," he said, thoughtfully; "there's no doubt about it."

"I don't know, my dear," said Mrs Wilton, plaintively. "It seems so strange, when she was so ill and in such trouble."

"Bah! Sham! Like all women, kicking up a row about the first kiss, and wanting it all the time."

"James, my dear, you shouldn't say such things. It was no sham. She was in dreadful trouble, I'm sure, and I cannot help thinking about the pike pond. It haunts me—it does indeed. Don't you think that in her agony she may have gone and drowned herself?"

"Yes, that's it," said Wilton, with a scowl at his wife.

"Oh! Horrible! I was having dreadful dreams all last night. You do think so, then?"

"Yes, you've hit it now, old lady. She must have jumped down from her window on to the soft flower-bed, and then gone and fetched the ladder, and put it up there, and afterwards gone and called Claud to come down and go hand in hand with her, so as to have company."

"Jumped down—the ladder—what did she want a ladder for, James, dear?"

"What do people want ladders for? Why, to come down by."

"But she was down, dear. I—I really don't know what you mean. You confuse me so. But, oh, James, dear, you don't mean that about Claud?"

"Why not? Depend upon it, they're at the bottom of that hole where the pig was drowned, and the pike are eating bits out of them."

"James!—Oh, what a shame! You're laughing at me."

"Laughing at you? You'd make a horse laugh at you. Such idiocy. Be quiet if you can. Don't you see how worried and busy I am? And look here— if anyone calls out of curiosity, you don't know anything. Refer 'em to me."

"Yes, my dear. But really it is very shocking of the young people. It's almost immoral. But you think they will get married directly?"

"Trust Claud for that. Fancy the jade going off in that way. Ah, they're all alike."

"No, James; I would sooner have died than consented to such a proceeding."

"Not you. Now be quiet."

"Going out, dear?"

"Only round the house for a few minutes. By the way, have you examined Eliza—asked her what Kate has taken with her?"

"Yes, dear. Nothing at all but her hat, scarf, and cloak. Such a shabby way of getting married."

"Never mind that," said Wilton; and he went into the hall, through the porch and on to the place where the ladder had been found.

There was little to find there but the deep impressions made by the heels, except that a man's footprints were plainly to be seen; and Wilton returned to his wife, rang the bell, and assuming his most judicial air waited.

"Send Miss Kate's maid here," he said, sternly.

"Yes, sir."

"Stop. Look here, Samuel, you are my servant, and I call upon you to speak the whole truth to me about this matter, one which, on further thought, I feel it to be my duty to investigate. Now, tell me, did you know anything about this proceeding on Mr Claud's part?"

"No, sir; 'strue as goodness, I didn't."

"Mr Claud did not speak to you about it?"

"No, sir."

"Didn't you see him last night?"

"No, sir; I went up to his room to fetch his boots to bring down and dry, but the door was locked, but when I knocked and asked for them he did say something then."

"Yes, what did he say?"

Samuel glanced at his mistress and hesitated.

"Don't look at me, Samuel," said Mrs Wilton; "speak the whole truth."

"Yes; what did he say?" cried Wilton, sternly.

"Well, sir, he told me to go to the devil."

Wilton coughed.

"That will do. Go and fetch Miss Wilton's maid."

Eliza came, looking red-eyed and pale, but she could give no information, only assure them that she did not understand it, but was certain something must be wrong, for Miss Kate would never have taken such a step without consulting her.

And so on, and so on. A regular examination of the servants remaining followed in quite a judicial manner, and once more Kate's aunt and uncle were alone.

"There," he said; "I think I have done my duty, my dear. Perhaps, though, I ought to drive over to the station and make inquiries there; but I don't see what good it would do. I could only at the most find out that they had gone to London."

"Don't you think, dear, that you ought to communicate with the police?"

"No; what for?"

"To trace them, dear. The police are so clever; they would be sure to find them out."

Wilton coughed.

"Perhaps we had better wait, my dear. I fully anticipate that they will come back to-night—or to-morrow morning, full of repentance to ask our forgiveness; and er—I suppose we shall have to look over it."

"Well, yes, my dear," said Mrs Wilton. "What's done can't be undone; but I'm sure I don't know what people will say."

"I shall be very stern with Claud, though, for it is a most disgraceful act. I wonder at Kate."

"Well, I did, my dear, till I began to think, and then I did not; for Claud has such a masterful way with him. He was always too much for me."

"Yes," said Wilton dryly; "always. Well, we had better wait and see if they come back."

"I am terribly disappointed, though, my dear, for we could have had such a grand wedding. To go off like that and get married, just like a footman and housemaid. Don't you remember James and Sarah?"

"Bah! No, I don't remember James and Sarah," said Wilton irascibly.

"Yes, you do, my dear. It's just ten years ago, and you must remember about them both wanting a holiday on the same day, and coming back at night, and Sarah saying so demurely: 'Please, ma'am, we've been married.'"

Wilton twisted his chair round and kicked a piece of coal on the top of the fire which required breaking.

"James, my dear, you shouldn't do that," said his wife, reprovingly. "You're as bad as Claud, only he always does it with his heel. There is a poker, my dear."

"I thought you always wanted it kept bright."

"Well, it does look better so, dear. But I do hope going off in the night like that won't give Kate a cold."

Wilton ground his teeth and was about to burst into a furious fit of anger against his wife's tongue, but matters seemed to have taken so satisfactory a turn since the previous day that the bite was wanting, and he planted his heels on the great hob, warmed himself, and started involuntarily as he saw in the future mortgages, first, second and third, paid off, and himself free from the meshes which he gave Garstang the credit of having spun round him. As for Claud, he could, he felt, mould him like wax. So long as he had some ready money to spend he would be quiet enough, and, of course, it was all for his benefit, for he would succeed to the unencumbered estates.

Altogether the future looked so rosy that Wilton chuckled at the glowing fire and rubbed his hands, without noticing that the fire dogs were grinning at him like a pair of malignant brazen imps; and just then Mrs Wilton let her work fall into her lap and gave vent to a merry laugh.

"What now?" said Wilton, facing round sharply. "Don't do that. Suppose one of the servants came in and saw you grinning. Just recollect that we are in great trouble and anxiety about this—this—what you may call it—escapade."

"Yes, dear; I forgot. But it does seem so funny."

"Didn't seem very funny last night."

"No, dear, of course not; and I never could have thought our troubles would come right so soon. But only think of it; those two coming back together, and Kate not having changed her name. There won't be a thing in her linen that will want marking again."

"Bah!" growled Wilton. "Yes, what is it?" he cried, as the footman appeared.

"Beg pardon, sir, but Tom Jonson had to go to the village shop for some harness paste, and it's all over the place."

"Oh, is it?" growled Wilton. "Of course, if Mr Tom Jonson goes out on purpose to spread it."

"I don't think he said a word, sir, but they were talking about it at the shop, and young Barker saw 'em last."

"Barker—Barker? Not—"

"Yes, sir, him as you give a month to for stealing pheasants' eggs. That loafing chap."

"He saw them last night? Here, go and tell Smith to fetch him here before me."

Samuel smiled.

"Do you hear, sir? Don't stand grinning there."

"No, sir; certainly not, sir," said the man, "but Tom Jonson thought you'd like to see him, sir, and he collared him at once and brought him on."

"Quite right. Bring him in at once. Stop a moment. Put two or three 'Statutes at Large' and 'Burns' Justice of the Peace' on the table."

The man hurriedly gave the side-table a magisterial look with four or fire pie-crust coloured quartos and a couple of bulky manuals, while Wilton turned to his wife.

"Here, Maria," he growled, in a low tone; "you'd better be off."

"Oh, don't send me away, please, dear," she whispered; "it isn't one of those horrid cases you have sometimes, and I do so want to hear."

"Very well; only don't speak."

"No, my dear, not a word," whispered Mrs Wilton, and she half closed her eyes and pinched her lips together, but her ears twitched as she sat waiting anxiously for the return of the footman, followed by the groom, who seemed to have had no little trouble in pushing and dragging a rough-looking lout of about eighteen into the room, where he stood with his smock frock raised on each side so as to allow his hands to be thrust deeply into his trousers pockets.

"Take your hat off," said Samuel, in a sharp whisper.

"Sheeawn't!" said the fellow, defiantly. "I arn't done nothin'."

Samuel promptly knocked the hat off on to the floor, which necessitated a hand being taken slowly from a pocket to pick it up.

"Here, don't you do that ag'in," cried the lad.

"Silence, sir. Stand up," cried Wilton.

"Mayn't I pick up my hat? I arn't done nothin'."

"Say 'sir'," whispered the footman.

"Sheeawn't. I arn't done nothin', I tell yer. No business to bring me here."

"Silence, sir," cried Wilton, taking up a pen and shaking it at the lad, which acted upon him as if it were some terrible judicial wand which might write a document consigning him to hard labour, skilly, and bread and water in the county jail. The consequence being that he stood with his head bent forward, brow one mass of wrinkles, and mouth partly open, staring at the fierce-looking justice of the peace.

"Listen to me: you are not brought here for punishment."

"Well, I arn't done nothin'," said the lad.

"I am glad to hear it, and I hope you will improve, Barker. Now, what you have to do is to answer a few questions, and if you do so truthfully and well, you will be rewarded."

"Beer?" said the lout, with a grin.

"My servant will give you some beer as you go out, but first of all I shall give you a shilling."

The fellow grinned.

"Shall I get the book and swear him, sir?" said Samuel, who was used to the library being turned into a court for petty cases.

"There is no need," said Wilton austerely. "Now, my lad, answer me."

"Yes, I sin 'em both last night."

"Saw whom?"

"Young Squire and his gal."

"Young Squire" made Mrs Wilton smile; "his gal" seemed to set her teeth on edge.

"Humph! Are you sure?" said Wilton.

"Sewer? Ay, I know young Squire well enough. Hit me many a time. Haw-haw! Know young Squire—I should think I do!"

"Say 'sir,'" whispered Samuel again.

"Sheeawn't," cried the fellow. "You mind your own business."

"Attend to me, sir," cried Wilton, in his sternest bench manner.

"Well, I am a-try'n' to, master, on'y he keeps on kedgin' me."

"Where did you see my son and—er—the lady?"

"Where did I sin 'em? Up road."

"Where were you?"

"Ahint the hedge."

"And what were you doing behind the hedge—wiring?"

"Naw. On'y got me bat-fowling nets."

"But you were hiding, sir?"

"Well, what o' that? 'Bliged to hide. Can't go out anywhere o' nights now wi'out summun watching yer. Can't go for a few sparrers but some on 'em says its pardridges."

"What time was it?"

"Hey?"

"What time was it?"

"I d'know; nine or ten, or 'leven. Twelve, may-be."

"Well?"

"Hey?"

"What then?"

"What then? Nothin' as I knows on. Yes, there weer; he puts his arm round her waist, and she give him a dowse in the faace."

"Humph! Which way did they go then?"

"Up road."

"Did you follow them?"

"What'd I got to follow 'em for? Shouldn't want nobody to follow me when I went out wi' a gal."

Wilton frowned.

"Did you see any carriage about, waiting?"

"Naw."

"What did you do then?"

"Waited till they was out o' sight."

"Yes, and what then?"

"Ketched sparrers, and they arn't game."

The lout looked round, grinning at all present, as if he had posed the magistrate in whose presence he was standing, till his eyes lit on Mrs Wilton, who was listening to him intently, and to her he raised his hand, passing the open palm upward past his face till it was as high as he could reach, and then descending the arc of a circle, a movement supposed in rustic schools to represent a most respectful bow.

"Ah, Barker, Barker!" said the recipient, shaking her head at him; "you never come to the Sunday school now."

"Grow'd too big, missus," said the lad, grinning, and then noisily using his cuff for the pocket-handkerchief he lacked.

"We are never too big to learn to be good, Barker," continued Mrs Wilton, "and I'm afraid you are growing a bad boy now."

"Oh, I don't know, missus; I shouldn't be a bad 'un if there was no game."

"That will do, that will do," said the Squire, impatiently. "That's all you know, then, sir?"

"Oh, no; I knows a lot more than that," said the lad, grinning.

"Then why the deuce don't you speak?"

"What say?"

"Tell me what more you know about Mr Claud and the lady, and I'll give you another shilling."

"Will yer?" cried the lad, eagerly. "Well, I've seed'd 'em five or six times afore going along by the copse and down the narrow lane, and I sin him put his arm round her oncet, and I was close by, lying clost to a rabbud hole; and she says, 'How dare you, sir! how dare you!' just like that I dunno any more, and that makes two shillin'."

"There; be off. Take him away, Samuel, and give him a horn of beer."

"Yes sir—Now, then, come on."

But the lad stood and grinned, first at the Squire and then at Mrs Wilton, rubbing his hands down his sides the while.

"D'yer hear?" whispered the footman, as the groom opened the door. "Come on."

"Sheeawn't."

"Come on. Beer."

"But he arn't give me the two shillings yet."

"Eh? Oh, forgot," said the Squire.

"Gahn. None o' your games. Couldn't ha' forgetted it so soon."

"There—Take him away."

Wilton held out a couple of shillings, and the fellow snatched them, bit both between his big white teeth, stuffed one in each pocket, made Mrs Wilton another bow, and turned to go; but his wardrobe had been sadly neglected, and at the first step one of the shillings trickled down the leg of his trousers, escaped the opening into his ill-laced boot, rattled on the polished oaken floor, and then ran along, after the fashion of coins, to hide itself in the darkest corner of the room. But Barker was too sharp for it, and forgetting entirely the lessons he had learned at school about ordering "himself lowly and reverently to all his betters," he shouted: "Loo, loo, loo!" pounced upon it like a cat does upon a mouse, picked it up, and thrust it where it could join its fellow, and turned to Mrs Wilton.

"Hole in the pocket," he said, confidentially, and went off to get the beer.

"Bah! Savage!" growled Wilton, as the door closed. "There, Maria, no doubt about it now."

"No, my dear, and we can sleep in peace."

But Mrs Wilton was wrong save and except the little nap she had after dinner while her husband was smoking his pipe; for that night, just before the last light was out—that last light being in the Squire's room where certain arrangements connected with hair and pieces of paper had detained Mrs Wilton nearly half an hour after her husband had announced in regular cadence that he was fast asleep—there came a long ringing at the hall door bell.

It was so utterly unexpected in the silence and solitude of the country place that Mrs Wilton sprang from her seat in front of the dressing-glass, jarring the table so that a scent-bottle fell with a crash, and injuring her knees.

"James—James!" she cried.

"Eh, what's the matter?" came from the bed, as the Squire sat up suddenly.

"Fire! Fire! Another stack burning, I'm sure."

Wilton sprang out of bed, ran to the window, tore aside the blind, flung open the casement, and looked down.

"Where is it?" he shouted, for he had more than once been summoned from his bed to rick fires.

"Where's what?" came in a familiar voice.

Wilton darted back, letting fall the blind.

"Slip on your dressing gown," he said, hastily, "and pull out those confounded things from your hair. They've come back."

"Oh, my dear, and me this figure!" cried the lady, and for the next ten minutes there was a hurried sound of dressing going on.

"Look sharp," said Wilton. "I'll go down and let them in. You'd better rouse up Cook and Samuel; they'll want something to eat."

"I won't be two minutes, my dear. Take them in the library; the wood ashes will soon glow up again. My own darlings! I am glad."

Mrs Wilton was less, for by the time the heavy bolts, lock, and bar had been undone, she was out of her room, and hurried to the balustrade to look down into the hall, paying no heed to the cool puff of wind that rushed upward and nearly extinguished the candle her husband had set down upon the marble table.

"My own boy!" she sighed, as she saw Claud enter, and heard his words.

"Thankye," he said. "Gone to bed soon."

"The usual time, my boy," said Wilton, in very different tones to those he had used at their last meeting. "But haven't you brought her?"

"Brought her?"

"Yes; where's Kate?"

"Fast asleep in bed by now, I suppose," said the young man sulkily.

"Oh, but you should have brought her. Where have you come from?"

"Fast train down. London. Didn't suppose I was going to stop here, did you, to be kicked?"

"Don't say any more about that, my boy. It's all over now; but why didn't you bring her down?"

"Oh, Claud, my boy, you shouldn't have left her like that."

"Brought her down—Kate—shouldn't have left," said the young man, excitedly. "Here, what do you both mean?"

"There, nonsense; what is the use of dissimulation now, my boy," said Wilton. "Of course we know, and—there—it's of no use to cry over spilt milk. We did not like it, and you shouldn't have both tried to throw dust in our eyes."

"Look here, guv'nor, have you been to a dinner anywhere to-night?"

"Absurd, sir. Stop this fooling. Where did you leave Kate?"

"In bed and asleep, I suppose."

"But—but where have you been, then?"

"London, I tell you. Shouldn't have been back now, only I couldn't find Harry Dasent. He's off somewhere, so I thought I'd better come back. I say, is she all right again?"

"I knew it! I knew it!" shrieked Mrs Wilton. "I said it from the first. Oh, James, James!—The pond—the pond! She's gone—she's gone!"

"Who's gone?" stammered Claud, looking from father to mother, and back again.

"Kate, dear; drowned—drowned," wailed Mrs Wilton.

"What!" shouted Claud.

"Look here, sir," said his father, catching him by the arm in a tremendous grip, as he raised the candle to gaze searchingly in his son's face; "let's have the truth at once. You're playing some game of your own to hide this—this escapade."

"Guv'nor!" cried the young man, catching his father by the arm in turn; "put down that cursed candle; you'll burn my face. You don't mean to say the little thing has cut?"

Chapter Eighteen

James Wilton stood for a few moments staring searchingly at his son. Then, in a sudden access of anger, he rushed to the library door, flung it open, came back, caught the young man by the shoulders, and began to back him in.

"Here, what are you doing, guv'nor? Leave off! Don't do that. Here, why don't you answer my question?"

"Hold your tongue, idiot! Do you suppose I want all the servants to hear what is said? Go in there."

He gave him a final thrust, and then hurried out to hasten upstairs to where Mrs Wilton stood holding on by the heavy balustrade which crossed the hall like a gallery, and rocking herself to and fro.

"Oh, James, I knew it—I knew it!" she sobbed out. "She's dead—she's dead!"

"Hush! Hold your tongue!" cried her husband. "Do you want to alarm the house? You'll have all the servants here directly. Come along."

He drew her arm roughly beneath his, and hurried her down the stairs into the library, thrust her into her son's arms, and then hurried to the hall table for the candle, ending by shutting himself in with them.

"Oh, Claud, Claud, my darling boy!" wailed Mrs Wilton.

"If you don't hold your tongue, Maria, you'll put me in a rage," growled Wilton, savagely. "Sit in that chair."

"Oh, James, James, you shouldn't," sobbed the poor woman, "you shouldn't," as she was plumped down heavily; but she spoke in a whisper.

"Done?" asked Claud, mockingly. "Then, now p'raps you'll answer my question. Has she bolted?"

"Silence, idiot!" growled his father, so fiercely that the young man backed away from trim in alarm. "No, don't keep silence, but speak. You contemptible young hound, do you think you can impose upon me by your question—by your pretended ignorance? Do you think you can impose upon me, I say? Do you think I cannot see through your plans?"

"I say, mater, what's the guv'nor talking about?" cried Claud.

"She's dead—she's dead!"

"Who's dead? What's dead?"

"Answer me, sir," continued Wilton, backing his son till he could get no farther for the big table. "Do you think you can impose upon me?"

"Who wants to impose on you, guv'nor?"

"You do, sir. But I see through your miserable plan, and I tell you this. You can't get the money into your own hands to make ducks and drakes of, for I am executor and trustee and guardian, and if there's any law in the land I'll lock up every shilling so that you can't touch it. If you had played honourably with me you would have had ample, and the estate would have come to you some day, cleared of incumbrances, if you had not killed yourself first."

"I don't know what you're talking about," cried Claud, angrily. "Who's imposing on you? Who's playing dishonourably? You behaved like a brute to me, and I went off to get out of it all, only I didn't want to be hard on ma, and so I came back."

"Oh, my darling boy! It was very, very good of you."

"Be quiet, Maria. Let the shallow-brained young idiot speak," growled Wilton. "Now, sir, answer me—have you gone through some form of marriage?"

"Who with?" said the young man, with a grin.

"Answer my question, sir. Have you gone through some form of marriage?"

"I? No. I'm free enough, guv'nor."

"You have not?" cried Wilton, aghast. "You mean to tell me that you have taken that poor girl away somewhere, and have not married her?"

"No, I don't mean to tell you anything of the sort. Here, mother, is the pater going mad?"

"Silence, Maria; don't answer him."

"Yes, do ma. What does it all mean? Has Kitty bolted?"

"She's drowned—she's drowned, my boy."

"Nonsense, ma! You're always thinking someone is drowned. Then she has bolted. Oh, I say!"

"No, sir; she has not bolted, as you term it in your miserable horsey slang. You've taken her away—there; don't deny it. You've got her somewhere, and you think you can set me at defiance."

"Do I, guv'nor?"

"Yes, sir, you do. But I've warned you and shown you how you stand. Now, look here; your only chance is to give up and do exactly as I tell you."

"Oh, is it?" said the young man mockingly.

"Yes, sir, it is. Now then, be frank and open with me at once, and I may be able to help you out of the miserable hole in which you have plunged us."

"Go ahead, then. Have it your own way, guv'nor."

"No time must be lost—that is, if you are not deceiving me and have already had the ceremony performed."

"I didn't stand on ceremony," said Claud, with a laughing sneer; "I gave her a few kisses, and a nice row was the result."

"Will you be serious, sir?"

"Yes, I'm serious enough. Where has she gone?"

"Where have you taken her?"

"I haven't taken her anywhere, guv'nor."

"Do you mean to tell me, sir, that you did not go up a ladder to her window?"

"Hullo!"

"Bring her down and take her right away?"

"I say, guv'nor," cried Claud, with such startling energy that his father's last suspicion was swept away; "is it so bad as that?"

"Then you didn't take her off?"

"Of course I didn't. Take her off? What, after that scene? Likely. What nonsense, guv'nor! Do you think she'd have come?"

"Claud, you amaze me, my boy," cried Wilton, who looked staggered, but his incredulity got the better of him directly. "No; only by your effrontery," he continued. "You are trifling with me; worse still, you are trifling with a large fortune. Come, it will pay you best to be frank. Where is she?"

"At the bottom of the pike pond, for all I know—a termagant," cried Claud; "I tell you I haven't seen her since the row."

"Then she is drowned—she's drowned."

"Be quiet, Maria!" roared Wilton. "Now, boy, tell me the truth for once in a way; did you elope with Kate?"

"No, guv'nor, I did not," cried the young man. "I never had the chance, or I'd have done it like a shot."

Wilton's jaw dropped. He was quite convinced now, and he sank into a chair, staring at his son.

"I—I thought you had made short work of it," said Wilton, huskily.

"Then she really has gone?" said Claud in a whisper.

"Yes, yes, my dear," burst out Mrs Wilton. "I knew it! I was right at first."

"Where has she gone, then, mother?"

"Hold your tongue, woman!" cried Wilton, angrily. "You don't know anything about it—how could she get a ladder there? Footsteps on the flower-bed, my boy. A man in it. I thought it was you."

"And all that money gone," cried Claud.

"No, not yet, my boy. There, I beg your pardon for suspecting you. It seemed so much like your work. But stop—you are cheating me; it was your doing."

"Have it your own way, then, guv'nor."

"You were seen with her last night."

"Eh? What time?" cried Claud.

"I don't know the time, sir, but a man saw you with her. Come, you see the risk you run of losing a fortune. Speak out."

Claud spoke in, but what he said was his own affair. Then, after a minute's thought, he said; "I say, would it be old Garstang, guv'nor?"

"No, sir, it would not be John Garstang," cried Wilton, with his anger rising again.

"No; I have it, guv'nor," cried Claud, excitedly. "I went up, meaning to have a turn in town with Harry Dasent, but he was out. That's it; he hasn't a penny in the world, and he has been down here three times lately. I thought he'd got devilish fond of her all at once; and twice over he let out about Kitty being so good-looking. That's it; he's got her away."

"No, no, my dear; she wouldn't have gone away with a man like that," sobbed Mrs Wilton. "She didn't like him."

"No; absurd," cried Wilton.

"But he'd have gone away with her, guv'nor."

"You were seen with her last night."

"Oh, was I? All right, then. If you say so I suppose I was, guv'nor, but I'm going back to London after ferreting out all I can. You're on the wrong scent, dad,—him! I never thought of that."

"You're wrong, Claud; you're wrong."

"Yes, mother, deucedly wrong," cried the young man fiercely. "Why didn't I think of it? I might have done the same, and now it's too late. Perhaps not. She'd hold out after he got her away, and we might get to her in time. No, I know Harry Dasent. It's too late now."

"Look here, Claud, boy, I want to believe in you," said Wilton, who was once more impressed by his son's earnestness; "do you tell me you believe that Harry Dasent has taken her away by force?"

"Force, or some trick. It was just the sort of time when she might listen to him. There; you may believe me, now."

"Then who was the lady you were seen with last night? Come, be honest. You were seen with someone. Who was it?"

"Mustn't kiss and tell, guv'nor," said Claud, with a sickly grin.

"Look here," said Wilton huskily. "There are a hundred and fifty thousand pounds at stake, my boy. Was it Kate?"

"No, father," cried the young man earnestly; "it wasn't, 'pon my soul."

"Am I to believe you?"

"Look here, guv'nor, do you think I want to fool this money away? What good should I be doing by pretending I hadn't carried her off? I told you I'd have done it like a shot if I had had the chance; and what's more, you'd have liked it, so long as I had got her to say yes. I did not carry her off, once for all. It was Harry Dasent, and if he has choused me out of that bit of coin, curse him, if I hang for it, I'll break his neck!"

"Oh! Claud, Claud, my darling," wailed Mrs Wilton, "to talk like that when your cousin's lying cold and motionless at the bottom of that pond!"

Chapter Nineteen

For the better part of two days Pierce Leigh went about like one who had received some terrible mental shock; and Jenny's pleasant little rounded cheeks told the tale of the anxiety from which she suffered, while her eyes followed him wistfully, and she seemed never weary of trying to perform little offices for him which would distract his attention from the thoughts which were sapping his vitality.

The life at the quiet little cottage home was entirely changed, for brother and sister were playing parts for which they were quite unsuited in a melancholy farce of real life, wearing masks, and trying to hide their sufferings from each other, with a miserable want of success.

And all the time Leigh was longing to open his heart to the loving, affectionate little thing who had been his companion from a child, his confidante over all his hopes, and counsellor in every movement or plan. She had read and studied with him, helped him to puzzle out abstruse questions, and for years they had gone on together leading a life full of happiness, and ready to laugh lightly over money troubles connected with the disappointment over the purchase of the Northwood practice through a swindling, or grossly ignorant, agent.

"Don't worry about it, Pierce dear," Jenny had said, "it is only the loss of some money, and as it's in the country we can live on less, and wear out our old clothes over again. I do wish I could cut up and turn your coats and trousers. You men laugh at us and our fashions, but we women can laugh at you and yours. Granted that our hats and dresses are flimsy, see how we can re-trim and unpick, and make them look new again, while your stupid things get worn and shiny, and then they're good for nothing. They're quite hopeless, for I daren't try to make you a new coat out of two old ones."

There was many a merry laugh over such matters, Jenny's spirits rising, as the country life brought back the bloom of health that had been failing in Westminster; and existence, in spite of the want of patients, was a very happy one, till the change came. This change to a certain extent resembled that in the yard of the amateur who was bitten by the fancy for keeping and showing those great lumbering fowls—the Brahmas, so popular years ago.

He had a pen of half-a-dozen cockerels, the result of the hatching of a clutch of eggs laid by a feathered princess of the blood royal; and as he watched them through their infancy it was with high hopes of winning prizes—silver cups and vases, at all the crack poultry shows. And how he tended and pampered his pets, watching them through the various stages passed by this kind of fowl—one can hardly say feathered fowl in the earlier stages of their existence, for through their early boyhood, so to speak, they run about in a raw unclad condition that is pitiful to see, for they are almost "birds of a feather" in the Dundreary idea of the singularity of plumage; and it is not until they have arrived pretty well at full growth that they assume the heavy massive plumage that makes their skeleton lanky forms look so huge. These six young Brahmas masculine grew and throve in their pen, innocent, happy, and at peace, till one morning their owner gazed upon them in pride, for they were all that a Brahma fancier could wish to see— small of comb, heavy of hackle, tail slightly developed, broad in the beam, short-legged, and without a trace of vulture hock. "First prize for one of them," said the owner, and after feeding them he went to town, and came back to find his hopes ruined, his cockerels six panting, ragged, bleeding wrecks, squatting about in the pen, half dead, too much exhausted to spur and peck again.

For there had been battle royal in that pen, the young birds engaging in a furious melée. For what reason? Because, as good old Doctor Watts said, "It is their nature to." They did not know it till that morning, but there was the great passion in each one's breast, waiting to be evoked, and transform them from pacific pecking and scratching birds into perfect demons of discord.

There was wire netting spread all over the top of their carefully sanded pen, and till then they had never seen others of their kind. It was their world, and as far as they knew there was neither fowl nor chicken save themselves. The memory of the mother beneath whose plumage they had nestled had passed away, for the gallinaceous brain cavity is small.

That morning, a stray, pert-looking, elegantly spangled, golden Hambro' pullet appeared upon the wall, looked down for a moment on the pen of full-grown, innocent young Brahmas, uttered the monosyllables "Took, took!" and flew away.

For a brief space, the long necks of the cockerels were strained in the direction where that vision of loveliness had appeared for a brief instant; the fire of jealous love blazed out, and they turned and fought almost to the death. It would have been quite, had there been strength.

The owner of these six cripples did not take a prize.

So at Northwood, women, save as sister or friend, had been non-existent to Pierce Leigh. Now the desire to rend his human brother was upon him strong.

Jenny knew it, and for more than one reason she trembled for the time that must come when Pierce should first meet Claud Wilton, for it had rapidly dawned upon her that the long-deferred grand passion of her brother was the stronger for its sudden growth.

In her anxiety, she went out during those two days a great deal for the benefit of her health, but really on the qui vive for the news that she felt must soon come of Claud's proceedings with his cousin; and twice over she had started the subject of their projected leaving, making Leigh raise his eyebrows slightly in wonder at the sudden change in his sister's ideas. But it was not till nearly evening that, during her brother's temporary absence, she heard the news for which she was waiting.

One of Leigh's poor patients called to see him—one of the class suffered by most young doctors, who go through life believing they are very ill, and that it is the duty of a medical man to pay extra attention to their ailments, and lavish upon them knowledge and medicine to the fullest extent, without a thought of payment entering their heads.

Betsy Bray was the lady in question, and as was her custom, Jenny saw the woman, ready to hear her last grievance, and tell her brother when he returned.

Betsy was fifty-five, and possessed of the strong constitution which bears a great deal of ease; but in her own estimation she was very bad. From frequenting surgeries, she had picked up a few medical terms, and larded her discourse with them and others of a religious tendency, her attendance at church dole-giving, and other charitable distributions being of the most regular description.

"Doctor at home, miss?" she said, plaintively, as she slowly and plumply subsided upon the little couch in the surgery, the said piece of furniture groaning in all its springs, for Betsy possessed weight.

"No, Mrs Bray. He has gone to call on the Dudges, at West Gale."

"Ah, he always is calling on somebody when I've managed to drag my weary bones all this way up from the village."

"I am very sorry. What is the matter now?" said Jenny, soothingly.

"Matter, miss? What's allus the matter with me? It's my chronics. Not a wink of sleep have I had all the blessed night."

"Well, I must give you something."

"Nay, nay, my dear; you don't understand my troubles. It's the absorption is all wrong; and you'd be giving me something out of the wrong bottles. You just give me a taste of sperrits to give me strength to get home again, and beg and pray o' the doctor to come on and see me as soon as he comes home, if you don't want me to be laid out stark and cold afore another day's done." ·

"But I have no spirits, Mrs Bray."

"Got none? Well, I dessay a glass o' wine might do. Keep me alive p'raps till I'd crawled home to die."

"But we have no wine."

"Dear, dear, dear, think o' that," said the woman fretfully. "The old doctor always had some, and a drop o' sperrits, too. Ah, it's a hard thing to be old and poor and in bad health, carrying your grey hairs in sorrow to the grave; and all about you rich and well and happy, rolling in money, and marrying and giving in marriage and wearing their wedding garments, one and all. You've heard about the doings up at the Manor House?"

"Yes, yes, something about them, Mrs Bray; but I'll tell my brother, and he will, I know, come and see you."

"Yes, you tell him; not as I believe in him much, but poor people must take what they can get—He's come back, you know?"

"My brother? No; he would have come straight in here."

"Your brother? Tchah, no!" cried the woman, forgetting her "chronics" in the interest she felt in the fresh subject. "You're always thinking about your brother, and if's time you began to think of a husband. I meant him at the Manor—young Claud Wilton. He's come back."

"Come back?" cried Jenny excitedly.

"Yes; but I hear he arn't brought his young missus with him. Nice goings on, running away, them two, to get married. But I arn't surprised; he fell out with the parson long enough ago about Sally Deal, down the village, and parson give it him well for not marrying her. Wouldn't be married here out o' spite, I suppose. Well, I must go. You're sure you haven't got a drop o' gin in the house?"

"Quite sure," said Jenny quickly; "and I'll be sure and tell my brother to come."

"Ay, do; and tell him I say it's a shame he lives so far out of the village. I feel sometimes that I shall die in one of the ditches before I get here, it's so far. There, don't hurry me so; I don't want to be took ill here. I know, doctors aren't above helping people out of the world when they get tired of them."

"Gone!" cried Jenny at last, with a sigh of relief; and then, with the tears rising to her eyes, "Oh, what shall I do? What shall I do? If they meet—if he ever gets to know!"

She hurried upstairs, put on her hat and jacket, and came down looking pale and excited, but without any very definite plans. One idea was foremost in her mind; but as she reached the door she caught sight of her brother coming with rapid strides from the direction opposite to that taken by the old woman who had just gone.

"Too late!" she said, with a piteous sigh; and she ran upstairs hurriedly, and threw off her things.

She had hardly re-arranged her hair when she heard her brother's voice calling her.

"Yes, dear," she said, and she ran down, to find him looking ghastly.

"Who was that went away from here?" he said huskily.

She told him, but not of her promise to send him over.

"I'll go to her at once," he said.

"No, no, Pierce, dear; she is not ill. Pray stay at home; there is really no need."

"Why should I stay at home?" he said, looking at her suspiciously.

"I—I am not very well, dear. You have been so dull, it has upset me. I wish you would stay in with me this evening; I feel so nervous and lonely."

"Yes, I will," he said; "but I must go there first."

"No, no, dear; don't, please, don't go," she pleaded, as she caught his arm. "Please stay. She is not in the least ill, and I want you to stop. There, I'll make some tea directly, and we'll sit over it and have a long cosy chat, and it will do us both good, dear."

"Jenny," he cried harshly, "you want to keep me at home."

"Yes, dear, I told you so; but don't speak in that harsh way; you frighten me."

"I'm not blind," he cried. "Don't deny it. You've heard from that old woman what I have just found out. He has come back."

"Pierce!" she cried; and she shrank away from him, and covered her face with her hands.

"Yes," he said wildly, and there was a look in his ghastly face which she had never seen before. "I knew it; and you are afraid that I shall meet him and wring his miserable neck."

"Oh, Pierce, Pierce," she cried piteously, as she threw herself at his feet; "don't, don't, pray don't talk in this mad way."

"Why not?" he said, with a mocking laugh. "It is consistent. There, get up; don't kneel there praying to a madman."

She sprang up quickly and seized him by the shoulder, and then threw herself across his knees and her arms about his neck.

"It is not true," she cried passionately. "You are not mad; you are only horribly angry, and I am frightened to death for fear that you should meet and be violent."

"Violent! I could kill him!" he muttered, with a hard look in his eyes. "Good God, what a profanation! He marry her! She must have been mad, or there has been some cruel act of violence. Jenny, girl, I will see him and take him by the throat and make him tell me all. I have fought against it. I have told myself that she is unworthy of a second thought, but my heart tells me that it is not so. There has been some horrible trick played upon her; she would not—as you have said—she could not have gone off of her own will with that miserable little hound."

"Yes, yes, that is what I think," she said, hysterically. "So wait patiently, dear, and we shall know the truth some day."

"Wait!" he cried, with a mocking laugh. "Wait! With my brain feeling as if it were on fire. No, I have waited too long; I ought to have gone off after him at once, and learned the truth."

"No, no, dear; you two must not meet. Now then, listen to me."

"Some day, little bird," he said, lifting her from his knee, as he rose; then kissing her tenderly he extricated himself from her clinging hands as gently as he could, and rushed out.

"O, Pierce, Pierce!" she cried. "Stay, stay!"

But the only answer to her call as she ran to the door was the heavy beat of his feet in the gloom of the misty evening.

"And if they meet he'll find out all," she wailed piteously. She paused, waiting for a few moments, and then searched in her pocket and brought out a tiny silver whistle, which she placed in the bosom of her dress, after flinging the ribbon which was in its ring over her head.

A minute later, with her cloak thrown on and hood drawn over her head, she had slipped out of the cottage, and was running down the by-lane in the direction of the Manor House.

Chapter Twenty

The soft light of the moon attracted Kate to her bedroom window, where she drew up the blind, and after standing gazing at the silvery orb for some minutes, she unfastened and threw open the casement, drew a chair forward, to sit there letting the soft air of the late autumn night give its coolness to her aching brow.

For the silence and calm seemed to bring rest, and by degrees the dull throbbing of her head grew less painful, the strange feeling of confusion which had made thinking a terrible effort began to pass away, and with her eyes fixed upon the skies she began to go over the events of the day, and to try and map out for herself the most sensible course to pursue. Go from Northwood she felt that she must, and at once; though how to combat the will of her constituted guardian was not clear. Garstang, in his encounter with Wilton, had put the case only too plainly, and there was not the vestige of a doubt in her mind as to the truth of his words. It had all been arranged in the family, and whatever might have been her cousin's inclinations at first, he showed only too plainly that he looked upon her as his future wife.

She shuddered at the thought; but the weak girl passed away again, and her pale cheeks began to burn once more with indignant anger, and the throbbing of her brow returned, so that she was glad to rest her head upon her hand.

By degrees the suffering grew less poignant, and as the pain and mental confusion once more died out she set herself to the task of coming to some decision as to what she should do next day, proposing to herself plan after plan, building up ideas which crumbled away before that one thought: her uncle was her guardian and trustee, and his power over her was complete.

What to do?—what to do? The ever recurring question, till she felt giddy.

It seemed, knowing what he did, the height of cruelty for Garstang to have gone and left her, but she was obliged to own that he could do nothing more than upbraid his relatives for their duplicity.

But he had done much for her; he had thoroughly endorsed her own ideas as to her position and her uncle's intentions; and at last, with the tears suffusing her eyes, as she gazed at the moon rising slowly above the trees, she sat motionless for a time, thinking of her happy life in the past; and owning to herself that the advice given to her was right, she softly closed the casement, drew down the blind, and determined to follow out the counsel.

"Yes, I must sleep on it—if I can," she said softly. "Poor Liza is right, and I am not quite alone—I am never alone, for in spirit those who loved me so well must be with me still."

There were two candles burning on the dressing-table, but their light troubled her aching eyes, and she slowly extinguished both, the soft light which flooded the window being ample for her purpose.

Crossing the room to the side furthest from the door, she bent down and bathed her aching forehead for a few minutes before beginning to undress, and was then about to loosen her hair when she was startled by a faint tap outside the window which sounded as if something had struck the sill.

She stopped, listening for a few minutes, but all was still, and coming to the conclusion that the sound had been caused by a rat leaping down somewhere behind the wainscot of the old room, she raised her hands to her head once more, but only for them to become fixed as she stood there paralysed by terror, for a shadow suddenly appeared at the bottom of the blind—a dark shadow cast by the moon; and as she gazed at it in speechless fear, it rose higher and higher, and looked monstrous in size.

She made an effort to cast off the horrible nightmare-like sense of terror, but as she realised that to reach the door she must pass the window it grew stronger.

The bell!

That was by the bed's head, and for the time being she felt helpless, so completely paralysed that she could not even cry for help.

What could it mean? Someone had placed a ladder against the window sill and climbed up, and at the thought which now flashed through her brain the helpless feeling passed away, and the hot indignation made her strong, and gave her a courage which drove away her childish fear.

How dare he! It was Claud, and she knew what he would say—that he had come there when all was still in the house and no one could know, to ask her forgiveness for the scene that day.

Drawing herself up, she was walking swiftly towards the door, with the intention of going at once to Liza's chamber, when there was a fresh movement of the shadow on the blind, and the dread returned, and her heart throbbed heavily.

Claud was a short-haired, smooth-faced boy—the shadow cast on the blind was the silhouette of a broad-shouldered, bearded man.

It was plain enough now—burglars must be trying to effect an entry, and in another moment she would have cried aloud for help, but just then there was a light tap on one of the panes, the shadow grew smaller and darker, as if the face had been pressed close to the window, and she heard her name softly uttered twice.

"Kate! Kate!"

She mastered her fear once more, telling herself it must be Claud; and she went slowly to the door; laid her hand upon the bolt to turn it, but paused again, for once more came the low distinct voice—

"Kate! Kate!"

She uttered a spasmodic cry, turned sharply round, and half ran to the window with every pulse throbbing with excitement, for she felt that the help she had prayed for last night had come.

Chapter Twenty One

There was no hesitation on the part of Kate Wilton. The dread was gone, and she rapidly drew up the blind and opened the casement window.

"You?" she said quickly, as she held out her hands, which were caught at once and held.

"Yes; who should it be, my child? Were you afraid that insolent young scoundrel would dare to do such a thing?"

"At first," she faltered, and then quickly, "I hardly knew what to think; I was afraid someone was going to break in. Oh, Mr Garstang, why have you come?"

He uttered a little laugh.

"For the same reason, I suppose, that would make a father who knew his child was in peril act in the same way."

"It is very, very kind of you; but you will be heard, and it will only cause fresh trouble."

"It can cause no greater than has come to us, my child. I was half-way to London, but I could not go on; so I got out at a station ten miles away, walked into the village close by, and found a fly and a man to drive me over. I wanted to know how you were getting on. Have you seen them again?"

"No. I came straight to my room, and have not left it since."

"Good girl! That was very brave of you. Then you took my advice."

"Of course."

"And Master Claud?"

He felt her start and shudder.

"Don't talk about him, please. But there, I am very grateful to you for being so kind and thoughtful, and for your brave defence."

"Brave nonsense, my child!" he said bluntly. "I did as any man of right feeling would have done if he found a ruffian insulting a weak, helpless girl. Kate, my dear, my blood has been boiling ever since. I could not go back and leave you in this state; I was compelled to come and see you and have a little consultation about your future. I felt that I must do it before seeing James

Wilton again. Not a very reputable way, this, of coming to a man's house, even if he is a connection of mine; not respectful to you, either, my child, but I felt certain that if I came to the door and asked to see you I should have been refused entrance."

"Yes, yes," said Kate, sadly. "I should not have been told of your coming, or I would have insisted upon seeing you."

"You would! Brave girl! I like to hear you speak out so firmly. Well, there was nothing for it but for me, middle-aged man as I am, to play the daring gallant at the lady's window—lattice, I ought to say."

"Please don't talk like this, Mr Garstang," said Kate. "It does not sound like you to be playful in your manner."

"Thank you, my child, you are right; it does not I accept the reproof. Now, then, to be businesslike. You have been thinking deeply, of course, since you have been alone?"

"Yes, very, very seriously about my position. Mr Garstang, it is impossible for me to stay here."

"Quite impossible. The conduct to you of your aunt and uncle makes them—no matter what promises they may give you—quite unworthy of your trust. Well?"

"I have pretty well decided that I shall go away to-morrow with Eliza, our old nurse and maid."

"A most worthy woman, my dear. You could not do better; but—"

"But what?" said Kate, nervously.

"I do not wish to alarm you, but do you fully realise your position here?"

"Yes, and that is why I have decided to go."

"Exactly; but you do not fully grasp my meaning. What about your uncle?"

"You mean that he will object?"

"Exactly."

"But if I am firm, and insist, he will not dare to detain me," said the girl warmly.

"You think so? Well, think again, my child. He is your guardian and trustee; he will absolutely refuse, and will take any steps which he considers right to prevent your leaving. I am afraid that by the power your poor father left in his hands he will consider himself justified in keeping you quite as a prisoner until you obey his wishes."

"Mr Garstang, surely he dare not proceed to such extremities!"

"I am afraid that he has the power, and I grieve to say he is in such a position that he is likely to be reckless in his desire to gain his ends."

Kate drew a deep breath, and gazed appealingly in the speaker's face.

"As a solicitor and the husband of your aunt's late sister, James Wilton naturally came to me for help in his money affairs, and I did the best I could for him. I found that he had been gambling foolishly on the Stock Exchange, instead of keeping to his farms, and was so involved that immediate payments had to be made to save him from absolute ruin."

"But my father surely did not know of this?"

"Not a word. He kept his own counsel, and of course until the will was read I had no idea of what arrangements your father had made; in fact, I was somewhat taken aback, for I thought it possible that he would have made me one of your trustees. But that by the way. I helped your uncle all I could as a monetary agent, and found clients who were willing to advance him money on his estate, which is now deeply mortgaged. These moneys are now wanted, for the interest has not been fully paid for years. In short, James Wilton is in a desperate condition, and my visits here have been to try and extricate him from his monetary tangle in which he finds himself. Now do you begin to grasp what his designs are?"

"Yes, I see," said Kate, sadly; "it is to get some of the money which should be mine, to pay his debts."

"Exactly, and the simplest way to do so is to marry you to Claud."

"No: there is a simpler way, Mr Garstang. If my uncle had come to me and told me his position I should have felt that I could not have done a more kindly deed than to help my father's brother by paying his debts."

"Very kind and generous of you, my child; but he would not believe it possible, and I must say to you that, after what has passed, you would not be doing your duty to the dead by helping your uncle to this extent. Kate, my dear, since I have been talking to you it has occurred to me that there is but one way out of your difficulty."

"Yes, what is it?" she cried eagerly.

"Of course, you cannot marry your cousin?"

"Mr Garstang!" she cried indignantly.

"It is impossible, of course; and if you stay here you will have to submit to endless persecution and annoyance, such as a highly strung, sensitive girl like you are will be unable to combat."

"You do not know me yet, Mr Garstang."

"Indeed? I think I do, as I have known you from a child. You are mentally strong, but you have been, and under these circumstances will be, further sapped by sickness, and it would need superhuman power to win in so cruel a fight. You must not risk it, Kate, my child. You must go."

"Yes, I feel that I know I must go, but how can I? You, as a lawyer, should know."

"A long and costly litigation, or an appeal to the Court of Chancery might save you, and a judge make an order traversing your father's will, but I should shrink from such a course; I know too well the uncertainties of the law."

"Then your idea for extricating me from my difficult position is of no value," she said, despairingly.

"You have not heard it yet," he said, "because I almost shrink from proposing such a thing to your father's child."

"Tell me what it is," she said firmly.

"You desire me to?"

"Of course."

"It is this—a simple and effective way of checkmating one who has proved himself unworthy. My idea was that you should transfer the guardianship to me."

"Willingly, Mr Garstang; but can it be done?"

"It must and shall be done if you are willing, my child," he said firmly, "but it would necessitate a very unusual, a bold and immediate step oh your part."

"What is that, Mr Garstang?" she said quietly.

"You would have to place yourself under my guardianship at once."

"At once?" she said, starting slightly.

"Yes. Think for yourself. It could not be done slowly and legally, for at the first suspicion that I was acting against him, James Wilton would place you immediately completely out of my reach, and take ample care that I had no further communication with you."

"Yes," she said quietly; "he would."

"Yes," he said, repeating her words, and speaking in a slow, passionless, judicial way; "if the thing were deferred, or if he were besieged, he would redouble his pressure. Kate, my dear, that was my idea; but it must sound almost as mad to you as it does to me. Yes, it is impossible; I ought not to have proposed such a thing, and yet I can not find it in my heart to give up any chance of rescuing you from your terrible position."

He was silent, and she stood there gazing straight before her for a few moments before turning her eyes upon his.

"Tell me plainly what you mean, Mr Garstang."

"Simply this: I did mean that you should take the opportunity of my being here and leave at once. I have the fly waiting, and I could take you to my town house and place you in the care of my housekeeper and her daughter. It would of course be checkmating your uncle, who could be brought to his knees; and then as the price of your pardon you could do something to help him out of his difficulties. Possibly a moderate payment to his creditors might free him on easy terms. But there, my child, the project is too wild and chimerical. It must almost sound to you like a romance."

She stood there gazing full in his eyes as he ceased speaking; and at the end of a minute he said gently, "There, I must not keep you talking here in the cold night air. Your chest is still delicate; but strange as the visit may seem, I am after all glad I have come, if only to give you a little comfort—to show you that you are not quite alone in the world. There, say good-night, and, of course, you will not mention my visit to anyone. I must go now and catch the night mail at the station. To-morrow I will see a very learned old barrister friend, and lay the matter before him so as to get his advice. He may show me some way out of the difficulty. Keep a good heart. I must show you that you have one who will act as an uncle should. But listen to me," he said, as he took her cold hand in his, "you must brace yourself up for the encounters to come. Even if I find that I can assist you, the law moves slowly, and it may be months before you can come out of prison. So no flinching; let James Wilton and that scoundrel Claud know that they have a firm, mentally strong woman to deal with; and now God bless you, my child! Good-night!"

He let her hand fall, and lowered himself a round of the ladder; but she stood as if carved in marble in the bright moonlight, without uttering a word.

"Say good-night, my dear; and come, be firm."

She made no reply.

"You are not hurt by my proposal?" he said quietly.

"No," she said at last, "I was trying to weigh it. I must have time."

"Yes, you must have time. Think it over, my child; it may strike you differently to-morrow, or you may see it in a more impossible light. So may I. You know my address: Bedford Row will find me. I am well known in London. Write to me if you require help, and at any cost I will come and see you, even if I bring police to force my way. Now, good-night, my dear. Heigho! Why did not I have a daughter such as you?"

"Let me think," said Kate gravely.

"No; this is no time for thinking, my child. Once more, good-night."

"No," said Kate firmly. "I will trust you, Mr Garstang. You must not leave me to be kept a prisoner here."

"Possibly they would not dare; and I must warn you that you are taking a very unusual step."

"Not in trusting you, sir," she said firmly. "Treat me as you have treated the daughter who might have been born to you, and save me at once from the position I am in. Wait while I go and waken Eliza. She must be with us."

"Your maid?" he said.

"Yes, I can not leave her here."

"They will not keep her a prisoner," he said quietly, "and she can join us afterwards. No, my child, if you go with me now it must be alone and at once. I will not put any pressure on you. Come or stay. You still have me to work for you as far as in me lies. Which shall it be? Your hat and cloak, or good-night?"

"Don't leave me, Mr Garstang. I am weak and hysterical still. I feel now, after the chance of freedom you have shown me, that I dare not face to-morrow alone."

"Then you will come?" he said, in the same low passionless way.

"I will."

Five minutes after, John Garstang was helping her carefully to descend the ladder, guarding her every footstep so that she could not fall; and as they reached the ground, he quietly offered her his arm.

"What a beautifully calm and peaceful night!" he said gravely. "Do you feel the cold?"

"No; my cheeks are burning," she answered.

"Ah! yes, a little excitement; but don't be alarmed. The fly is waiting about half a mile away. A sharp walk will bring back the correct circulation. Almost a shame, though, my child, to take you from the clear pure air of the country to my gloomy house in Great Ormond Street. Not very far from your old home."

"Don't talk to me, please, Mr Garstang," she said painfully.

"I most, my dear; and about everything that will take your attention from the step you are taking. Are your shoes pretty stout? I must not have you suffering from wet feet. By the way, my dear, you were nineteen on your last birthday. You look much older. I thought so yesterday. Dear, dear, ii my poor wife had lived, how she would have blessed me for bringing her a daughter to our quiet home! How you would have liked her, my dear! A sweet, good, clever woman—so different to Maria Wilton. Well, well, a good woman, too, in spite of her weakness for her boy."

He chatted on, with Kate walking by him in silence, till the fly was reached, with the horse munching the grass at the road side, and the driver asleep on the box, but ready to start into wakefulness at a word.

An hour later, Kate sat back in the corner of a first-class carriage, when her strength gave way, and she burst into a hysterical fit of sobbing. But she heard Garstang's words:

"I am glad to see that, my child. Cry on; it will relieve your overburdened heart. You will be better then. You have done right; never fear. To-morrow you can rest in peace."

Chapter Twenty Two

Jenny was almost breathless when she reached the park palings of the Manor House, some little distance from the gate at the end of the avenue; and here she paused for a few moments beneath an oak which grew within the park, but which, like many others, spread out three or four huge horizontal boughs right across the boundary lane, and made the way gloomy even on sunny days.

She looked sharply back in the direction by which she had come, but the evening was closing in more and more gloomy, and the mist exceedingly closely related to a rain, was gathering fast and forming drops on the edges of dead leaves and twigs, beside making the grass overhanging the footpath so wet that the girl's feet and the lower parts of her skirts were drenched.

No one was in sight or likely to be in that secluded spot, and having gained her breath, she started off once more, heedless of the sticky mud of the lane, and followed it on, round by the park palings, where the autumn leaves lay thick and rustled as her dress swept over them. In a few minutes she reached a stile in the fence, where a footpath—an old right of way much objected to by Squire Wilton, as the village people called him—led across the little park, passing the house close by the end of the shrubbery, and entering another lane, which curved round to join the main road right at the far end of the village, a good mile away from the Doctor's cottage.

There were lights in the drawing-room and dining-room, making a dull glow on the thickening mist, as Jenny halted at the end of the shrubbery, and all was still as death, till a dog barked suddenly, and was answered by half a dozen others, pointers and retrievers, in the kennel by the stables. This lasted in a dismal, irritating chorus, which made the girl utter little ejaculations suggestive of impatience, as she waited for the noise to end.

She glanced round once more, but the evergreens grew thickly just over an iron hurdle fence, and she satisfied herself that as she could only indistinctly see the shrubs three or four yards away, it was impossible for her to be seen from the house.

The barking went on in a full burst for a few minutes. Then dog after dog finished its part; the sextette became a quartette, a trio, a duet; and then a deep-voiced retriever performed a powerful solo, ending it with a prolonged bay, and Jenny raised her hand to her lips, when the hill chorus burst out again, and the girl angrily stamped her foot in the wet grass.

"Oh, what a cold I shall catch," she muttered. "Why will people keep these nasty dogs?"

The barking went on for some minutes, just as before, breaking off by degrees into another solo; but at last all was still, the little sighs and ejaculations Jenny had kept on uttering ceased too. Then she raised her head quickly, and a shrill chirp sounded dead and dull in the misty air, followed at intervals by two more.

It was not a regular whistle, but a repetition of such a call as a night bird might utter in its flight as it floated over the house.

The mist seemed to stifle the call, and the girl was about to repeat it, but it was loud enough for the dogs to hear, and they set up a fierce baying, which lasted till there was a loud commotion of yelps and cries, mingled with the rattling of chains, the same deep-mouthed dog breaking out in a very different solo this time, one suggestive of suffering from the application of boot toes to its ribs.

Then quiet, and Jenny with trembling hand once more raised the little silver whistle to her lips, and the shrill chirps rang out in their former smothered way.

"Oh," sighed Jenny. "It will be a sore throat—I'm sure it will. I must go back; I dare not stay any longer. Ugh! How I do hate the little wretch. I could kill him!"

The girl's pretty little white teeth grated together, and once more she stamped her foot, following up this display of irritation by stamping the other.

"Cold as frogs," she muttered, "and the water's oozy in my boots. Wretch!"

"Ullo!" came in a harsh whisper, followed by the cachination which often accompanies a grin. "You've come, then!"

There was a rustle of the bushes before her, and the dimly seen figure of Claud climbed over the iron hurdle, made a snatch at the girl's arm with his right and a trial to fling his left about her waist, but she eluded him.

"Keep off," she said sharply; "how dare you!"

"Because I love you so, little dicky-bird," he whispered.

"I thought you didn't mean to come."

"No, you didn't, pet. I heard you first time, but I had to go out and kick the dogs. They heard it, too, and thought it was poachers. Only one, though—come after me!"

"You!" she said, contemptuously. "You, sir! Who would come after you?"

"Why, you would."

"Such vanity!"

"Then what did you come for?"

"To bring you back this rubbishing little whistle."

"Nonsense; you'd better keep that."

"I tell you I don't want it. Take it, sir."

"No, I shan't take it. Keep it."

"There it is, then," she cried; and she threw it at him.

"Gone in among the hollies," he said. "Well, I'm not going to prick myself hunting for it in the dark. What a little spit-fire it is! What's the matter with you to-night?"

"Matter enough. I've come to tell you never to make signals for me to come out again."

"Why? I say, what a temper you are in to-night. Here, let me help you over, and we'll go round to the arbor. You'll get your feet wet standing there."

"They are wet, and I shall catch a cold and die, I hope."

"Oh, I say, Jenny!"

"Silence, sir! How dare you speak to me like that!"

"Come over, then, into the arbor."

"I have told you again and again that I never would!"

"You are a little tartar," he whispered. "You get prettier every day, and peck and say nastier things to me. But there, I don't mind; it only makes me love you more and more."

"It isn't true," she cried furiously. "You're a wicked story-teller, and you know it."

"Am I?"

"Yes; that's the same miserable sickly tale you have told to half-a-dozen of the silly girls in the village. I know you thoroughly now. How dare you follow me and speak to me? If I were to tell my brother he'd nearly kill you."

"Quite, p'raps, with a drop out of one of his bottles."

"I can never forgive myself for having listened to the silly, contemptible flattery of the cast-off lover of a labourer's daughter."

"Oh, I like that, Jenny; what's the good of bringing all that up? That's been over ever so long. It was only sowing wild oats."

"The only sort that you are ever likely to have to sow. I know all now—everything; so go to her, and never dare to speak to me again."

"What? Go back to Sally? Well, you are a jealous little thing."

"I, jealous—of you?" she said, with contempt in her tone and manner.

"Yes, that's what's the matter with you, little one. But go on; I like it. Shows me you love me."

"I? Ha, ha, ha!" laughed Jenny derisively. "Do you think I don't know everything?"

"I daresay you do. You're such a clever little vixen."

"Do you suppose it has not reached my ears about your elopement with your cousin?"

"I don't care what you've heard; it ain't true. But I say, don't hold me off like this, Jenny; you know I love you like—like anything."

"Yes, anything," she retorted angrily; "any thing—your dogs, your horses, your fishing-rods and gun."

"Oh, I say."

"You miserable, deceitful trickster, I ought not to have lowered myself to even speak to you, or to come out again to-night, but I wanted to tell you what I thought about you, and it's of no use to treat such thick-skinned creatures as you with contempt."

"Well, you are wild to-night, little one. Don't want me to show my teeth, too, and go, do you?"

"Yes, and the sooner the better, sir; go back to your wife."

"Go back to my wife!" he cried, in tones which carried conviction to her ears. "Oh, I say; you've got hold of that cock-and-bull story, have you?"

"Yes, sir, I have got hold of the miserable cock-and-bull story, as you so elegantly turn it."

"Oh, I don't go in for elegance, Jenny; it ain't my way; but as for that flam, it ain't true."

"You dare to tell me that, when the whole place is ringing with it, sir!" she cried, angrily.

"The whole place rings with the noise when that muddle-headed lot got pulling the bells in changes. But it's only sound."

"Don't, pray don't try to be witty, Claud Wilton; you only fail."

"All right; go on."

"Do you dare to tell me that you did not elope with your cousin the other night?"

"Say slope, little one; elope is so old-fashioned."

"And I suppose you've married her for the sake of her money."

"Do you?" he said, sulkily; "then you suppose jolly well wrong. It's all a lie."

"Then you haven't married her?"

"No, I haven't married her, and I didn't slope with her; so now then."

"Do you dare to tell me that you did not go up to London?"

"No, I don't, because I did."

"With her, in a most disgraceful, clandestine manner?"

"No; I went alone with a very jolly good-tempered chap, whom everybody bullies and calls a liar."

"A nice companion; and pray, who was that?"

"This chap—your sweetheart; and I came back with him too."

"Then where is your cousin?"

"How should I know?"

"She did go away, then, the same night?"

"Yes. Bolted after a row we had."

"Is this true?"

"Every blessed word of it; and I haven't seen her since. Now, tell me, you're very sorry for all you've said."

"Tell me this; has she gone away with some one else?"

"What do you want to know for?"

"I want to find out that you are not such a wicked story-teller as I thought."

"Well, I have told you that."

"Who can believe you?"

"You can. Come, I say; I thought you were going to be really a bit loving to me at last when I heard the whistle. It's been like courting a female porcupine up to now."

"You know whom your cousin has gone with?"

"Pretty sure," he said, sulkily.

"Who is it?"

"Oh, well, if you must know, Harry Dasent."

"That cousin I saw here?"

"Yes, bless him! Only wait till we meet."

"Oh!" ejaculated Jenny, and then she turned to go; but Claud caught her arm.

"No, no; you might say something kind now you've found out you're wrong."

"Very well then, I will, Claud Wilton. First of all, I never cared a bit for you, and—"

"Don't believe you. Go on," he said, laughing.

"Secondly, take my advice and go away at once, for if my brother should meet you there will be a terrible scene. He believes horrible things of you, and I know he'll kill you."

"Phew!" whistled Claud. "Then he has found out?"

"Take my advice and go. He is terrible when he is roused, and I don't know what he'd do."

"I say, this ain't gammon, is it?"

"It is the solemn truth. Now loose my arm; you hurt me."

"Well, it's all right, then, and perhaps it's for the best I am going off to-night to hunt out Harry Dasent. I should have gone before, but I had to be about with the guv'nor, making inquiries."

"Then loose my arm at once, and go before it is too late."

"It is too late," thundered a voice out of the gloom. "Jenny—sister—is this you?"

Chapter Twenty Three

Jenny uttered a faint cry, and staggered against the iron hurdle, bringing down a shower of drops upon her head.

Leigh, after his words, uttered first in menace, then in a bitterly reproachful tone, paid no more heed to her, but turned fiercely upon Claud.

"Now, sir," he cried; "have the goodness to—You scoundrel! You dog!"

He began after the fashion taught by education, but nature was too strong. He broke off and tried to seize Claud by the throat; but, active as the animal mentioned, the young fellow avoided the onslaught, placed one hand upon the hurdle, and sprang over among the shrubs.

Leigh followed him in time to receive blow after blow, as the branches through which Claud dashed sprang back, cutting him in the face and drenching him with water. Guided, though, by the sounds, he followed as quickly as he could, till all at once the rustling and crackling of branches ceased, and he drew up short on the soft turf of a lawn, listening for the next movement of his quarry, but listening in vain.

A minute later the dogs began barking violently, and Leigh's thoughts turned to his sister. Then to Claud again, and he hesitated as to whether he should go to the house and insist upon seeing him. But his reason told him that he could not leave Jenny there in the wet and darkness, and with his teeth set hard in his anger and despair, he tried to find his way back to the place where he had come over into the garden, missing it, and coming to the conclusion that his sister had fled, for though he peered in all directions on crossing the hurdles, he could see no sign of her in the misty darkness.

As it happened he was not above a dozen yards from where she stood clinging to the dripping iron rail; and when with an angry exclamation he turned to make for the pathway, her plaintive voice arose:

"Please take me with you, Claud," she said. "I am so faint and cold!"

He turned upon her with a suppressed roar, caught her by the arm, dragged it under his, and set off through the dripping grass with great strides, but without uttering a word.

She kept up with him as long as she could, weeping bitterly the while, and blinding herself with her tears so that she could not see which way they went. Twice over she stumbled and would have fallen, had not his hold been so tight upon her arm, and at last, totally unable to keep up with him, she was about to utter a piteous appeal, when he stopped short, for they had reached the wet and muddy stile.

Here he loosed her arm, and sprang over into the road.

"Give me your hands," he cried, and she obeyed, and then as he reached over, she climbed the stile, stepping on to the top rail at last.

"Jump," he said, sharply; and she obeyed, but slipped as she alighted, one foot gliding over the muddy surface, and in spite of his strong grasp upon her hands, she fell sideways, and uttered a sharp cry.

"No hysterical nonsense, now, girl," he cried. "Get up!"

"I—I can't, Pierce. Oh, pray, don't be so cruel to me, please."

"Get up!" he cried, more sternly.

"My ankle's twisted under me," she said, faintly. "I—I—!"

A piteous sigh ended her speech, and she sank nerveless nearly to the level, but a sudden snatch on his part saved her from falling prone.

Then bending down, he raised her, quite insensible, in his arms, drew her arm over his shoulders, and strode on again, the passionate rage and indignation in his breast nerving him so that she seemed to possess no weight at all.

For another agony had come upon him, just when life seemed to have suddenly become unbearable, and there were moments when it appeared to be impossible that the bright girl who had for years past been to him as his own child could have behaved in so treacherous, so weak and disgraceful a way as to have listened to the addresses of the young scoundrel who seemed to have blasted his life.

"And she always professed to hold him in such contempt," he said to himself. "Great heavens! Are all women alike in their weakness and folly?"

He reached the cottage at last, where all was now dark; but the door yielded to his touch, and he bore her in, and laid her, still insensible, upon the sofa.

Upon striking a light, and holding a candle toward her face, he uttered a deep sigh, for she was ghastly pale, her hair was wet and clinging to her temples, and he could see that she was covered with the sticky, yellowish clay of the field and lane. But he steeled his breast against her. It was her punishment, he felt; and treating her as if she were some patient and a stranger, he took off her wet cloak and hood, threw them aside, and proceeded to examine for the injury.

But little examination was necessary, and his brow grew more deeply lined as he quickly took out a knife, slit her wet boot from ankle to toe, and set her foot at liberty.

Then lighting another candle, he walked sharply into his surgery, and returned with splints and bandages, to find her eyes open, and that she was gazing at him wildly.

"Where am I? What is the matter?" she cried, hysterically. "This dreadful pain and sickness!"

"At home. Lie still," he said, coldly. "Your ankle is badly hart."

"Oh!" she sighed, and the tears began to flow, accompanied by a piteous sobbing, for the meaning of it all came back.

He went out again, and returned with a glass containing some fluid, then passing his hand beneath her head, he raised her a little.

"Drink this," he said.

"No, no, I can not bear it. You hurt me horribly."

"I can not help it. Drink!"

He pressed the glass to her lips, and she drank the vile ammoniacal mixture.

"Now, lie still. I will not hurt you more than I can help, but I must see if the bone is broken, and set it."

"No, no, not yet Pierce," she sobbed; "I could not bear it while I am in this state. Let me tell you—let me explain to you first."

"Be silent!" he cried, angrily. "I do not want to hear a word I must see to your ankle before it swells up and the work is impossible."

"Never mind that, dear. I must tell you," she cried, piteously.

"I know all I want to know," he said, bitterly; "that the sister I have trusted and believed in has been cruelly deceiving me—that one I trusted to be sweet and true and innocent has been acting a part that would disgrace one of the village wenches, for to be seen even talking to that young scoundrel under such circumstances would rob her of her character. And this is my sister! Now, lie still. I must bandage this hurt."

"Oh, Pierce, dear Pierce! You are hurting me more than I can bear," she sobbed; for he had gone down on one knee as he spoke, and began manipulating the injured joint.

"I can not help it; you must bear it. I shall not be long."

"I—I don't mean that, dear; I can bear that," she moaned. "It is your cruel words that hurt me so. How can you say such things to me?"

"Be silent, I tell you. I can only attend to this. If it is neglected, you may be lame for life."

"Very well," she said, with a passionate cry; "let me be lame for life—let me die of it if you like, but you must, you shall listen to me, dear."

"I will not listen to you now—I will not at any time. You have killed my faith in you, and I can never believe or trust in you again."

"But you shall listen to me," she cried; and with an effort that gave her the most acute pain, she drew herself up and embraced her knees. "You shall not touch me again until you listen to me. There!"

"Don't behave like a madwoman," he said, sternly. "Lie back in your place; you are injuring yourself more by your folly."

"It is not folly," she cried; "I will not be misjudged like this by my own brother. Pierce, Pierce, I am not the wicked girl you think."

"I am glad of it," he said, coldly; "even if you are lost to shame."

"Shame upon you, to say such words to me."

"Perhaps I was deceived in thinking I found you there to-night with your lover."

"My lover!" she cried, hysterically.

"Now, will you lie down quietly, and let me bandage your ankle, or must I stupefy you with chloroform?"

"You shall do nothing until you have listened to me," she cried, wildly. "He is not my lover. I never had a lover, Pierce. I went there to-night to tell him to go away, for I was afraid for you to meet him. I shivered with dread, you were so wild and strange."

"Were you afraid I should kill him," he said, with an angry glare in his eyes.

"Yes, or that he might kill you. Pierce, dear, if I have deceived you, it was because I loved you, and I was fighting your fight."

Indeed! he said, bitterly.

"He has been watching for me, and coming here constantly ever since we came to the house. I couldn't go down the village, or for a walk without his meeting me. He has made my life hateful to me."

"And you could not appeal to your brother for help and protection?"

"I was going to, dear, but matters happened so that I determined to be silent. No, no, don't touch me till you have heard all. I found how you loved poor Kate."

"Will you be silent!" he raged out.

"No, not if I die for it. I found out how you loved Kate, and I soon knew that they meant her for that—that dreadful boy, while all the time he was trying to pay his addresses to me. Then I made up my mind to give him just a little encouragement—to draw him on, so as to be able to let Kate see how utterly contemptible and unworthy he was, for I could lead him on until she surprised us together some day, when all would have been over at once, for she would never have listened to him. Do you hear me, Pierce? I tried to fool him, but he has fooled me instead, and robbed me of my own brother's love."

"What do you mean by fooling you?" he cried, with his attention arrested at last.

"We have been all wrong, dear; I found it out to-night. He did not take Kate away."

"What! Why, they were seen together by that poaching vagabond, Barker, the fellow the keeper shot at and I attended. He watched them."

"No, dear; it was not Kate with him then: it was I. Kate is gone, and he is in a rage about it."

"Gone? With whom?"

"With—with—oh! Pierce, Pierce! say some kind word to me; tell me you love and believe me, dear. I am hot the wicked creature you think, and—and—am I dying? Is this death?"

He laid her back quickly, and hurriedly began to bathe her temples, but ceased directly.

"Better so," he muttered; and then with trembling hands, which rapidly grew firmer, he examined the injury, acting with such skill that when a low sigh announced that the poor girl was recovering her senses, he was just laying the injured limb in an easy position, before rising to take her hand in his.

Chapter Twenty Four

Kate Wilton needed all her strength of mind to bear up against the depression consequent upon her self-inflicted position. As she sat back in a corner of the carriage, dimly lit by a lamp in which a quantity of thick oil was floating to and fro, she could see that Garstang in the corner diagonal to hers was either asleep or assuming to be so, and for the moment this relieved her, for she felt that it was from kindness and consideration on his part.

But the next minute she was in agony, reproaching herself bitterly for what now presented the aspect of a rashly foolish action on her part.

Then, with her mental suffering increasing, she tried to combat this idea, telling herself that she had acted wisely, for it would have been madness to have stayed at Northwood and exposed herself to the risk of further insult from her cousin, now that she knew for certain what were her uncle's designs. For she knew that appeal to her aunt would be useless, that lady being a slave to the caprices of her son and the stern wishes of her husband, and quite ready to believe that everything they said or did was right.

And so on during the slow night journey toward London, her brain growing more and more confused by the strangeness of her position, and the absence of her natural rest, till the swaying to and fro of her thoughts seemed to be somewhat bound up with that of the thick oil in the great glass bubble of a lamp and with the stopping of the train and the roll and clang of the great milk tins taken up at various stations.

At last her fevered waking dream, as it seemed to her, was brought to an end by Garstang suddenly starting up as if from sleep to rub his condensed breath off the window-pane and look out.

"London lights," he said.—"Asleep, my dear?"

"No, Mr Garstang. I have been awake thinking all the while."

"Of course you would be. What an absurd, malapropos question. There, you see what it is to be a middle-aged, unfeeling man. I'm afraid we do get very selfish. Instead of trying to comfort you, and chatting pleasantly, I curl up like a great black cat and go to sleep."

She made no reply. The words would not come.

"Cold, my dear?"

"No. I feel hot and feverish."

"Nervous anxiety, of course. But try and master it. We shall soon be home, and you can have a good cup of tea and go to bed. A good long sleep will set you right, and you will not be thinking of what a terrible deed you have committed in coming away in this nocturnal clandestine manner. That sounds grand, doesn't it, for a very calm, sensible move on life's chess-board—one which effectually checks James Wilton and that pleasant young pawn his son. There, there, don't fidget about it, pray. I have been thinking, too, and asking myself whether I have done my duty by Robert Wilton's child in bringing you away, and I can find but one answer—yes; while conscience says that I should have been an utter brute to you if I had left you to be exposed to such a scandalous persecution."

"Thank you, Mr Garstang," said Kate, frankly, as she held out her hand to him. "I could not help feeling terribly agitated and ready to reproach myself for taking such a step. You do assure me that I have done right?"

"What, in coming with me, my dear?" he said, after just pressing her hand and dropping it again. "Of course I do. I was a little in doubt about it at first, but my head feels clearer after my nap, and I tell you, as an experienced man, that you have done the only thing you could do under the circumstances. This night journey excites and upsets you a bit, but I'm very much afraid that some of them at Northwood will be far worse, and serve them right."

"Poor 'Liza will be horror-stricken," said Kate. "I wish I had begged harder for you to bring her too."

"Ah, poor woman! I am sorry for her," said Garstang, thoughtfully; "servants of that devoted nature are very rare. It is an insult to call them servants; they are very dear and valuable friends. But just think a moment, my dear. To have roused her from sleep and told her to dress and come with you—to join you in your flight would have seemed to her then so mad a proceeding that it would have resulted in her alarming the house, or at least in upsetting our project. She would never have let you come."

"I am afraid you are right," said Kate, with a sigh.

"I am sure of it, my child; but you must communicate with her at once. She must not be kept in suspense an hour longer than we can help. Let me see, I must contrive some way of getting a letter to her.—Ah, here we are."

For the train had slowed while they were talking, and was now gliding gently along by the platform of the great dimly lighted station.

A porter sprang on to the footboard as he let down the window.

"Luggage, sir?"

"No. Is the refreshment room open?"

"Yes, sir."

"That will do, then," said Garstang, and he slipped a coin into the man's hand. "Now, then, my dear, we'll go and have a hot cup of tea at once."

"I really could not touch any now, Mr Garstang," said Kate.

"That's what I daresay you said about your medicine when you were a little girl; but I must be doctor, and tell you that it is necessary to take away that nervous shivering and agitation; and besides, have a little pity on me."

She smiled faintly as he handed her out of the carriage, and suffered herself to be led to where the cheerless refreshment room was in charge of a couple of girls, who looked particularly sleepy and irritable, but who had been comforting themselves with that very rare railway beverage, a cup of freshly made tea.

"There, I am sure you feel better for that," said Garstang, as he drew his companion's arm through his and led her out of the station, ignoring the offers of cabman after cabman. "A nice, little, quick walk will circulate your blood, and then we'll take a cab and go home."

She acquiesced, and he took her along at a brisk pace through the gas-lit streets, passing few people but an occasional policeman who looked at them keenly, and the men busy in gangs sweeping the city streets; but at the end of a quarter of an hour he raised his hand to the sleepy looking driver of a four-wheeler, handed his companion in, gave the man his instructions, and then followed, to sit opposite to her, and drew up the window, when the wretched vehicle went off with the glass jangling and jarring so that conversation became difficult.

"There!" said Garstang, merrily; "now, my dear, I am going to confess to a great deal of artfulness and cunning."

She looked at him nervously.

"This is a miserable cab, and I could have obtained a far better one in the station, but now you have come away it's to find peace, quiet, and happiness, eh?"

"I hope so, Mr Garstang."

"Yes, and you shall have those three necessities to a young girl's life, or John Garstang will know the reason why. So to begin with I was not going to have James Wilton and his unlicked cub coming up to town some time this morning, enlisting the services of a clever officer, who would question the porters at the terminus till he found the man who asked me about luggage, and then gather from that man that he called cab number nine millions and something to drive us away. Then, as they keep a record of the cabs which take up and where they are going, for the benefit of that stupid class of passengers who are always leaving their umbrellas and bags on seats, that record would be examined, number nine millions and something found, questioned, and ready to endorse the entry as to where we were going; and the next thing would have been Uncle James and Cousin Claud calling at my house, insisting upon seeing you, and consequently a desperate row, which would upset you and make me say things again which would cause me to repent. Now do you see?"

"Yes," she said, gravely; "they will not follow us now."

"I hope not, but it is of no use to be sure. I am taking every precaution I can; and I shall finish by getting out where I told the man—Russell Square; and we will walk the rest of the way."

Kate did not speak, for a vague terror was beginning to oppress her, which her companion's bright cheery way had hard work to disperse.

"It is of no use to be sure about anything, but if they do find out that you have come with me, these proceedings will throw them off the scent. Your uncle does not know that I have a house in Great Ormond Street. Of course he knows of my offices in Bedford Row, and of my place at Chislehurst, where Harry Dasent lives with me—when he condescends to be at home. Come, you seem brighter and more cheerful now, but you will not be right till you have had a good long sleep."

Very little was said for the rest of the journey, the cab drawing up at the end of the narrow passage close to Southampton Row, where there was no thoroughfare for horses; and after the man was paid, Garstang led his companion along the pavement as if about to enter one of the houses, going slowly till the cab was driven off. Then, increasing his pace, he led the way into the great square, along one side, making for the east, and finally stopped suddenly in front of a grim-looking red-brick mansion in Great Ormond Street—a house which in the gloomy morning, just before dawn, had a prison-like aspect which made the girl shiver.

"Strange how cold it is just before day," said Garstang, leading the way up the steps, glancing sharply to right and left the while. The next moment a latch-key had opened the ponderous door, and they stood in a great hall dimly seen to be full of shadow, till Garstang struck a match, applied it beneath a glass globe, and revealed the proportions of the place, which were ample and set off by rich rugs, and old oak presses full of blue china, while here and there were pictures which looked old and good.

"Welcome home, my child," said Garstang, with tender respect. "It looks gloomy now, but you are tired, faint, and oppressed with trouble. This way."

He led the girl to a door at the foot of a broad staircase, opened it, entered the room, and once more struck a match, to apply it to a couple of great globes held up by bronze figures on the great carved oak mantelpiece, and as the handsome, old-fashioned room lit up, he stopped and applied a match to the paper of a well-laid fire, which began to burn briskly, and added the warmth and glow of its flames and the cheery crackle of the wood to the light shed by the globes.

"There," he continued, drawing forward a great leather-covered easy chair to the front of the fire, "take off your hat, but keep your cloak on till the room gets warmer. It will soon be right."

She obeyed, trying to be firm, but her hands trembled a little as she glanced at her strange surroundings the while, to see that the room was heavily but richly furnished, much of the panelled oak wall being taken up by great carved cabinets, full of curious china, while plates and vases were ranged abundantly on brackets, or suspended by hooks wherever space allowed. These relieved the heaviness of the thick hangings about a stained-glass window and over the doors, lying in folds upon the thick Persian carpet, while as the fire burned up a thousand little reflections came from the glaze of china, and wood polished as bright as hands could make it.

"You did not know I was quite a collector of these things, my dear. I hope you will take an interest in them by-and-by. But to begin with, let me say this—that I hope you will consider this calm old house your sanctuary as well as home, that you are its mistress as long as you please, and give your orders to the servants for anything that seems to be wanting."

"You are very good to me, Mr Garstang," faltered Kate, who felt that the vague terror from which she had suffered was dying away.

"Good? Absurd! Now, then, you will not mind being left alone for a few minutes? I am going to awaken my housekeeper and her daughter. Rather an early call."

As he spoke a great clock over the mantelpiece began to chime musically, and was followed by the hour in deep, rich, vibrating tones.

"It's a long time since I was up at five in the morning," said Garstang, cheerily. "Hah! a capital fire soon. Becky is very clever at laying fires. You will find her and her mother rather quaint, but they are devoted to me. Excellent servants. I never see anyone else's house so clean. There, I shall not be long."

He smiled at her pleasantly, and left the room, while, as the door closed, and the heavy folds of the portiere dropped down, Kate sank back in her chair, and the tears which had been gathering for hours fell fast. Then she drew herself up with a sigh, and hastily wiped her eyes, as if relieved and prepared to meet this new change of fate.

Garstang's few minutes proved to be nearly a quarter of an hour, during which, after a glance or two round the room, Kate sat thinking, with her ideas setting first in one direction, then ebbing in the other, the feeling that she had done wrong predominating; but her new guardian's reappearance changed their course again, and she could feel nothing but gratitude to one whose every thought seemed to be to make her position bearable.

"I could not be cross with them," he said, as he entered; "but it is an astonishing thing how people who have neither worry nor trouble in the world can sleep. Now those two have nothing on their minds but the care of this house, which came to me through an old client, and in which I very seldom live! and I believe they pass half their time drowsing through existence. If the truth were known, they were in bed by nine o'clock last night, and they were so soundly asleep that the place might have been burned down without their waking."

"It seems a shame to disturb them," said Kate, with a faint smile.

"What? Not at all, my child. Do them good; they want rousing out of their lethargy. I have told them to prepare a bedroom for you, and I should advise you to retire as soon as they say it is ready. There is no fear of damp, for the rooms are constantly having fires in them, and Sarah Plant is most trustworthy. Go and have a good long sleep, and some time in the afternoon we will have a discussion on ways and means. You will have to go shopping, and I shall have to play guardian and carry the parcels. By the way, you will want some money. Have you any?"

"I have a few pounds, Mr Garstang."

"Perhaps that will do for the present; if not, please bear in mind that you have unlimited credit with your banker. I am that banker till you can declare yourself independent, so have no compunction whatever about asking for what you need Is there anything more that I can do for you?"

"No, Mr Garstang; only to contrive a way of getting Eliza here."

"Oh, yes, of course, I will not forget that; but we must be careful. We don't want any more quarrelling. It is bad for you, and it upsets me. Ah, they're ready."

For at that moment there was a soft tapping at the door.

"Your bedroom is the one over this, and I hope you will find it comfortable. No trees to look out upon; no flowers; no bright full moon; plenty of bricks, mortar, and chimney-pots; but there are rest and peace for you, my child; so go, and believe that I am ready to fight your battles and to make you happy here. I can if you will only help."

"I shall try, Mr Garstang," she said, with a faint smile.

"Then *c'est un fait accompli*," he replied, holding out his hand. "Good-night—I mean, good morning. Sarah is waiting to show you to your room."

She placed her hand in his for a few moments, and then with heart too full for words she hurried to the door and passed through into the hall, to find a strange-looking, dry, elderly woman standing on the skin mat at the foot of the stairs, holding a massive silver bedroom candlestick in her hand, and peering at her curiously, but ready to lower her eyes directly.

"This way, please, miss," she said, in a lachrymose tone of voice; and she began to ascend the low, wide, thickly-carpeted stairs, holding the candle before her, and showing her gaunt, angular body against a faint halo of light.

Kate followed, wondering, and feeling as if she were in a dream, while Garstang was slowly walking up and down among his cabinets, rubbing his hands softly, and smiling in a peculiar way.

"Promises well," he said softly; "promises well, but I have my work cut out, and I have not reckoned with Harry Dasent yet."

He stopped short, thinking, and then involuntarily raised his eyes, to find that he was exactly opposite a curious old Venetian mirror, which reflected clearly the upper portion of his form.

He started slightly, and then stood watching the clearly seen image of his face, ending by smiling at it in a peculiar way.

"Not so very old yet," he said softly; "a woman is a woman, and it only depends upon how you play your cards."

"But there is Harry. Ah, I must not reckon without him."

Chapter Twenty Five

Kate's conductress had stopped at a door on the first floor, above which an old portrait hung, so that when the woman held the candle which she carried above the level of her head, the bodily and mentally weary girl felt that two people were peering cautiously at her, and she gladly entered the old-fashioned, handsomely-furnished room, and stood by the newly-lit fire, which, with the candles lit on the chimney-piece and dressing-table, gave it a cheerful welcoming aspect.

She could not have explained why, but the aspect of the woman would suggest dead leaves, and the saddened plaintive tone of her voice brought up the sighing of the wind in the windows of the old house at Northwood.

"I took some of the knobs of coal off, miss, for Becky always will put on too much," said the woman plaintively, as she took her former attitude, holding the candle on high, and gazed at the new-comer. "I always say to her that when she gets married and pays for coals herself she'll know what they cost, though I don't know who'd marry her, I'm sure. I'll put 'em back if you like."

"There will be plenty of fire—none was needed," said Kate, wearily. "I only want to rest."

"Of course you do, miss," said the woman, still watching her, with face wrinkled and eyes half closed. "And you needn't be afraid of the bed. Everything's as dry as a bone. Becky and me slep' in it two nights ago. We sleep in a different bed every night so as to keep 'em all aired, as master's very particular about the damp."

"Thank you; I am sure you have done what is necessary," said Kate, who in her low nervous state was troubled by the woman's persistent inquiring stare.

"Is there anything I can do for you, miss?"

"Thank you, no. I am very tired, and will try and sleep."

"Because I can soon get you a cup of tea, miss."

"Not now, thank you. In the morning. I will not trouble you now."

"It's to-morrow morning a'ready, my dear, and nothing's a trouble to me," said the woman, despondently, "'cept Becky."

"Thank you very much, but please leave me now."

"Yes, miss, of course. There's the bells: one rings upstairs and the other down, so it will be safest to ring 'em both, for it's a big house—yes," she continued, thoughtfully, "a very big house, and there's no knowing where Becky and me may be."

"Ah," sighed Kate, as at last she was relieved from the pertinacious curious stare, for the door had closed; but as she sank wearily in a lounge chair the housekeeper seemed photographed upon her brain, and one moment she was staring at her with candle held above her head, the next it was the face of the handsome woman above the door, peering inquiringly down as if wondering to see her there.

The candles burned brightly and the fire crackled and blazed, and then there was a peculiar roaring sound as of the train rushing along through the black night; the room grew darker, and shrank in its proportions till it was the gloomy first-class carriage, with the oil washing to and fro in the thick glass bubble lamp, while John Garstang sat back in the corner, and Kate started up, to shake her head and stare about her wonderingly, as she mentally asked herself where she was, and shivered as she recognised the fire, and the candles upon the mantelpiece.

She glanced round at the turned-down bed, looking inviting beneath the thick dark hangings, and felt that it would be better to lie down and rest, but thought that she would first fasten the door.

She rose, after waiting for a few moments to let her head get clearer, and walked on over the soft carpet toward the dark door, which kept on receding as she went, while the power seemed to be given her to see through it as if it were some strange transparency. Away beyond it was John Garstang, waving her on towards him, always keeping the same distance off, till it grew darker and darker, and then lighter, for the fire was blazing up and the wood was crackling, as there was the sound of a poker being placed back in the fender; and there, as she opened her eyes widely, stood the woman with the chamber candlestick held high above her head, gazing at her in the former inquiring way.

"It is a part of a nightmare-like dream," said Kate to herself; "my head is confused with trouble and want of rest;" and as in a troubled way she lay back in the chair, she fully expected to see the face of the woman give place to that over the door, and then to John Garstang moving slowly on and on and beckoning her to come away from Northwood Manor House, where her aunt and uncle were trying to hurry her off to the church, where Claud was waiting, and Doctor Leigh and his sister stood in deep mourning, gazing at her with reproachful eyes.

As her thoughts ran in that way she mentally pictured everything with a vividness that was most strange, and she was rapidly gliding back into insensibility when the woman spoke, and she started back, with her head quite clear, while a strange feeling of irritability and anger made her features contract.

"Awake, miss?" said the woman, plaintively.

"Yes, yes; why did you come back? I will ring when I want you—both bells."

"There was the fire, miss; I couldn't let that go out I was obliged to come every hour, and I left it too long now, and had to start it with a bundle of wood."

Kate sat up and stared back at her, then round the room, to see that the candles were burning—four—on mantelpiece and dressing-table.

"Didn't hear me set the fresh ones up, miss, did you?" said the woman, noticing the direction of her eyes. "T'others only burned till twelve."

"Burned till twelve—come every hour? Why, what time is it?"

"Just struck three, miss. Breakfast will be ready as soon as you are; but you'd ha' been a deal better if you'd gone to bed. I did put you a clean night-dress, and it was beautifully aired. Becky held it before the kitchen fire ever so long, for it only wanted poking together and burned up well."

"I—I don't understand," faltered Kate. "Three o'clock?"

"Yes, miss; and as black as pitch outside. Reg'lar London fog, but master's gone out in it all the same. He said he'd be back to dinner, and you wasn't to be disturbed on no account, for all you wanted was plenty of sleep."

"Then I have been thoroughly asleep?"

"Yes, miss; about ten hours I should say; but you'd have been a deal better if you'd gone to bed. It do rest the spine of your back so."

Kate rose to her feet, staggered slightly, and caught at the chair back, but the giddy sensation passed off, and she walked to the window.

"Can't see nothing out at the back, miss," said the woman, shaking her head, sadly. "Old master hated the tiles and chimney-pots, and had double windows made inside—all of painted glass, but you couldn't see nothing if they weren't there. It's black as night, and the fog comes creeping in at every crack. What would you like me to do for you, miss?"

"Nothing, thank you."

"Then I'll go and see about the breakfast, miss. I s'pose you won't be long?"

Kate drew a deep breath of relief once more, and trying to fight off the terrible sensation of depression and strangeness which troubled her, she hurried to the toilet table, which was well furnished, and in about half-an-hour went out on to the broad staircase, which was lit with gas, and glanced round at the pictures, cabinets, and statues with which it was furnished. Then, turning to descend, she was conscious of the fact that she was not alone, for, dimly seen, there was a strange, ghastly-looking head, tied up with a broad white handkerchief, peering round the doorway of another room, but as soon as its owner found that she had attracted attention she drew back out of sight, and Kate shuddered slightly, for the face was wild and strange in the half-light.

The staircase looked broader and better as she descended to the room into which she had been taken on her arrival, and found that it was well lit, and a cheerful fire blazing; but she had hardly had time to glance round when the woman appeared at the door.

"Breakfast's quite ready, miss," she said. "Will you please to come this way?"

She led the way across the hall, but paused and turned back to a door, and pushed it a little way open.

"Big lib'ry, miss. Little lib'ry's upstairs at the back-two rooms. There's a good fire here. Like to see it now?"

"No, not now."

"This way then, miss," and the woman threw open a door on the other side.

"Dining-room, miss. There ain't no drawing-room; but master said this morning that if you wished he'd have the big front room turned into one. I put your breakfast close to the fire, for it's a bit chilly to-day."

Kate thought she might as well have said "to-night," as she glanced round the formal but richly furnished room, with its bright brass fireplace, and breakfast spread on a small table, and looking attractive and good.

"I made you tea, miss, because I thought you'd like it better; but I'll soon have some coffee ready if you prefer it. Best tea, master's wonderfully particular about having things good."

"I prefer tea," said Kate, quietly, as she took her place, feeling more and more how strange and unreal everything appeared.

And now the magnitude of the step she had taken began to obtrude itself, mingled with a wearying iteration of thoughts of Northwood, and what must have been going on since the morning when her flight was first discovered. Her uncle's anger would, she knew, be terrible! Then her cousin! She could not help picturing his rage when he found that she had escaped him. What would her aunt and the servants think of her conduct? And then it was that there was a burning sensation in her cheeks, as her thoughts turned to Leigh and his sister, the only people that during her stay at Northwood she had learned to esteem.

And somehow the burning in her cheeks increased till the tears rose to her eyes, when, as if the heat was quenched, she turned pale with misery and despair, for she felt how strongly that she had left behind in Jenny Leigh one for whom she had almost unknowingly conceived a genuine sisterly affection.

From that moment the struggle she had been having to seem calm, and at home, intensified, and she pushed away cup and saucer and rose from the table, just as the housekeeper, who had been in and out several times, reentered.

"But you haven't done, miss?" she said, plaintively.

"Yes, thank you; I am not very well this morning," said Kate, hastily.

"As anyone could see, miss, with half an eye; but there's something wrong, of course."

"Something—wrong?" faltered Kate.

"Yes, miss," said the woman in an ill-used tone. "The tea wasn't strong enough, or the sole wasn't done to your liking."

"Don't think that, Mrs—Mrs—"

"Plant's my name, miss—Sarah Plant, and Becky's Becky. Don't call me Mrs, please; I'm only the servant."

"Well, do not think that, Sarah Plant. Everything has been particularly nice, only I have no appetite this morning—I mean, to-day."

"You do mean that, miss?"

"Of course I do."

"Thank you kindly, miss. I did try very hard, for master was so very particular about it. He always is particular, almost as Mr Jenour was; but this morning he was extra, and poor, dear, old master was never anything like it. Then if you please, miss, I'll send Becky to clear away, and perhaps you'd like to go round and see your new house. I hope you will find everything to your satisfaction."

"My new house?"

"Yes, miss; master said it was yours, and that we were to look upon you as mistress and do everything you wished, just as if you were his daughter come to keep house for him. This way please, miss."

Kate was ready to say that she wished to sit down and write, for her heart was full of self-reproach, and she longed to pour out her feelings to her old confidential maid; but the thought that it would be better perhaps to fall in with Garstang's wishes and assume the position he had arranged for her to occupy, made her acquiesce and follow the housekeeper out of the room.

The woman touched a bell-handle in the hall, and then drew back a little, with a show of respect, as her eyes, still eagerly, and full of compassion, scanned the new mistress she had been told to obey.

"Will you go first, ma'am?"

"No: be good enough to show me what it is necessary for me to see."

"Oh, master said I was to show you everything you liked, miss—I mean, ma'am. It's a dreadfully dark day to show you, but I've got the gas lit everywhere, and it does warm the house nicely and keep out the damp."

Kate longed to ask the woman a few questions, but she shrank from speaking, and followed her pretty well all over the place until she stopped on the first floor landing before a heavy curtain which apparently veiled a window.

"I hope you find everything to your satisfaction, ma'am—that the house has been properly kept."

"Everything I have seen shows the greatest care," said Kate.

"Thank you, ma'am," said the woman, and her next words aroused her companion's attention at once, for the desire within her was strong to know more of her new guardian's private life, though it would have been, she felt, impossible to question. "You see, master is here so very seldom that there is no encouragement for one to spend much time in cleaning and dusting, and oh, the times it has come to me like a wicked temptation to leave things till to-morrow; but I resisted, for I knew that if I did once, Becky would be sure to twice. You see, master is mostly at his other house when he isn't at his offices, where he just has snacks and lunches brought in on trays; but it's all going to be different now, he tells me, and the house is to be kept up properly, and very glad I am, for it has been like wilful waste for such a beautiful place never hardly to be used, and never a lady in it in my time."

"Then Mrs Garstang did not reside here?"

"Oh, no, ma'am! nor old master's lady neither—not in my time."

"Mr Garstang's father?"

"Oh, no, ma'am: Mr Jenour, who had it before master, and—and died here—I mean there," said the woman, in a whisper, and she jerked her head toward the heavy curtain. "It was Mr Jenour's place, and he collected all the books and china and foreign curiosities. I'll tell you all about it some day, ma'am."

"Thank you," said Kate, quietly. "I will go down to the library now; I wish to write."

"There's pen, ink and paper in there, ma'am," said the woman, jerking her head sideways; "and you can see the little lib'ry at the same time."

"I would rather leave that till another time."

"Hah!" came in a deep low sigh, as if of relief, and Kate turned quickly round in surprise, just catching sight of the face with the handkerchief bound round it that she had seen before.

It was drawn back into one of the rooms instantly, and Kate turned her questioning eyes directly upon the housekeeper.

"It's only Becky, ma'am—my gal. She's been following us about to peep at you all the time. I did keep shaking my head at her, but she would come."

"Is she unwell—face-ache?" asked Kate.

"Well, no, ma'am, not now. She did have it very bad a year ago, but it got better, and she will keep tied up still for fear it should come back. She says it would drive her mad if it did; and if I make her leave off she does nothing but mope and cry, so I let her keep on. She's a poor nervous sort of girl, and she has never been right since she lost the milkman."

"Lost the milkman?" said Kate, wonderingly.

"He went and married someone else, ma am, as had money to set him up in business. Females has a deal to put up with in this life, as well I know. Then you won't go and see the little lib'ry to-day, ma'am?"

"No, not to-day," said Kate, with an involuntary shiver which made the woman look at her curiously, and the deep sigh of relief came again from the neighbouring room.

"Cold, ma'am?"

"Yes—no. A little nervous and upset with travelling," said Kate; and she went down at once to the library, took a chair at the old-fashioned morocco-covered table, glanced round at the well-filled bookcases, and the solid rich air of comfort, with the glowing fire and softened gaslight brightening the place, and taking paper stamped with the address she began to write rapidly, explaining everything to her old maid, pleading the urgency of her position for excuse in leaving as she had, and begging that "dear old nurse" would join her at once.

She paused from time to time to look round, for the silence of the place oppressed her; and in her nervous anxious state, suffering as she was from the feeling that she had done wrong, there were moments when she could hardly refrain from tears.

But she finished her long, affectionate letter and directed it, turning round to sit gazing into the fire for a few minutes, hesitating as to whether she should do something that was in her mind.

There seemed to be no reason why she should not write to Jennie Leigh, but at the same time there was a something undefined and strange which held her back from communication; but at last decision had its way, and feeling firmer, she turned to the table once more and began to write another letter.

"Why should I have hesitated?" she said, softly; "I'm sure she likes me very much, and she will think it so very strange if I do not write." But somehow there was a slight deepening of tint in her cheeks, and a faint sensation of glow as she wrote on, her letter being unconsciously couched in very affectionate terms; while when she had concluded and read it over she found that she had been far more explanatory than she had intended, entering fully into her feelings, and the horror and shame she had felt on discovering the way in which her cousin had been thrown with her, detailing his behaviour; and finally, in full, the scene in which Mr Garstang had protected her and spoken out, to the unveiling of the family plans.

"Pray don't think that I have acted foolishly, dear Jenny," she said in a postscript. "It may seem unmaidenly and strange, but I was driven to act as I did. I dared not stay; and beside being in some way a relative, Mr Garstang is so fatherly and kind that I have felt quite safe and at rest. Pray write to me soon. I shall be so glad to hear, for I fear that I shall be rather lonely; and tell your brother how grateful I am to him for his attention to me. I am much better and stronger now, thanks to him."

The glow in her cheeks was a little deeper here, and she paused with the intention of re-writing the letter and omitting all allusion to Doctor Leigh, but she felt that it would seem ungrateful to one to whose skill she owed so much; and in spite of a sensation of nervous shrinking, the desire to let him see she was grateful was very strong.

So the letter was finished and directed.

But still she hesitated, and twice over her hand was stretched out to take and destroy the missive, while her brain grew troubled and confused.

"I can't think," she said to herself at last with a sigh; "my brain seems weary and confused;" and then she started from her chair in alarm, for Garstang was standing in the room, the thick curtains and soft carpet having deadened his approach; and in fact, he had been there just within the heavy portiere watching her for some minutes.

Chapter Twenty Six

The first two pages of Chapter XXVI, are missing from the scan. We will continue to try to find what was upon them.

the best way, but it was the best way that offered, was it not?"

"Of course; yes," she said eagerly.

"Yes, decidedly it was," he said, still speaking in the same quiet, thoughtful way. "You set me thinking, too, my dear, whether I have done right by you in bringing you here. Yes," he said, turning upon her sharply, "I am sure I have, if I treat it as a temporary asylum. Yes, it is right, my child: but perhaps we ought to set to at once—if you feel equal to it, and now that we have time and no fear of interruption—and go over what distant relations or what friends you have, and invite the most suitable, that is to say, the one you would prefer—always supposing this individual possesses the firmness to protect you. Then he or she shall be sent for, and you shall go there."

"I do not wish to be ungrateful to you, Mr Garstang."

"You ungrateful! It isn't in your nature, my dear. But what do you think of my suggestion?"

"I think it is right, and what I should do," she replied.

"Very well then, you shall do it, my dear child; but you cannot, of course, do it to-night. It is a very important step, and you must choose deliberately, and after due and careful thought. In the meantime, Great Ormond Street is your temporary resting-place, where you are quite safe, and can make your plans in peace. As for me, I am your elderly relative, and we, I mean Mrs Plant and I, are delighted to have the monotony of the place relieved by your coming. Now, is this right?—does it set your little fluttering heart at rest?"

"Yes, thank you, Mr Garstang. I—I am greatly relieved."

"Very well then, let us set all 'the cares that infest the day,' as the poet has it, aside, and have a calm, restful evening. You need it, and I must confess that I do not feel in my customary fettle, as the country folk call it. Why, you look better already. I see how it is. Your mind is more at ease."

She smiled.

"That's right; and by the way, man-like I did not think of it till I reached my office to see some letters. I did tell Mrs Plant to try and make everything right for you here, but it never occurred to me that a lady is not like a man."

She looked at him wonderingly.

"I mean that a man can get along with a clean collar, a tooth-brush, and a pocket-comb, while a lady—"

He stopped and smiled.

"Now, look here, my child," he said, "I will leave you for a few minutes while you ring and have up Mrs Plant. You can give her what instructions you like about immediate necessities, and they can be fetched while we are at dinner. Other things you can obtain at leisure yourself."

"Thank you, Mr Garstang," said Kate, with the look of confidence in her eyes increasing, as she rose from her seat and laid her hands in his.

"No, no, please don't," he said, with a pleasant smile, as he gently returned the pressure of her hands, and then dropped them. "Let's see, dinner in half an hour." He looked at his watch. "Don't think me a gourmet, please, because I think a good deal of my dinner; for I work very hard, and I find that I must eat. There, I'll leave you for a bit."

He laid his book on the table, nodded and smiled, and walked out of the room, while with the tears rising to her eyes Kate stood gazing after him, feeling that the cloud hanging over her was lightening, and that she was going to find rest.

She rang, and Sarah Plant appeared with her head on one side, looking more withered than ever, and to her was explained the needs of the moment.

"Yes, ma'am," said the woman, plaintively; "of course I'll go, only there's the dinner, and if I wait till afterwards the shops will be shut up. I don't think you or master would like Becky to wait table with her face tied up, and if I make her take the handkerchief off she'll go into shrieking hysterics, and that will be worse. And then—would you mind looking out, ma'am?"

She walked slowly across to the window, and drew aside one of the heavy curtains.

Kate followed her, looked, and turned to the woman.

"Draw up the blind," she said.

There was a feeble smile, and a shake of the head.

"It is up, ma'am, and it's been like that all day—black as pitch. Plagues of Ejup couldn't have been worse."

"Oh, it is impossible for you to go," said Kate, quickly. "What am I to do?"

"Well, ma'am, if you wouldn't mind, I think I could tell you. You see, master come to this place when Mr Jenour died, and there hasn't been a thing taken away since. It's just as it used to be when Mrs Jenour was alive, years before. There's drawers and drawers and wardrobes full of everything a lady can want; and there's never a week goes by that I don't spend hours in going over and folding and airing, and I spend shillings and shillings every year in lavender. So if you wouldn't mind—"

Sarah Plant did not finish her sentence, but stood looking appealingly at the visitor.

"It is impossible for you to go out, Mrs Plant."

"Sarah, if you wouldn't mind, ma'am, and it's very good of you to say so."

"Well, then, Sarah," said Kate, smiling, and feeling more at ease, "you shall help me to get over the difficulty. Now go and see to your duties. I do not wish Mr Garstang to be troubled by my visit."

"Troubled, my dear young lady! I'm sure he'd be pleased to do anything. I'm not given to chatter and gossip, and, as I've often told Becky, if she'd been more obedient to me, and not been so foolish as to talk to milkmen, she'd have been a happier girl. But I can't help telling you what I heard master say this morning to himself, after he'd been giving me my orders: 'Ah,' he says, quite soft like, 'if I had had a child like that!' and of course, miss, he meant you."

Speaking dramatically, this formed Sarah Plant's exit, but Kate called her back.

"Would you mind and see that these two letters are posted? Have you any stamps?"

"There's lots, ma'am, in that little stand," said the woman, pointing to the table; and a couple being affixed the woman took the letters out with her.

About half an hour later Garstang entered, smiling pleasantly, and offering his arm.

"Dinner is waiting," he said, and he led his guest into the dining-room, where over a well-served meal, with everything in the best of taste, he laid himself out to increase the feeling of confidence he saw growing in Kate's eyes.

His conversation was clever, if not brilliant; he showed that he had an amply stored mind, and his bearing was full of chivalrous respect; while feeling more at rest, Kate felt drawn to him, and the magnitude of her step grew less in her troubled eyes.

The dinner was at an end, and they were seated over the dessert, Garstang sipping most temperately at his one glass of claret from time to time, and for some minutes there had been silence, during which he had been gazing thoughtfully at the girl.

"The most pleasant meal I have had for years," he said suddenly, "and I feel loath to break the charm, but it is time for the lady of the house to rise. Will you make the curiosity place the drawing-room, and when the tea has been brought up, send for me? I shall be longing to come, for I enjoy so little of the simple domestic."

Sarah Plant's words came to Kate's mind, "Ah, if I had had a child like that!" and the feeling of rest and confidence still grew, as Garstang rose and crossed the room to open the door for her.

"By the way, there is one little thing, my dear child," he said gravely.

Kate started, and her hand went to her breast.

"Don't be alarmed," he said, smiling, "a mere trifle in your interest. You are rapidly getting over the shock caused by the troubles of the past twenty-four hours or so, but you are not in a condition to bear more."

"My uncle!" cried Kate, excitedly.

"Exactly," said Garstang firmly. "You see, the very mention of trouble sends the blood rushing to your heart. Those letters that were lying on the hall table ready for posting: is it wise to send them and bring him here post haste, with his gentlemanly son? Yes, I know neither is to him, but he would know where you were as soon as he saw your letter in the bag."

"Mr Garstang, you do not think he would dare to open a letter addressed to my maid?"

"Yes," said Garstang, quietly; "unfortunately I do."

Chapter Twenty Seven

Claud Wilton took to the search for his cousin with the greater eagerness that he found it much more pleasant to be where he was not likely to come in contact with Pierce Leigh, for there was something about that gentleman's manner which he did not like. He knew of his ability in mending bones, for he had become aware of what was done when one labourer fell off a haystack, and when another went to sleep when riding on the shafts of a wagon, dived under the wheels, and had both his legs broken; but all this was suggestive of his ability to break bones as well, and recalling a horse-whipping, received in the hunting field, from the brother of a young lady to whom he had been too polite, he scrupulously avoided running further risks. Consequently, after the unpleasant interruption of his meeting with Jenny Leigh, he lost no time in getting up to town, being pretty well supplied with money by his father, who was to follow next day.

"I'm short of cash, my boy," said Wilton; "but this is a case in which we must not spare expense."

"Go to Scotland Yard, and set the detectives to work?"

"In heaven's name no, boy! We must be our own detectives, and hunt them out. Curse the young scoundrel. I might have known he would be after no good. An infernal poacher on our preserves, boy."

"Yes, guv'nor; and he has got clear off with the game."

"Then you must run him down, and when you have found out where he is, communicate with me; I must be there at the meeting."

"What? Lose time like that! No, guv'nor; I'll half kill him—hang me if I don't."

"No, no! I know you feel ready to—a villain—but that won't do. You'll only frighten the poor girl more, and she'll cling to him instead of coming away with you."

"But, guv'nor—"

"Don't hesitate, boy; I tell you I'm right. Let's get Kate away from him, and then you may break every bone in his skin if you like."

"But I want to give him a lesson at once."

"Yes, of course you do—but Kate and her fortune, my boy. Once you're on the scent, telegraph to me. I'll come and stay at Day's, in Surrey Street."

"Suppose they're gone abroad, guv'nor?"

"Well, follow them—all round the world if it's necessary. By the way, you've always been very thick with Harry; now, between men of the world, has there ever been any affair going on? You know what I mean."

"Lots, dad."

"Ah!—Ever married either of them?"

"Not he."

"That's a pity," said Wilton, "because it would have made matters so easy. Well, there, be off. The dog-cart's at the door."

Claud slapped his pocket, started for the station, and went up to stay at a bigger hotel than the quiet little place affected by his father; and about twelve o'clock the next day he presented himself at Garstang's office, where Barlow, the old clerk, was busy answering letters for his employer to sign.

"Morning, Barlow," said Claud, "Mr Harry in his room?"

"Mr Harry, sir? No, sir. I thought he was down with you, shooting and hunting."

"Eh? Did he say that he was going down to Northwood?"

"Well, dear me! Really, Mr Claud Wilton, sir, I can't be sure. I think I did hear him say something about Northwood; but whether it was that he was going there or had come back from there I really am not sure. Many pheasants this season?"

"Oh, never mind the pheasants," cried Claud, impatiently. "When was that?"

"Dear me now," said the man, thoughtfully; "now when was that—Monday, Tuesday, Wednesday—?"

"Thursday, Friday, Saturday," cried Claud, impatiently. "What a dawdling old buffer you are! Come, when was it: you must know?"

"Really, sir, I can't be sure."

"Was it this week?"

"I shouldn't like to say, sir."

"Well, last week then?"

"It might have been, sir."

"Yah!" growled Claud. "Think he's down at Chislehurst?"

"He may be, sir."

"Yes, and he may be at Jericho."

"Yes, sir; but you'll excuse me, there was a knock."

The clerk shuffled off his stool, and went to the door to admit a fresh visitor in the person of Wilton pere.

"Ah, Claud, my boy! You here?"

"Yes, father, I'm here; just come," said the young man, sulkily.

"Well, found them?"

"Do I look as if I had found them, dad? No."

"Tut-tut-tut!" ejaculated Wilton, who looked pale and worn with anxiety. "Mr Garstang in, Mr Barlow?"

"Yes, sir," said the clerk; "shall I say you are here?"

"Ye-es," said Wilton. "Take in my card, and say that I shall be obliged if he will give me an interview."

The old clerk bowed, and left the outer office for the inner, while Wilton turned to his son, to say hastily, "You may as well come in with me as you are here."

"Thanks, no; much obliged. What made you come here? You don't think he's likely to know?"

"Yes, I do," said Wilton, in a low voice. "I believe young Harry's carried her off, and that he's backing him up. You must come in with me: we must work together."

"Mr Garstang will see you, gentlemen," said the old clerk, entering.

"Gentlemen!" muttered Claud angrily, to his father.

"Yes, don't leave me in the lurch, my boy," whispered Wilton; and Claud noted a tremor in his father's voice, and saw that he looked nervous and troubled.

Wilton made way for his son to pass in first, the young man drew back for his father, and matters were compromised by their entering together, Garstang, who looked perfectly calm, rising to motion them to seats, which they took; and then there was silence for a few moments, during which Claud sat tapping his teeth with the ivory handle of the stick he carried, keeping his eyes fixed the while upon his father, who seemed in doubt how to begin.

"May I ask why I am favoured with this visit, gentlemen?" said Garstang, at last.

This started Wilton, who coughed, pulled himself together, and looking the speaker fully in the face, said sharply,

"We came, Mr John Garstang, because we supposed that we should be expected."

"Expected?" said Garstang, turning a little more round from his table, and passing one shapely leg over the other, so that he could grasp his ankle with both hands. "Well, I will be frank with you, James Wilton; there were moments when I did think it possible that you might come; I will not say to apologise, but to consult with me about that poor girl's future. How is she?"

Father and son exchanged glances, the former being evidently taken a little aback.

"Well," said Garstang, without pausing for an answer to this question; "I am glad you have come in a friendly spirit; I shall be pleased to meet you in the same way, so pray speak out. Let us have no fencing. Tell me what you propose to do."

Wilton coughed again, and looked at his son.

"You must see," said Garstang firmly, "that a fresh arrangement ought to be made at once. Under the circumstances she cannot stay at Northwood, and I will own that I am not prepared to suggest any relative of her father who seems suitable for the purpose. The large fortune which the poor child will inherit naturally acts as a bait, and there must be no risk of the poor girl being exposed to the pertinacious advances of every thoughtless boy who wishes to handle her money."

"I say, look here," cried Claud, "if you want to pick a quarrel, say so, and I'll go."

"I have no wish to pick a quarrel, young man," replied Garstang, sternly; "and I should not have spoken like this if you had not sought me out. Perhaps you had better stay, sir, and hear what your father has to propose, unless he has already taken you into his confidence."

"Well, he hasn't," said Claud, sulkily. "Go on, guv'nor, and get it over."

"Yes, James Wilton, go on, please, as your son suggests, and get it over. My time is valuable, and in such a case as this, between relatives, I shall be unable to make a charge for legal services. Now then, once more, what do you propose?"

"About what?" said Wilton, bluntly.

"About the future home of your niece?"

"Ah, that's what I've come about," said Wilton, gazing at the other sternly. "Where is she?"

Garstang looked at him blankly for a few moments.

"Where is she?" he said at last. "What do you mean?"

"What I say: where is Kate Wilton?"

"Where is she?" cried Garstang, changing his manner, and speaking now with a display of eagerness very different from his calm dignified way of a few minutes before. "Why, you don't mean to say that she has gone?"

"Yes, I do mean to say that she has gone."

"Bravo!" cried Garstang, putting down the leg he had been nursing, and giving it a hearty slap. "The brave little thing! I should not have thought that she had it in her."

"That won't do, John Garstang," said Wilton, sourly; "and it's of no use to act. The law's your profession—not acting. Now then, I want to know where she is."

"How should I know, man? She was not placed in my charge."

"You know, sir, because it was in your interest to know. This isn't the first time I've known you play your cards, but you're not playing them well: so you had better throw up your hand."

"Look here, James Wilton," said Garstang, looking at him curiously; "have you come here to insult me with your suspicions? If this young lady has left your roof, do you suppose I have had anything to do with it?"

"Yes, I do, and a great deal," cried Wilton, angrily. "You can't hoodwink me, even if you can net me and fleece me. Do you think I am blind?"

"In some things, very," said Garstang, contemptuously—

"Then I'm not in this. I see through your plans clearly enough, but you are checked. Where is that boy of yours?"

"I have no boy," said Garstang, contemptuously.

"Well, then, where is your stepson?"

"I do not know, James Wilton. Harry Dasent has long enough ago taken, as your son here would say, the bit in his teeth. I have not seen him since he came down to your place. But surely," he cried, springing up excitedly, "you do not think—"

"Yes, I do think, sir," cried Wilton, rising too; "I am sure that young scoundrel has carried her off. He has been hanging about my place all he could since she has been there, and paying all the court he could to her, and you know it as well as I do, the scoundrel has persuaded her that she was ill-used, and lured her away."

"By Jove!" said Garstang, softly, as he stood looking thoughtfully at the carpet, and apparently hardly hearing a word in his stupefaction at this announcement,

"Do you hear what I say, sir?" cried Wilton, fiercely, for he was now thoroughly angry; "do you hear me?"

"Yes, yes, of course," cried Garstang, making an effort as if to rouse himself. "Well, and if it is as you suspect, what then? Reckless as he is, Harry Dasent would make her as good a husband as Claud Wilton, and a better, for he is not related to her by blood."

"You dare to tell me that!" thundered Wilton.

"Yes, of course," said Garstang, coolly. "Why not?"

"Then you do know of it; you are at the bottom of it all; you have helped him to carry her off."

"I swear I have not," said Garstang, quietly. "I would not have done such a thing, for the poor girl's sake. It may be possible, just as likely as for your boy here, to try and win the girl and her fortune, but I swear solemnly that I have not helped him in any way."

"Then you tell me as a man—as a gentleman, that you did not know he had got her away?"

"I tell you as a man, as a gentleman, that I did not know he had got her away. What is more, I tell you I do not believe it. Tell me more. How and when did she leave? When did you miss her?"

"Night before last—no, no, I mean the next morning after you had left. She had gone in the night."

Garstang's hand shot out, and he caught Wilton by the shoulder with a fierce grip, while his lip quivered and his face twitched, as he gazed at him with a face full of horror.

"James Wilton," he said, in a husky voice, "you jump at this conclusion, but did anyone see them go?"

"No: no one."

"You don't think—"

"Think what, man? What has come to you?"

"She was in terrible trouble, suffering and hysterical, when she went up to her room," continued Garstang, with his voice sinking almost to a whisper, and with as fine a piece of acting as could have been seen off the stage. "Is it possible that, in her trouble and despair, she left the house, and—"

He ceased speaking, and stood with his lips apart, staring at his visitor, who changed colour and rapidly calmed down.

"No, no," he said, and stopped to dear his voice. "Impossible! Absurd! I know what you mean; but no, no. A young girl wouldn't go and do that just because her cousin kissed her."

"But she has been ill, and she was very weak and sensitive."

"Oh, yes, and the doctor put her right. No, no. She wouldn't do that," said Wilton, hastily. "It's as I say. Come, Claud, my lad, we can do no good here, it seems. Let's be moving. Morning, John Garstang; I am going to get help. I mean to run her down."

"You should know her best, James Wilton, and perhaps my judgment has been too hasty. Yes, I think I agree with you: so sweet, pure-minded, and well-balanced a girl would never seek refuge in so horrible a way. We may learn that she is with some distant relative after all."

"Perhaps so," said Wilton hastily. "Come, Claud, my lad," and he walked straight out, without glancing to right or left, and remained silent till they were crossing Russell Square.

"I say, guv'nor," said Claud, who passed his tongue over his lips before speaking, as if they were dry, "you don't think that, do you? It's what the mater said."

"No, no, impossible. Of course not. She couldn't. I think, though, we may as well get back," and for the moment he forgot all about the ladder planted against the sill.

And as they walked on they were profoundly unconscious of the fact that Garstang's grave elderly clerk was following them at a little distance, and looking in every other direction, his employer having hurried him out with the words:

"See where they go."

John Garstang then seated himself before the good fire in his private room, and began to think of the interview he had just had, while as he thought he smiled.

Chapter Twenty Eight

Kate gave way most unwillingly, but felt obliged to yield to what she felt was a common-sense view of the question.

"If you write now we shall be having endless trouble," said Garstang. "Your uncle will come here, and I shall be compelled to give you up."

"But I would refuse to go," said Kate, with spirit.

Garstang smiled, and shrugged his shoulders.

"Will you give me credit, as an old lawyer, my dear child, for knowing a little of the law?"

"Of course," she cried.

"Well, let me tell you that if James Wilton finds out where you are, I foresee endless troubles. You know his projects?"

Kate nodded quickly.

"To compass those plans, he will stop at nothing, even force. But supposing I defeat him in that, for I tell you frankly I should make every effort, he would set the law to work. If I get the best counsel I can, we shall have a long, wearisome lawsuit, and probably your late father's estate will be thrown into Chancery. You will become a ward of the Lord Chancellor, and the inroads made upon your fortune will be frightful."

"I don't think I should care," said Kate, looking at him wistfully, "so long as I could be at peace."

"Have you thought out any relative or friend whom you feel that you can trust, and to whom you would like to go?"

"No; not yet," said Kate, wearily; "and I have tried very hard."

"Then don't try, my child," he said, with a smile, "and then perhaps the idea will come. I ought to say, though," he added, playfully, "do try hard, so as not to succeed, for I do not want you to go. It is as if a change had come over my life, and like the man in one of the old plays, I had discovered a long-lost child."

"Pray don't treat it lightly, Mr Garstang," said Kate. "All this troubles me terribly. I feel so helpless."

"Believe me that if I talk lightly, I think very, very seriously of your position," said Garstang, quickly. "I know how painful it must be for you to neglect your friends, those to whom you would write, but really I am obliged to advocate reticence for the present. I will have your letters posted if you desire me to, but I am bound to show you the consequences which must follow."

Kate sighed, and looked more and more troubled.

"To put it more plainly," continued Garstang, "my position is that I have an extensive practice, with many clients to see, and consequently I must be a great deal away. Now suppose one morning, when I am out, James Wilton and his son present themselves. What will you do?"

Kate shivered, and gazed at him helplessly.

"I shall not feel best pleased to come back home to dinner, and find you gone."

"My position is terrible," said Kate. "I almost wish I were penniless."

"Come, come, not so terrible; it is only that of a prisoner who has her cell door barred inside, so that she can open it when she pleases. May I try and advise you a little?"

"Yes, pray, pray do, Mr Garstang."

"Well, my advice is this—even if it causes your poor old nurse great anxiety. She will be content later on, when she learns that it was for your benefit. My advice is for you to try and settle down here for a while, so as to see how matters shape themselves, or till you have decided where it would be better for you to go."

She looked at him wistfully.

"Could I not take apartments somewhere, and have Eliza up to keep house for me?"

"Well—yes," he said, thoughtfully. "It would be risky, for every movement of your old servant will be jealously watched just now. It would be better later on. What do you think?"

"That I do not wish to seem ungrateful for your kindness, neither do I feel justified in putting you to great trouble and expense."

"Pooh, pooh," he said, merrily, "I am not so poor that I can not afford myself a few pleasures. But proper pride is a fine thing. There, you shall be independent, and pay me back everything when you come of age."

He glanced at his watch, for breakfast had been over some time, and they had sat talking.

"I am keeping you, Mr Garstang," she said.

"Well, I like to be kept, but I have several appointments to-day. Have a good quiet think while I am gone, and we will talk it over again to-night."

"No," said Kate, quietly, "you will be tired then. I will take your advice, Mr Garstang."

"Yes?" he said, raising his eyebrows a little.

"I will stay here for a time, where, as you say, I can be at rest and safe from intrusion. We will see what time brings forth."

"Spoken like a thoughtful, wise little woman," said Garstang, without the slightest display of elation. "By the way, you find plenty of books to read?"

"Oh, yes, and I have been studying the old china."

"A very interesting subject; but music—you are fond of music. We must see about that."

He nodded and smiled, and then she saw that he became very calm and thoughtful, as if immersed in his business affairs.

Once more she was quite alone, thinking that she had been a whole week in the solemn old house, and a few minutes later the housekeeper entered to clear away the breakfast things.

"Is there anything I can do for you, ma'am?" said the woman sadly, when she had finished her task, Kate noticing the while that there was an occasional whisper outside the door, as the various articles were handed out.

"No, I think not, this morning, Sarah," said Kate, with a smile which proved infectious, for the woman stood staring at her for a few moments as if in wonder, and then her own countenance relaxed stiffly, as if she had not smiled in years, till her face looked nearly cheerful.

"You are handsome, ma'am," she said; "I haven't seen you look like that before since you've been here."

"Why does not Becky come in to help you to clear away?" said Kate, to change the conversation, and Sarah Plant's face grew stern and withered again, as she shook her head.

"She's such a sight, ma'am, with that handkercher round her head."

"I should not mind that; I have not fairly seen her since I came."

"No, ma'am, and you won't if she can help it. You mayn't mind, but she do. She always hides herself when anybody's about. Poor girl, she's been in trouble almost ever since she was born. There's sure to be something in this life. Not as I complains of master. It was just the same with old master, and when he died it made Becky ever so much worse. You see, ma'am, old master's wife was ill for a long time, and that made the house dull and quiet; and then she died, and old master was never the same again. He spent scores o' thousands o' pounds on furniture, and books, and china, and did everything he could to make the place nice, but he never held up his head again. And then somehow his money went wrong, and new master used to come to help him out of his troubles, but it was no use; old master never had the blinds pulled up again; and that made Becky and me different to most folk, for it used to be like being shut up in a cupboard, and we never hardly went out. Becky ain't been out of the house for years, and years, and years."

"We must make the house more cheerful now, Sarah."

The woman looked at her in astonishment, and then shook her head.

"Well, ma'am, I will say that it has seemed different since you came; but no—it's beautifully furnished, and I never see a better kitchen in my life—but make it cheerful? No, ma'am, it ain't to be done."

"We shall see," said Kate, smiling, and the woman's face relaxed once more as she gazed at the fair, intellectual countenance before her as if it were some beautiful object which gave her real pleasure; but as Kate's smile died away her own features looked cloudy, and she shook her head.

"No, ma'am, it's my belief as this was meant to be a dull house before the big trouble came. Me and Becky used to say to one another it was just as if the sun had gone out, but we never expected what came at last, or I believe we should have run away."

The moment before Kate had been thinking of dismissing the housekeeper to her work, but this hint at something which had happened enchained her attention, and the woman went on.

"You see, old master kept on getting from bad to worse, spite of Mr Garstang's coming and seeing to his affairs; and one day the doctor says to me: 'It's of no use, Mrs Plant, I can do nothing for a man who shuts himself up and sets all the laws of nature at defiance.' Those were his very words, ma'am; I recollected them because I never quite knew what they meant; but the doctor evidently thought master had done something wrong, though I don't think he ever did, for he was such a good man. Then came that morning, ma'am. I may as well tell you now. Becky used to sleep with me then, same as she does now, but that was before she had face-ache and fits. I remember it as well as can be. It was just at daylight in autumn time, when the men brings round the ropes of onions, and I nudged her, and I says,

'Time to get up, Becky,' and she yawned and got up and went down, for she always dressed quicker than I could. And there I was, dressing, and thinking that master had told me that Mr Garstang was coming at ten o'clock, and I was to send him into the library at once, and breakfast was to be ready there.

"I'd just put on my cap, ma'am, and was going down, when I heard the horridest shriek as ever was, and sank down in a chair trembling, for I felt as sure as sure that burglars were in the house, and they were murdering my poor Becky. I was that frightened I got up and tottered to the door, and locked and bolted it, for I said they shouldn't murder me. But, oh, dear; what I did suffer! 'Pretty sort of a mother you are,' I says to myself, 'taking care of yourself, and letting poor Becky be cut to pieces p'raps to hide their crime.'

"That went to my heart like a knife, ma'am, and I unfastened the door again and went out and listened, and all was still as still. You know how quiet it can be in this house, ma'am, don't you?"

Kate nodded.

"So I stood trembling there at the very top of the house, for we used to sleep up there, then, before Becky took to wanting to be downstairs, where she wasn't so likely to be seen; and though I listened and I listened, there wasn't a sound, and I give it to myself again. 'Why,' I says, 'a cat would scratch if you tried to take away its kitten to drown it'—as well I know, ma'am, for I've tried—'and you stand there doing nothing about your own poor girl.' That roused me, ma'am, and I went down, with the staircase all gloomy, with the light coming only from the sooty skylight in the roof; and there were the china cupboards and the statues in the dark corners all seeming to look down at something on the first floor. I was ready to drop a dozen times over, but I felt that I must go, even if I died for it; and down I went, step by step, peeping before me, and ready to shriek for help directly I saw what it was.

"But there was nothing that I could see, and I stopped on the first floor, looking over the banisters and trying to make out whether the hall door was open; but no, I couldn't see anything, and I went along sideways, looking down still, till I saw that the dining-room door was open, and it seemed to me that the shrieking must have come from there. I was just opposite to the door leading into the two little lib'ries—you know, ma'am, where the big curtain is—and I was taking another step sideways, meaning to look a little more over and then go and call up master, who didn't seem to have heard, when I caught my foot on something, and cried out and fell. And then I found it was poor Becky, who had just crawled out of the doorway on her hands and knees.

"For just a minute I couldn't say a word, but when I did, and asked her what was the matter, she only knelt there, clinging to my gownd, and staring up at me with a face that was horrible to behold.

"'What is it—what is it?' I kept on saying, but she couldn't speak, only kneel there, staring at me till I took her by the shoulders and shook her well. 'Why don't you speak?' I says. 'What is it?'

"She only said 'Oh'—a regular groan it was, and she turned her head slowly round to look back at the little lib'ry passage, and then she turned back and hid her face in my petticoats.

"'Tell me what it is, Becky,' I says, more gently, for it didn't seem that any harm was coming to us, but she couldn't speak, only point behind her toward the little lib'ry door, and this made me shiver, for I knew there must be something dreadful there. At last, though, for fear she should think I was a coward, I tried to get away from her, but she clung to me that tight that I couldn't get my gownd clear for ever so long. But at last I did, and I went into the little lobby through the door; but there was nothing there, and the lib'ry door was shut close; and I was coming back when I felt Becky seize me by the arm and point again, and then I saw what I hadn't seen before; there were footmarks on the carpet fresh made, and I saw that Becky must have made 'em when she had gone to the lib'ry door; and there was the reason for it, just seen by the light which came from the little skylight—there it was, stealing slowly under the bottom of the mat."

Chapter Twenty Nine

Kate Wilton looked at the woman in horror.

"Yes, ma'am," Sarah continued, "there it was, and when I opened the door I could only get it a little way, for something was just inside, and as I stood there trembling, there came out a nasty wet smell of gunpowder, just as if water had been upset on the hob.

"I didn't want any telling, ma'am; I knew, and poor Becky knew, that master had shot himself with something and was lying there.

"I waited for just about a minute, ma'am, for my senses seemed to be quite gone, and I was as bad as poor Becky; but I got to be a little sensible soon, and began to feel that I must do something. I called to Becky to come and help me, but it was no use; she was just as if she was stunned, and could only stare at me, shivering all the while. So I felt that I must do what there was to do myself, and I went back to the door, and pushed and pushed till I could just squeeze myself through the narrow slit I made; and then I dursen't look round, but stood with my back to it for ever so long before I could feel that he might be alive, and that I ought to go for the doctor.

"I looked round then, feeling as I turned that I should be obliged to shriek out, but I didn't. Poor master, he was lying on his side, with his hand under his head, just quiet and calm, as if he had only gone to sleep. It made me wonder what I had been frightened at, and I went down on one knee and took the hand which was by his side, touching a pistol."

"Yes?" said Kate, breathlessly, for the woman paused.

"Yes, ma'am, it was quite cold. He must have shot himself early in the night, and I knew it was no good to go to fetch a doctor then. Leastwise I think that's what I felt, for I didn't *go*, but crept out very softly and shut the door; and then I took hold of poor Becky's arm and led her down to the kitchen, where she went off into a dead faint, and came to, and fainted over again—fit after fit, so that I was busy for hours and didn't know how time went, till all at once there was a double knock at the door, which I knew was Mr Garstang come.

"I went up and let him in, and he looked at me so strange.

"'What is it?' he said; 'your master?'

"'Yes, sir,' I says, 'and I was to show you in as soon as you came.'

"He nodded, and went up at once, neither of us saying another word. Then he went in through the door gently, and came out again, looking horribly shocked.

"'When did you find him?' he says; and I told him. 'Poor fellow!' he says, 'I am not surprised. Sarah Plant, you must go and tell the police;' and I did, and there was an inquest, and at last the poor old master was to be buried, with only Mr Garstang to follow him, for he had no relations or friends.

"I sat in my bit of noo black, and Becky just opposite me, waiting while they'd gone to the cemetery, for no one asked me to go, and I sat there looking at Becky, who began crying as she heard them carrying the coffin downstairs and never stopped all that time. And I thought to myself, 'We two will have to go out into the world, and nobody won't take us with poor Becky like that;' and my heart was so full, miss—ma'am, that I began to cry, too; but I'm afraid it was for myself, not for poor master. Last of all, the carriage came back, and I let Mr Garstang in, looking terribly cut up.

"'Bring me a little tea, Sarah,' he says, and I went and got it, and had a cup, too, wanting it as I did badly, and by-and-by he rung for me to fetch the tray.

"I got to the door with it, when he calls me back.

"'Sarah,' he says, 'your poor master has no relations left, and by the papers I hold, everything comes to me.'

"'Yes, sir; so I s'posed,' I says to him, 'and you want me and Becky to go at once.'

"He looked at me with that nice soft smile of his, and he says, 'Why should you think that? No,' he says, 'I want everything to stay just as it is; I won't have a thing moved, and I should be very glad if you and Becky would stay and keep the house for me.'

"I couldn't answer him, ma'am, for I was crying bitterly; but I knew him, what a good man he was, and that me and Becky had found a friend. Seven years ago, ma'am, and never an unkind word from him when he came, which wasn't often. He only told me not to gossip about the place, and I said I wouldn't, and never did till I talked to you, ma'am, and as for poor Becky, she never speaks to no one. Perhaps, ma'am, you'd like to come upstairs, and see the marks."

"See the marks?" stammered Kate.

"Yes, ma'am, where old master lay. You've never been in the little lib'ry, but if you like I'll show you now. There's only a little rug to move, and there it is, quite plain."

"No, no, I do not wish to see," said Kate, shuddering. "So there has been a terrible tragedy here?"

"Yes, ma'am, and that's what makes the place so dull and still. I often fancy I can see poor old master gliding about the staircase and passages; but it's all fancy, of course."

"All fancy, of course," said Kate, softly. "But it is very terrible for such a thing to have happened here."

"Yes, ma'am, that's what I often think; and there's been times when I'm low-spirited; and you know there are times when one does get like that Becky's enough to make anyone dumpy, at the best of times, 'specially towards night, when she's sitting there with her face tied up and her eyes staring and looking toward the door, as if she fancied she was going to see master come in; for she will believe in ghosts, and it's no use to try to stop her. Ah, she's a great trial, ma'am."

"Poor girl!" said Kate.

"Thankye, ma'am. It's very good of you to say so," sighed the woman; "and it is nice to have a lady here to talk to. It's quite altered the place. There have been times, and many of them, when I felt that I must take poor Becky away and get another situation, but it would be ungrateful to new master, who's a dear good man, and never an unkind word since with him I've been. It isn't everyone who'd keep a servant with a girl like Becky about the house. But he never seems to mind, being a busy man, and I s'pose he must see that the only way in which Becky's happy is in cleaning and polishing things. I believe if she woke up in the middle of the night and remembered that she hadn't dusted something she'd want to get up and do it; and she would, too, if she dared. But go about the house in the middle of the night without me, ma'am? No; wild horses wouldn't drag her."

Sarah Plant ceased speaking, for she suddenly woke to the fact that Kate was gazing at the fire, with her thoughts evidently far away; and the woman stole softly from the room. But as the door clicked faintly Kate started and looked about her, half disposed to call her back, for the narrative she had heard made her position seem terribly lonely.

She restrained herself, though, and sat trying to think and turn the current of her thoughts, telling herself that she had no cause for anxiety save on Eliza's account. For Garstang could not have been more fatherly and considerate to her. His words, too, were wise and right. To let her uncle know where she was must result in scenes that would be stormy and violent; and she determined at last to let herself be guided entirely by her self-constituted guardian.

"Yes, he is right. He is all that is kind and fatherly in his way, and I, too, should be ungrateful if I murmured against my position. It will not be for long. In less than two years I shall be of age, and fully my own mistress."

She paused to think, for a doubt arose.

Would she be her own mistress? She had heard her father's will read, but it was at a time when she was distracted with grief, and save that she grasped that she was heiress to a large fortune, which was to remain invested in her father's old bank, she knew comparatively nothing as to the control her uncle possessed. Yes; she recalled that he was sole executor and guardian until she married.

"And I shall never marry," she sighed; but as the words were breathed, scenes at the old Manor came back; the pleasant little intimacy with Jenny Leigh, her praise of her brother, and that brother's manly, kindly attentions to his patient, his skill having achieved so much in bringing her back to health.

Yes, he had always been the attentive, courteous physician, and neither word nor look had intimated that he was anything else; but these things are a mystery beyond human control, and as Kate Wilton sat and thought, it was with Pierce Leigh present with her in spirit, and she felt startled; for the tell-tale blood was mantling her cheeks, and she hurriedly rose to do something to change the current of her thoughts.

"Poor Mr Garstang," she said, softly; "he shall not find me ungrateful. He, too, has suffered. If he had had a daughter like this!"

She recalled his words, evidently not intended for her ears. Wifeless—childless—wealthy, and yet solitary.

Her heart warmed towards him, and she was ready to call herself selfish for intruding her wishes upon one whose sole thought seemed to be to protect her and make her life peaceful.

"He shall not find me selfish," she said to herself, "and I will be guided by him and do what he thinks right."

She went out into the solemn-looking hall and began to ascend the great staircase, taking a fresh interest in the place, which seemed now as if it would be her home perhaps for months. The pictures and statues interested her, and she paused before a cabinet of curious old china, partly to try and admire, partly to think of how ignorant she was of all these matters, and a few minutes after, found herself close to the heavy curtain, beyond which was the door leading into the little library.

A strange thrill ran through her, and she turned to hurry into her own room, with her cheeks growing pale. But the blood flowed back, and with a feeling of self-contempt she walked straight to the curtain, drew it aside, passed through an archway, and turned the handle of a door. This opened upon a passage, whose walls were covered with venerable looking books, a dim skylight above showing the faded leather and worn gilding upon their backs. There was another door at the end, and as the woman's narrative forced itself back to her attention there was a fresh thrill which chilled her; but she went on firmly, opened the door, and passed through to find herself in the first of two rooms connected by a broad opening dimly lit by a stained-glass window, and completely covered with books, all old and evidently treasures of a collector.

Once more she shuddered, for she was standing upon one of several small Persian rugs dotted about the dark polished floor, and from the woman's description she knew that she must be where the former owner of the house had lain dead.

But the sensation of dread was momentary, and the warm flush of life came back to her cheeks as she said softly:

"What is there to fear?" and then found herself repeating:

"'There is no Death! What seems so is transition;
  This life of mortal breath
Is but a suburb of the life elysian
  Whose portal we call Death.'

"Oh, father—father!" she moaned softly; "but I am so lonely without you;" and she sank into a chair, to weep bitterly.

The tears brought relief and firmness, and drying her eyes, she went slowly from room to room, thinking of him who had once trod those boards—a sad and solitary man.

Somehow her thoughts brought her back to Garstang, who seemed so noble and chivalrous in his conduct to her, and how that he, too, was a sad and solitary man, for she had heard in the past that his marriage had proved unhappy.

A few minutes later, when she let the curtain drop behind her, and stood once more on the staircase, a change had come over her, and in spite of the slight redness and moisture remaining in her eyes, she looked brighter and more at rest, till she caught a glimpse of a strangely wild pair of staring eyes gazing at her from one of the dark doorways in horror and wonder, till their owner grasped the fact that she was observed, and fled.

"Poor Becky!" thought Kate, as she smiled sadly? "I must try and make friends with her now."

Chapter Thirty

The days passed calmly enough with Kate Wilton, and no more was said on either side about communicating with anyone. Garstang was there at breakfast, and left till dinner time, when he returned punctually.

Kate read and worked, and waited for him to speak, striving the while by her manner to let her guardian see that she was trying to show her gratitude to him for all that he had done. And so a fortnight glided by, and then, unable to bear it longer, she determined to question him.

That evening Garstang came in looking weary and careworn. There was evidently some trouble on the way, and as she rose to meet him she felt that she must not speak that night, for her new guardian had cares enough of his own to deal with.

But he began at once as he took her hands, smiling gravely as he looked in her eyes.

"Well, my poor little prisoner," he said, half-banteringly, "aren't you utterly worn out, and longing, little bird, to begin beating your breast against the bars of your cage?"

"No," she said, gently; "I am getting used to it now."

"Brave little bird!" he said, raising both her hands to his lips and kissing them, before letting them fall; "then I shall come back some evening and hear you warbling once again. I have not heard you sing since the last evening I spent in Bedford Square long months ago."

He saw her countenance change, and he went on hastily:

"By the way, has Sarah Plant bought everything for you that you require?"

"Oh, yes," she said; "far more."

"That's right. I am so ignorant about such matters. Pray do not hesitate to give her orders. Do you know," he continued, as he sat down and began to warm his hands, gazing the while with wrinkled brow at the fire, "I have been doing something to-day in fear and trembling."

"Indeed?" she said, anxiously.

"Yes," he said, thoughtfully, as he took up the poker and began to softly tap pieces of unburned coal into glowing holes. "My conscience has been smiting me horribly about you, my child. I come back after fidgeting all day about your being so lonely and dull, with nothing but those serious books about you—by the way, did they send in that parcel from the library?"

"Yes. Thank you for being so thoughtful about me, Mr Garstang."

"Oh, nonsense! But I think, my child, we could get rid of that formal Mr Garstang. Do you think you could call me guardian, little maid?"

"Yes, guardian," she said, smiling at him, as he turned to look at her anxiously.

"Hah! Come, that's better," he cried; and he set down the poker and rubbed his hands softly, as he gazed once more thoughtfully at the fire. "That sounds more as if you felt at home, and I shall dare to tell you what I have done. You see, I have been obliged to beg of you not to go out for a bit without me, and I have not liked to propose taking you of an evening to any place of entertainment—not a theatre, of course yet awhile, but a concert, say."

"Oh no, Mr Garstang!" she said, hastily, with the tears coming to her eyes.

He coughed, and looked at her in a perplexed way.

"Oh no, guardian," she said, smiling sadly.

"Hah! that's better. Of course not; of course not. Forgive me for even referring to it. But er—you will not feel hurt at what I have done?"

She looked at him anxiously.

"Yes," he said, speaking as if he had been suddenly damped. "I ought not to have done it yet. It will seem as if I were making it appear that you will have to stop some time."

"What have you done?" asked Kate, gravely.

"Well, my child, I know how musical you used to be, and as I was passing the maker's to-day the thought struck me that you would like a piano. 'It would make the place less dull for her,' I said, and—don't be hurt, my dear—I—I told him to send a good one in."

"Mr Garstang!—guardian!" she said, starting up, with the tears now beginning to fall.

"There, there, fought to have known better," he cried, catching up the poker, and beginning to use it hurriedly. "Men are so stupid. Don't take any notice, my dear. I'll counter-order it."

"No, no," she said gently, as she advanced to him and held out her hand "I am not hurt; I am pleased and grateful."

"You are—really?" he cried, letting the poker drop, and catching her hand in his.

"Of course I am," she said, simply. "How could I be otherwise? Don't think me so thoughtless, and that I do not feel deeply all your kindness."

"Kindness, nonsense!" he said, dropping her hand again, and turning away. "But will it help to make the time pass better?"

"Yes, I shall be very glad to have it."

"And, er—you'll sing and play to me sometimes when I come back here?"

"Yes," she said, smiling through her tears; "and I would to-night, now that you have come back tired and careworn, if it were here."

"Tired and careworn? Who is?"

"You are. Do you think I could not see?"

He looked at her with his eyes full of admiration, and then turned to the fire again.

"I am most grateful, guardian," she said. "But shall I have to be a prisoner long?"

"Hah!" he said with a sigh, and as if not hearing her question, "you are right, my child. I have had a very, very worrying day."

"I thought so," said Kate, resuming her seat, and looking at him in a commiserating way. "I hope it is nothing very serious."

"Serious?" he said, turning to her, sharply. "Well, yes it is, but I ought not to worry you about it."

"They say that sometimes relief comes in speaking of our troubles."

"But suppose one gets relief, and the other pain?" he said, looking at her quickly.

"Then it is something about me?"

He turned and looked at the fire again.

"Please tell me, guardian," she said.

"Only make you unhappy, my dear, just when you are getting back to your old self."

She looked at him in a troubled way for some moments, and then with a sudden outburst:

"You have seen Uncle James?"

He did not answer for a while, but sat gazing at the fire.

"Yes," he said, at last; "I have seen your Uncle James."

"And he knows I am here," she cried, clasping her hands, and looking at him in horror.

He turned slowly and met her eyes.

"Then you don't repent the step you have taken, and want to go back to Northwood?" he said.

"How could I when you have protected me as you have, and saved me from so much suffering and insult?"

"Hah!" he said, with a sigh of relief, "thank you, my child. I was afraid that you would be ready to return to him."

"Mr Garstang!" she cried.

"Guardian."

"Then, guardian, how could you think it? If I have seemed dull and unhappy, surely it was not strange, considering my position."

"Of course not; but I was flattering myself with the belief that you were really getting reconciled to your fate."

"I am reconciled," said Kate, warmly; "but I can not help longing to take my old nurse by the hand again, and to see my friends."

"Friends?" he said, looking at her curiously.

"Yes; I made two friends down there whose society was pleasant to me, and whom I have missed."

"Indeed! I did not know."

"But tell me, is uncle coming? Does he know I am here?" cried Kate, excitedly.

"No, he is not coming, my child, and he does not know you are here," said Garstang, watching her searchingly.

"Ah!" ejaculated the girl, with a sigh of relief. "I could not—I dare not meet him."

"That is what I felt. You can not meet him for some time to come, but there are unpleasant complications, my dear, which trouble me a great deal."

"Yes?" said Kate, excitedly.

"Such as will, I fear, make it necessary for you to remain still secluded."

"But, Mr Garstang, suppose that he should come to see you one day when you were out, and he were shown in to me."

"Ah, yes," he said, dryly, watching her troubled face narrowly, "what I once said: that would be awkward."

"Oh, it would be horrible," cried Kate, springing to her feet. "I could not go back with him. And he has a right to claim me, and he would insist."

She began to pace the room excitedly, with her hands clasped before her.

"Yes, my child, it would be horrible," said Garstang, gently, "and that is why, in spite of its giving you pain, I have been so particular lest by any letter of yours he should learn where you were."

"But he might come as I said—to see you, in your absence," she cried.

"No, my dear," he said, reaching out one hand as she was passing the back of his chair; and she stopped at once, and placed hers trustingly within. "Don't be alarmed. I am an old man of the world, and for years past I have had to set my wits to work to battle with other people's. Uncle James does not know that you are here, and unless you tell him he is not likely to know, for the simple reason that he is not aware that I have such a place."

Kate uttered a sigh of relief, and let her hand rest in his.

"Poor fellow, he is horribly disappointed, and he is leaving no stone unturned to trace you, and his hopeful son is helping him and watching me."

"Oh!" ejaculated Kate, excitedly. "Yes, but they do not know of this place, and are keeping an eye upon my offices in Bedford Row and my house down in Kent. I little thought when my poor old friend and client died and this place fell to me that it would one day prove so useful. So there, try and stop this fluttering of the pulses, little maid; so long as we are careful, and you wish it, you can remain in sanctuary. Now let's dismiss the tiresome business altogether. I am glad, though, that you are pleased about the piano."

"No, no; don't dismiss it yet," cried Kate, eagerly. "Tell me what he said."

"Humph!" said Garstang, frowning; "shall I? No; better not."

"Yes, please; I can not help wanting to know."

"But I'm afraid of upsetting you, my dear."

"It will not now; I am growing firmer, Mr Garstang, my guardian," she said. "Better tell me than leave me to think, and perhaps lie awake to-night imagining things that may not be true."

"Well, yes—that would be bad," he said, nodding his head. "There, sit down then, and draw your chair to the fender. Your face is burning, but your hands are cold. That's better," he continued, as he took up the poker again, and sat forward, gazing at the fire, and once more tapping the pieces of coal into the glowing caverns. "You see, he has been to me three times."

"And I did not know!" cried Kate.

"No, you did not know, my dear, because I did not want to upset you. What do you think he says?"

"That I fled to you, and placed myself under your protection?"

"Wrong," said Garstang, looking round and smiling in the beautiful face across the hearth, as he played the part of an amiable fatherly individual to perfection. "Shall I say guess again?"

"No, no, pray don't trifle with me, guardian."

"Trifle with you?" he cried, growing stern of aspect. "No. There, it must come out. He did not say that, and he did not accuse me of fetching you away, for he and Master Claud are upon a wrong scent."

"Yes—yes," said Kate, eagerly.

"They say that Harry Dasent made an excuse of his friendship with Claud to go down to Northwood with another object in view."

"Yes—what?" she said, looking at him wonderingly.

"You, my child."

"Me?" she cried, aghast.

"Well, to speak more correctly, your money, my dear; and that, despairing of winning you in a straightforward way, he either came and caught you in the humour for being persuaded to leave with him, having on his other visits paved the way by making love to you—"

"Oh!" ejaculated Kate; "I never noticed anything particular in his manner to me—yes, I did, once or twice he was very, very attentive."

"Indeed," said Garstang, frowning.

"But you said 'either,'" cried Kate, anxiously.

"Yes; either that he had persuaded you to elope with him, or he had climbed to your window and by some means forced you to come away."

"What madness!" cried Kate.

"Yes, and there's more behind; they accuse me of conniving at it, and say they are sure you are married, and that I know where you are."

"Mr Dasent!" exclaimed Kate, gazing at Garstang wonderingly.

"Yes, Harry Dasent," he said, drawing himself up. "He is my poor dead wife's son, my dear, and it so happens that he is giving colour to the idea by his absence from home on one of his reckless, ne'er-do-weel expeditions; but between ourselves, my child, I'd rather see you married to Claud Wilton, your cousin, than to him; and," he added warmly, "I think I would sooner follow you to your grave than—Yes—what is it?"

"I beg pardon, sir," said the housekeeper, "but the dinner's spoiling, and I've been waiting half an hour and more for you to ring."

"Then bring it up directly, Mrs Plant, for we are terribly ready."

"Yes, sir."

"At least I am, my dear; I was faint for want of it when I came in. Shall we shelve the unpleasant business now?"

"It is so dreadful," said Kate.

"Well, yes, it is; so it used to be with the poor folks who were besieged by the enemy. You are besieged, but you have a strong castle in which to defend yourself, and you can laugh your enemies to scorn. Really, Kate, my child, this is something like being cursed by a fortune."

She nodded her head quickly.

"Money is useful, of course, and I once had a very eager longing to possess it; but, like a great many other things, when once it is possessed it is—well, only so much hard cash, after all. It won't buy the love and esteem of your fellow-creatures. Do you know, my dear, if it were not for something I should be ready to say to you—'Let Uncle James have your paltry fortune and pay off his debts.' That's what he wants, not you. As for Claud, he'd break your heart in a month."

"Could I deliver the money over to him?" said Kate, looking anxiously in her new guardian's face.

"Oh, yes, my dear, that would be easy enough. And then—I tell you what: I have plenty, and I'm tired of the worry and care of a solicitor's life. Why shouldn't I take a few years' holiday and go on the Continent with my adopted daughter and her old maid? Paris, Berlin, Vienna, Switzerland, Italy, Egypt—what would you say to that? It would be delightful."

"Yes," said Kate, eagerly, "and then I could be at rest. No," she said, suddenly, with the colour once more rising in her cheeks, "that would be impossible."

"Yes," said Garstang, watching her narrowly, as she averted her face, to gaze now in the fire. "Castles in the air, my dear."

"Yes," she said, dreamily, "castles in the air;" but she was seeing golden castles in the glowing fire, and her face grew hotter as, in spite of herself, she peopled one of those golden castles in a peculiar way which made her pulses begin to flutter, and she felt that she dared not gaze in her companion's face.

"Yes, castles in the air, my child," said Garstang again. "For that fortune was amassed by your father for the benefit of his child and her husband, and she must not lightly throw it away to benefit a foolish, grasping, impecunious relative."

"The dinner is served, sir," said Mrs Plant.

Garstang rose and offered his arm, which Kate took at once.

"We may dismiss the unpleasant business now," he said, with a smile.

"Yes, yes, of course," she said.

"But tell me, you do feel satisfied and safe—at rest?"

"Quite," she said, looking smilingly in his face.

"Then now for dinner," he said, leading her to the door.

That evening John Garstang sat over his modest glass of wine alone, fitting together the pieces of his plans, and as he did so he smiled and seemed content.

"No," he said, softly, "you will not pocket brother Robert's money, friend James, for I hold the winning trump. What beautiful soft wax it is to mould! Only patience—patience! The fruit is not quite ripe yet. A hundred and fifty thou—a hundred and fifty thou!"

Chapter Thirty One

"If I could only get poor Pierce to believe in me again!" sighed Jenny, as she lay back in an easy chair at the cottage, after a month of illness; for in addition to the violent sprain from which she had suffered, the exposure had brought on a violent rheumatic cold and fever, from which she was slowly recovering.

"But he doesn't believe in me a bit now, even after all I've suffered. Oh, how I should like to punish that wretched boy before I go!"

She was sitting close to the window, where she could look down the road toward the village, her eyes dull, her face listless, thinking over the past—her favourite way of making herself miserable, as she had no heart attachment, or disappointment, as a mental "pièce de résistance" to feast upon during her illness.

Everything had gone so differently from the way she had planned. Pierce was to marry Kate Wilton, and be rich and happy ever afterwards; she intended to be what she called a nice, little, old maiden aunt, to pet and tend all her brother's children, for, of course, Kate and Pierce would have her to live with them; but it was all over—Kate had gone, no one knew where; Pierce, who had always loved her so tenderly, scarcely ever spoke to her as he used. He was quiet, grave, and civil, but never walked up and down the garden with his arm round her waist, laughing and joking with her, and talking about the prince who was to come some day to carry her off to his palace. It was all misery and wretchedness.

"I'm sure nobody could have been so ill and suffered so much before," she said, "and I'm growing so white, and thin, and ugly, and old looking, and I'm sure I shall have to go about with a crutch; and it's so lonely with Pierce always going out to see old women and old men who are not half so bad as I am; and I wish I was dead! Oh, dear, oh, oh, dear, I wonder whether it hurts much to die. If it does, I'll ask Pierce to give me some laudanum to put me out of my misery, and—Oh, who's that?"

A carriage had drawn up at the gate, and she leaned forward to see.

"Mrs Wilton's carriage," she said, quickly growing interested, "and poor Pierce out. Oh, dear, how vexatious it is, when he wants patients so badly! I wonder who's ill now. It can't be that little wretch, because I saw him ride by an hour ago, and stare at the place; and it can't be Mr Wilton, because he always goes over to Dixter market on Fridays. It must be Mrs Wilton herself."

"If you please, miss, here's Missus Wilton," said the tall, gawky girl, just emancipated from the village schools to be Jenny's maid-of-all-work and nurse, and the lady in question entered with her village basket upon her arm.

"Ah! my dear child!" she cried, bustling across the room, putting her basket on the table, and then bobbing down to kiss Jenny, who sat up, frowning and stiff. "No, no, don't get up."

"I was not going to, Mrs Wilton," said Jenny, coldly; "I can't."

"Think of that, now," cried the visitor, drawing a chair forward, and carefully spreading her silks and furs as she sat down; "and I've been so dreadfully unneighbourly in not coming to see you, though I did not know you had been so bad as this. You see, I've had such troubles of my own to attend to that I couldn't think of anything else; but it all came to me to-day that I had neglected you shamefully, and so I said to myself, I'd come over at once, as Mr Wilton and my son were both out, and bring you a bit of chicken, and a bottle of wine, and the very last bunch of grapes before it got too mouldy in the vinery, and here I am."

"Yes, Mrs Wilton," said Jenny, stiffly; "but if you please, I am not one of the poor people of the parish."

"Why, no, my dear, of course not; but whatever put that in your head?"

"The wine, Mrs Wilton."

"But it's the best port, my dear—not what I give to the poor."

"And the bit of chicken, Mrs Wilton," said Jenny, viciously.

"But it isn't a bit, my dear; it's a whole one," said the lady, looking troubled.

"A cold one, left over from last night's dinner," said Jenny, half hysterically.

"Indeed, no, my dear," cried the visitor, appealingly; "it isn't a cooked one at all, but a nice, young Dorking cockerel from the farm."

"And a bunch of mouldy grapes," cried Jenny, passionately, bursting into a fit of sobbing, "just as if I were widow Gee!"

"Why, my dear child, I—oh, I see, I see; you're only just getting better, and you're lonely and low, and it makes you feel fractious and cross, and

I know. There, there, there, my poor darling! I ought to have come before and seen you, for I always did like to see your pretty, little, merry face, and there, there, there!" she continued, as she knelt by the chair, and in a gentle, motherly way, drew the little, thin invalid to her expansive breast, kissing and fondling and cooing over her, as she rocked her to and fro, using her own scented handkerchief to dry the tears.

"That's right. Have a good cry, my dear. It will relieve you, and you'll feel better then. I know myself how peevish it makes one to be ill, with no one to tend and talk to you; but you won't be angry with me now for bringing you the fruit and wine, for indeed, indeed, they are the best to be had, and do you think I'd be so purse-proud and insulting as to treat you as one of the poor people? No, indeed, my dear, for I don't mind telling you that I'm only going to be a poor woman myself, for things are to be very sadly altered, and when I come to see you, if I'm to stay here instead of going to the workhouse, there'll be no carriage, but I shall have to walk."

"I—I—beg your pardon, Mrs Wilton," sobbed Jenny. "I say cross things since I have been so ill."

"Of course you do, my precious, and quite natural. We women understand it. I wish the gentlemen did; but dear, dear me, they think no one has a right to be cross but them, and they are, too, sometimes. You can't think what I have to put up with from Mr Wilton and my son, though he is a dear, good boy at heart, only spoiled. But you're getting better, my dear, and you'll soon be well."

"Yes, Mrs Wilton," said Jenny, piteously, "if I don't die first."

"Oh, tut, tut, tut! die, at your age. Why, even at mine I never think of such a thing. But, oh, my dear child, I want you to try and pity and comfort me. You know, of course, what trouble we have been in."

"Yes," said Jenny. "I have heard, and I'm better now, Mrs Wilton. Won't you sit down?"

"To be sure I will, my dear. There: that's better. And now we can have a cozy chat, just as we used when you came to the Manor. Oh, dear, no visitors now, my child. It's all debt and misery and ruin. The place isn't the same. Poor, poor Kate!"

"Have you heard where she is, Mrs Wilton?"

"No, my dear," said the visitor, tightening her lips and shaking her head, "and never shall. Poor dear angel! I am right. I'm sure it's as I said."

Jenny looked at her curiously, while every nerve thrilled with the desire to know more.

"I felt it at the first," continued Mrs Wilton. "No sooner did they tell me that she was gone than I knew that in her misery and despair she had gone and thrown herself into the lake; and though I was laughed at and pooh-poohed, there she lies, poor child. I'm as sure of it as I sit here."

"Mrs Wilton!" cried Jenny, in horrified tones. "Oh, pray, pray, don't say that!" and she burst into a hysterical lit of weeping.

"I'm obliged to, my dear," said the visitor, taking a trembling hand in hers, and kissing it; "but don't you cry and fret, though it's very good of you, and I know you loved the sweet, gentle darling. Ah, it was all a terrible mistake, and I've often lain awake, crying without a sound, so as not to wake Mr Wilton and make him cross. Of course you know Mr Wilton settled that Claud was to marry her, and when he says a thing is to be, it's no use for me to say a word. He's master. It's 'love, honour, and obey,' my dear, when you're a married lady, as you'll find out some day."

"No, Mrs Wilton, I shall never marry."

"Ah, that's what we all say, my child, but the time comes when we think differently. But as I was telling you, I thought it was all a mistake, but I had to do what Mr Wilton wished, though I felt that they weren't suited a bit, and I know Claud did not care for her. I'd a deal rather have seen him engaged to a nice little girl like you."

"Mrs Wilton!" said Jenny, indignantly.

"Oh, dear me, what have I said?" cried the lady, smiling. "He's wilful and foolish and idle, and fond of sport; but my boy Claud isn't at all a bad lad — well, not so very — and he'll get better; and I'm sure you used to like to have a talk with him when you came to the Manor."

"Indeed I did not!" cried Jenny, flushing warmly.

"Oh, very well then, I'm a silly old woman, and I was mistaken, that's all. But there, there, we don't want to talk about such things, with that poor child lying at the bottom of the lake; and they won't have it dragged."

"But surely she would not have done such a thing, Mrs Wilton," cried Jenny, wildly.

"I don't know, my dear. They say I'm very stupid, but I can't help, thinking it, for she was very weak and low and wretched, and she quite hated poor Claud for the way he treated her. But I never will believe that she eloped with that young Mr Dasent."

"Neither will I," cried Jenny, indignantly. "She would not do such a thing."

"That she would not, my dear; and I say it's a shame to say it, but my husband will have it that he has carried her off for the sake of her money. And as I said to my husband, 'You thought the same about poor Claud, when the darling boy was as innocent as a dove.' There, I'm right, I'm sure I'm right. She's lying asleep at the bottom of the lake."

Jenny's face contracted with horror, and her visitor caught her in her arms again.

"There, there, don't look like that, my dear. She's nothing to you, and I'm a very silly old woman, and I dare say I'm wrong. I came here to be like a good neighbour, and try and comfort you, and I'm only making you worse. That's just like me, my dear. But now look here. You mustn't go about with that white face. You want change, and you shall come over to the Manor and stay for a month. It will do you good."

"No," said Jenny, quietly. "I can not come, thank you, Mrs Wilton. My brother would not permit it."

"But he must, for your sake. Oh, these men, these men!"

"It is impossible," said Jenny, holding out her hand, "for we are going away."

"Going away! Well, I am sorry. Ah, me! It's a sad world, and maybe I shall be gone away, too, before long. But you might come for a week. Why not to-morrow?"

Jenny shook her head, and the visitor parted from her so affectionately that no further opposition was made to the basket's contents.

Chapter Thirty Two

Jenny had not been seated alone many minutes after the carriage had driven off, dwelling excitedly upon her visitor's words respecting Kate's disappearance, when the front door was opened softly, and there was a tap on the panel of the room where she sat.

"Who's there? Come in."

"Only me," said a familiar voice, and, hunting whip in hand, Claud Wilton stood smiling in the doorway.

"You!" cried Jenny, with flaming cheeks. "How dare you come here?"

"Because I wanted to see you," he said. "Just met the mater, and she told me how bad you'd been, and that you talked about dying. I say, you know, none of that nonsense."

"What is that to you, sir, if I did?"

"Oh, lots," he said, twirling the lash of his whip as he stood looking at her. "If you were to pop off I should go and hang myself in the stable."

"Go away from here directly. How dare you come?" cried Jenny, indignantly.

"Because I love you. You made me, and you can't deny that."

"Oh!" ejaculated the girl, as her cheeks flamed more hotly.

"I can't help it now. I've been ever so miserable ever since I knew you were so bad; and when the old girl said what she did it regularly turned me over, and I was obliged to come. I say, I do love you, you know."

"It is not love," she cried hotly; "it is an insult. Go away. My brother will be here directly."

"I don't care for your brother," said the young man, sulkily. "I'm as good as he is. I wanted to see how bad you were."

"Well, you've seen. I've been nearly dead with fever and pain, and it was all through you that night."

"Yes, it was all through me, dear."

"Silence, sir; how dare you!"

"Because I love you, and 'pon my soul, I'd have been ten times as bad sooner than you should."

"It is all false—a pack of cruel, wicked lies."

"No, it ain't. I know I've told lots of lies to girls, but then they were only fools, and I've been a regular beast, Jenny, but I'm going to be all square now; am, 'pon my word. I didn't use to know what a real girl was in those days, but I've woke up now, and I'd do anything to please you. There, I feel sometimes as if I wish I were your dog."

"Pah! Go and find your rich cousin, and tell her that."

"—My rich cousin," he cried, hotly. "She's gone, and jolly go with her. I know I made up to her—the guv'nor wanted me to, for the sake of her tin—but I'm sick of the whole business, and I wouldn't marry her if she'd got a hundred and fifty millions instead of a hundred and fifty thousand."

"And do you think I'm so weak and silly as to believe all this?" she cried.

"I d'know," he said, quietly. "I think you will. Clever girl like you can tell when a fellow's speaking the truth."

"Go away at once, before my brother comes."

"Shan't I wouldn't go now for a hundred brothers."

"Oh," panted Jenny. "Can't you see that you will get me in fresh trouble with him, and make me more miserable still?"

"I don't want to," he said, softly, "and I'd go directly if I thought it would do that, but I wouldn't go because of being afraid. I say, ain't you precious hard on a fellow? I know I've been a brute, but I think I've got some good stuff in me, and if I could make you care for me I shouldn't turn out a bad fellow."

"I will not listen to you. Go away."

"I say, you know," he continued, as he stood still in the doorway, "why won't you listen to me and be soft and nice, same as you were at first?"

"Silence, sir; don't talk about it. It was all a mistake."

"No, it wasn't. You began to fish for me, and you caught me. I've got the hook in me tight, and I couldn't get away if I tried. I say, Jenny, please listen to me. I am in earnest, and I'll try so hard to be all that is square and right. 'Pon my soul I will."

"Where is your cousin?"

"I don't know—and don't want to," he added.

"Yes you do, you took her away."

"Well, it's no use to swear to a thing with a girl; if you won't believe me when I say I don't know, you won't believe me with an oath. What do I want with her? She hated me, and I hated her. There is only one nice girl in the world, and that's you."

"Pah!" cried Jenny, who was more flushed than ever. "Look at me."

"Well, I am looking at you," he said, smiling, "and it does a fellow good."

"Can't you see that I've grown thin, and yellow, and ugly?"

"No; and I'll punch any fellow's head who says you are."

"Don't you know that I injured my ankle, and that I'm going to walk with crutches?"

"Eh?" he cried, starting. "I say, it ain't so bad as that, is it?"

"Yes; I can't put my foot to the ground."

"Phew!" he whistled, with a look of pity and dismay in his countenance; "poor little foot."

"I tell you I shall be a miserable cripple, I'm sure; but I'm going away, and you'll never see me again."

"Oh, won't I?" he said, smiling. "You just go away, and I'll follow you like a shadow. You won't get away from me."

"But don't I tell you I shall be a miserable cripple?"

"Well," he said, thoughtfully; "it is a bad job, and perhaps it'll get better. If it don't I can carry you anywhere; I'm as strong as a horse. Look here, it's no use to deny it, you made me love you, and you must have me now—I mean some day."

"Never!" cried Jenny, fiercely.

"Ah, that's a long time to wait; but I'll wait. Look here, little one," he cried, passionate in his earnestness now, "I love you, and I'm sorry for all that's gone by; but I'm getting squarer every day."

"But I tell you it is impossible. I'm going away; it was all a mistake. I can't listen to you, and I tell you once more I'm going to be a miserable, peevish cripple all my life."

"No, you're not," said the lad, drawing himself up and tightening his lips. "You're not going to be miserable, because I'd make you happy; and I like a girl to be sharp with a fellow like you can; it does one good. And as to being a cripple, why, Jenny, my dear, I love you so that I'd marry you to-morrow, if you had no legs at all."

Jenny looked at him in horror, as he still stood framed in the doorway; but averted her eyes, turning them to the window, as she found how eagerly he was watching her, while her heart began to beat rapidly, as she felt now fully how dangerous a game was that upon which she had so lightly entered. Rough as his manner was, she could not help feeling that it was genuine in its respect for her, though all the same she felt alarmed; but directly after, the dread passed away in a feeling of relief, and a look of malicious glee made her eyes flash, as she saw her brother coming along the road.

But the flash died out, and in repentance for her wish that Pierce might pounce suddenly upon the intruder, she said, quickly:

"Mr Wilton, don't stop here; go—go, please, directly. Here's my brother coming."

She blushed, and felt annoyed directly after, angry with herself and angry at her lame words, the more so upon Claud bursting out laughing.

"Not he," cried the lad. "You said that to frighten me."

"No, indeed; pray go. He will be so angry," she cried.

"I don't care, so long as you are not."

"But I am," she cried, "horribly angry."

"You don't look it. I never saw you seem so pretty before."

"But he is close here, and—and, and I am so ill—it will make me worse. Pray, pray, go."

"I say, do you mean that?" he said, eagerly. "If I thought you really did, I'd—"

"You insolent dog! How dare you?" roared Pierce, catching him by the collar and forcing him into the room. "You dare to come here and insult my sister like this!"

"Who has insulted her?" cried Claud, hotly.

"You, sir. It is insufferable. How dare you come here?"

"Gently, doctor," said Claud, coolly; "mind what you are saying."

"Why are you here, sir?"

"Come to see how your sister was."

"What is it to you, puppy? Leave the house," cried, Pierce, snatching the hunting whip from the young man's hand, "or I'll flog you as you deserve."

"No, you won't," said Claud, looking him full in the eyes, with his lips tightening together. "You can't be such a coward before her, and upset her more. Ask her if I've insulted her."

"No, no, indeed, Pierce; Mr Wilton has been most kind and gentlemanly—more so than I could have expected," stammered Jenny, in fear.

"Gentlemanly," cried Pierce scornfully. "Then it is by your invitation he is here. Oh, shame upon you."

"No, it isn't," cried Claud stoutly. "She didn't know I was coming, and when I did come she ordered me off—so now then."

"Then leave this house."

"No, I won't, till I've said what I've got to say; so put down that whip before you hurt somebody, more, perhaps, than you will me. You're not her father."

"I stand in the place of her father, sir, and I order you to go."

"Look here, Doctor, don't forget that you are a gentleman, please, and that I'm one, too."

"A gentleman!" cried Pierce angrily, "and dare to come here in my absence and insult my sister!"

"It isn't insulting her to come and tell her how sorry I am she has been ill."

"A paltry lie and subterfuge!" cried Pierce.

"No, it isn't either of them, but the truth, and I don't care whether you're at home, Doctor, or whether you're out I came here to tell her outright, like a man, that I love her; and I don't care what you say or do, I shall go on loving her, in spite of you or a dozen brothers.—Now give me my whip."

His brave outspoken way took Pierce completely aback, and the whip was snatched from his hand, Claud standing quietly swishing it round and round till he held the point in his fingers, looking hard at Jenny the while.

"There," he said, "I don't mean to quarrel; I'm going now. Good-bye, Jenny; I mean it all, every word, and I hope you'll soon be better. There," he said, facing round to Leigh. "I shan't offer to shake hands, because I know that you won't but when you like I will. You hate me now, like some of your own poisons, because you think I'm after Cousin Kate, but you needn't. There, you needn't flinch; I'm not blind. I smelt that rat precious soon. She never cared for me, and I never cared for her, and you may marry her and have her fortune if you can find her, for anything I'll ever do to stop it—so there."

He nodded sharply, stuck his hat defiantly on his head, and marched out, leaving Pierce Leigh half stunned by his words; and the next minute they heard him striding down the road, leaving brother and sister gazing at each other with flashing eyes.

Chapter Thirty Three

For some moments neither spoke.

"Was this your doing?" cried Leigh, at last, and he turned upon his sister angrily.

At that moment Jenny was lying back, trembling and agitated, with her eyes half closed, but her brother's words stung her into action.

"You heard what Mr Claud Wilton said," she retorted, angrily. "How dare you speak to me like this, Pierce, knowing what you do?"

He uttered an impatient ejaculation.

"Yes, that is how you treat me now," she said, piteously; "your troubles have made you doubting and suspicious. Have I not suffered enough without you turning cruel to me again?"

"How can you expect me to behave differently when I find you encouraging that cad here? It is all the result of the way in which you forgot your self-respect and what was due to me."

"That's cruel again, Pierce. You know why I acted as I did."

"Pah!" he exclaimed; "and now I find you encouraging the fellow."

"I was as much taken by surprise as you were, dear," she said.

"And to use the fellow's words, do you think I am blind? It was plain enough to see that you were pleased that he came."

"I was not," she cried, angrily now. "I tell you I was quite taken by surprise. I was horrified and frightened, and I was glad when I saw you coming, for I wanted you to punish him for daring to come."

Leigh looked at his sister in anger and disgust.

"If I can read a woman's countenance," he said, mockingly, "you were gratified by every word he said to me."

"I don't know—I can't tell how it was," she faltered with her pale cheeks beginning to flame again, "but I'm afraid I was pleased, dear."

"I thought so," he cried, mockingly.

"I couldn't help liking the manly, brave way in which he spoke up. It sounded so true."

"Yes, very. Brave words such as he has said in a dozen silly girls' ears. And he told you before I came that he loved you?"

"Yes, dear."

"And you told him that his ardent passion was returned," he sneered.

"I did not. I could have told him I hated him, but I could not help feeling sorry, for I have behaved very badly, flirting with him as I did."

"And pity is near akin to love, Jenny," cried Leigh, with a harsh laugh, "and very soon I may have the opportunity of welcoming this uncouth oaf for a brother-in-law, I suppose. Oh, what weak, pitiful creatures women are! People cannot write worse of them than they prove."

Jenny was silent, but she looked her brother bravely in the face till his brows knit with anger and self-reproach.

"What do you mean by that?" he cried, angrily.

"I was only thinking of the reason why you speak so bitterly, Pierce."

"Pish!" he exclaimed; and there was another silence.

"Mrs Wilton came this afternoon and brought me a chicken and some wine and grapes," said Jenny, at last.

"Like her insolence. Send them back."

"No. She was very kind and nice, Pierce. She was full of self-reproach for the way in which poor Kate Wilton was treated."

"Bah! What is that to us?"

"A great deal, dear. She is half broken-hearted about it, and says it was all the Squire's doing, and that she was obliged. He wished his son to marry Kate."

"The old villain!"

"And she says that poor Kate is lying drowned in the lake."

Leigh started violently, and his eyes looked wild with horror, but it was a mere flash.

"Pish!" he ejaculated, "a silly woman's fancy. The ladder at the window contradicted that. It was an elopement and that scoundrel who was here just now was somehow at the bottom of it. He helped."

"No," said Jenny, quietly, "he was not, I am sure. There is some mystery there that you ought to probe to the bottom."

"That will do," he said, sharply, and she noticed that there was a peculiar startled look in her brother's eyes. "Now listen to me. You will pack up your things. Begin to-night. Everything must be ready by mid-day to-morrow."

"Yes, dear," she said, meekly. "Are you going to send me away?"

"No, I am going to take you away. I cannot bear this life any longer."

"Then we leave here?"

"Yes, at once."

"Have you sold the place?"

"Bah! Who could buy it?"

"But your patients, Pierce?"

"There is another man within two miles. There, don't talk to me."

"Won't you confide in me, Pierce?" said Jenny, quickly. "I can't believe that we are going because of what has just happened. You must have heard some news."

He frowned, and was silent.

"Very well, dear," she said, meekly. "I am glad we are going, for I believe you will try and trace out poor Kate."

"A fly will be here at mid-day," he said, without appearing to hear her words, and her eyes flashed, for all told her that she was right and that the sudden departure was not due to the encounter with Claud. But that meeting had sealed his lips in anger, just when he had reached home full of eagerness to confide in his sister that he had at last obtained a slight clew to Kate's whereabouts.

For he had been summoned to the village inn to attend a fly-driver, who had been kicked by his horse. The man was a stranger, and the injury was so slight that he was able to drive himself back to his place, miles away. But in the course of conversation, while his leg was being dressed, he had told the Doctor that he once had a curious fare in that village, and he detailed Garstang's proceedings, ending by asking Leigh if he knew who the lady was.

Chapter Thirty Four

"Here! Hi! Hold hard!"

Pierce Leigh paid no heed to the hails which reached his ears as he was crossing Bedford Square one morning; but he stopped short and turned angrily when a hand was laid heavily upon his shoulder, to find himself face to face with Claud Wilton, who stood holding out his hand.

"I saw you staring up at Uncle Robert's old house, but it's of no use to look there."

"What do you mean, sir?" said Leigh sternly.

"Get out! You know. Well, aren't you going to shake hands?"

There was something so frank and open in the young man's look and manner that Leigh involuntarily raised his hand, and before a flash of recollection could telegraph his second intent it was seized and wrung, vigorously.

"That's better, Doctor," cried Claud. "How are you?"

"Oh, very well," said Pierce shortly.

"Well, you don't look it. No, no, don't give a fellow the cold shoulder like that. I say, I came ever so long ago and called on the new people here, for I thought perhaps she might have been to her old home, but it was only a fancy. No go; she hadn't been there."

"You will excuse me, Mr Wilton," said Pierce, coldly; "I am busy this morning—a patient. I wish you good day."

"No, you don't. I've had trouble enough to find you, so no cold shoulder, please. It's no good, for I won't lose sight of you now. I say: it was mean to cut away from Northwood like you did."

"Will you have the goodness to point out which road you mean to take, Mr Wilton," said Leigh, wrathfully, "and then I can choose another?"

"No need, Doctor; your road's my road, and I'll stick to you like a 'tec'."

Leigh's eyes literally flashed.

"There, it's of no use for you to be waxy, Doctor, because it won't do a bit of good. I've got a scent like one of my retrievers; and I've run you down at last."

"Am I to understand then, sir, that you intend to watch me?" said Leigh, sternly.

"That's it. Of course I do. I've been at it ever since you left the old place. When I make up my mind to a thing I keep to it—stubborn as pollard oak."

"Indeed," said Leigh, sarcastically; "and now you have found me, pray what do you want?"

"Jenny!" said Claud, with the pollard oak simile in voice and look.

"Confound your insolence, sir!" cried Leigh, fiercely. "How dare you speak of my sister like that?"

"'Cause I love her, Doctor, like a man," and there was a slight quiver in the speaker's voice; but his face was hard and set, and when he spoke next his words sounded firm and stubborn enough. "I told her so, and I told you so; and whether she'll have me some day, or whether she won't, it's all the same, I'll never give her up. She's got me fast."

In spite of his anger, Leigh could not help feeling amused, and Claud saw the slight softening in his features, and said quickly: "I say, tell me how she is."

"My sister's health is nothing to you, sir, and I wish you good morning."

He strode on, but Claud took step for step with him, in spite of his anger.

"It's of no use, Doctor, and you can't assault me here in London. I shall find out where you live, so you may just as well be civil. Tell me how she is."

Leigh made no reply, but walked faster.

"Her health nothing to me," said Claud, in a low, quick way. "You don't know; and I shan't tell you, because you wouldn't believe, and would laugh at me. I say, how would you like it if someone treated you like this about Kate?"

"Silence, sir! How dare you!" thundered Leigh, facing round sharply and stopping short.

"Don't shout, Doctor; it will make people think we're rowing, and collect a crowd. But I say, that was a good shot; had you there. Haven't found her yet, then?"

"My good fellow, will you go your way, and let me go mine?"

"In plain English, Doctor, no, I won't; and if you knock me down I'll get up again, put my hands in my pockets, and follow you wherever you go. I shan't hit out again, though I am in better training and can use my fists quicker than, you can, and I've got the pluck, too, as I could show you. Do just what you like, call me names or hit me, but I shan't never forget you're Jenny's brother. Now, I say, don't be a brute to a poor fellow. It ain't so much of a sin to love the prettiest, dearest, little girl that ever breathed."

"Will you be silent?"

"Oh, yes, if you'll talk to a fellow. You might be a bit more feeling, seeing you're in the same boat."

"You insufferable cad!" cried Leigh, furiously.

"Yes, that's it. Quite right—cad; that's what I am, but I'm trying to polish it off, Doctor. I say, tell me how she is. She was so bad."

"My sister has quite recovered."

"Hooray!" cried Claud, excitedly. "But, I say—the ankle. How is it?"

"Look here, my good fellow, you must go. I will not answer your questions. Are you mad or an idiot?"

"Both," said Claud, coolly. "I say, you know, about that ankle. I believe you were so savage that night that you kicked it and broke it."

"What!" cried Leigh, excitedly. "My good fellow, what do you take me for?"

"Her brother, with an awful temper. Her father would not treat me like you do, if he was alive. It was a cowardly, cruel act for a man to do."

"You are quite mistaken, sir," said Leigh, coldly, as he wondered to himself that he should be drawn out like this. "My sister was unfortunate enough to sprain her ankle."

"Glad of it," said Claud, bluntly. "I was afraid it was your doing, and whenever I see you it sets my monkey up and makes me want to kick you. Well, you've told me how she is, and that's some pay for all my hunting about in town. I say, there's another chap down at Northwood stepped into your shoes already. The mater has had him in for the guv'nor's gout. He caught a cold up here with the hunting for Kate. It turned to gout, and I've had all the hunting to do. Now you and I will join hands and run her down."

Leigh made an angry gesture, which was easy enough to interpret—"How am I to get rid of this insolent cad?"

Claud laughed.

"You can't do it," he said. "I say, Doctor, sink the pride, and all that sort of thing. It's of no use to refuse help from a fellow you don't like, if he's in earnest and means well. Now, just look here. 'Pon my soul, it's the truth. Kate Wilton has got a hundred and fifty thou., and your sister hasn't got a penny. I'm not such a fool as you think, for I can read you like a book. You were gone on Cousin Kate long before you were asked to our house, and you'd give your life to find her; and, mind, I don't believe it's for the sake of her money. Well, I'm doing all I can to find her, and have been ever since you came away. Why? I'll tell you. Because it will please little Jenny, who about worships you, though you don't deserve it. And I tell you this, Doctor: if I had found her I'd have come and told you straight—if I could have found you, for Jenny's sake."

Leigh looked at him fixedly, trying hard to read the young man's face, but there was no flinching, no quivering of eyelid, or twitch about the lips. Claud gazed at him with a straightforward, dogged look which carried with it conviction.

"Look here," sud Claud, "I haven't found out where she is."

"Indeed?" said Leigh, guardedly.

"But I've found out one thing."

With all the young doctor's mastery of self, he could not help an inquiring glance.

Claud saw it, and smiled.

"She did not go off with Harry Dasent I found out that."

Leigh remained silent.

"Ara now look here. I've gone over it all scores of times, trying to think out where she can be, and that there's some relation or friend she bolted off to so as to get away from us, but I can't fix it on anyone, and go where I will, from our cousins the Morrisons down to old Garstang—who's got the guv'nor under has thumb, and could sell us up to-morrow if he liked—I can't get at it. But the scent seems to be most toward old Garstang, and I mean to try back there. The guv'nor said it was his doing, to help Harry Dasent, but that's all wrong. Those two hate one another like poison, and I can't make out any reason which would set Garstang to work to get her away. He'd do it like a shot to get her money, but he can't touch that, for I've read the will again. Nobody but her husband can get hold of that bit of booty, and I wish you may get it. I do, 'pon my soul. Still, I'm growing to think more and more that foxy Garstang's the man."

They had been walking steadily along side by side while this conversation was going on, and at last, fully convinced that Claud would not be shaken off, and even if he were would still watch him, Leigh walked straight on to his new home, and stopped short at a door whereon was a new brass plate, while the customary red bull's-eyes were in the lamp like danger signals to avert death and disease—the accidents of life's great railway.

"Now, Mr Wilton," he said, shortly, "you have achieved your purpose and tracked me home."

"And no thanks to you," said Claud, with one of his broad grins. "Won't ask me in, I suppose?"

"No, sir, I shall not."

"All right I didn't expect you would. Of course I should have found you out some time from the directories."

"My name is not in them, sir."

"Oh, but it soon would be, Doctor. I say, shall you tell her you have seen me?"

"For cool impudence, Mr Claud Wilton," said Leigh, by way of answer, "I have never seen your equal."

"'Tisn't impudence, Doctor," said Claud, earnestly; "it's pluck and bull-dog. I haven't been much account, and I don't come up to what you think a fellow should be."

"You certainly do not," said Leigh, unable to repress a smile.

"I know that, but I've got some stuff in me, after all, and when I take hold I don't let go."

He gave Leigh a quick nod, and thrusting his hands into his pockets, walked right on, without looking back, Leigh watching him till he turned a corner, before taking out a latch-key and letting himself into the house.

"The devil does not seem so black as he is painted, after all," he said, as he wiped his feet, and at the sound Jenny, quite without crutches, came hurrying down the stairs.

"Oh, Pierce, dear, have you been to those people in Bedford Street? They've been again twice, and I told them you'd gone."

"Ugh!" ejaculated Leigh. "What a head I have! Someone met me on the way, and diverted my thoughts. I'll go at once."

And he hurried out.

Chapter Thirty Five

It was a splendid grand piano whose tones rang, through the house, and brought poor Becky, with her pale, anaemic, tied-up face, from the lower regions, to stand peering round corners and listening till the final chords of some sonata rang out, when she would dart back into hiding, but only to steal up again as slowly and cautiously as a serpent, and thrust out her head from the gloom which hung forever upon the kitchen stairs, when Kate's low, sweet voice was heard singing some sad old ballad, a favourite of her father's, one which brought up the happy past, and ended often enough in the tears dropping silently upon the ivory keys.

Such a song will sometimes draw tears from many a listener; the melody, the words, recollections evoked, the expression given by the singer, all have their effect; and perhaps it was a memory of the baker (or milkman) which floated into poor, timid, shrinking Becky, for almost invariably she melted into tears.

"She says it's like being in heaven, ma'am," said Sarah Plant, giving voice upstairs to her child's strained ideas of happiness. "And really the place don't seem like the same, for, God bless you! you have made us all so happy here."

Kate sighed, for she did not share the happy feeling. There were times when her lot seemed too hard to bear. Garstang was kindness itself; he seemed to be constantly striving to make her content. Books, music, papers, fruit, and flowers—violets constantly as soon as he saw the brightening of her eyes whenever he brought her a bunch. Almost every expressed wish was gratified. But there was that intense longing for communion with others. If she could only have written to poor, amiable, faithful Eliza or to Jenny Leigh, she would have borne her imprisonment better; but she had religiously studied her new guardian's wishes upon that point, yielding to his advice whenever he reiterated the dangers which would beset their path if James Wilton discovered where she was.

"As it is, my dear child," he would say again and again, "it is sanctuary; and I'm on thorns whenever I am absent, for fear you should be tempted by the bright sunshine out of the gloom of this dull house, be seen by one or other of James Wilton's emissaries, and I return to find the cage I have tried so hard to gild, empty—the bird taken away to another kind of captivity, one which surely would not be so easy to bear."

"No, no, no; I could not bear it!" she cried, wildly. "I do not murmur. I will not complain, guardian; but there are times when I would give anything to be out somewhere in the bright open air, with the beautiful blue sky overhead, the soft grass beneath my feet, and the birds singing in my ears."

"Yes, yes, I know, my poor dear child," he said, tenderly. "It is cruelly hard upon you, but what can I do? I am waiting and hoping that James Wilton on finding his helplessness will become more open to making some kind of reasonable terms. I am sure you would be willing to meet him."

"To meet him again? Oh, no, I could not. The thought is horrible," she cried. "He seems to have broken faith so, after all his promises to my dying father."

"He has," said Garstang, solemnly; "but you misunderstand me; I did not mean personally meet him, but in terms, which would be paying so much money—in other words, buying your freedom."

"Oh, yes, yes," she cried, wildly, "at any cost. It is as you said one evening, guardian; I am cursed by a fortune."

"Cursed indeed, my dear. But there, try and be hopeful and patient, and we will have more walks of an evening. Only to think of it, our having to steal out at night like two thieves, for a dark walk in Russell Square sometimes. I don't wonder that the police used to watch us."

"If I could only write a few letters, guardian!"

"Yes, my dear, if you only could. I cannot say to you, do not, only lay the case before you once again."

"Yes, yes, yes," she said, hastily wiping away a few tears. "I am very, very foolish and ungrateful; but now that's all over, and I am going to be patient, and wait for freedom. I am far better off than many who are chained to a sick bed."

"No," he said, gently, shaking his head at her; "far worse off. Sickness brings a dull lassitude and indifference to external things. The calm rest of the bedroom is welcome, and the chamber itself the patient's little world. You, my dear, are in the full tide of life and youth, with all its aspirations, and must suffer there, more. But there; I am working like a slave to settle a lot of business going through the courts; and as soon as I can get it over we will take flight somewhere abroad, away from the gilded cage, out to the mountains and forests, where you can tire me out with your desires to be in the open air."

"I—I don't think I wish to leave England," she said, hesitatingly, and with the earnest far-off look in her eyes that he had seen before.

"Well, well, we will find some secluded place by the lakes, where we are not likely to be found out, and where the birds will sing to you. And, here's a happy thought, Kate, my child—you shall have some fellow prisoners."

"Companions?" she said, eagerly.

"Yes, companions," he replied, with a smile; "but I meant birds—canaries, larks—what do you say to doves? They make charming pets."

"No, no," she said, hastily; "don't do that, Mr Garstang. One prisoner is enough."

He bowed his head.

"You have only to express your wishes, my child," he said.—"Then you are going to try and drive away the clouds?"

"Oh, yes, I am going to be quite patient," she said, smiling at him; and she placed her hands in his.

"Thank you," he said, gently; and for the first time he drew her nearer to him, and bent down to kiss her forehead—the slightest touch—and then dropped her hands, to turn away with a sigh.

And the days wore on, with the prisoner fighting hard with self, to be contented with her lot. She practiced hard at the piano, and studied up the crabbed Gothic letters of the German works in one of the cases. Now and then, too, she sang about the great, gloomy house, but mostly to stop hurriedly on finding that she had listeners, attracted from the lower regions.

But try how she would to occupy her thoughts, she could not master those which would bring a faint colour to her cheeks. For ever and again the calm, firm countenance of Pierce Leigh would intrude itself, and the colour grew deeper, as she felt that there was something strange in all this, especially when he of whom she thought had never, by word or look, given her cause to think that he cared for her. And yet, in her secret heart, she felt that he did. And what would he think of her? He could not know anything of her proceedings, but little of her reasons for fleeing from her uncle's care.

Chapter Thirty Six

The memories of her slight friendship with the Leighs—slight in the rareness of their meetings—grew and grew as the days passed on, till Kate Wilton found herself constantly thinking of the brother and sister she had left at Northwood. Jenny's bright face was always obtruding itself, seeming to laugh from the pages of the dull old German book over which she pored; and it became a habit in her solitary life to sit and dream and think over it, as it slowly seemed to change; the merry eyes grew calm and grave, the broad forehead broader, till, though the similarity was there, it was the face of the brother, and she would close the book with a startled feeling of annoyance, feeling ready to upbraid herself for her want of modesty—so she put it—in thinking so much of one of whom she knew so little.

At such times she began to suffer from peculiar little nervous fits of irritation, which were followed by long dreamy thoughts which troubled her more than ever, respecting what the Leighs would think of her flight.

Music, long talks with Sarah Plant, efforts to try and draw out poor Becky, everything she could think of to take her attention and employ her mind, were tried vainly. The faces of the brother and sister would obtrude more and more, as her nervous fretfulness increased, and rapidly now the natural struggle against her long imprisonment increased.

She tried hard to conceal it from Garstang, and believed that he did not notice it, but it was too plain. Her efforts to appear cheerful and bright at breakfast time and when he came back at night, grew forced and painful; and under his calm smiling demeanour and pleasant chatty way of talking to her about current events, he was bracing himself for the encounter which he knew might have to take place at any moment.

It was longer than he anticipated, but was suddenly sprung upon him one evening after an agonising day, when again and again Kate had had to fight hard to master the fierce desire to get away from the terrible solitude which seemed to crush her down.

She knew that she was unwell from the pressure of her solitary life upon her nerves; the thoughts which troubled her magnified themselves; and now with terrible force came the insistent feeling that she had behaved like a weak child in not bravely maintaining her position at her uncle's house, and forcing him to fulfill his duty of protector to his brother's child.

"Is it too late? Am I behaving like a child now?" she asked herself, and at last with a wild outburst of excitement she determined that her present life must end.

She had calmed down a little just before Garstang returned that evening, and the recollection of his chivalrous treatment and fatherly attention to her lightest wants made her shrink from declaring that in spite of everything she must have some change; for, as she had told herself in her fit of excitement that afternoon, if she did not she would go mad.

She was very quiet during dinner, and he carefully avoided interrupting the fits of thoughtfulness in which from time to time she was plunged, but an hour later, when he came after her to the library from his glass of wine, he saw that her brows were knit and that the expected moment had come.

"Tired, my dear?" he said, as he subsided into his easy chair.

"Very, Mr Garstang," she said, quickly; and the excited look in her eyes intensified.

"Well, I don't like parting from you, my child," he said; "I have grown so used to your bright conversation of an evening, and it is so restful to me, but I must not be selfish. Go to bed when you feel so disposed. It is the weather, I think. The glass is very low."

"No," said Kate quickly, "it is not that; it is this miserable suspense which is preying upon me. Oh, guardian, guardian, when is all this dreadful life of concealment to come to an end?"

"Soon, my child, soon. But try and be calm; you have been so brave and good up to now; don't let us run risks when we are so near success."

"You have spoken to me like that so often, and—and I can bear it no longer. I must, at any risk now, have it put an end to."

"Ah!" he sighed, with a sad look; "I am not surprised to hear you talk so. You have done wonders. I would rather have urged you to be patient a little longer, my dear, but I agree with you; it is more than a bright young girl can be expected to bear. I have noticed it, though you have made such efforts to conceal it; the long imprisonment is telling upon your health, and makes you fretful and impatient."

"And I have tried so hard not to be," she cried, full of repentance now.

"My poor little girl, yes, you have," he said, reaching forward to take and pat her hand. "Well, give me a few hours to think what will be best to do, and then we will decide whether to declare war against James Wilton and cover ourselves with the shield of the law, or go right away for a change. You will give me a few hours, my dear, say till this time to-morrow?"

"Oh, yes," she said, with a sigh of relief. "Pray forgive me; I cannot help all this."

"I know, I know," he said, smiling. "By the way, to-morrow is my birthday; you must try and celebrate it a little for me."

She looked at him wonderingly.

"I mean, make Sarah Plant prepare an extra dinner, and I will bring home plenty of fruit and flowers; and after dinner we will discuss our plans and strike for freedom. Ah, my dear, it will be a great relief to me, for I have been growing very, very anxious about you. Too tired to give me a little music?"

"No, indeed, no," she said eagerly. "Your words have given me more relief than I can tell."

"That's right," he said, "but to be correct, I ought to ask you to read to me, to be in accord with the poem. But no, let it be one of my favourite songs, and in that way,

"'The night shall be filled with music,
    And the cares which infest the day
Shall fold their tents like the Arabs,
    And as silently steal away.'"

"Longer than I expected," said Garstang, as she left him that night for her own room. "Now let us see."

In accordance with his wish, Kate tried to quell the excitement within her breast by entering eagerly into the preparations for the evening's repast, but the next day passed terribly slowly, and she uttered a sigh of relief when the hands of the clock pointed to Garstang's hour of returning.

He came in, smiling and content, laden with flowers and fruit, part of the former taking the shape of a beautiful bouquet of lilies, which he handed to her with a smile.

"There," he cried; "aren't they sweet? I believe, after all, that Covent Garden is the best garden in the world. I'm as pleased as a child over my birthday. Here, Mrs Plant, take this fruit, and let us have it for dessert."

The housekeeper came at his call, and smiled as she took the basket he had brought in his cab, shaking her head sadly as she went down again.

"Hah!" ejaculated Garstang; "and I must have an extra glass of wine in honour of the occasion. It is all right, my dear," he whispered, with a great show of mystery. "Plans made, cut and dried. We'll have them over with the dessert."

Kate gave him a grateful look, and took up and pressed her bouquet to her lips, while Garstang went to a table drawer and took out a key.

"You have never seen the wine cellar, my dear. Come down with me. It is capitally stored, but rather wasted upon me."

He went into the hall and lit a chamber candle, returning directly.

"Ready?" he said, as she followed him down the dark stairs to the basement, Becky being seen for a moment flitting before them into the gloom, just as Garstang stopped at a great iron-studded door, and picked up a small basket from a table on the other side of the passage.

The door was unlocked, and opened with a groan, and Garstang handed his companion the candlestick.

"Don't you come in," he said; "the sawdust is damp, and young ladies don't take much interest in bottles of wine. But they are interesting to middle-aged men, my dear," he continued as he walked in, his voice sounding smothered and dull. Then came the chink of a bottle, which he placed in the wine basket, and he went on to a bin farther in.

"Don't come," he cried; "I can see. That's right. Our party to-night is small," and he came out with the two bottles he had fetched, stamped the sawdust off his feet, re-locked the door, and led the way upstairs, conveying the wine into the dining-room.

Ten minutes later they were seated at the table, and Garstang opened the bottle of champagne he had fetched himself.

"There, my dear," he said; "you must drink my health on this my birthday," and in spite of her declining, he insisted. "Oh, you must not refuse," he said. "And, as people say, it will do you good, for you really are low and in need of a stimulus."

The result was that she did sip a little of the sparkling wine, with the customary compliments, and the dinner passed off pleasantly enough. At last she rose to go.

"I will not keep you long, my dear," he said. "Just my customary glass of claret, and by that time my thoughts will be in order, and I can give you my full news."

Kate went into the library, growing moment by moment more excited, and trying hard to control her longing to hear Garstang's plans, which were to end the terrible life of care. It seemed as if he would never come, and he did not until some time after the housekeeper had brought in the tea things and urn.

"At last," she said, drawing a deep breath full of relief, for there was a step in the hall, the dining-room door was heard to close, and directly after Garstang entered, and she involuntarily rose from her seat, feeling startled by her new guardian's manner, though she could not have explained the cause.

"I have been growing so impatient," she said hastily, as he came to where she stood.

"Not more so than I," he said; and she fancied for the moment that there was a strange light in his eyes.

But she drove away the thought as absurd.

"Now," she cried; "I am weary with waiting. You have devised a way of ending this terrible suspense?"

"I have," he said, taking her hands in his; and she resigned them without hesitation.

"Pray tell me then, at once. What will you do?"

"Make you my darling little wife," he whispered passionately; and he clasped her tightly in his arms.

Chapter Thirty Seven

For a few moments Kate Wilton was passive in Garstang's arms. The suddenness of the act—the surprise, stunned her, and his words seemed so impossible that she could not believe her hearing. Then horror and revulsion came; she knew it was the truth, and like a flash it dawned upon her that all that had gone before, the chivalrous behaviour, the benevolence and paternal tenderness, were the clever acting of an unscrupulous man— the outcome of plans and schemes, and for what? To obtain possession of the great fortune by which she felt more than ever that she was cursed.

With a faint cry of horror she thrust him back with both hands upon his breast, and struggled wildly to escape from his embrace.

But the effort was vain; he clasped her tightly once again, in spite of her efforts, and covered her face, her neck, her hair, with his kisses.

"Silly, timid little bird!" he whispered, as he held her there, horrified and panting; "what ails you? The first kisses, of course. There, don't be so foolish, my darling child; they are the kisses of him who loves you, and who is going to make you his wife. Come, have I not been tender and patient, and all that you could wish, and is not this an easy solution of the difficulties by which you are surrounded?"

"Mr Garstang, loose me, I insist!" she cried. "How dare you treat me so!"

"I have told you, my beautiful darling. Come, come, be sensible; surely the love of one who has worshipped you from the first time he met you is not a thing to horrify you. Am I so old and repulsive, that you should go on like this? Only a few hours ago you were pressing my hands, holding your face to mine for my kisses; while now that I declare myself you begin struggling like a newly-captured bird. Why, Kate, my darling, I am talking to you like a poetic lover in a sentimental play. Really, dry lawyer as I am, I did not know that I could rise to such a flow of eloquence. Yes, pet, and you are acting too. There, that is enough for appearances, and there is no one to see, so let's behave like two sensible matter-of-fact people. Come and sit down here."

"I wish to go—at once," she cried, striving hard to be firm, feeling as she did that everything, in her hopeless state, depended upon herself.

"We'll talk about that quietly, when you have seated yourself. No—you will not?" he cried playfully. "Then you force me to show you that you must," and raising her in his arms, he bore her quickly to the couch, and sat beside her, pinioning her firmly in his grasp.

"There," he said, "man is the stronger in muscles, and woman must obey; but woman is stronger in the silken bonds with which she can hold man, and then he obeys."

She sat there panting heavily, ceasing her struggles, as she tried to think out her course of action, for she shrank from shrieking aloud for help, and exposing her position to the two women in the house.

"That's better," he said; "now you are behaving sensibly. Don't pretend to be afraid of me. Now listen—There, sit still; you cannot get away. If you cry out not a sound could reach the servants, for I have sent them to bed; and if a dozen men stood here and shouted together their voices could not be heard through curtains, shutters, and double windows. There, I am not telling you this to frighten you, only to show you your position."

She turned and gazed at him wildly, and then dragged her eyes away in despair as he said, caressingly.

"How beautiful you are, Kate! That warm colour makes you more attractive than ever, and tells me that all this is but a timid girl's natural holding back from the embraces of the man whom she has enslaved. There is no ghastly pallor, your lips are not white, and you do not turn faint, but are strong and brave in your resistance; so now let's talk sense, little wifie. You fancy I have been drinking; well, I have had a glass or two more than usual, but I am not as you think, only calm and quiet and ready to talk to you about what you wished."

"Another time—to-morrow. Mr Garstang, I beg of you; pray let me go to my own room now."

"To try the front door on the way, and seek to do some foolish thing? There, you see I can read your thoughts, my darling. So far from having exceeded, I am too sensible for mat; but you could not get out of the house, for the door is locked, and I have the key here. There; to begin; you would like to leave here to-night?"

"Yes, yes, Mr Garstang; pray let me go."

"Where? You would wander about the streets, a prey to the first ruffian who meets you. To appeal to the police, who would not believe your story;

and even if they did, where would you go? To-morrow back to Northwood, to be robbed of your fortune; to go straight to that noble cousin's arms. No, no, that would not do, dear. Now, let's look the position in the face. I am double your age, my child. Well, granted; but surely I am not such a repellent monster that you need look at me like that I love you, my pretty one, and I am going to marry you at once. As my wife, you will be free from all persecution by your uncle. He will try to make difficulties, and refuse to sign papers, and do plenty of absurd things; but I have him completely under my thumb, and once you are my wife I can force him to give up all control of you and yours."

"To-morrow—to-morrow," she said, pleadingly, as she felt how hopeless it was to struggle. "I am sick and faint, Mr Garstang; pray, pray let me go to my room now."

"Not yet," he said playfully, and without relaxing his grasp; "there is a deal more to say. You have to make me plenty of promises, that you will act sensibly; and I want these promises, not from fear, but because you love me, dear. Silent? Well, I must tell you a little more. I made up my mind to this, my child, when I came to you that night. 'I'll marry her,' I said; 'it will solve all the difficulties and make her the happiest life.'"

"No, no, it is impossible, Mr Garstang," she cried. "There, you have said enough now. You must—you shall let me go. Is this your conduct towards the helpless girl who trusted you?"

"Yes," he said laughingly, "it is my conduct towards the helpless girl who trusted me; and it is the right treatment of one who cannot help herself."

"No," she cried desperately; "and so I trusted to you, believing you to be worthy of that trust."

"And so I am, dear; more than worthy. Kate, dearest, do you know that I am going to make you a happy woman, that I give you the devotion of my life? Every hour shall be spent in devising some new pleasure for you, in making you one of the most envied of your sex. I am older, but what of that? Perhaps your young fancy has strayed toward some hero whom your imagination has pictured; but you are not a foolish girl. You have so much common sense that you must see that your position renders it compulsory that you should have a protector."

"A protector!" she cried bitterly.

"Yes; I must be plain with you, unless you throw off all this foolish resistance. Come, be sensible. To-morrow, or the next day, we will be married, and then we can set the whole world at defiance."

"Mr Garstang, you are mad!" she cried, with such a look of repugnance in her eyes that she stung him into sudden rage.

"Mad for loving you?" he cried.

"For loving me!" she said scornfully. "No, it is the miserable love of the wretched fortune. Well, take it; only loose me now; let me go. You are a lawyer, sir, and I suppose you know what to do. There are pens and paper. Loose me, and go and sit down and write; I promise you I will not try to leave the room; lock the door, if you like, till you have done writing."

"It is already locked," he said mockingly; and he smiled as he saw her turn pale.

"Very well," she said calmly; "then I cannot escape. Go and write, and I will sign it without a murmur. I give everything to you; only let me go. It is impossible that we can ever meet again."

"Indeed!" he said, laughing. "Foolish child, how little you know of these things! Suppose I do want your money; do you think that anything I could write, or you could sign, would give it me without this little hand? Besides, I don't want it without its mistress—my mistress—the beautiful little girl who during her stay here has taught me that there is something worth living for. There, there, we are wasting breath. What is the use of fighting against the inevitable? Love me as your husband, Kate. I am the same man whom you loved as your guardian. There, I want to be gentle and tender with you. Why don't you give up quietly and say that you will come with me like a sensible little girl, and be my wife?"

"Because I would sooner die," she said, firmly.

"As young ladies say in old-fashioned romances," he cried mockingly. "There, you force me to speak very plainly to you. I must; and you are wise enough to see that every word is true. Now listen. You have not many friends; I may say I, your lover, am the only one; but when you took that step with me one night, eloping from your bedroom window, placing yourself under my protection, and living here secluded with me in this old house for all these months, what would they say? Little enough, perhaps nothing; but there is a significant shrug of the shoulders which people give, and which means much, my child, respecting a woman's character. You see now that you must marry me."

"No," she said calmly; "I trusted myself to the guardianship of a man almost old enough to be my grandfather. He professed to be my father's friend, and I fled to him to save myself from insult. Will the world blame me for that, Mr Garstang?"

"Yes, the world will, and will not believe."

"Then what is the opinion of the world, as you term it, worth? Now, sir, I insist upon your letting me go to my room."

As she spoke, she struggled violently, and throwing herself back over the head of the couch made a snatch at the bell-pull, with such success that the smothered tones of a violent peal reached where they were.

Garstang started up angrily, and taking advantage of her momentary freedom, Kate sprang to the door and turned the key, but before she could open it he was at her side.

"You foolish child!" he said, in a low angry voice; "how can you act—"

Half mad with fear, she struck at him, the back of her hand catching him sharply on the lips, and before he could recover from his surprise, she had passed through the door and fled to her room, where she locked and bolted herself in, and then sank panting and sobbing violently upon her knees beside her bed.

Chapter Thirty Eight

"Yes; what is it?"

Kate Wilton raised her head from where it rested against the bed as she crouched upon the floor, and gazed round wonderingly, conscious that someone had called her by name, but with everything else a blank.

There was a tapping at the door.

"Yes, yes," said Kate; and she hurried across the room.

"If you please, ma'am, breakfast is waiting, and master's compliments, and will you come down?"

"Yes; I'll be down directly," she cried; and then she pressed her hands to her head and tried to think, but for some moments all was strange and confused, and she wondered why she should have been sleeping there upon the floor, dressed as she was on the previous night, the flowers she had worn still at her breast.

The flowers crushed and bruised!

They acted as the key to the closed mental door, which sprang open, and in one flash of the light which flooded her brain she saw all that had passed before she fled there, and then knelt by the bedside, praying for help, and striving to evolve some means of escape, till, utterly exhausted, nature would bear no more, and she fell asleep, to be awakened by the coming of the housekeeper.

And she had told her that she would be down directly. What should she do?

Hurrying to the bell, she rang, and then waited with beating heart for the woman's footsteps, which seemed an age in coming; but at last there was a tap at the door.

"Did you ring, ma'am?"

"Yes; I am unwell I am not coming down."

"Can I do anything for you, ma'am?"

"No."

Kate stood thinking for a few moments with her hands to her throbbing brows, for her head was growing confused again, and mental darkness seemed to be closing in; but once more the light came, and she tore the crushed flowers from her breast, put on her bonnet and mantle, and then, hurriedly, her gloves.

She felt that she must get away from that house at once; she could not determine then where she would go; that would come afterwards; she could not even think then of anything but escape.

Her preparations took but a few minutes, and then she went to the door and listened.

All was still in the house as far as she could make out, and timidly unfastening the door, she softly opened it, to look out on the great landing, but started back, for in the darkest corner there was a figure.

Only one of the statues, the one just beyond the great curtain over the archway leading to the little library; and gaining courage and determination, she stepped out, and cautiously looked down into the sombre hall.

Everything was still there, and she could just see that the dining-room door was shut, a sign that Garstang was within, at his solitary breakfast.

Her breath came and went as if she had been running, and she pressed her hand upon her side to try and subdue the heavy throbbing of her heart.

If she could only reach the front door unheard, and steal out!

She drew back, for there was a faint rattling sound, as of a cover upon a dish; then footsteps, and as she drew back she could see the housekeeper cross the hall with a small tray, enter the dining-room, whose door closed behind her, and the next minute come out, empty-handed, re-cross the hall, and disappear. Then her voice rose to where Kate stood, as she called to her daughter.

Garstang must be in the dining-room, at his breakfast; and, desperate now in her dread, Kate drew a deep breath, walked silently over the soft carpet to the head of the stairs, and with her dress rustling lightly, descended, reached the hall, seeing that the door appeared to be in its customary state, and the next moment she would have been there, trying to let herself out, when she was arrested by a faint sound, half-ejaculation, half-sigh, and turning quickly, there, upon the staircase, straining over the balustrade to watch her, was Becky, with the sunlight from a stained-glass window full upon her bandaged face.

Making an angry gesture to her to go back, Kate was in the act of turning once more when a firm hand grasped her wrist, an arm was passed about her waist, and with a sudden drag she was drawn into the library and the door closed, Garstang standing there, stern and angry, between her and freedom.

"Where are you going?" he cried.

"Away from here," she said, meeting his eyes bravely. "This is no place for me, Mr Garstang. Let me pass, sir."

"That is no answer, my child," he said. "Where are you going? What are your plans?"

She made no answer, but stepped forward to try and pass him; but he took her firmly and gently, and forced her to sit down.

"As I expected, you have no idea—you have no plans—you have nowhere to go; and yet in a fit of mad folly you would fly from here, the only place where you could take refuge; and why?"

"Because I have found that the man I believed in was not worthy of that trust."

"No; because in a maddening moment, when my love for you had broken bounds, I spoke out, prematurely perhaps, but I obeyed the dictates of my breast. But there, I am not going to deliver speeches; I only wish to make you understand fully what is your position and mine. I said a great deal last night, enough to have taught you much; above all, that our marriage is a necessity, for your sake as much as mine. No, no; sit still and be calm. We must both be so, and you must talk reasonably. Now, my dear, take off that bonnet and mantle."

She made no reply.

"Well, I will not trouble about that now. You will see the necessity after a few minutes. First of all, let me impress upon you the simple facts of your position here. In the first place, you are kept here by the way in which you have compromised yourself. Yes, you have; and if you drove me to it I should openly proclaim that you have been my mistress, and were striving to break our ties in consequence of a quarrel."

She made no reply, but her eyes seemed to blaze.

"Yes," he said, with a smile; "I understand your looks. I am a traitor, and a coward, and a villain; that is, I suppose, the interpretation from your point of view; but let me tell you there are thousands of men who would be ten times the traitor, coward and villain that you mentally call me, to win you and your smiles, as I shall."

He stood looking down at her with a proud look of power, and she involuntarily shrank back in her seat and trembled.

"In the second place," he continued, "I take it from your manner that you mean for a few days to be defiant, and that you will try to escape. Well, try if you like, and find how vain it is. I have you here, and in spite of everything I shall keep you safely. I will be plain and frank. For your fortune and for yourself I love you with a middle-aged man's strong love for a beautiful girl who has awakened in him passions that he thought were dead. You will try and escape? No, you will not; for now, for the first time, I shall really cage the lovely little bird I have entrapped. You will keep to your room, a prisoner, till you place your hands in mine, and tell me that you are mine whenever I wish. You will appeal to my servants? Well, appeal to them. You will try and escape by your window? Well, try. You must know by now that it opens over a narrow yard, and an attempt to descend from that means death; but there are ways of fastening such a window as that, and this will be done, for I want to live and love, and your death would mean mine."

He paused and looked down at her in calm triumph, but her firm gaze never left his, and her lips were tightly drawn together.

"I could appeal to your pity, but I will not now. I could tell you of my former loveless marriage, and my weary life with the wretched woman who entrapped me; but you will find all that out in time, and try to recompense me for the early miseries of my life, and for your cruel coldness now. There, I have nearly done. I have gambled over this, my child, and I have won, so far as obtaining my prize. To obtain its full enjoyment, I have treated you as I have since you have been here, during which time I have taught you to love me as a friend and father. I am going to teach you to love me now as a husband—a far easier task."

"No!" she cried, angrily. "I would sooner die."

"Spare your breath, my dear, and try and school yourself to the acceptance of your fate. Claud Wilton is in town, hunting for you, and do you think I will let that young scoundrel drag you into what really would be a degrading marriage? I would sooner kill him. Come, come, be sensible," he cried, speaking perfectly calmly, and never once attempting to lessen the distance between them. "I startled you last night. See how gentle and tender I am with you to-day. I love you too well to blame you in any way. I love you, I tell you; and I know quite well that the passion is still latent in your breast; but I know, too, that it will bud and blossom, and that some day you will wonder at your conduct toward one who has proved his love for you. I cannot blame myself, even if I have been driven to win you by a coup. Who would not have done the same, I say again? You have charmed me by your beauty, and by the beauties of your intellect; and once more I tell you gently and lovingly that you must now accept your fate, and look upon me as a friend, father, lover, husband, all in one. Kate, dearest, you shall not repent it, so be as gentle and kind to me as I am to you."

He ceased, and she sat there gazing at him fixedly still.

"Now," he said, changing his manner and tone, "we must have no more clouds between us. You need not shrink and begin beating your wings, little bird. I will be patient, and we will go on, if you wish it, where we left off last evening when you came here from the dining-room. I am guardian again until you have thought all this over, and are ready to accept the inevitable. We must not have you ill, and wanting the doctor."

A thrill ran through her, and as if it were natural to turn to him who came when she was once before sorely in need of help, she recalled the firm, calm face of Pierce Leigh; but a faint flush coloured her cheek, as if in shame for her thought.

Garstang saw the brightening of her face, and interpreted it wrongly.

"A means of escape from me?" he said. "What a foolish, childish thought! Too romantic for a woman of your strength of mind, Kate. No, I shall not let you leave me like that. There, you must be faint and hungry; so am I. Take off your things, and come and face your guardian at the table, in the old fashion. No? You prefer to go back to your room this morning? Well, let it be so. Only try and be sensible. It is so childish to let the servants be witnesses to such a little trouble as this. There, your head is bad, of course; and you altered your mind about going for a walk."

He opened the door for her to pass out, and then rang the bell.

"Mrs Plant answered the bell last night," he said, meaningly. "Poor woman, she had gone to bed, and came here in alarm; so she knows that you were taken ill and went to your room. I would not let her come and disturb you, as you were so agitated.—Ah, Mrs Plant, your mistress does not feel equal to staying down to breakfast. Go and get a tray ready, and take it up to her in her room."

The woman hurried to carry out Garstang's wishes, and Kate rose to her feet, while he drew back to let her pass.

"The front door is fastened," he said, with a quiet smile, "and there is no window that you can open to call for help. Even if you could, and people came to inquire what was the matter, a few words respecting the sick and delirious young lady upstairs would send them away. It is curious what a wholesome dread ordinary folk have of an illness being infectious. Will you come down to dinner, or sooner, dearest?" he said, sinking his voice to a whisper, full of tenderness. "I shall be here, and only too glad to welcome you when you come, sweet dove, with the olive branch of peace between us, and take it as the symbol of love."

A prisoner, indeed, and the chains seemed to fetter and weigh her down as, without a word, her eyes fixed and gazing straight before her, she walked by him into the hall, mastered the wild agonising desire to fling herself at the door and call for help, and went slowly to the stairs, catching sight of the pale bandaged face peering over the balustrade and then drawn back to disappear.

But as Kate saw it a gleam of hope shot through the darkness. Poor Becky—letters—appeals for help to Jenny Leigh. Could she not get a message sent by the hand of the strange-looking, shrinking girl?

She went on steadily up towards her room, without once turning her head, feeling conscious that Garstang was standing below watching her; but by the time she reached the first landing there was the sound of a faint cough and steps crossing to the dining-room, and she breathed more freely, and glanced downward as she turned to ascend the second flight.

The hall was vacant, and looking toward the doorway through which Becky had glided, she called to her in a low, excited whisper:

"Becky! Becky!"

But there was no reply, and hurrying up the rest of the way she followed the girl, entered the room into which she had passed, and found her standing in the attitude of one listening intently.

"Becky, I want to speak to you," she whispered; but the girl darted to a door at the other end, and was gliding through into the dressing-room, through which she could reach the staircase.

This time Kate was too quick for her, and caught her by the dress, the girl uttering a low moan, full of despair, and hanging away with all her might, keeping her face averted the while.

"Don't, don't do that," whispered Kate, excitedly. "Why are you afraid of me?"

"Let me go; oh! please let me go."

"Yes, directly," whispered Kate, still holding her tightly; "but please, Becky, I want you to help me. I am in great trouble, dear—great trouble."

"Eh?" said the girl, faintly, "you?"

"Yes, and I do so want help. Will you do something for me?"

"No, I can't," whispered the girl. "I'm no use; I oughtn't to be here; don't look at me, please; and pray, pray let me go."

"Yes, I will, dear; but you will help me. Come to my room when your mother has been."

The girl turned her white grotesque face, and stared at her with dilated eyes.

"You will, won't you?"

Becky shook her head.

"Not to help a poor sister in distress?" said Kate, appealingly.

"You ain't my sister, and I must go. If he knew I'd talked to you he'd be so cross."

With a sudden snatch the girl released her dress and fled, leaving Kate striving hard to keep back her tears, as she went on to the broad landing and reached her room, thinking of the little library and the account she had heard of the former occupant, who found life too weary for him, and had sought rest.

Her first impulse was to lock her door, but feeling that she had nothing immediate to fear, and that perhaps a display of acquiescence in Garstang's plans might help her to escape, she sat down to think, or rather try to think, for her brain was in a whirl, and thought crowded out thought before she had time to grasp one.

But she had hardly commenced her fight when there was a tap at the door, and Sarah Plant entered with a breakfast tray, looking smiling and animated.

"I'm so sorry, ma'am; but I've made you a very strong cup of tea, and your breakfast will do you good. There. Now let me help you off with your things."

"No, no, never mind now. Mrs Plant, will you do something to help me?"

"Of course, I will, ma'am. There isn't anything I wouldn't do for you."

"Why are you smiling at me in that way?"

"Me smiling, ma'am? Was I? Oh, nothing."

"I insist upon your telling me. Ah, you know what has taken place."

"Well, well, ma'am, please don't be angry with me for it. You did give the bell such a peal last night, you quite startled me."

"Then you do know everything?"

"Well, yes, ma'am; you see, I couldn't help it. Me and poor Becky always knew that you were to be the new missis here from the day you came."

"No, it is impossible. I must go away from here at once."

"Lor', my dear, don't you take it like that! Why, what is there to mind? Master is one of the dearest and best of men; and think what a chance it is for you, and what a home."

"Oh, silence; don't talk like that! I tell you it is impossible."

"Ah, that's because you're thinking about Master being a bit older than you are. But what of that? My poor dear man was twice as old as me, and he never had but one fault—he would die too soon."

"I tell you it is impossible, my good woman," cried Kate, imperiously. "I have been entrapped and deceived, and I call upon you, as a woman, to help me."

"Yes, ma'am, of course I'll help you."

"Ah! then wait here while I write a few lines to one of my father's old friends."

"A letter? Yes, ma'am; but if you please, Master said that all letters were to be taken to him."

"As they were before?" said Kate, with a light flashing in upon her clouded brain.

"Yes, ma'am; he said so a week or two before you came."

"Planned, planned, planned!" muttered Kate, despairingly.

"Yes, ma'am, and of course I must take them to him. You see, he is my master, and I will say this of him—a better and kinder master never lived. Oh, my dear, don't be so young and foolish. You couldn't do better than what he wishes, and make him happy, and yourself, too."

"Will you help me, woman, to get away from here? I will pay you enough to make you rich if you will," said Kate, desperately.

"I will do anything I can for you, ma'am, that isn't going against Master; of that you may be sure."

"Then will you post a couple of letters for me?" cried Kate, desperately.

"No, ma'am, please, I mustn't do that."

"Go away," cried Kate, fiercely now. "Leave me to myself."

"Oh, my dear, don't, pray, go on like that I know you're young, and the idea frightens you; but it isn't such a very dreadful thing to be married to a real good man."

Kate darted to the door, flung it open, and stood with flashing eyes, pointing outward.

"Oh, yes, ma'am, of course I'll go; but do, pray, take my advice. You see, you're bound to marry him now, and—"

The door was closed upon her, and Kate began to pace up and down, like some timid creature freshly awakened to the fact of its being caged, and grown desperate at the thought.

"Helpless, and a prisoner!" she groaned to herself. "What shall I do? Is there no way of escape?" And once more the thought of Jenny Leigh and her brother came to her mind, and the feeling grew stronger that she might find help there.

But it seemed impossible unless she could write and stamp a letter and throw it from the window, trusting to some one to pick it up and post it.

No; the idea seemed weak and vain, and she cast it from her, as she paced up and down, with her hands clasped and pressed to her throbbing breast.

"There is no help—no help!" she moaned, and then uttered a faint cry of alarm, for the door behind her was softly opened, and the idea that it was Garstang flashed through her brain as she looked wildly round.

Becky's white tied-up face was just thrust in, and the door held tightly to, as if about to act as a perpendicular guillotine and shave through her neck.

Chapter Thirty Nine

Kate uttered a gasp of relief on finding her fear needless, and darted towards the door, when, to her despair, the grotesque head was snatched back.

"Becky! Becky!" she cried piteously, as the door was closing; and she stood still, not daring to approach.

Her action had its effect, for the door was slowly pressed open again, and the bow of the washed-out cotton handkerchief which bandaged the woman's face gradually appeared, the ends, which stuck up like a small pair of horns, trembling visibly. Then by very small degrees the woman's forehead and the rest of the face appeared, with the eyes showing the white all round, as their owner gazed at the prisoner with her usual scared look intensified.

"Pray come in, Becky," said Kate, softly; and she drew back towards a chair, so as to try and inspire a little confidence.

The head was slowly shaken, and the door drawn once more tightly against the woman's long thin neck.

"Whatcher want?" she said, faintly.

"I want you to come in and talk to me," said Kate in a low, appealing tone. "I want you to help me."

"Dursn't."

"Yes, yes, you dare. Pray, pray don't say that I have no one to ask but you. Oh, Becky, Becky, I am so unhappy. If you have a woman's heart within your breast, have pity on me!"

"Gug!"

A spasm contracted the pallid face as a violent sob escaped from her lips, and the tears began to flow from the dilated eyes, and were accompanied by unpleasant sniffs.

"Don't make me cr-cr-cry, miss, please."

"No, no, don't cry, Becky dear, pray," whispered Kate, anxiously.

"You make me, miss—going on like that; and d-don't call me dear, please. I ain't dear to nobody; I'm a miserable wretch."

"I always pitied you, Becky, but you never would let me be kind to you."

"N-no, miss. It don't do no good. On'y makes me mis'rable."

"But I must be; I will be kind to you, Becky, and try and make you happy," whispered Kate.

"Tain't to be done, miss, till I die," said the woman, sadly; and then there was a triumphant light in her eyes, and her face lit up as she said more firmly, "but I'm going to be happy then."

"Yes, yes, and I'll try to make you happy while you live; but you will help me, dear?"

The poor creature shook her head.

"Yes, you will—I'm sure you will," pleaded Kate. "But pray come in."

"Dursn't, miss."

"But I am in such trouble, Becky."

"Yes, I know; he wants to marry you, and he's going to keep you locked up till he does. I know."

"Yes, yes; and I want to get away."

"But you can't," whispered the woman, and she withdrew her head, and Kate in her despair thought she had gone. But the head reappeared slowly. "Nobody watching," she whispered.

"I must go away, and you must help me, Becky," whispered Kate.

"It's no good. He won't let you, miss. But don't you marry him."

"Never!" cried Kate.

"Hush, or they'll hear you; and mother's siding with him, and going to help him. She says he's an angel, but he's all smooth smiles, and talks to you like a saint, but he's a horrid wretch."

"Yes, yes. But now listen to me."

"Yes, I'm a-listening, miss. It's all because you're so pretty and handsome, and got lots o' money, aintcher?"

"Yes, unhappily," sighed Kate.

"That's what he wants. He got all poor old master's money, and the house and furniture out of him."

"He did?" whispered Kate, excitedly.

"Yes, miss; I know. Mother says it's all nonsense, and that we ought to love him, because he's such a good man. But I know better. Poor old master used to tell me when I took him up his letters: 'Ah, Becky, my poor girl, you are disappointed and unhappy,' he says, 'but I'm more unhappy still. That man won't be satisfied till he has ground the last farthing out of me, and there's nothing left but my corpse.' I didn't believe him, and I said, 'Don't let him have it, sir.' 'Ah, Becky,' he says, 'I'm obliged; signed papers are stronger than iron chains,' he says, 'and he's always dragging at the end. But he shall have it all, and heavy pounds o' flesh at the end, and the bones too.' I didn't know what he meant, miss; and I didn't believe as anyone could be as unlucky as me. But I believed him at last, when I went to his room and found him dead on the floor; and then I knew he must be worse than I was, for I couldn't have done what he did."

"Becky," whispered Kate, fixing the trembling woman with her eyes, "I can understand how people who are very unhappy seek for rest in death. Do you wish to come here some morning, and find me lying dead?"

"Oh, miss!" cried the woman, excitedly, pushing the door more open; "don't, please don't you go and do a thing like that. You're too young and beautiful, and—oh, oh, oh! Please don't talk so; I can't abear it—pray!"

"Then help me, Becky, for I tell you I would sooner die."

"What, than marry him?"

"Yes, than marry this dreadful man."

"Then—then," whispered the woman, after withdrawing her head to gaze back, "I feel that I dursn't, and p'raps he'll kill me for it—not as I seem to mind much, and mother would soon get over it, for I ain't o' no use—but I think I will try and help you. You want to get away?"

In her wild feeling of joy and excitement, Kate sprang toward the door, and she would have flung her arms round the unhappy woman's neck. But before she could reach her the head was snatched back, and the fastening gave a loud snap, while when she opened it, Becky had disappeared and her mother was coming up the stairs to fetch the breakfast tray.

"And not touched a bit, my dear," said the housekeeper, with a reproachful shake of the head. "Now you must, you know; you must, indeed. And do let me advise you, my dear. Mr Garstang is such a good man, and so indulgent, and it's really naughty of you to be so foolish as to oppose his wishes."

Kate turned upon her with a look that astounded the woman, who stood with parted lips, breathless, while a piece of bread was broken from the loaf on the tray, and a cup of tea poured out and placed aside.

"Take away that tray," said Kate, imperiously; "and remember your place. Never presume to speak to me again like that."

"No, ma'am—certainly not, ma'am," said the woman, hastily. "I beg your pardon, ma'am, I am sure."

"Leave the room, and do not come again until I ring."

"My!" ejaculated the woman, as soon as she was on the landing, "to think of such a gentle-looking little thing being able to talk like that! P'raps master's caught a tartar now."

There was a gleam of hope, then, after all. Poor Becky was not the vacant idiot she had always appeared. Kate felt that she had made one friend, and trembling with eagerness she went to the writing-table and wrote quickly a few lines to Jenny Leigh, briefly explaining her position, and begging her to lay the matter before her brother and ask his help and advice.

This she inclosed and directed, and then sat gazing before her, conjuring the scene to follow at the cottage, and the indignation of Leigh. And as she thought, the warm blood tinged her pale cheeks once more, and she covered her face with her hands, to sit there sobbing for a few minutes before slowly tearing up the letter till the fragments were too small ever to be found and read by one curious to know their contents.

Gladly as she would have seen Pierce Leigh appear and insist upon her taking refuge with his sister, she felt that she could not send such an appeal to those who were comparative strangers; and though she would not own to it even to herself, she felt that there were other reasons why she could not write.

An hour of intense mental agony and dread passed, and she had to strive hard to keep down the terrible feeling of panic which nearly mastered her, and tempted her to rush down the stairs to try once more to escape, or to go to one of the front windows, throw it open, and shriek for help.

"It would be an act of madness," she sighed, as she recalled Garstang's words respecting the sick lady. "And they would believe him!" she cried, while the feeling of helplessness grew and grew as she felt how thoroughly she was in Garstang's power.

Then came the thought of her aunt and uncle, her natural protectors, and she determined to write to them. James Wilton would fetch her away at once, for he was her guardian; and surely now, she told herself, she was woman enough to insist upon proper respect being paid to her wishes. She could set at defiance any of her cousin's advances; and her conduct in leaving showed itself up in its strongest colours, as being cowardly—the act of a child.

With a fresh display of energy she wrote to her aunt, detailing everything, and bidding her—not begging—to tell her uncle to come to her rescue at once. But no sooner was the letter written than she felt that her aunt would behave in some weak, foolish way, and there would be delay.

She tore up that letter slowly, and after hiding the pieces, she sat there thinking again, with her brow wrinkled, and the look of agony in her face intensifying.

"I have right on my side. He is my guardian, and he dare not act otherwise than justly by me. I am no longer the weak child now."

And once more she took paper, and wrote this time to James Wilton himself, telling him that Garstang had lured her away by the promise of protection, but had shown himself in the vilest colours at last.

"He must—he shall protect me," she said, exultantly, and she hastily directed the letter.

But as she sat there with the letter in her hand, she shrank and trembled. For in vivid colours her imagination painted before her the trouble and persecution to which she would expose herself. She knew well enough what were James Wilton's aims, and that situated as he was, he would stand at nothing to gain them. It was in vain she told herself that anything would be preferable to staying there at John Garstang's mercy, the horror of rushing headlong back to her guardian, and the thoughts of his triumphant looks as he held her tightly once again, proved too much for her, and this letter was slowly torn up and the pieces hidden.

As she sat there, with every nerve on the rack, a strange feeling of faintness came over her, and she started up in horror at the idea of losing her senses, and being at this man's mercy. And as she walked hurriedly to and fro, trembling as she felt the faintness increasing, some relief came, for she grasped the fact that her faintness was due to want of food, and it was past mid-day.

There was the bread close at hand, though, and turning to it she began to crumble up the pieces and to eat, though it was only with the greatest difficulty that she accomplished her task.

But it had the required effect—the sensation of sinking passed off. And now she set herself the task of trying to think of some one among the very few friends she had known before her father's death to whom she could send for help; but there did not occur to her mind one to whom she could apply in such a strait. There were the people at the bank, and the doctor who had attended her father in his last illness, but they were comparatively such strangers that she shrank from writing to them; and at last, unnerved, and with her mind seeming to refuse to act, she sat there feeling that there was not a soul in the world whom she could trust but the Leighs. She could send to Jenny, who would, she knew, be up in arms at once; but there was her brother. She could not, she dared not, ask him; and it would be, she felt, asking him. It would be so interpreted if she wrote.

And then came the question which sent a shiver through her frame— what must he think of her, and would he come to her help as he would have done before she committed so rash an act?

Kate's weary ponderings were interrupted by a tap at the door, which produced a fit of trembling, and she glided to it to slip the bolt, which had hardly passed into its socket before the housekeeper's voice was heard.

"I beg your pardon, ma'am, but lunch is ready, and master would be glad to know if you are well enough to come down."

A stern negative was the reply, and for about a quarter of an hour she was undisturbed. Then came another tap, and the rattling of china and glass.

"If you please, ma'am, I've brought your lunch."

She hesitated for a few moments. The desire was strong to refuse to take anything, but she felt that if she was to keep setting Garstang at defiance till she could escape, she must have energy and strength. So, unwillingly enough, she unfastened the door, the housekeeper entered with a tray, and set it down upon the table.

"Can I bring you up anything more, ma'am, and would you like any wine?"

"No," was the abrupt answer, in tones that would bear no reply, and the woman went away, the door being fastened after her.

The lunch tray looked dainty enough, but it remained untouched for a time. A desperate resolve had come upon the prisoner, and once more seating herself, she wrote a piteous letter to Jenny, imploring help, directed it, and placed it ready for giving to poor Becky when she came again. Stamps she had none, but she had a little money, and doubtless the girl would dispatch her note in safety.

The desperate step taken, she felt more at ease, and feeling that her state of siege must last for a couple of days longer, she sat down and once more forced herself to eat, but she shrank from touching the water in the carafe, looking at it suspiciously, and preferring to partake of some that was in the room.

The tray was fetched in due time, and the housekeeper smiled her satisfaction; but she went off without a word, and Kate felt that she would go straight to Garstang and report that the lunch had been eaten.

She winced at this a little, but felt that it was inevitable, and feeling in better nerve she went to the door, which she had fastened, opened it a little, and stood there to watch for the coming of Becky.

But the hours glided by, and with a creeping sense of horror she saw the wintry evening coming rapidly on, and thought of the night.

Whenever a footstep was heard she was on the qui vive, but each time it was the mother. The daughter, who had before this seemed to be always gliding ghost-like about the place, was now invisible, and as Kate watched she saw the housekeeper light the hall jets and then descend to the kitchen region.

Twice over she shrank back and secured the door, for she heard Garstang cough slightly, and saw him cross the hall from library to dining-room, and in each case she let some minutes elapse before she dared open and peer out again. The last time it was to be aware of the fact that the dinner hour had come once more, and soon after the woman began to ascend the stairs, Kate retiring within and slipping the bolt, to stand and listen for the message she knew would be delivered.

"Master's compliments, and are you well enough to come down, ma'am?"

The brief negative sent the messenger down again, and the prisoner was left undisturbed for a few minutes, when there was the sound of a tray being brought to the door, but this time it was refused entrance.

Kate watched again eagerly now, feeling that in all probability Becky would try to see her while her mother was occupied in the dining-room, but the time passed on and there was no sign of her, and thoughts of desperate venturing to try and reach the front door attacked the listener, but only to be dismissed.

"It would only be to expose myself to insult," she said, and growing more and more despondent, she once more closed and secured the door, expecting that there would be a fresh message sent up.

In due time there was another tap at the door, but no request for her to come down.

"I have brought you up some tea, ma'am."

Kate hesitated about admitting the woman, for the memory of the scene at the same hour on the previous night flashed across her, but instinctively feeling that the messenger was alone, she unfastened the door and let her in.

"Master's compliments, ma'am, and he hopes that your quiet day's rest will have done you good. He says he will not trouble you to see him to-night, but he hopes you will be yourself again in the morning. Good-night, ma'am; I won't disturb you again. The things can be left on the side-table. Is there anything else I can do?"

"No, I thank you," said Kate, coldly.

"Very good, ma'am."

The woman went back to the door, and Kate's last hope of her turning a friend to help her died out, for she heard her sigh and say softly, evidently to be heard:

"Poor dear master; it's very sad."

"Good-night!" said Kate, involuntarily repeating the woman's words. "God help me and protect me through the long night watches, and inspire me with the thought that shall bring me help. How can I dare to sleep?"

The answer came from Nature—imperative, and who knew no denial; for once more the prisoner awoke, wondering to find that it was morning and that she must have slept for many hours in a chair.

Chapter Forty

In the hope that an opportunity would soon come, and to be ready at any moment, one of Kate's first acts that morning was to write plainly a few words on a sheet of paper, begging Becky to post her letter, and inclosing it with the note in another envelope, which she directed to the woman herself. This she placed in the fold of her dress, where she could draw it out directly, and waited.

The housekeeper was not long before she made her appearance with the breakfast tray, and was respectful in the extreme.

"Master thought, ma'am, that perhaps you might like your breakfast alone this morning, but he hopes to see you at lunch. He is so unwell that he is not going out this morning."

"Staying to watch for fear I should escape," thought Kate, and a nervous shiver ran through her; but rest seemed to have given her mental strength, and after breakfast she felt disposed to ridicule the idea of her being kept there against her will. "It must be possible to get away," she thought. It only wanted nerve and determination, for there was but the wall of the house between her and safety.

Soon after breakfast the housekeeper appeared again, to remove the breakfast things.

"Would you mind me coming to tidy up your room, ma'am, while you are here, or would you prefer my waiting till you go down?"

"Do it now," said Kate, quietly; and to avoid being spoken to, she took up a book and held it as if she were reading. But all the time she was noting everything, with her senses on the alert, and the next minute her heart began to throb wildly, for she saw the woman go to the door, pass out the tray, and it was evident that some order was given.

Becky was there, and Kate sat trembling, her excitement increasing when the next minute there was a light tap at the door, and Becky was admitted to assist in rearranging the room.

This went on for about a quarter of an hour, with Becky carefully minding not to glance at the prisoner, who, with head bent, watched her every movement, on the hope of her being left alone for a few minutes.

But as the mother was always near at hand, the opportunity did not come; and at last, with the envelope doubled in her hand, Kate began to feel that she might give up this time, and would have to wait till she could see the woman passing her room.

The disappointment was terrible, and Kate's heart sank in her despair as the housekeeper suddenly said:

"There, that will do—get on downstairs."

She stood back for her daughter to pass her, and then followed to the door, where a whispered conversation ensued.

"What? Left the brush?"

"Yes; other side of the room."

"Be quick, then. Fetch it out."

The housekeeper was passing through the door as she spoke, and Becky reappeared, to cross the room hurriedly, with her face lighting up as she gave the prisoner a meaning look, drew something from her bosom, and thrust it into Kate's hand, and took the note offered to her.

"Now, Becky!" came from outside.

The woman darted to the door.

"Well?"

"Can't find it. Tain't there."

The door closed, and Kate was once more alone, to eagerly examine the tiny packet handed to her.

It was square, about an inch across, roughly tied up with black worsted, and proved to be a sheet of note paper, doubled up small, and containing the words, written in an execrable hand:

"You run away. Come down at twelve o'clock, and I'll let you out threw the airy."

Letter rarely contained such hope as this, and the receiver, as she sat there, with her pulses bounding in her excitement, saw no further difficulty. Her lonely position in London, the want of friends to whom she could flee, the awkward hour of the night—these all seemed to be trifles compared to the great gain, for in a few hours she would be free.

She carefully destroyed the note, burning it in the fireplace, and then sat thinking, after opening and gazing out of the window, to realise how true Garstang's words had been. But they were of no consequence now, for the way of escape was open, and she repented bitterly that she had dispatched her letter to Jenny. Then once more a feeling akin to shame made her flush, as she thought of Leigh and what he would feel on hearing the letter read by his sister.

The day passed slowly on. A message came, asking if she would come down to lunch, and she refused. Later on came another message, almost a command, that she would be in her usual place at dinner, and to this she made no reply, for none seemed needed; but she determined that she would not stir from her room.

Then more and more slowly the time glided on, till it was as if night would never come.

But she made her preparations, so as to be ready when midnight did arrive. They were simple enough, and consisted in placing, bonnet, mantle, and the fewest necessaries. Her plans were far more difficult: where to go?

She sat and thought of every friend in turn, but there was a difficulty in the way in each case; and in spite of trying hard to avoid it, as the last resource, she seemed to be driven to take refuge with Jenny Leigh; and in deciding finally upon this step she forced herself to ignore the thought of her brother, while feeling exhilarated by the thought that the course pursued would be the one most likely to throw Garstang off her track, for Northwood would be the last place he would credit her with fleeing to.

Her head grew clearer now, as her hope of escape brightened, and the plans appeared easier and easier, and the way more clear.

For it was so simple. Garstang and the housekeeper would by that time be asleep, and all she would have to do would be to steal silently down in the darkness to where Becky would be waiting for her. She would take her into the basement, and she would be free. If she could persuade her, she would take the poor creature with her. She would be a companion and protection, and rob her night journey of its strange appearance.

The rest seemed to be mere trifles. She would walk for some distance, and then take a cab to the railway terminus at London Bridge, and wait till the earliest morning train started. The officials might think it strange, but she could take refuge in the waiting room.

And now, feeling satisfied that her ideas were correct, she thought of her letter to Jenny. This would only be received just before her arrival, but it would have prepared her, and all would be well. The only dread that she had now was that she might encounter anyone from the Manor House at the station. On the way, the station fly would hide her from the curious gaze, but the thought made her carefully place a veil ready for use.

Then came a kind of reaction; was it not madness to go to Northwood? Her uncle would soon know, and as soon as he did, he would insist upon her going back, and then—

Kate reached no farther into the future, for there was a knock at the door, and the housekeeper appeared, smiling at her, and handed her a note.

She saw at a glance that it was in Garstang's handwriting, and she refused to take it, whereupon the woman placed it upon the table, close to her elbow, and left the room.

For quite half an hour, Kate sat there determined not to open the letter, and trying hard not even to look at it; but human nature is weak, and unable to control the desire to know its contents, and excusing herself on the plea that perhaps it might have some bearing upon her plans for that night—a bearing which would force her to alter them—she took it up, opened it, and then sat gazing at it in despair.

It was a large envelope, and the first thing which fell from it was her letter to Jenny, apparently unopened, but crumpled and soiled as if it had been held in a hot and dirty hand; while the other portion of the contents of the envelope was a letter from Garstang, calling her foolish and childish and asking her if she thought his threats so vain and empty that he had not taken precautions against her trying such a feeble plan as that.

"I can not be angry with you," he concluded, "I love you too well; but I do implore you, for your sake as well as my own, to act sensibly, and cease forcing me to carry on a course which degrades us both. Come, dearest, be wise; act like a woman should under the circumstances. You know well how I worship you. Show me in return some little pity, and let me have its first fruits in your presence at the dinner-table this evening. I promise you that you shall have no cause to regret coming down. My treatment shall be full of the most chivalrous respect, and I will wait as long as you wish, if only you will give me your word to be my wife."

Was there any other way of sending the letter? Could she cast it from the window, in the hope of its being picked up and posted? She feared not, and passed the weary minutes thinking that she must give it up. But she roused herself after a time. The mother had evidently taken the letter from Becky, and handed it to Garstang; but the flight was Becky's own proposal, and now, after getting into trouble as she would have done over the letter, she would be the more likely to join in the flight.

Dinner was announced, but she refused to go down, and after partaking of what was sent up, she waited and waited till bed-time was approaching, giving the housekeeper cause to think from her actions that she was going to bed, and fastening her door loudly as the woman left the room after saying good-night.

And now came the most crucial time. She knew from old experience what Garstang's habits were. He would read for about half an hour after the housekeeper had locked and barred the front door; and then go up to his room, which was in the front, upon the second floor; and she stood by the door, listening through the long leaden minutes for the sharp sound of the bolts and the rattle of bar and chain. Her brow was throbbing, and her hands felt damp in the palms with the dread she felt of some fresh development of Garstang's persecution, and she would have given anything to have unbolted and opened her door, so as to stand in the darkness and watch, but shivered with fear at the very thought.

At last, plainly heard, came the familiar sounds, and now she pictured what would follow—the extinguishing of the staircase and hall lights, as the housekeeper and her child went up to bed in the attic, and the place left in darkness, save where a faint bar of rays came from beneath the library door. Half an hour later that door would be opened, and Garstang would pass up. Then there would be nearly an hour to wait before she dared to steal away.

The agony and suspense now became so unbearable that Kate felt that she must do something or she would go mad; and at last she softly threw back the bolt, opened the door, and looked out.

All was dark, and after listening intently, she glided out inch by inch till she reached the balustrade and peered down into the hall.

Exactly as she had pictured, there were a few faint rays from the library door, and just heard there was the smothered sound of a cough.

She stole back to listen, but first closed and bolted the door hastily, put on bonnet, veil, and mantle, and then put out the candles burning upon her dressing-table.

This done, she crept back to the door and stood there, waiting to hear some sound, or to see the gleam of a candle when Garstang went up, but she waited in vain.

The half-hour must have long passed, and she was fain to confess that since her coming she had never once heard him go up to bed. The thick carpets, the position of her door, would dull sound and hide the light passing along the landing, and when another half-hour had passed she mustered up sufficient courage to once more slip the bolt.

It glided back silently, but the hinges gave a faint crack as she opened them, and she then stood fast, with her heart beating violently, ready to fling the door to and fasten it again. But all was still, and at last once more, inch by inch, she crept out silently till she was able to gaze down into the hall.

The breath she drew came more freely now, for the faint bar of light from the library was no longer there, and in the utter silence of the place she knew that the door must be wide open, and the fire nearly extinct, for all at once there was the faint tinkling sound of dying cinders falling together.

He must have gone up to bed.

For a few moments Kate Wilton felt ready to hurry down the stairs, but she checked the desire. It was not the appointed time, and she stole back, closed the door, and forced herself to sit down and wait Becky had said twelve o'clock, and it would be folly to go down earlier.

Never had the place seemed so silent before. The distant roll of a cab sounded faint in the extreme, and it was as if the great city was for the time being dead. And now her heart sank again at the thought of her venture. She was going to plunge into the silence and darkness of the streets, so it seemed to her then; and the idea was so fraught with fear that she felt she must resign herself to her fate, for she dared not.

The faint striking of a clock sent a thrill through her, and once more she felt inspired with the courage to make the attempt. Becky would have stolen down, and be waiting, and perhaps after the trouble of the letter business be quite ready to go with her. "Yes, she must go," she said; and now, with every nerve drawn to its highest pitch of tension, she opened the door, and stood for a few moments listening.

All was perfectly still, and hesitating no longer, she walked silently and swiftly to the staircase, caught at the hand-rail, and began to descend, her dress making a faint rustling as it passed over the thick carpet.

Her goal was the door leading to the kitchen stairs, and the only dread she had now was that she might in the darkness touch one of the hall chairs, and make it scrape on the polished floor; but she recalled where each stood, and after a momentary pause, feeling convinced that she could make straight for the spot, she went on down into the darkness, reached the mat, and then found that there was a faint, dawn-like gleam coming from the fan-light over the door.

Then her heart seemed to stand still, for just before her there was something shadowy and dark.

"One of the statues," she thought for the moment, and then turned to flee, but stopped.

"Becky," she whispered, and a hand touched her arm.

Chapter Forty One

A wild, despairing cry escaped Kate Wilton's lips, as the firm grasp of a man's hand closed upon and prisoned her wrist.

"Hush, you foolish girl," was whispered, angrily, and she was caught by a strong arm thrown round her, the wrist released, and a hand was clapped upon her lips. "Do you want to alarm the house?"

Her only reply was to struggle violently and try to tear the hand from her mouth, but she was helpless, and the arm round her felt like iron.

"It is of no use to struggle, little bird," was whispered. "Are you not ashamed to drive me to watch you like this, and prevent you from perpetrating such a folly? What madness! Try to leave the house at midnight, by the help of that wretched idiotic girl, and trust yourself alone in the street. Truly, Kate, you need a watchful guardian. Now, as you prefer the darkness, come and sit down with me; I want a quiet talk with you. Kate, my dear, you force me to all this, and you must listen to reason now. There, it is of no use to struggle. Come with me quietly and sensibly, or I swear that I will carry you."

Her answer was another frantic struggle, while, wrenching her head round, she freed herself from the pressure of his hand, and uttered another piercing scream.

"Silence!" he cried, fiercely; and he was in the act of raising her from the floor, when she writhed herself nearly free, and in his effort to recover his grasp, he caught his foot on the mat and nearly fell.

It was Kate's opportunity. With one hand she thrust at him, with the other struck at him madly, ran to the stairs, and bounded up, just reaching her room as a light gleamed from above and showed Garstang a dozen steps below, too late to overtake her before her door was dashed to and fastened.

Then, as she stood there, panting and ready to faint with horror, she heard Garstang's angry voice and the whining replies of the housekeeper, while, though she could not grasp a word, she could tell by the tones that the woman was being abused for coming down, and was trying to make some excuse.

How that night passed Kate Wilton hardly knew, save that it was one great struggle to master a weak feeling of pitiful helplessness which prompted her to say, "I can do no more."

At times, from utter mental exhaustion, she sank into a kind of stupor, more than sleep, from which she invariably started with a faint cry of horror and despair, feeling that she was in some great peril, and that the darkness was peopled with something against which she must struggle in spite of her weakness. It was a nightmare-like experience, constantly repeated, and the grey morning found her feverish and weak, but in body only. Despair had driven her to bay, and there was a light in her eyes, a firmness in her words, which impressed the housekeeper when she came at breakfast time.

"Master's compliments, ma'am, and he is waiting breakfast," she said; "and I beg your pardon, ma'am, but I thought I ought to tell you he is very angry. I never saw him like it before; and if you would be ruled by me, I'd go down and see him. You have been very hard to him, I know; and you can't, I'm sure, wish to hurt the feelings of one who is the best of men."

Kate sat looking away from her in silence, and this encouraged the woman to proceed.

"He was very cross when he found out that you had been persuading poor Becky to post a letter for you. He suspected her, and had her into the lib'ry and made her confess; and then he took the letter away from her. But that was nothing to what he was when he found that instead of going to bed Becky had come down again and was waiting to try and let you out I thought he would have turned her into the street at once. But oh, my dear, he is such a good man, he wouldn't do that. But he said it was disgracefully treacherous of her. And between ourselves, my dear, it was quite impossible. Master has, I know, taken all kinds of precautions to keep you from going away. He told me that it was only a silly fit of yours, and that you didn't mean it; and, oh, my dear, do pray, pray be sensible. Think what a good chance it is for you to marry one of the noblest and best of—"

Sarah Plant ceased speaking, and stood with her lips apart, gazing blankly at the prisoner, who had slowly turned her head and fixed her with her indignant eyes.

"Silence, you wretched creature!" she said, in a low, angry whisper. "How dare you address me like this! Go down to your master, and tell him that I will see him when he has done his breakfast."

"Oh, please come now, ma'am."

"Tell him to send me word when he is at liberty, and I will come."

Kate pointed to the door, and the woman hurried out.

She returned in a few minutes, though, with a breakfast tray, which she set down without a word, and once more Kate was alone; but she started at a sound she heard at the door, and darted silently to it to slip the bolt; but before her hand could reach it there was a faint click, and she knew that the key had been taken out and replaced upon the other side. She was for the first time locked in, and a whispering told her that Garstang was there.

The struggle with her weakness had not been without its result. An unnatural calmness—the calmness of despair—had worked a change in her, and she was no longer the frightened, trembling girl, but the woman, ready to fight for all that was dear in life. She knew that she was weak and exhausted in body, and sat down with a strange calmness to the breakfast that had been brought up, eating and drinking mechanically, but thinking deeply the while of the challenge which she felt that she had sent down to Garstang, and collecting her forces for the encounter.

Quite an hour had passed before she heard a sound; and then the key was turned in the lock, and the housekeeper appeared.

"Master is in the library, ma'am," she said, "and will be glad to see you now."

This was said with a meaning smile, which said a great deal; but Kate did not even glance at her. She walked calmly out of her room, descended the staircase, and went straight into the library, where Garstang met her with extended hands.

"My dearest child," he began.

She waved him aside, and walked straight to her usual place, and sat down.

"Ah!" said Garstang, as if to himself; "more beautiful than ever, in her anger. How can she wonder that she has made me half mad?"

"Will you be good enough to sit down, Mr Garstang?" she said, gazing firmly at him.

"May I not rather kneel?" he said, imploringly.

"Will you be good enough to understand, Mr Garstang," she continued, with cutting contempt in her tones, "that you are speaking to a woman whose faith in you is completely destroyed, and not to a weak, timid girl."

"I can only think one thing," he whispered, earnestly, "that I am in the presence of the woman I worship, one who will forgive me everything, and become my wife."

"Your wife, sir? I have come here this morning, repellent as the task is, to tell you what you refuse to see—that your proposals are impossible, and to demand that you at once restore me to the care of my guardian."

"To be forced to marry that wretched boy?" he cried, passionately; "never!"

"May I ask you not to waste time by acting, Mr Garstang?" she said, with cutting irony. "You call me 'My dear child!' You are a man of sufficient common sense to know that I am not the foolish child you wish me to be, and that your words and manner no longer impose upon me."

"Ah, so cruel still!" he cried; but she met his eyes with such scathing contempt in her own that his lips tightened, and the anger he felt betrayed itself in the twitching at the corners of his temples.

"You have unmasked yourself completely now, sir, and by this time you must understand your position as fully as I do mine. You have been guilty of a disgraceful outrage."

"My love—I swear it was my love," he cried.

"Of gold?" she said, contemptuously. "Is it possible that a man supposed to be a gentleman can stoop to such pitiful language as this? Let us understand each other at once. Your attempts to replace the fallen mask are pitiful. Come, sir, let us treat this as having to do with your scheme. You wish to marry me?"

"Yes; I adore you."

She rose, with her brow wrinkling, her eyes half closed, and the look of contempt intensifying.

"Perhaps I had better defer what I wished to say till to-morrow, sir?"

He turned from her as if her words had lashed him, but he wrenched himself back and forced himself to meet her gaze.

"In God's name, no!" he cried, passionately; "say what you have to say at once, and bring this folly to an end."

She resumed her seat.

"Very well; let us bring this folly to an end. I am ready to treat with you, Mr Garstang."

"Hah!" he cried, with a mocking laugh. "An unconditional surrender?"

"Yes, sir; an unconditional surrender," she said calmly. "You have been playing like a gamester for the sake of my fortune."

"And your beautiful self," he whispered.

"For my miserable fortune; and you have won."

"Yes," he said, "I have won. I am the conqueror; but Kate, dearest—"

She rose slowly from her seat.

"Will you go on speaking without the mask, Mr Garstang?" she said, coldly; and she heard his teeth grit together, as he literally scowled at her now, with a look full of threats for the future.

"I am your slave, I suppose," he said, bitterly; but she remained standing.

"I wish to continue talking to Mr Garstang, the lawyer," she said, coldly. "If this is to continue it is a waste of words."

He threw himself back in his chair, and she resumed hers.

"Now, sir, you are a solicitor, and learned in these matters; can you draw up some paper which will mean the full surrender of my fortune to you? and this I will sign if you set me at liberty."

"No," he said, quietly, "I can not draw up such a paper."

"Why?"

"Because it would be utterly without value."

"Very well, then, there must be some way by which I can buy my liberty. The money will be mine when I come of age."

"Yes, there is one way," he said, gazing at her intently.

"What is that, sir?"

"By signing the marriage register."

"That I shall never do," she said, rising slowly. "Once more, Mr Garstang, I tell you that this money is valueless to me, and that I am ready to give it to you for my liberty."

"And I tell you the simple truth—that you talk like the foolish child you are. You cannot give away that which you do not possess. It is in the keeping of your uncle, and the law would not allow you to give it away like that."

"Does the law allow you to force me to be your wife, that you may, as my husband, seize upon it?"

"The law will let you consent to be my wife," he said, wincing slightly at her words.

"I have told you my decision," she said, coldly.

"Temporary decision," he said, smiling.

"And," she continued, "I shall wait until your reason has shown you that we are not living in the days of romance. Your treatment would be horrible in its baseness if it were not ridiculous. I own that I was frightened at first, but a night's calm thought has taught me how I stand, has given me strength of mind, and I shall wait."

"And so shall I," he said, gazing at her angrily as he leaned forward; but she did not shrink from his eyes, meeting them with calm contemptuous indifference; and he sprang up at last with an angry oath.

"Once more, Kate," he said, "understand this: you must and shall be my wife. You may try and set me at defiance, shut yourself up in your room, and keep on making efforts to escape, but all is in vain. I weighed all this well before I put my plans in execution. You hear me?"

"Every word," she said, coldly. "Now hear me, Mr Garstang. I shall never consent to be your wife."

"We shall see that," he cried.

"I shall not shut myself up in my room, and I shall make no further attempt to leave this house. It would be too ridiculous. Sooner or later my uncle will trace me, and call you to account. I shall keep nothing back, and if he thinks proper to prosecute you for what you have done I shall be his willing witness."

"Then you would go back to Northwood?" he said, with a laugh.

"Yes; if my uncle were here I should return with him at once. I was an impressionable, weak girl when I listened to you that night I had faith in you then. Events since have made me a woman."

She rose again, and took a step or two to cross the room, and he sprang up to open the door.

"We shall see," he said, with an angry laugh.

"Thank you," she said, calmly. "I was not going upstairs." And to his utter amazement she passed beyond him to one of the bookshelves, took down the volume she had been studying, and returned to her seat.

He stood gazing at her, utterly confounded; but she calmly opened the book, and, utterly ignoring his presence, sat reading and turning over the leaves.

There was a profound silence in the room for a few minutes, save that the clock on the chimney-piece kept on its monotonous tick; and then Garstang strode angrily to the door, went out, and closed it heavily behind him, while Kate uttered a low, deep sigh, and with her face ghastly and eyes closing, sank back in her chair.

The tension had been agonising, and she felt as if something in her brain was giving way.

Chapter Forty Two

"Still obstinate?"

Kate turned her head and looked gravely at Garstang, but made no reply.

A week had passed since the scene in the library, and during that period she had calmly resumed her old position in the house, meeting her enemy at the morning and evening meals; and while completely crushing every advance by her manner, shown him that she was waiting in full confidence for the hour of her release.

She never once showed her weakness, or let him see traces of the misery or despair which rendered her nights, sleeping or waking, an agony; she answered him quietly enough whenever he spoke on ordinary subjects, but at the slightest approach to familiarity, or if he showed a disposition to argue about the folly, as he called it, of her conduct, she rose and left the room, and somehow her manner impressed him so, that he dared not try to detain her.

He felt, as she had told him, that it was no longer the weak girl with whom he was contending, but the firm, imperious woman; while her confidence in her own power increased as she, on more than one occasion, realised the fact that she had completely mastered.

But the position remained the same, and as soon as she was alone the battle with another enemy commenced. Despair was always making its insidious approaches, sapping her very life, and teaching her that her triumph was but temporary; and she shuddered often as she thought of the hour when her strength and determination would fail.

Another week commenced, and she noted that there was a marked change in Garstang. Consummate actor as he was, he had returned to his former treatment, save that he no longer played the amiable guardian, but the chivalrous gentleman, full of deference and respect for her slightest wish. He made no approaches. There was nothing in his behaviour to which the most scrupulous could have objected; but knowing full well now that he had only covered his face with a fresh mask, she was more than ever on her guard, never relaxing her watchfulness of self for a moment.

She could only feel that he was waiting his time, that it was a siege which would be long, but undertaken by him in the full belief that sooner or later she would surrender.

That he left the house sometimes she felt convinced; but how or when she never knew, and the greater part of his time was passed in the library, where he evidently worked hard over what seemed to be legal business. Japanned tin boxes had made their appearance, and she had more than once seen the table littered with papers and parchments; but all these disappeared into the boxes at night, and the evenings were spent much as of old, though the conversation was distant and brief.

At last, about a fortnight after the setting in of the fresh regime, she was descending the stairs one afternoon, when she had proof of Garstang's having been away, for a latch-key rattled in the door, he entered, and stood with it open, while a cabman brought in a large deed box, set it down in the hall, and the door was closed and locked. After this, Garstang lifted the box to bear it into the library, when he caught sight of Kate descending to enter the inner room, the one into which he had ushered her on the morning of her coming, and in which he now passed a great deal of his time.

As their eyes met she saw that he looked pale and haggard, and it struck her at the moment that something had occurred to disturb him. Her heart leaped, for naturally enough she felt that it must be something relating to her, and in the momentary fit of exultation she felt that help was coming, and hurried into the room to hide the agitation from which she was suffering.

And now for the first time since her attempt to escape, she caught sight of Becky, passing down from the upper part of the staircase, but the glance was only momentary. As soon as she saw that she was observed, the pale-faced woman drew back.

There she stood, panting heavily as if suffering from some severe exertion. For she felt that Garstang would follow her in, that there would be a scene; but the minutes went by, and all was quite still, and by degrees her firmness was restored; but instinctively she felt that something was about to happen, and the dread of this, whatever it might be, set her longing to escape.

And now once more the idea came that it was absurd for her to be in prison there, when it seemed as if she had only to open the door and step out, or else descend to the basement, wait till one of the tradesmen came down the area, and then seize that opportunity to go.

But she had tried it and failed. The doors were always locked, save when tradesmen or postmen came; and then there was the area gate. No one ever came down.

The dinner time came, and she calmly took her place. Garstang was quietly cordial, though a little more silent than customary to her; but it was plain enough that he was suffering from some unusual excitement, when he addressed the housekeeper. For he found fault with nearly everything, and finally dismissed her in a fit of anger.

"Servants are so thoughtless," he said, with an apologetic smile. "That woman knows perfectly well what I like, and yet if I do not go into a fit of anger with her now and then, she grows dilatory and careless. But there, I beg your pardon; I ought to have waited until we were alone."

Kate rose soon after and went into the library, where, as she sat reading, she was dimly conscious of voices in the passage; and assuming that the housekeeper was again being taken to task, she forced herself to think only of her book, and soon after silence and the closing of the dining-room door told her that Garstang had gone back to his wine.

His stay after dinner had grown longer now, and it was quite half-past nine before he joined her, sometimes partaking of a cup of tea, but more often declining it, and sitting in silence gazing at the fire.

Upon this occasion she sat until the housekeeper brought in the tea tray, placed it upon its table, while a low, hissing sound outside told her that the urn was waiting; and Kate found herself thinking that Becky must be there until her mother fetched it, and she wondered whether it would be possible to get a few words with the woman again, and if she would be too frightened to try and post another letter.

Kate looked up suddenly and found that the housekeeper was watching her in a peculiar manner, but turned hurriedly away in confusion, and fetched the tea-caddy to place beside the tray. And again Kate found that she was watching her, and it seemed to her that it was with a pitying look in her eyes. This idea soon gave place to another. The woman wanted to talk to her, and her theme would be Garstang.

"That will do, Mrs Plant," she said; when the woman darted another peculiar look at her, and Kate saw the woman's lips move, but she said nothing aloud, and left the room, leaving its occupant thoughtful and repentant. For it struck her that the woman's eyes had a pitying sympathetic aspect, and that perhaps a few words of appeal to her better feelings would be of no avail, and that help might come through her after all.

Should she ring and try?

A few minutes' thought, and the idea grew less and less vivid, till it died away.

"She dare not, even if she would," thought Kate; and calmly and methodically she proceeded to make the tea, just casually noticing that the screw which held in its place the ornamental knob on the lid of the silver tea-pot had been off and was secured in its place again with what appeared to be resin.

It was a trifle which seemed to be of no importance then, as she turned on the hot water from the urn, rinsed out the pot made the tea and sat thinking while she gave it time to draw. Her thoughts were upon the old theme, the way of escape, or to find a way of sending letters to both Jenny and her uncle.

She started from her reverie, poured out a cupful, took up her book again, grew immersed in it, and sat back sipping her tea from time to time, till about half the cup was finished, before she noticed that it had a peculiar flavour, but concluded that it was fresh tea, and she had made it a little too strong.

The old German book was interesting, and she still read on and sipped her tea till she had finished the cup, and then sat frowning, for the last spoonful or two had the peculiar flavour intensified.

It was very strange. The tea was very different. She smelt the dregs in her cup, and the odour was strongly herbaceous.

She tasted it again, and it was stronger, while the flavour was now clinging to her palate.

She sat thinking for a few moments, laid her book aside, and let a little water from the urn flow into the spare cup, and examined it.

Pure and tasteless, just boiled water; there was nothing there; so she drew the pot to her side, opened the lid and smelt it.

The odour was plain enough. A dull, vapid, flat scent, which seemed familiar, but she could not give it a name.

"What strange tea!" she thought; and then the mystery was out, for she caught sight of the fastening of the lid handle. It was as it usually appeared; but the screw was loose, and it turned and rattled in her fingers. The dark, resinous patch which had held it firmly had gone, melted by the heat and steam, and hence the peculiar flavour of the tea.

"How stupid!" she exclaimed; and rising from her seat, she rang the bell.

The housekeeper was longer than usual in answering, and Kate was about to ring again, when the woman appeared, looking nervous and scared.

"Did you ring, ma'am?" she asked; and her voice sounded weak and husky.

"Yes; look at that tea-pot, Mrs Plant; smell the tea."

"Is—is anything the matter with it, ma'am?" faltered the woman.

"Matter? Yes! How could you be so foolish! I noticed that something had been used to fasten the knob on the lid."

"Yes—yes, ma'am; it has worn loose. The screw has got old."

"What did you use to fasten it with—resin?"

"I—I did not do anything to it, ma'am," faltered the woman, whose face was now ghastly.

"Someone did, and it melted down into the tea. It tastes horrible. Take the pot, and wash it out I must make some fresh."

"Yes, ma'am," said the woman eagerly, glancing from the tea-pot to her and back again. "You had better make some fresh, of course."

She uttered a sigh, as if relieved, but Kate saw that her hands trembled as she took up the pot.

"There, be quick. I shall not complain to Mr Garstang, and get you another scolding."

"Thank you, ma'am—no ma'am," said the woman faintly, and she glanced behind her toward the door, and then caught at the table to support herself.

"What is the matter? Are you unwell?" asked Kate.

"N-no, ma'am—a little faint and giddy, that's all," she faltered. "I—am gettin' better now—it's going off."

"You are ill?" said Kate kindly. "Never mind the tea. I will go to the cellaret and get you a little brandy. There, sit down for a few moments. Yes, sit down; your face is covered with cold perspiration. Are you in the habit of turning like this?"

The woman did not answer, but sat back in the chair into which she had been pressed, moaning slightly, and wringing her hands.

"No-no," she whispered wildly; "don't go. He's there. I dursen't. I shall be better directly. Miss Wilton, I couldn't help it, dear; he—he did it. Don't say you've drunk any of that tea!"

It was Kate's turn to snatch at something to support her, as the horrible truth flashed upon her; and she stood there with her face ghastly and her eyes wild and staring at the woman, who had now struggled to her feet.

For some moments she could not stir, but at last the reaction came, and she caught the housekeeper tightly by the arm, and placed her lips to her ear.

"You are a woman—a mother; for God's sake, help me! Quick, while there is time. Take me with you now."

"I can't—I can't," came back faintly; "I daren't; it's impossible."

Kate thrust the woman from her, and with a sudden movement clapped her hands to her head to try and collect herself, for a strange singing had come in her ears, and objects in the room seemed a long distance off.

The sensation was momentary and was succeeded by a feeling of wild exhilaration and strength, but almost instantaneously this too passed off; and she reeled, and saved herself from falling by catching at one of the easy chairs, into which she sank, and sat staring helplessly at the woman, who was now speaking to someone—she could not see whom—but the words spoken rang in her ears above the strange metallic singing which filled them.

"Oh, sir, pray—pray, only think! For God's sake, sir!"

"Curse you, hold your tongue, and go! Dare to say another word, and— do you hear me?—go!"

Kate was sensible of a thin cold hand clutching at hers for a moment; then a wave of misty light which she could not penetrate passed softly before her eyes, and this gradually deepened; the voices grew more and more distant and then everything seemed to have passed away.

Chapter Forty Three

"Curse you! Do you hear what I say?" roared Garstang, furiously; "leave the room!"

"No, sir, I won't!" cried the housekeeper, as she stood sobbing and wringing her hands by Kate's side. "It's horrible; it's shameful!"

"Silence!"

"No, I won't be silenced now," cried the woman. "You're my master, and I've done everything you told me up to now, for I thought she was only holding back, and that at last she'd consent and be happy with you; but you're not the good man I thought you were, and the poor dear knew you better than I did; and I wouldn't leave her now, not if I died for it—so there!"

"Come, come," said Garstang, hurriedly; "don't be absurd, Sarah. You are excited, and don't know what you are saying."

"I never knew better what I was saying, sir," cried the woman, passionately. "Absurd! Oh, God forgive you—you wicked wretch! And forgive me too for listening to you to-day. You took me by surprise, you did, and I didn't see the full meaning of it all. Oh, it's shameful!—it's horrible! And I believe you've killed her; and we shall all be hung, and serve us right, only I hope poor Becky, who is innocent as a lamb, will get off."

"Look here, Sarah, my good woman; you are frightened, and without cause."

"Without cause? Oh, look at her—look at her! She's dying—she's dying!"

"Hush, you silly woman! There, I won't be cross with you; you're startled and hysterical. Run into the dining-room and fetch the brandy from the cellaret."

"No. If you want brandy, sir, fetch it yourself. I don't stir from here till this poor dear has come to, or lies stiff and cold."

Garstang ground his teeth, and rushed upon the woman savagely, but she did not shrink; and he mastered himself and took a turn or two up and down the room before facing her again, and beginning to temporise.

"Look here, Sarah," he said, in a low, husky voice; "I've been a good friend to you."

"Yes, sir, always," said the woman, with a sob.

"And I've made a home here for your idiot child."

"Which she ain't an idiot at all, sir, but she ain't everybody's money; and grateful I've always been for your kindness, and you know how I've tried to show it. Haven't I backed you up in this? Of course, you wanted to marry such a dear, sweet, young creature; but for it to come to that! Oh! shame upon you, shame!"

Garstang made a fierce gesture, but he controlled himself and stopped by her again.

"Now just try and listen to me, and let me talk to you, not as my old servant, but as my old friend, whom I have trusted in this delicate affair, and whom I want to go on trusting to help me."

"No, sir, no. You've broken all that, and I'll never leave the poor dear—there!"

"Will you hear me speak first?" said Garstang, making a tremendous effort to keep down his rage.

"Yes, sir, I'll listen," said the woman; "but I'll stop here."

"Now, let me tell you, then—as a friend, mind—how I am situated. It is vital to me that we should be married at once, and you must see as a woman, that for her reputation's sake, after being here with me so long, she ought to give up all opposition. Now, you see that—"

"I'd have said 'Yes' to it yesterday, sir," said the woman, firmly; "but I can't say it to-night."

"Nonsense! I tell you it is for her benefit. I only want her to feel that further resistance is useless. There, now, I have spoken out to you. You see it is for the best. To-morrow or next day we shall be married by special license. I have made all the arrangements."

"Then, now go and make all the arrangements for the poor dear's funeral, you bad, wicked wretch!" cried the woman passionately, as she sank on her knees and clasped Kate about the waist. "Oh, my poor dear, my poor dear, he has murdered you!"

"Silence, idiot!" cried Garstang, in a fierce whisper. "Can't you see that she is only asleep?"

"Asleep? Do you call this sleep? Look at her poor staring eyes. Feel her hands.—No, no, keep back. You shan't touch her."

She turned upon him with so savage and cat-like a gesture that he stopped short with his brows rugged and his hands clenched.

There was a few moments' pause, but the woman did not wince; and Garstang felt more than ever that he must temporise again. He burst into a mocking laugh.

"Oh, you silly woman," he said. "All this nonsense about a girl's holding off for a time. You've often heard her say how she liked me. You know she came here of her own free will. And I know you feel that I mean to marry her as soon as I can persuade her to come to the church. What a storm you are making about nothing! She has taken something. Well, you consented to its being given her; and you are going as frantic as if I had poisoned her."

"I know, I know," cried the woman, "and I was a vile wretch to consent to help you."

"Stuff and nonsense, Sarah, old friend. Now look here; suppose instead of its being a harmless sleeping draught, it had been the effect of her drinking an extra glass or two of champagne. Would you have gone on then like this?"

"It's of no use for you to talk; I know what a smooth winning tongue you've got, as would bring a bird down out of a tree; but I know you thoroughly now; and Becky was right; you're a base man, and you did worry and worry poor dear Mr Jenour till he shot himself. You robbed him till you'd got everything that was his, and now you've murdered this poor darling girl."

"That will do," cried Garstang, stung now to the quick. "If you will be a fool you must suffer for it. Now, listen to me, woman; this is my house, and this is my wife. She came to me, and she is mine. I have told you that I will take her to the church. Now, go up to your room—I am desperate now—and if you dare to make a sound or to leave it till to-morrow morning, I'll shoot you and your girl too."

The woman stared at him, her lips parted, and with dilated eyes.

"You know what this place is. Not a sound can reach the outside. You have not a soul who would come to inquire after you, and the world would never know what had become of you. Now go."

She stood up, trembling like a leaf, fascinated by his fierce eyes, and began to walk slowly round to the other side of the table, sidewise, so as to keep as far from him as she could.

"Hah!" he said, through his set teeth, "you understand me then at last. Upstairs with you at once," and as he spoke he stepped quickly to Kate's side, dropped on one knee, and took hold of her icy hand. But he sprang to his feet, half stunned, the next moment, for with a wild cry, the woman threw open the door as if to escape from him, but tore out the key.

"Becky! Becky!" she shrieked.

"Yes, mother!" came from where the tied-up face was stretched over the balustrade on the first floor.

"Lock yourself in master's room, open the window, and shriek murder until the police come."

"Damnation!" roared Garstang; and he rushed at and seized the woman, who clung to one of the bookshelves, bringing it down with a crash, and a shriek came from the upper floor.

"Stop her," roared Garstang. "There, I give in. Here, Becky, your mother will speak to you."

"Lock yourself in the room, but don't scream till I tell you, or he comes," cried the woman.

"That will do," said Garstang, savagely, and he loosed his hold, with the result that the woman ran back to the insensible girl, and once more clasped her in her arms.

Garstang began to pace up and down the room, but paused at the door, to reach out and see Becky's white face and eyes displaying the white rings round them, peering down from above.

At the sight of him she rushed to his bedroom, and stood half inside, ready to lock herself in if he attempted to ascend.

A wild cry from Sarah Plant took Garstang back to her side.

"I knew it—I knew it!" she cried, bursting into a passionate fit of sobbing; "you've killed her. Look at her, sir, look. Oh, my poor dear, my poor dear! God forgive me! What shall I do?"

A chill of horror ran through Garstang, and he bent down over his victim, trembling violently now, as he raised one eyelid with his finger, then the other, bent lower so that his cheek was close to her lips, and then caught her hand, and tried to feel her pulse.

"No, no; she is only sleeping," he said, hoarsely.

"Sleeping!" moaned the woman, hysterically; "do you call that sleep?"

Garstang drew a deep breath, and his horror increased.

"Help me to lay her on the couch," he said, huskily.

"No, no, I'm strong enough," groaned the woman. "Oh, my poor dear—my poor dear! he has murdered you."

She rose quickly, and in her nervous exaltation, passed her arms round the helpless figure, and lifted it like a child, to bear it to the couch, and lay it helplessly down.

"Oh, help, help!" she groaned, in a piteous wail. "A doctor—fetch a doctor at once."

"No, no, go for brandy—for cold water to bathe her face."

"I don't leave her again," cried the woman, passionately; "I'd sooner die."

Garstang gazed down at them wildly for a few moments, and then rushed across into the dining-room, obtained the brandy, a glass, and a carafe of water, and returned, to begin bathing Kate's temples and hands, but without the slightest result, save that her breathing became fainter, and the ghastly symptoms of collapse slowly increased.

"She's going—she's going!" moaned the shuddering woman, who knelt by the couch, holding Kate tightly as if to keep her there. "We've poisoned her! we've poisoned her!"

The panic which had seized upon Garstang increased, as he gazed wildly at his work. Strong man as he was, and accustomed to control himself, he began now to lose his head; and at last, thoroughly aghast, he caught the housekeeper by the shoulder and shook her.

"Don't leave her," he said, in a husky whisper. "I'm going out."

"What!" cried the woman, turning and catching his arm; "going to try and escape, and leave me here?"

"No, no," he whispered; "a doctor—to fetch a doctor."

"Yes, yes," moaned the woman; "a doctor—fetch a doctor; but it is too late—it is too late!"

Garstang hardly heard her words, as he bent down and took a hurried look at Kate's face. Then hurrying to the door, he caught sight of Becky still watching.

"Go down and help your mother," he cried, excitedly; and unfastening the door, he rushed out.

Chapter Forty Four

Pierce Leigh returned home after a long weary day of watching. From careful thought and balancing of the matter, he had long come to the conclusion that Claud Wilton's ideas were right, and that John Garstang knew where his cousin was. But suspicion was not certainty, and though he told himself that he had no right or reason in his conduct, he could not refrain from spending all the time he could spare from his professional work in town—work that was growing rapidly—in trying to get some news of the missing girl.

He was more amenable now, and ready to discuss the matter with his sister, who remained Kate's champion and declared that she was sure there was some foul play in the matter; but he would not give way, and laughed bitterly whenever Jenny aired her optimism, and said she was sure that all would end happily after all.

"Silly child!" he said bitterly. "If Miss Wilton was the victim of foul play—which I do not believe—she could have found some means of communicating with her friends."

"But she had no friends, Pierce," cried Jenny. "She told me so more than once."

"She had you."

"Oh, I don't count, dear; I was only an acquaintance, and it had not had time to ripen into affection on her side. I soon began to love her, but I don't think she cared much for me."

"Ah, it was a great mistake," sighed Leigh.

"What was?" cried Jenny sharply.

"Our going down to Northwood. I lost a thousand pounds by the transaction."

"And gained the dearest girl in the world to love."

"Don't talk absurdly, child," said Leigh, firmly. "I beg that you will not speak to me in that tone about Miss Wilton. Has Claud been again?"

"I beg that you will not speak to me in that tone about Mr Wilton," said Jenny, with a mischievous look at her brother, who glanced at her sharply.

"Claud Wilton is not such a bad fellow after all, I begin to think. All that horsey caddishness will, I daresay, wear off."

"I am sorry for the poor woman who has to rub it off," said Jenny.

"You did not tell me if he had called."

"Yes, he did call."

"Jenny!"

"I didn't ask him to call, and he did not come to see me," said the girl demurely. "He wanted you, and left his card. I put it in the surgery. I think he said he had some news of his cousin."

"Indeed?" said Leigh, starting. "When was this?"

"Yesterday evening. But Pierce, dear, surely it is nothing to you. Don't go interfering, and perhaps make two poor people unhappy."

Leigh turned upon her angrily.

"What a good little girl you would be, Jenny, if you had been born without a tongue."

"Yes," she said, "but I should not have been half a woman, Pierce, dear."

"Did he say when he would come again?"

"No."

"Did he say more particularly what his news was?"

"No, dear, and I did not ask him, knowing how particular you are about my being at all intimate with him."

He gave her an angry glance, but she ignored it.

"Anyone else been?"

"Yes; there was a message from Mrs Smithers, saying she hoped you would drop in after dinner and see her. Her daughter came—the freckly one. The buzzing in her mother's head had begun again, and Miss Smithers says she is sure it is the port wine, for it always comes after her mother has been drinking port wine for a month."

"Of course. She eats and drinks twice as much as is good for her.—Did young Wilton say anything about Northwood?"

"Yes," said Jenny, carelessly. "The new doctor has got the parish work, but he isn't worked to death. Oh, by the way, there's a letter on the chimney-piece."

Leigh rose and took it eagerly, frowning as he read it.

"Bad news, Pierce, dear?"

"Eh? Bad? Oh, dear no; I have to meet Dr Clifton in consultation at three to-morrow, at Sir Montague Russell's."

"Oh! I say, Pierce dear, how rapidly you are picking up a practice!"

"Yes," he said, with a sigh; and then with an effort to be cheerful, "How long will dinner be?"

"Half an hour," said Jenny, after a glance at the clock, "and then I hope they will let you have a quiet evening. You have not been at home once this week."

"Ah, yes, a quiet evening would be pleasant."

"Thinking, Pierce dear?" said Jenny, after a pause.

"Yes," he said dreamily, as he sat back with his eyes closed. "I can't make it all fit. He rarely goes to the office, I have found that out; and from what I can learn he must be living in the country. The house I saw him go to has all the front blinds drawn down, and last time I rode by I saw a woman at the gate, but I could not stop to question her—I have no right."

"No, dear, you have no right," said Jenny, gravely. "That was only a fancy of yours. But how strangely things do come to pass!"

Leigh started, and gazed at his sister wonderingly.

"What do you mean?" he said.

"I was only replying to your remarks, dear, about your suspicions of this Mr Garstang."

"I? My remarks?" he said, looking at her strangely. "I said nothing."

"Why, Pierce dear, you did just now."

"No, not a word. I was asleep when you spoke."

"Asleep?"

"Yes. What is there strange in that? A man must have rest, and I have been out for the last three nights with anxious cases. Was I talking?"

"Yes, dear," said Jenny, rising, to go behind the chair and lay her soft little hands upon her brother's head. "Talking about that shut-up house, and this Mr Garstang. I thought it was not possible, and that it was very wild of you to take a house in this street so as to be near and watch him, but nothing could have been better. You are getting as busy as you used to be in Westminster. But Pierce, dear," she whispered softly, "don't you think we should be happier if we were in full confidence with one another—as we were once?"

"No," he said, gloomily, "I shall never be happy again."

"You will, dear, when some day we meet Kate, and all this mystery about her is at an end."

"Meet Miss Wilton and her husband," he said, bitterly.

"No, dear; if I know anything of women you will never meet Kate Wilton's husband. Pierce, dear, I am your sister, and I have been so lonely lately, ever since we came to London. You have never quite forgiven me all that unhappy business. Don't you think you could if you tried?"

He sat perfectly silent for a few moments, and then reached round, took her in his arms, and kissed her long and lovingly.

In an instant she was clinging to his neck, sobbing wildly, and he had hard work trying to soothe her.

But she changed again just as quickly, and laughed at him through her tears.

"There," she cried, "now I feel ten years younger. Five minutes ago I was quite an old woman. But, Pierce, you will confide in me now, and make me quite as we used to be?"

"Yes," he said.

She wound her arms tightly round his neck, and laid her face to his.

"Then confess to me, dear," she whispered. "You do dearly love Kate Wilton?"

He was silent for some moments, and then slowly and dreamily his words were breathed close to her ear.

"Yes; and I shall never love again."

Jenny turned up her face and kissed him, but hid it, burning, directly after in his breast.

"Pierce dear," she whispered, "I have no one else to talk to like this. May I confess something now to you?"

"Why not?" he said, gently. "Confidence for confidence."

She was silent in turn for some time. Then she spoke almost in a whisper.

"Will you be very angry, Pierce, if I tell you that I think I am beginning to like Claud Wilton very much?"

"Like—him?" he cried, scornfully.

"I mean love him, Pierce," she said, quietly.

"Jenny! Impossible!"

"That's what I used to think, dear, but it is not."

"You foolish baby, what is there in the fellow that any woman could love?"

"Something I've found out, dear."

"In Heaven's name, what?"

"He loves me with all his heart."

"He has no heart."

"You don't know him as I do, Pierce. He has, and a very warm one."

"Has he dared to make proposals to you again?"

"No, not a word. But he isn't like the same. It was all through you, Pierce. I made him love me, and now he looks up to me as if I were something he ought to worship, and—and I can't help liking him for it."

"Oh, you must not think of it," cried Leigh.

"That's what I've told myself hundreds of times, dear, but it will come, and—and, Pierce, dear, it's very dreadful, but we can't help it when the love comes. Do you think we can?"

She slipped from him, and dashed the tears from her eyes, for her quick senses detected a step, and the next moment a quiet-looking maid-servant announced the dinner.

No more was said, but the manner of sister and brother was warmer than it had been for months; and though he made no allusions, there was a half-reproachful, half-mocking smile on Leigh's lips when his eyes met Jenny's.

The dinner ended, he went into their little plainly-furnished drawing-room to steal half-an-hour's rest before hurrying off to make the call as requested; and he had not left the house ten minutes when there was a hurried ring at the bell.

Jenny clapped her hands, and burst into a merry laugh.

"I am glad," she cried. "No; I ought to be sorry for the poor people. But how they are finding out what a dear, clever, old fellow Pierce is! I wonder who this can be?"

She was not kept long in doubt, for the servant came up.

"If you please, ma'am, there's that gentleman again who called to see master."

"What gentleman?" said Jenny, suddenly turning nervous—"Mr Wilton?"

"Yes, ma'am."

"Did you tell him your master was out?"

"Yes, ma'am, and he said would you see him just a moment?"

"I'll come down," said Jenny, turning very hard and stiff; and it seemed to be a different personage who descended to Leigh's consulting room, where Claud was walking up and down with his hat on.

"Ah, Miss Leigh!" he cried, excitedly, as he half ran to her, with his hands extended.

But Jenny did not seem to see them; only standing pokeresque, and gazing at the young fellow's hat.

"Eh? What's the matter? Oh, I beg your pardon," he cried, catching it off confusedly; "I'm so excited, I forgot. But I can't stop; I'll come in again by and by and see your brother. Only tell him I've found her."

"Found Kate Wilton?" cried Jenny, dropping her formal manner and catching him by the arm, his hand dropping upon hers directly.

"Yes, I'm as sure as sure. I've been on the scent for some time, and I never could be sure; but I'm about certain now, and I want your brother to come and help me, for he has a better right than I have to be there."

"My brother, Mr Wilton?" said Jenny, in a freezing tone.

"Oh, I say, please don't," he whispered earnestly; "I am trying so hard to show you that I'm not such a cad as you used to think, and when you speak to me in that way it makes me feel as if there's nothing, left to do but enlist, and get sent off to India, or the Crimea, or somewhere, to be killed out of the way."

"Tell me quickly, where is she?"

"I can't yet. I'm not quite sure."

"Pah!"

"Ah, you wait a bit, and you'll see; and if I do find her I shall bring her here."

"Here?" cried Jenny, excitedly.

"Yes, why not? she likes you better than anybody in the world; he likes, her, and—. Here, I can't stop. Good-bye; tell him I'll be back again as soon as I can, for find her I will to-night."

"But Mr Wilton—Claud!"

"Ah!" he cried excitedly, turning to her.

"Tell me one thing."

"Everything," he cried, wildly, "if you'll speak to me like that. Someone I thought had got her; I'm about sure now, but—I'd give anything to stop—but I can't."

He rushed out into the street, and Jenny returned to her room and work, trembling with a double excitement, one moment blaming herself for being too free with her visitor, the next forgetting everything in the news.

"Oh, Pierce, dear Pierce! if it is only true," she muttered, as her work dropped from her hands, and she sat hour after hour longing for her brother's return. This was not till ten, when she was trembling with excitement, and in momentary expectation of seeing Claud Wilton return first.

Chapter Forty Five

Jenny was standing at the window, watching the people go by, when a cab drew up and Leigh sprang out, to let himself in with his latch-key; and she was half-way down to meet him as he was coming up.

"Pierce," she whispered excitedly. "Claud Wilton has been. He has, he is sure, found Kate; and he is coming again to fetch you to where she is."

Leigh staggered, and caught at the balustrade to save himself from falling.

"Where is she?" he panted.

"I—don't know; he was not quite sure, but he is coming again. He says no one but you has a right to be there when she is found; and Pierce—Pierce—he is going to bring her here!"

Leigh stood gazing straight before him, feeling as if he could hardly breathe, and he followed his sister into the drawing-room, but had hardly sunk into a chair when there was a tremendous peal at the bell.

"Here he is!" cried Jenny; and Leigh sprang from his seat to hurry down, but restrained himself, and to his sister's despair, stood waiting.

"Pierce, dear," she whispered, "pray go."

"I have no right," he said huskily; and Jenny wrung her hands and tried vainly for what she deemed the correct words to say.

The painful silence was broken by the appearance of the maid.

"A gentleman to see you, sir; very important."

"Mr Wilton?" cried Jenny.

"No, ma'am, a strange gentleman," said the girl. "Someone very bad."

Leigh exhaled his pent-up breath with a sigh of relief, and went quickly down to where his visitor was waiting, looking wild and ghastly.

Garstang!—the man he had been watching for months without result, but who looked at him as one whom he had never met before.

"Will you come with me directly?" he cried. "My house—only in the next street. I'd better tell you at once, so that you may bring some antidote with you. I need not explain—a young lady—my wife—a foolish quarrel—a little jealousy—and she has taken some of that new sedative, Xyrania—a poisonous dose, I fear."

"A young lady—my wife," rang in Leigh's ears like the death knell of all hopes. Then he was right: this man had carried her off with her consent, and it had come to this.

"Do you not hear me, sir?" cried Garstang; "Mr— I don't know your name; I came to the first red lamp. You are a doctor?"

"Yes, yes, of course," cried Leigh, hastily.

"Then, for God's sake, come on before it is too late!"

Leigh was the calm, cold, collected physician once again, and he spoke in a strange tone that he did not know as his own.

"Xyrania," he said; and he went to a case of bottles and jars, took down one of the former, poured a small quantity into a phial, corked it, and said solemnly—

"Lead the way, sir—quick; but I must tell you that an overdose of that drug means sleep from which there is no awaking."

Garstang uttered a low, harsh sound, and motioned towards the door, leading the way; while Leigh followed him, with his brain feeling, in addition to the terrific crushing weight of depression as if all the world were nothing now, confused and strange, as he wondered that the man did not recognise him; and too much stunned to grasp the fact that he who had filled so large a measure of his thoughts for months had never met him face to face—probably had never heard of him, save as some doctor in practice at Northwood.

Then, as they hurried along the pavement, and at the end of another hundred yards turned into Great Ormond Street, Leigh felt oppressed by another thought—that after all, Kate, if it were she he was being taken to see, must have been for months past in the house he had so often gazed at in passing, with an intense desire to enter, but had always crushed down that desire, telling himself that it was insane.

Meanwhile Garstang was talking to him in a hurried excited tone, uttering words that hardly reached his companion's understanding; but he caught fragments about "unhappy temper—insomnia—indulgence in the potent drug—his agony and despair"—and then he cried wildly, as he paused at the door of the familiar house with its overhanging eaves, and inserted the latch-key:

"Doctor—any fee you like to demand, but you must save my wife's life."

"Must save his wife's life!" groaned Leigh, mentally, as his heart gave what seemed to be one heavy throb. Then he stepped into the great gloomy hall.

Chapter Forty Six

"His wife!"

The words kept repeating themselves in Pierce Leigh's brain like the beating of some artery charged to bursting, and the agony seemed greater than he could bear; while the revelation which had been so briefly made told of misery and a terrible despair which had driven the woman he loved to this desperate act. But for one thought he would have rushed madly away to try and forget everything by a similar act, for the means were at home, ready to his hand, his suffering being more than he could bear.

But there was that thought; she was in peril of her life, and the husband had flown unconsciously to him for help. He might be able to save her—make her owe that life to him—and this thought fought against his weakness, and for the time being made him strong enough to follow Garstang to the library door, just as poor Becky darted away and disappeared through the doorway leading to the basement.

As Leigh entered and saw Kate lying motionless upon the sofa, with the housekeeper kneeling by her side, a pang shot through him which seemed to cleave his heart; then as it passed away he was the calm stern physician once more.

"You had better go, sir," he said sharply, "and leave me with the nurse."

"No: do your work," said Garstang harshly; "I stay here."

Leigh made no answer, but took the housekeeper's place, to examine the sufferer's dilated pupils and test the pulsation, and then he turned quickly to Garstang.

"Where are the bottle and glass?" he said sharply.

"What bottle—what glass?" replied Garstang, taken by surprise.

"The symptoms seem to accord with what you say, but I want to make perfectly sure. Where is the drug she took?"

"Oh, it was in the tea, sir, there," cried the housekeeper.

Garstang turned upon her with a savage gesture, and Leigh saw it. His suspicions were raised.

"Here, sir," said the woman, pointing to the pot.

"Oh yes," said Garstang hurriedly: "she took it in her tea."

"She did not, sir!" cried the woman desperately.

"Hold your tongue!" roared Garstang.

"I won't, doctor, if I die for it," cried the woman. "He drugged her, poor dear. I was obliged to do as he said."

"The woman's mad," cried Garstang. "Go on with your work."

A savage instinct seemed to drive Leigh, on hearing this, to bound at Garstang, seize him by the throat and strangle him; but a glance at Kate checked it, and the physician regained the ascendancy.

He poured a little of the tea into a clean cup, smelt, tasted, and spat it out.

"Quite right," he said firmly. "Don't let that tea-pot be touched again."

Garstang winced, for the words were to him charged with death, a trial for murder, and the silent evidence of the crime.

"Here, you help me," said Leigh, quickly; and he rinsed out the cup with water from the urn, poured a couple of teaspoonfuls from a bottle into the cup, and kneeling by the couch while the housekeeper held the insensible girl's head, tried to insert the spoon between the closely set teeth.

The effort was vain, and he was forced to trickle the antidote he tried to administer through the teeth, but there was no effort made to swallow; the insensibility was too deep.

"Better?" said Garstang, after watching the doctor's efforts to revive his patient for quite half an hour.

"Better?" he said, fiercely. "Can you not see, man, that she is steadily passing away?"

"No, no, she seems calmer, and more like one asleep. Oh, persevere, doctor!"

"I want help here—the counsel and advice of the best man you can get. Send instantly for Sir Edward Lacey, Harley Street."

"No," said Garstang, frowning darkly. "You seem an able practitioner. It is a matter of time for the effects of the potent drug to die out, is it not?"

"Yes, of course; but I fear the worst."

"Go on with what you are doing, doctor; I have faith in you."

At that moment Leigh felt that nothing more could be done—that nature was the great physician; and he once more knelt down by the side of the couch for a time, while a terrible silence seemed to have fallen on the place, even the housekeeper looking now as if she were turned to stone, and dared not move her lips as she intently watched the calm white face upon the pillow.

"I can do no more," said Leigh at last, in a hoarse whisper. "God help me! How weak and helpless one feels at a time like this!"

The words came involuntarily from his lips, for at that moment he seemed to be alone with the sufferer, his patient once again, whose life he would have given his own to save.

"Oh, come, come, doctor!" said Garstang, breaking in harshly upon the terrible stillness, and there was a forced gaiety in his tone. "It was a little sleeping draught; surely the effects will soon pass off. You are taking too serious a view of the case."

"I take the view of it, sir," said Leigh, gravely, as he bent lower over the marble face before him, fighting hard to control the wild desire to press his lips to the temple where an artery throbbed, "I take the view given to us by experience. You had better send for further help at once."

"No, no. It is only making an expose, where none is necessary. I will not believe that she is so bad. You medical men are so prone to magnify symptoms."

"Indeed?" said Leigh, who dared not look at the speaker, but bent once more over his patient. "You came and told me that your wife was dying."

"His wife, sir?" cried the housekeeper, indignantly. "It's a wicked lie!"

Garstang turned savagely upon the woman, but he had to face Leigh, who sprang to his feet with a wild exaltation making every pulse throb and thrill.

"Not his wife!" he cried fiercely.

"No, sir, and never would be."

"Curse you!" roared Garstang, making at her; but Leigh thrust him back.

"Then there has been foul play here."

"How dare you?" cried Garstang. "I called you in to—But go on with your work, sir. Can you not see that the woman drinks?—she is mad drunk now. Hysterical, and does not know what she is saying. The lady is my wife, and I insist upon your attending to your professional duties or leaving the house. Is this the conduct of a physician?"

"It is the conduct of a man, sir, who finds himself face to face with a scoundrel."

"You insolent hound!"

"John Garstang—"

"John Garstang!"

"Yes, John Garstang; you see I know you! It is true then that you have abducted this lady, or lured her into this place, where you have kept her secluded from her friends. There is no need to ask the reason. I can guess that."

"You—you—" cried Garstang, ghastly now in his surprise. "Who are you that you dare to speak to me like this?"

"I, sir, am the physician you called in to see his old patient, dying, I fear, from the effects of the drug you have administered," said Leigh, with unnatural calmness; "the man whose instinct tempts him to try and crush out your wretched life as he would that of some noxious beast. But we have laws, and whatever the result is here, my duty is to hand you over to the police."

"Oh, doctor! doctor!" cried the woman wildly, from behind the couch. "Quick, quick! Look! Oh, my poor, poor child!"

Leigh sprang back to the couch and fell upon his knees, for a violent twitching had convulsed the girl's motionless form.

Garstang, his face wild with fear, stood gazing down over the doctor's shoulder, and then strode quickly to the back of the library, bent over a table, and took something from a drawer, before striding back, to stand looking on, trembling violently now, as he witnessed the strange convulsions, which gradually died out, and a low gasping sound escaped the sufferer's lips.

Garstang drew a long, deep breath, turned quickly, and made for the door; but as he reached it Leigh's hand was upon his collar, and he was swung violently round and back into the room.

He nearly fell, but recovered himself, and stood with his hand in his breast.

"Stand away from that door," he cried.

"To let you escape?" said Leigh, firmly. "No; whether that convulsion means death or life to your victim, sir, you are my prisoner till the police are here. You—woman, go to the door, and send for or fetch the police."

The housekeeper started forward, but with one heavy swing of the arm Garstang sent her staggering back, and then approached Leigh slowly, with a half-crouching movement, like some beast about to spring.

"Stand away from that door, and let me pass," he said, huskily.

"Go back and sit down in that chair," said Leigh sternly; and he now stepped slowly and watchfully toward him.

"Stand away from that door," said Garstang again.

"Hah!" ejaculated Leigh, as he caught a glimpse of something in the man's hand; and he sprang at him to dash it aside, when there was a flash, a loud report, and as a puff of smoke was driven in his face, Leigh spun round suddenly, and fell half across the farther table with a heavy thud.

At the same moment, Garstang thrust a pistol into his breast, darted to and flung open the door, to run right into the hall, where he was seized by a man, and a tremendous struggle ensued, Garstang striving fiercely to escape, his adversary to force him back toward the staircase; chairs were driven here and there, one of the marble statues fell with a crash, and twice over Garstang nearly shook his opponent off.

But he was wrestling with a younger man, who was tough, wiry, and in good training, while, in spite of the desperate strength given for the moment by fear, Garstang was portly, and his breath came and went in gasps.

"Here, you girl, open the door; call help—can't hold him!" came in gasps.

A low wailing sound was the only response, and poor Becky, who was by the front door, with her face tied up, covered it entirely with her hands, and seemed ready to faint.

The struggle went on here and there, and once more there was the gleam of a pistol and a voice rang out:

"Ah! coward, fight fair."

As utterance was given to these words the speaker made a desperate spring to try and catch the pistol, his weight driving Garstang back, whose heels caught against a heavy fragment of the broken piece of statuary, and its owner went down with the back of his head striking violently against another piece of the marble.

The next moment, fainting and exhausted, his adversary was seated on the fallen man's chest, wresting the pistol from his grasp.

"Thought he'd done me. Here, you're a pretty sort of a one, you are! Why didn't you call the police?"

"Oh, I dursen't! I dursen't!" sobbed Becky.

"You dursen't, you dursen't!" grumbled the speaker. "Hi! help, somebody! Hi, Kate! are you in there? What, Doctor! Then you've got here, after all. I did go to your house."

For Pierce Leigh suddenly appeared at the library door, where he stood, supporting himself by the side.

Chapter Forty Seven

"I say, he didn't shoot you, did he?"

"Yes—through the arm," said Leigh faintly. "Better directly. Can you keep him down, Wilton?"

"Oh yes, I'll keep the beggar down," said Claud, cocking the pistol. "Do you hear, you sir? You move a hand and as sure as I've got you here, I'll fire. Send for a doctor someone."

"No, no," cried Leigh, a little more firmly; "not yet;" and he drew a handkerchief from his pocket and folded it with one hand. "Tie this tightly round my arm."

"You take the pistol then—that's it—and let the brute have it if he stirs. I won't get off him. Kneel down."

Leigh obeyed after taking the pistol, and Claud bound the handkerchief tightly round his arm.

"Hurt you?"

"Yes; but the sickness is going off. Tighter: it will stop the bleeding."

"All right; but I say, we had better have in a doctor," said Claud excitedly.

"Not yet. We don't want an expose," said Leigh anxiously.

"Shall I go for one, sir?" said the housekeeper.

"No. How is she now?" said Leigh anxiously.

"Just the same, sir," said the woman, stifling her sobs.

"I'll come in a moment or two. Go back; there is nothing to fear now."

A burst of hysterical sobbing came from the front door, where Becky was crouching down, with her face buried in her hands.

"Take her with you," said Leigh hastily; and he stood before Garstang while Becky walked into the library, shivering with dread.

"Here, you hold up, what's your name," cried Claud. "You behaved like a trump. It's all right; he can't hurt you now."

"No," said Leigh, in a harsh whisper, as the two women passed in and the door swung to; "nor anyone else. Look."

"Eh?" said Claud wonderingly. "What at?"

"Don't you see?" said Leigh, bending down and turning Garstang's head a little on one side.

"Ugh!" ejaculated Claud. "Blood! I didn't mean that. Why, he must have hit his head on that bit of marble."

"Yes," answered Leigh, after a brief examination, "the skull is fractured. We must get him away from here."

"Not dangerous, is it, doctor?" said Claud, aghast.

Leigh made no answer, but rose to his feet and sat down on one of the hall chairs.

"What is it—faint?" said Claud.

"Yes—get me—something—he cannot move."

"She seems to be more like sleeping now, sir," said the housekeeper, appearing at the door. "Oh, no, no; don't let him get up!"

"It's all right, old lady. Here, got any brandy? The doctor's hurt, and faint."

"Yes, sir; yes, sir," said the woman, glancing in a horrified way, at the two injured men, as she passed into the dining-room, from which she returned directly with a decanter and glass.

"It's port wine, sir," she said in a trembling voice; and she poured out a glass.

Leigh drained it, and rose to his feet.

"I will come back directly," he said.

"That's right. I say, I don't quite like his looks."

Leigh bent over the prostrate man, but said nothing, and passed into the library, where he spent five minutes in attendance upon Kate; and at the end of that time he rose with a sigh of relief.

"Will she come to, sir?" whispered the housekeeper, with her voice trembling.

"Yes, I think the worst is over. The medicine I gave her is counteracting the effects of the drug."

"Oh, oh, oh!" burst out Becky; and she flumped down on the carpet and caught one of Kate's hands, to lay it against her cheek and hold it there, as she rocked herself to and fro.

"Becky! Becky! you mustn't," whispered her mother.

"Let her alone; she will do no harm," said Leigh, quietly.

"Are—are you going to send for the police, sir?" faltered the woman.

"No, certainly not yet," replied Leigh; and he went back into the hall.

"I say," said Claud, in a voice full of awe, "I'm jolly glad you've come. He ain't dying, is he?"

For answer Leigh went down on one knee, and made a fresh examination.

"No," he said at last; "but he is very bad. I cannot help carry him, but he must be got into one of the rooms."

"Fetch that old girl out, and we'll carry him," said Claud; and after a moment or two's thought Leigh went to the library, stood for a while examining his patient there, and then signed to Becky and her mother to follow him.

Under his directions a blanket was brought, passed under the injured man, and then each took a corner, and he was borne into the dining-room and laid upon a couch.

"I don't like to call in police, or a strange surgeon," Leigh whispered to Claud. "We do not want this affair to become public."

"By George, no!" said Claud, hastily.

"Then you must help me. I can do what is necessary; and these women can nurse him."

"But I can't help you," protested the young man. "If it was a horse I could do something. Don't understand men."

"I do, to some extent," said Leigh, smiling faintly. Then, to the woman, "You can go back now. Call me at once if there is any change."

The two trembling women went out, and after another feeble protest Claud manfully took off his coat, and acting under Leigh's instructions, properly bandaged the painful wound made by Garstang's bullet, which had struck high up in Leigh's arm, and passed right through, a very short distance beneath the skin.

"A mere nothing," said Leigh, coolly, as the wound was plugged and bandaged, the table napkins coming in handy. "Why, Wilton, you'd make a capital dresser."

"Ugh!" ejaculated the young man, with a shudder. "I should like to be down on one. Sick as a cat."

"Take a glass of wine, man," said Leigh, smiling.

"I just will," said Claud, gulping one down. "Thank you, since you are so pressing, I think I will take another. Hah! that puts Dutch courage in a fellow," he sighed, after a second goodly sip. "It's good port, Garstang. Here's bad health to you—you beast."

He drank the rest of his wine.

"I say, doctor, you don't expect me to help timber his head, do you?"

Leigh nodded, as he drew his shirt-sleeve down over his bandages.

"But the brute would have shot me, too."

"Yes, but he's hors de combat, my lad, and you don't want to jump on a fallen enemy."

"Don't know so much about that, doctor," said the young man, dryly, "but you ought."

"Perhaps so," replied Leigh, "but I am what you would call crotchety, and I must treat him as I would a man who never did me harm. Come, your wine has strung you up. Let's get to work."

"Must I? Hadn't you better put the beggar out of his misery? He isn't a bit of good in the world, and has done a lot of harm to everyone he knows."

"Bad fracture," said Leigh, gravely, as he passed his hand round the insensible man's head, "but not complicated. He must have fallen with tremendous violence."

"Of course he did," said Claud. "He had my weight on him, as well as his own. Can he hear what we say?"

"No, and will not for some time to come. Now, take the scissors out of my pocket-book, and cut away all the hair round the back. There, cut close: don't be afraid."

"Afraid! Not I," said Claud, with a laugh, "I'll take it all off, and make him look like a—what I hope he will be—a convict."

He began snipping away industriously, talking flippantly the while, to keep down the feeling of faintness which still troubled him.

"Fancy me coming to be old Garstang's barber! I say, doctor, you'd like to keep a lock of the beggar's hair, wouldn't you? I mean to have one."

"Mind what you are doing," said Leigh, quietly; and as Claud went on cutting he prepared bandages with one hand and his teeth, from another of the fine damask napkins; and in spite of the pain he suffered, bandaged the injury, and at last sank exhausted in a chair, but rose directly to go across to the library.

"How is she?" said Claud, anxiously, upon his return.

"The effects are passing off, and in two or three hours I hope she will come to."

"Then look here," said Claud, anxiously, "ought I to—I mean, ought you to send over to somebody and tell her how things are going on? She'll be horribly anxious."

Leigh frowned slightly.

"You mean my sister, of course," he said. "No; she is aware that I was called in to a case of emergency, but she does not know that it is here."

"Doesn't she know? I say, though, I'm a bit puzzled how you came here."

"This man fetched me."

"Fetched you? How came he to do that?"

"In ignorance of who I was, of course. But how came you here so opportunely?"

"Oh, I've been watching and tracking for long enough, till I ran him to earth; and I've been trying for days to get at him. Got hold of that woman with the tied-up head at last—only this evening—and was going to bribe her, but she let out everything to me, and after telling me everything, said she'd let me in. So I went for you, and as you were out I was obliged to try and get Kate away at once. You know the rest I say, this is what you call a climax, isn't it?"

Leigh sat gazing at him sternly, but Claud did not avoid his eyes, and went on.

"Now look here; of course he got her for the sake of her money, and she can't stop here. But she must be taken away as soon as she can be moved."

"Of course."

"Yes, of course," said Claud, firmly. "It isn't a time for stickling about ourselves; we've got to think about her, poor lass. Damn him! I feel as if I could go and tear all his bandages off—a beast!"

"What do you propose, then?" said Leigh, calmly.

"Well, for the present we'd better take her to your house. She must be in a horrid state, and the best thing for her is to find herself along with some one she loves. It will do her no end of good to find Jenny's—I beg your pardon, Miss Leigh's arms around her."

"Yes, you are quite right; and I could go to an hotel."

"Humph! Yes, I suppose you ought to, but I've been thinking of something else, if you don't mind. The guv'nor's shut up with his gout, so I think I ought to go home and fetch the mater. She talks a deal, but she's a jolly motherly sort, and was fond of Kate. There's no harm in her, only that she's a bit soft about her beautiful boy—me, you know," he said, with one of his old grins.

Leigh winced a little, and Claud's face grew solemn directly.

"I say," he said hastily, "it was queer that he should have come and fetched you, wasn't it?"

"Yes," said Leigh, "a curious stroke of fate, or whatever you may call it; and yet simple enough. It was in a case of panic; he was seeking a doctor, and my red lamp was the first he saw. But after all, it was the same when we were boys; if we had strong reasons, through some escapade, for wishing to avoid a certain person, he was the very first whom we met."

"Yes, Mr Wilton; what you propose is the best course that can be pursued, and I think it is our duty towards your cousin; we can arrange later on what ought to be done about this man. You and your relatives may or may not think it right to prosecute him, but you may rest assured that his injury will keep him a close prisoner for a long while to come."

"Yes, I suppose that fall was a regular crippler, but you have to think about prosecuting too. The law does not allow people to use pistols."

"We can discuss that by-and-by. Now, please, I shall be greatly obliged if you will go to my sister, and tell her as much as you think is necessary. If she has gone to bed she must be roused. Ask her to be ready to receive Miss Wilton, and then I think you ought to go down to Northwood and fetch Mrs Wilton."

"All right—like a shot," said Claud, eagerly. "I mean directly," he cried, colouring a little. "But, er—you mean this?"

"Of course," said Leigh, smiling; "why should I not? Let me be frank with you, if I can with a sensation of having a hole bored through my arm with a red-hot bar. A short time back I felt that if there was a man living with whom I could never be on friendly terms, you were that man; but you have taught me that it is dangerous to judge any one from a shallow knowledge of what he is at heart. I know you better now; I hope to know you better in the future. Will you shake hands?"

"Oh!" ejaculated Claud, seizing the hand violently, and dropping it the next instant as if it were red-hot. For Leigh's face contracted, and he turned faint from the agony caused by the jar. "What a thoughtless brute I am! Here, have another glass of that beast's wine."

"No, no, I'm better now. There, quick! It must be very late, and I don't want my sister to have gone to bed. I dare say she would sit up for me some time, though."

"Yes, I'm off," cried Claud, excitedly; "but let me say—no, no, I can't say it now; you must mean it, though, or you wouldn't have spoken like that."

He had reached the door, when Leigh stopped him.

"I'll go in first and see how your cousin is; Jenny would like the last report."

"Better, certainly," he said on his return; and Claud hurried out of the house.

"He said 'Jenny,'" he muttered, as he ran towards Leigh's new home. "'Jenny,' not 'my sister,' or 'Miss Leigh.' Oh, what a lucky brute I am! But I do wish I wasn't such a cad!"

Chapter Forty Eight

Before morning Kate was sufficiently recovered to be removed to Leigh's house; but it was days before her senses had fully returned, and her brain was thoroughly awake to the present and the past, to find herself lovingly attended by her aunt and Jenny Leigh, who was her companion down to Northwood, while Claud kept the doctor company in town and accompanied him as assistant every time he visited Great Ormond Street. For Leigh, in spite of his own injuries, continued to attend Garstang till he was thoroughly out of danger, though it was months before he was able to go to his office.

It was time he went there, for the place, and his country house in Kent, were in charge of his creditors' representatives, it having come like a crash on the monetary world that Garstang, the money-lender and speculator, had failed for a very heavy sum.

Poetic justice or not, John Garstang found himself bankrupt in health and pocket; his bold attempt to save his position by making Kate his wife being the gambler's last stroke.

As a matter of course, James Wilton was involved; led on by Garstang, he had mortgaged his property deeply, and the money was now called in, and ruin stared him in the face just at a time when he was prostrate with illness.

"It's jolly hard on the old man," said Claud one day when he had come up to town and called on Leigh, "for the guv'nor has lorded it down at Northwood all these years, and could have been doing it fine now if it hadn't been for old Garstang. He gammoned the guv'nor into speculating, and then gammoned him when he lost to go on with the double or quits game, and a nice thing Johnny must have made out of it. If it had been sheep or turnips, of course the old man would have been all there; but it was a fat turkey playing cards with a fox, and I suppose everything comes to the hammer."

"Very bad for your mother," said Leigh.

"Oh, I don't know. I say, may I light my pipe?"

"Oh, yes; smoke away while you have any brains left."

"Better smoke one's brains away than catch some infection in your doctor's shop. How do I know that some one with the epidemics hasn't been sitting in this chair?—ah! that's better. I say, it's a pity you don't smoke, Leigh."

"Is it? Very well, then, I'll have a cigar with you to help keep off the infection. I did have a rheumatic patient in that chair this morning."

"Eh? Did you? Oh, well, I'll risk that. Ah, now you look more sociable, and as if you hadn't got your back up because I called."

"I couldn't have had, because I was very glad to see you."

"Were you? Well, you didn't look it. You were saying about being bad for the mater. I don't believe she'll mind, if the guv'nor don't worry. She's about the most contented old girl that ever lived, if things will only go smooth. The crash comes hardest on poor me. It's Othello's occupation, gone, and no mistake, with yours truly. I say, don't you think I could turn surgeon? I have lots of friends in the Mid-West Pack, and if they knew I was in the profession I could get all the accidents."

"No," said Leigh, smiling; "you are not cut out for a doctor."

"I don't think I am cut out for anything, Leigh, and things look very black. I can farm, and of course if the guv'nor hadn't smashed I could have gone on all right. But it's heart-breaking, Leigh; it is, upon my soul. I haven't been home for weeks. Been along with an old aunt."

"Why, you oughtn't to leave a sinking ship, my lad."

"Well, I know that," said Claud, savagely; "and that's why I've come here."

"Why you've come here?" said Leigh, staring.

"Yes; don't pretend that you can't understand."

"There is no pretence. Explain yourself."

Claud Wilton had only just lit his pipe, but he tapped it empty on the bars, and sat gazing straight before him.

"I want to do the square thing," he said; "but I'm such an impulsive beggar, and I can't trust myself. I want you to send for your sister home; Kate's all right again; mother told me so in a letter; and she has got her lawyer down there, and is transacting business. Look here, Leigh: it isn't right for me to be down there when your sister's at the Manor. I can't see a shilling ahead now, and it isn't fair to her."

Leigh looked at him keenly.

"I shall have to marry Kate after all," continued Claud, with a bitter laugh. "Do you hear, hated rival? We can't afford to let the chance go. Oh, I say, Leigh, I wish you'd give me a dose, and put me out of my misery, for I'm about the most unhappy beggar that ever lived."

"Things do look bad for you, certainly," said Leigh. "How would it be if you tried for a stewardship to some country gentleman—you understand?"

"Oh, yes, I understand stock and farming generally; but who'd have me? Hanged if I couldn't go and enlist in some cavalry regiment; that's about all I'm fit for."

"Don't talk nonsense, my lad. Where are you staying?"

"Nowhere—just come up. I shall have to get a cheap room somewhere."

"Nonsense! You can have a bed here. We'll go and have a bit of dinner somewhere, and chat matters over afterwards. I may perhaps be able to help you."

"With something out of the tintry-cum-fuldicum bottle?"

"I have a good many friends; but there's no hurry. We shall see?"

Claud reached over, and gripped Leigh's hand.

"Thankye, old chap," he said. "It's very good of you, but I'm not going to quarter myself on you. If you have any interest, though, and could get me something to go to abroad, I should be glad. Busy now, I suppose?"

"Yes, I have patients to see. Be with me at six, and we'll go somewhere. Only mind, you will sleep here while you are in town. I want to help you, and to be able to put my hand on you at once."

The result was that Claud stayed three days with his friend; and on the third Leigh had a letter at breakfast from his sister, enclosing one from Mrs Wilton to her son, whose address she did not know, but thought perhaps he might have called upon Leigh.

"Eh? News from home?" said Claud, taking the note, and glancing eagerly at Leigh's letter the while. "I say, how is she?"

"My sister? Quite well," said Leigh, dryly.

Claud sighed, and opened his own letter.

"Poor old mater! she's such a dear old goose; she's about worrying herself to death about me, and—what!—oh, I say. Here, Leigh! Hurrah! There is life in a mussel after all."

"What do you mean?"

"Why, hark here. You know I told you that Kate had got her lawyer down there?"

"Yes," said Leigh, frowning slightly.

"Well, God bless her for the dearest and best girl that ever breathed! She has arranged to clear off every one of the guv'nor's present liabilities by taking over the mortgages, or whatever they are. The mater don't understand, but she says it's a family arrangement; and what do you think she says?"

Leigh shook his head.

"That she is sure that her father would not have seen his brother come to want God bless her. What a girl. Leigh, it's all over with you now. Intense admiration for her noble cousin, Claud, and—confound it, old fellow, don't look at me! I feel as if I should choke."

He went hurriedly to the window, and stood looking out for some minutes, before coming back to where Leigh sat gravely smoking his cigar.

Claud Wilton's eyes had a peculiarly weak look in them as he stood by Jenny's brother, and his voice sounded strange.

"I'm going down by the next train," he said. "This means the work at home going on as usual, and I shan't be a beggar now, Leigh. I say, old man, I am going to act the true man by hier. I may speak right out to her now?"

"Whatever had happened I should not have objected, for sooner or later I know you would have made her a home."

Claud nodded.

"And look here," he cried, "why not come down with me? Kate would be delighted to see you. Only you wouldn't bring Jenny back?"

"Take my loving message to my sister," said Leigh, ignoring his companion's other remark, "that I beg she will come home now at once."

"Because I'm going down?" pleaded Claud.

"Yes," said Leigh, gravely, "because you are going down."

A year and a half glided by, and Kate Wilton had become full mistress of her property, and other matters remained, as the lawyers say, "in statu quo," save that Jenny was back with her brother. James Wilton was very much broken, and his son was beginning to be talked of as a rising agriculturist. John Garstang was at Boulogne, and his stepson had married a wealthy Australian widow in Sydney.

Jenny had again and again tried to urge her brother to propose to Kate, but in vain.

"It is so stupid of you, dear," she said. "I know she'd say yes to you, directly. Of course any girl would if you asked her."

"Yes, I'm a noble specimen of humanity," said Leigh, dryly.

"I believe you're the proudest and most sensitive man that ever lived," cried Jenny, angrily.

"One of them, sis."

"And next time I shall advise her to propose to you. You couldn't refuse."

"You are too late, dear," he said, gravely, as he recalled a letter he had received a month before, in which he had been reproached for ignoring the writer's existence, and forcing her to humble herself and write.

There were words in that letter which seemed burned into his brain and he had a bitter fight to hold himself aloof. For in simple, heart-appealing language she had said: "Am I never to see you and tell you how I pray nightly for him who twice saved my life, and enabled me to live and say I am still worthy of being called his friend?"

Pride—honourable feeling—true manhood—whatever it was—he fought and won, for in his unworldly way he told himself that in his early struggles for a position he could not ask a rich heiress to be his wife.

"I know," Jenny often said, "that she wishes she had hardly a penny in the world."

It does not fall to many of us to have our fondest wishes fulfilled, but Kate Wilton had hers, though in a way which brought misery to thousands, though safety to more who have lived since.

For the great commercial crisis burst upon London. One of the great banks collapsed, and dragged others, like falling card houses, in its wake. Among others, Wilton's Joint Stock Bank came to the ground, and in its ruin the two-thirds left of Kate's money went out like so much burning paper, leaving only a few tiny sparks to scintillate in the tinder, and disappear.

"Oh, how horrible!" cried Jenny, when the news reached the Leighs. "What a horrid shame! I must go and see her now she is in such trouble."

"No," said Leigh, drawing himself up with a sigh of relief, "let me go first."

"Pierce!" cried Jenny, excitedly, as she sprang to her brother's breast, her face glowing from the result of shockingly selfish thoughts connected with Claud Wilton and matrimony, "and you mean to ask her that?"

He nodded, kissed her lovingly, and hurried to Kate Wilton's side.

The interview was strictly private, as a matter of course, but the consequences were not long in following, and among other things James Wilton made his will—the will of a straightforward, honest man.

There were people who said that the passing of the Limited Liability Act was mainly due to the way in which Kate Wilton's fortune was swept away. That undoubtedly was a piece of fiction, but out of evil came much good.